ALSO BY JONATHAN BUCKLEY

THE BIOGRAPHY OF THOMAS LANG

XERXES

GHOST MACINDOE

INVISIBLE

SO HE TAKES THE DOG

CONTACT

TELESCOPE

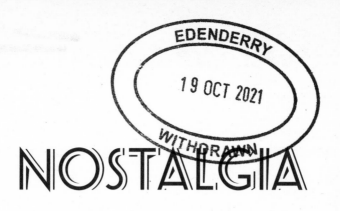
NOSTALGIA

JONATHAN BUCKLEY

Sort Of
BOOKS

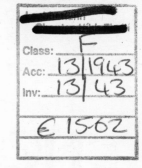

NOSTALGIA BY JONATHAN BUCKLEY

Published in 2013 by
Sort Of Books
PO Box 18678, London NW3 2FL
www.sortof.co.uk

Distributed by
Profile Books
3a Exmouth House, Pine Street,
London ECIR OJH

10 9 8 7 6 5 4 3 2

Typeset in Palatino, Syracuse, Seaside Resort and Mostra Nuova to a
design by Henry Iles

Printed in the UK by Clays Ltd, St Ives plc

448pp.

A CIP catalogue record for this book is available from the British Library

ISBN 978-1908745316

FOR SUSANNE HILLEN
AND BRUNO BUCKLEY

NOSTALGIA

THERE IS STILL PLENTY OF GOOD MUSIC
TO BE WRITTEN IN C MAJOR

ARNOLD SCHOENBERG

I.I

THE RECORDED HISTORY OF CASTELLUCCIO begins with the Etruscans, whose settlement was centred on the area now occupied by Piazza del Mercato, but it was not until the twelfth century that walls were first built around the town and its fortress – the Rocca – was raised at its highest point. In 1203 the *comune* of Castelluccio elected its first *podestà* (chief magistrate), whose residence was within the Rocca. Not long afterwards, an earthquake wrecked the fort and a new Palazzo del Podestà was constructed in the centre of the town. The fortress itself was rebuilt some time after 1360, when Ugo Bonvalori of Volterra became the *podestà*. The most notable feature of the new Rocca was the Torre del Saraceno, which remains the tallest structure in the town and incorporates, in its lower storeys, portions of the pre-earthquake fortress. By the end of the century the Bonvalori family had taken occupation of the

Rocca and had become, *de facto*, the ruling family of Castelluccio, a position they maintained until the 1470s, when Castelluccio came under Florentine control. The Rocca then fell into disuse.

Workshops and warehouses had taken occupancy of various parts of the fortress by the late eighteenth century. In 1787 extensive damage was caused by the explosion of a quantity of gunpowder that was being stored in the former dungeons. After another earthquake in 1846 the only substantial part of the Rocca left standing was the Torre del Saraceno.

Two different explanations are given for the name of the tower. Some believe that it comes from the effigy of a Saracen that was suspended from a gibbet in the courtyard of the Rocca for use as a jousting target. Local folklore prefers to attribute the name to the small basalt head that is embedded in the tower's northern façade. Though probably dating from the fourth century, the head is popularly said to depict a North African slave who was murdered by Muzio Bonvalori after insulting one of Muzio's half-sisters.

1.2

It's late in the afternoon, a mid-August Thursday. A man is at work on the roof of the Torre del Saraceno, fixing a pole to the parapet with steel bands. That done, he attaches a flag – the emblem of Saint Zeno: a boar, with one foreleg crooked – with a thin metal spar to hold it out in the breezeless air.

From the window of his *studiolo* Robert Bancourt watches the man for a minute, before returning to the email that has arrived from Max Jelinek, chairman of the Jelinek optical equipment company: *Dear Mr Bancourt – we understand perfectly that Mr Westfall's commitments do not permit him to undertake our proposed commission at this point in time. An artist of his standing is always in demand. We appreciate that. But we were so amazed by what Milton Jeremies showed us – for this portrait, we'll wait for as long as is necessary. November would be OK for Myrto – she could come to Italy for two or three days, maybe four. Would that work for Mr Westfall? Let me know what he says. As for the fee – let's just say that there'll be no problem on that score.* A photo of the wife has been attached to the email. Myrto's face is as taut as a football, and the eyes stare through the skin in a delirium of contentment; the teeth are an orthodontical masterclass, and she seems to have carbon fibre for hair. God knows what age she is: anywhere from 55 to 75.

Now the man is sitting on the parapet, legs dangling, talking on his phone as if he were lounging on a park bench rather than perched at an altitude of 34.5 metres, with nothing but air between his feet and the street; he types a text with a thumb while adjusting the fittings of the flag with his other hand; he waves to someone down on the street.

Robert's phone rings: it's Teresa. It's been another dull day in the office. 'So are you with your master this evening?' she asks. He is, as he'd told her this morning he would be. 'See you tonight, when he lets you go,' she says, like a woman resigned to her husband's stupid hobby.

On the bench there's a canvas to be stretched; Robert is stapling the canvas to the frame when the doorbell rings. 'Door!' shouts Gideon.

1.3

Claire Yardley steps out of the Albergo Ottocento onto Corso Garibaldi, and pauses to get her bearings from the map that the receptionist has given her: the building opposite is the old theatre; turning right will take her to Piazza del Mercato.

Within a couple of minutes she is on the square. She aligns the map with the landmarks – the church on the far side, on the right; the tower to its left – then walks towards the place marked by the red cross. There, as the receptionist had described, is the ironwork arch, clogged with wisteria; and there's the bar, the Alla Torre, with a second arch beyond it. The gates are closed with a chain that's been looped around the handles half a dozen times, but it's not padlocked. Through the arch, she sees a garden of shrubs and gravel paths; on the right, a small flight of steps, leading to double doors. Ring the top button, marked 5, she was told, but the top bell has no label. She hesitates, then presses; a full minute passes before a voice shouts out of the entryphone: '*Pronto*?'

Unnerved by the tone, she puts her mouth close to the door. 'Yes,' she says. 'Is that Mr Westfall?'

'No,' is the answer. 'Who is this?'

'I'd like to see Mr Westfall. Would that be possible?'

'You need to make an appointment,' she is told.

'I didn't know that,' she replies. Receiving no immediate response, she continues: 'Can I make an appointment to see him later?' she asks.

'He could see you on Saturday.'

A runnel of sweat sprints out of her hair and into an ear. 'I really would like to see him today. Is that not possible?'

'He could see you on Saturday,' the voice repeats. It's like talking to a computer.

'Saturday is too late,' she says. 'I've come from London. Is this evening out of the question? For a few minutes? That's all I need.' A young woman is sitting at a table outside the bar; she seems to be amused by the situation.

There is a pause, in which muttering can be heard in the entryphone. The voice instructs her: 'Wait there. I'll come down.'

A minute later, the doors are opened by a wiry individual, fair-haired, slim, not tall, probably mid-thirties, in jeans and white T-shirt and navy blue plimsolls. He has a small quiff, which contributes to a 1950s kind of look. This must be Robert.

He is looking at a woman who couldn't be more obviously English. The dress is a shapeless floral number, with a lot of pale and dusty pink in it, and the body is what you'd expect of a woman of her age – maybe forty – who doesn't believe in strenuous exercise; the face is so unremarkable that he'd struggle to recall it tomorrow; the hair – medium length, dark brown, straight – has been ordered into an approximate tidiness rather than styled. The eyes are an attractive green-grey, though, and the gaze is strong, even if the expression does suggest a customer who's had to queue for half an hour at the complaints desk.

'I'm Mr Westfall's assistant,' he says, offering a hand. There's a nervy tension in the handshake; and clearly he's not in the best of moods.

'Pleased to meet you,' she says.

'He can't be disturbed at the moment. I'm sorry,' he tells her, with a small smile that denotes immovableness. 'He's working. He never sees anyone in the afternoon.'

'And when he finishes working – what then?'

'He eats.'

'Straight away?'

'More or less.'

'I wouldn't take up much of his time,' she persists. 'I really do want to meet him. It would mean so much to me.' There is a wheedling tone in her voice, which she dislikes.

'Are you a painter?' he asks.

It's obvious that he thinks she cannot be an artist, so she answers: 'Yes, I am.'

He seems a little surprised, but not disbelieving; his mouth opens slightly; he is a fraction less resolute now.

'Just ten minutes?' she pleads. 'Five? I can come back any time this evening. Any time.' She smiles; it's too blatant an attempt to elicit sympathy, but it works.

'I'll have a word,' he says. 'Wait here.' He leaves the doors ajar; the young woman at the table, turning the pages of a magazine, is smirking; a brown dog emerges from the shrubbery, trots up the steps and, ignoring her, nudges open one of the doors with its head, a moment before Robert reappears.

'7.45,' he says. 'He can give you ten minutes.'

'That's fine. Thank you.'

'You're welcome,' he says, coolly. He steps back, taking hold of the door handles, and says: 'The name?'

'I'm sorry?'

'Your name.'

'Matilda,' she answers.

'I'm Robert. We'll see you later. 7.45. Don't be late. He has a thing about punctuality.'

'I won't be late,' she assures him. 'Thank you.'

The doors are already closed. The young woman gives a smile as Claire passes her table.

1.4

Gideon sits on a high stool in front of one of the easels. He is at work on a still life that has been commissioned by Niccolò Turone, formerly a test driver, nowadays the boss of a travel company which specialises in wildlife-watching expeditions. On the right-hand side of the picture, in front of a stack of cogs, there is a lizard, almost completed; Gideon is refining the colours of its tail when his assistant returns.

'She'll be back at a quarter to eight,' says Robert, on his way through the studio.

'Lord save me,' murmurs Gideon, changing his brush. 'Describe her,' he requests.

'My age, thereabouts. Catalogue clothes. Headmistress of a primary school in the depths of Surrey.'

'Really?'

'A guess. Says she's an artist.'

'Evening-class watercolourist?'

'Probably.'

'A treat awaits. She understands she's in the express lane?'

'That was made clear.'

'Good chap.'

'One other thing,' says Robert, at the door of his work room. 'Max Jelinek. He's proposing that the wife comes here in November. We have a photo. You might want to take a look.'

'Tell.'

'Severely rejuvenated face. Huge quantities of botox, plus knife work.'

'Not a chance.'

'Remuneration would be generous.'

'Of what order of generosity?'

'The fee would not be an issue.'

Gideon stops; he squints at the canvas as if it were a mirror. 'Oh Christ,' he sighs.

'So what shall I tell him?' asks Robert.

'Tell him I'd rather eat gravel for a year.'

'I'll tell him we'll let him know, at some unspecified point in the future.'

'Yes, do that,' says Gideon. 'But not November. Next year. We can keep the wolf from the door until then.' With a cocktail stick he applies three dots of colour to the lizard, and with each dot he mimics the *ching* of an old cash register.

I.5

WESTFALL, GIDEON. Born London, 1948. Attended Camberwell School of Art, 1968–72, prior to studying with Martin Calloway, 1973–75. First group exhibition: The New Classicism, Satler Gallery, London, 1978. Has exhibited widely in the USA and Europe; works are held in numerous private collections. Since 1993 he has lived in the central Italian town of Castelluccio.

[From *Who's Who in British Art: 1945 to the present*, edited by L. Andriessen & J. C. Myers, London, 2009.]

I.6

At 7.43pm Claire walks through the gate by the Alla Torre and there is Robert, on the steps, waiting. He checks his watch, gives her a gratified nod, says 'Good evening', and turns to lead her up the terracotta-tiled staircase. 'We're on the top floor,' he says, and nothing more. By the time they reach the second storey she's already six steps behind him; he doesn't turn round.

At the top landing he waits for her to catch up. A piano is playing inside. 'Is that him?' she asks.

'Yes,' Robert answers. 'In so far as it's his hi-fi.' This is said without a smile. 'Bach,' he adds. '*The Well-Tempered Clavier*, Book Two. One can never have too much of it, I say.' He knocks, then immediately takes a key from his pocket and opens the door. They are in a dark hallway, facing another door; again Robert knocks and opens.

This is her first sight of Gideon: he is sitting in an armchair, eyes closed. He lifts a hand, to signify that they should wait until the music has ended. Robert closes the door silently, takes a single step into the room; he peruses the ceiling, with his bottom lip pushed slightly out.

Claire looks around the room. CDs fill a dozen shelves beyond the armchair, which faces a pair of loudspeakers that are as high as her shoulders. As expected, there are pictures: a woman, naked, lying on her back on a mattress, against a bare brick wall; a ruin, perhaps a cathedral, with grass growing in the nave; objects – bottles and jars, mostly – on a tabletop; a man standing on a wide grey sandy beach. The last one appears not to be by the person who painted the other three.

The final chord evaporates, and Gideon aims the remote control at the CD player, with a conductor's gesture of termination. He raises himself from his seat, carefully, smoothly, as if out of respect for the silence that the music has become. He removes the disc from the player, and Robert says: 'Here's Matilda.'

Gideon puts the CD in its case; he files the disc on its rightful place. 'Thank you,' he says, and Robert departs, soundlessly. It's like paying a visit to a cardinal.

'So,' says Gideon, facing her at last. 'You're from London.'

'That's right.'

'Here on holiday?'

'Sort of.'

'In what way "sort of"?'

'It's partly a holiday, but mainly I've come to see you.'

In his face there is barely any visible acknowledgement of this statement; just enough for it to be understood that she would not be the first person to have come to Castelluccio primarily to meet Gideon Westfall. There is some resemblance to her father. The hands are her father's: the thick, strong fingers, with flat and wide nails, like plectrums. Gideon's hair has thinned as her father's had thinned, and the mix of grey and dark brown is her father's, as are the waves around the temples. The eyes are a version of her father's too: the same colour, the same suggestion of purpose; this is a man, she observes, who aims to impress himself upon people at the outset. He's larger than her father: both taller and heavier – fatter than in any of the photos she has found online. 'Robert tells me you're an artist,' he says.

'I'm not an artist,' she replies.

'You're not?'

'No.'

'But that's what you told Robert.' The eyes have taken on a surface-penetrating intensity; displeasure is rising.

'It is,' she admits. 'But I'm not.'

'So why did you lead Robert to believe that you were?' he demands. 'Explain, please.'

'You don't recognise me, do you?' she says.

'Why should I recognise you?'

'We've met. It's been a few years. Best part of twenty. I've changed a bit.' She waits for him to work it out, but he is not trying to work it out, so she tells him: 'I'm Claire. Claire Yardley.' It's quite impressive, the lack of reaction: he merely angles his head to the left a little, and fractionally narrows his eyes, as if he's looking at a picture which until this moment had not interested him; now he's spotted a mildly curious detail.

'Well, well, well,' he murmurs. 'You're Claire.' One corner of his mouth makes a wry upturn. 'Yes. Yes, I can see it.'

She offers a hand. 'Anyway,' she says, 'pleased to meet you.'

Her manner is that of a seconded police officer meeting a colleague with whom she's going to be working for a while. 'Likewise,' he says.

'Surprised?'

'Naturally.'

'Not too unpleasantly?'

'No. Not at all. But I can't say I'm altogether sure the subterfuge was necessary.'

'For all I knew, if I'd pressed the buzzer and said who I was, you'd have told me to go away.'

'Of course I wouldn't.'

'No "of course" about it. Eccentric artists and all that. And you did fend me off when I emailed.'

'I'm not eccentric, and I didn't fend you off.'

'Yes, you did.'

'I said I was busy. Which I am.'

'"Busy for the foreseeable future". That's not an invitation, is it?'

He appears to disregard this point; he looks at her closely, as if reasoning away a grain of doubt as to her identity. 'Do sit down,' he says, like a lawyer with a client, indicating his armchair. He props himself into an angle of the wall, beside a window; she has to twist in the chair to face him. 'So, you're on holiday?' he asks.

'I told you,' she replies. 'I've come to see you.'

'But not just to see me, surely?'

'I'll have a holiday while I'm at it. But you're the main reason.'

A momentary lowering of an eyebrow suggests that he finds this odd, and perhaps a little disturbing, as if she's revealed that she can name every address at which he's ever lived, plus the dates. 'You're here on your own?' he asks.

'Yes. I'm on my own.'

'And you're leaving tomorrow?'

'No. I'm here for a week.'

'Oh,' he says, and there's definitely some dismay here. 'But Robert said—'

'Yes. I might have given a misleading impression. I didn't want to wait until Saturday.'

His nose emits a faint snorting breath – the sound made by a chess-player who finds himself temporarily outmanoeuvred by a weaker opponent.

He watches her as she surveys the room: she has the look of someone searching for clues. Her demeanour has something of her father about it – the aura of blunt efficiency, of a mind that reaches conclusions too quickly. 'So,' she says, patting her thighs. 'This is where you live. It's nice.' The small smile is also evocative of her mother.

'I like it,' says Gideon.

She points to the painting of the naked woman on a mattress. 'That's yours, isn't it? I mean you painted it, yes?'

'Yes, I did.'

'And that one and that one,' she goes on, indicating the ruin and the bottles. 'But that one isn't you.' She points to the man on the beach.

'That's right,' he answers, as though commending a bright child's observation.

Irked, she scans the room again. The mouth, he now notices, is like her mother's, with its implication of obduracy, a propensity to sulk. 'You're staying at the Ottocento?' he asks.

'Yes.'

'Room OK?'

'Very comfortable.'

'Had a chance to explore the town?'

'Not yet.'

'Not much to see. That's one reason we like it.'

'We?'

'Myself and Robert.'

'Oh. Right,' she says.

'Not what you're thinking,' he tells her. 'He's my assistant. That's all. Many people made the same mistake, when we first arrived.'

'I wasn't thinking anything,' she says, which he can see, from the wavering of her eyes, is not true; she lacks her mother's opacity.

'You've hired a car, I take it?'

'No.'

'So how did you get here?'

'Train to Florence. Bus to Colle whatever it's called. Taxi to here.'

'Well, we can lend you a car. You'll want to explore the area. A day in Siena, certainly. Have you been to Siena?'

'Never.'

'Well, it's just over there,' he tells her, turning to the window. 'If you look—'

'Yes, I know. I have a guidebook,' she says, a little more sharply than intended.

Gideon looks out of the window, but she can tell he's not looking at what's out there. 'There are some nice walks around here,' he goes on, still gazing out.

'I'm sure.'

'I can give you a map. A detailed one. For walking.'

'Thank you,' she says. She is about to say that there's no need to find it right away, but already he is at a bookshelf. Within twenty seconds the map is in her hand. She thanks him again.

Looking at his watch, he says: 'I have to go, I'm afraid. But do drop round tomorrow.' And at this point the room's other door, beyond the loudspeakers, comes open and in trots a fudge-coloured and curly-coated dog, the one she saw earlier. Gideon beckons the dog to his side and gives its head a vigorous stroke, glad of the distraction. 'This is Trim,' he says.

'Nice dog,' she comments.

'A Lagotto Romagnolo.'

'He's beautiful.'

'He is,' says Gideon. He continues rubbing the dog's head and then there's a knock at the door and Robert enters, now wearing well-pressed chinos and a Prussian blue shirt.

I.7

'Meet my niece,' Gideon calls across the room. 'Robert, this is Claire; Claire, this is Robert.' The gestures would make you think that this was a little drama of his own devising, for the bemusement of his assistant.

'Hello,' says Robert; he stays by the door and raises a hand in greeting. He evinces no curiosity as to why her name should have changed; it's as though he's never seen her before, and has no interest in making her acquaintance.

'Now,' Gideon says to her, 'have you eaten?'

'I said I'd eat at the hotel,' she says.

She anticipates an attempt to persuade her to cancel, but instead Gideon merely asks her to excuse him for a moment, before leaving the room by the door beyond the speakers.

She had stood up when Robert came in; now she takes a couple of steps towards the window. 'Nice view,' she remarks, which he affirms with a nod. It's a pleasant landscape – nothing startling or luscious, but easy on the eye. 'What's that place?' she asks.

From halfway across the room he peers past her shoulder. 'The one on the near horizon?'

'Yes.'

'Cásole d'Elsa.'

'Anything to see there?'

'Castle, now the town hall. Handful of churches. Nothing remarkable.'

'And Siena is where?'

'Ninety degrees to the right. Out of range,' he answers. The dog, having followed Gideon out of the room, comes back; it butts Robert's leg with its muzzle and receives a couple of pats on the rump.

'Trim – is that as in "trim the grass", or is it short for something Italian?'

'As in "trim the grass".'

'Odd name,' she comments. The dog buffets her shins, so she gives its back a stroke; the fur is as soft as a lamb's fleece. 'We were in contact last year,' she reminds Robert. 'I emailed.'

'I remember,' he says. This may or may not be true; it's not possible to tell if he knows anything at all about her. He's not so much morose as absent.

Gideon returns, wearing a linen jacket that has a dozen creases to the square inch. 'Friendly chap, isn't he?' he says, pointing at the dog; perhaps this is a jibe at his assistant. 'Ready?' he asks Robert.

'Let's roll,' says Robert, with as much enthusiasm as an undertaker getting ready to drive the hearse. He leads the way down the stairs.

Gideon tells her they are going in her direction, so they'll walk with her as far as the hotel. Out on the piazza he pauses for a moment and looks around, as if to ascertain that everything is as it should be. Two old men are crossing the square arm in arm, and one of them raises a hand to Gideon; a dozen starlings, after wheeling around the church's weathervane, fly overhead and alight on the parapet of the tower. Gideon squints up at where the birds have settled. 'That's the Saracen's Tower,' he informs her. 'Thirteenth century. Roman foundations. All of this used to be a castle,' he explains, with a whirl of a hand, encompassing the piazza. A small man with a flattened nose passes them, and he shakes Gideon's hand, barely breaking stride. Gideon resumes his speech, as though Claire has come to Castelluccio to make a documentary about him. He loves the spirit of this place, he tells her; he uses the phrase *genius loci*. When he was a young man, he used to think that an artist shouldn't be at home anywhere, but Castelluccio has made him change his mind. He takes a deep breath, as if the street were exuding a heady vapour, like a fifty-year-old malt. They have almost reached the hotel. A priest, walking down the centre of the road, nods crisply at Robert and is repaid in kind.

'Prettier than where I live,' says Claire.

'And where's that?' Gideon enquires.

'Stockwell.'

'Ah,' says Robert; it's the first time he's opened his mouth since they left the apartment.

'You know it?'

'Been through it,' he answers.

'It has its good points,' she says.

Outside the hotel, Gideon stops. 'So, tomorrow,' he says. 'Do you want to come round for lunch? I take a break at one.'

'Sure.'

'One o'clock on the dot,' he says.

'On the dot,' she agrees.

'See you then,' says Gideon, departing. Robert shakes her hand, making it seem that he's doing it on behalf of his employer.

1.8

Most visitors to Castelluccio enter the town by its northern gate, the Porta di Volterra, because the main car park is situated there, as is the bus terminus. Via Matteotti rises gently from the Porta di Volterra to Piazza del Mercato, which is still the location of the weekly market, currently held on Wednesdays. The Torre del Saraceno, the highest structure in the town, rises over the northern side of the square, where parts of the fortress's walls have been incorporated into a number of the buildings. On the west side of the piazza stands the Loggia del Mercato, formerly a shelter for the market traders, and on the opposite side you'll see one of Castelluccio's four functioning churches, Santissimo Redentore.

From the southeast corner of Piazza del Mercato, Via dei Falcucci leads to the eastern gate, the Porta di Siena; halfway along Via dei Falcucci, Via San Lorenzo curves down to the derelict church of San Lorenzo. The main street of Castelluccio, Corso Garibaldi, runs from the southwest corner of Piazza del Mercato to the central square, Piazza Maggiore, 250 metres to the west, passing two significant buildings along the way: Palazzo

Campani, the largest private residence in the town; and the Teatro Gaetano, a nineteenth-century theatre, now defunct. On the corner of Corso Garibaldi and Piazza Maggiore you'll find the Caffè del Corso, which opened for business more than a century ago. Castelluccio's most important church, San Giovanni Battista, shares the southern side of Piazza Maggiore with its most important secular structure, the Palazzo Comunale, or town hall.

Behind the Palazzo Comunale you'll find another square, Piazza della Libertà, which fronts the southern gate, the Porta di Massa, from where Via dei Pellegrini and Via Santa Maria, following the arc of the best-preserved section of the old town walls, sweep westwards to the western gate, the Porta di Santa Maria. Adjacent to the gate is the church of Santa Maria dei Carmini. The small Piazza dei Carmini marks the terminus of Corso Diaz, which extends eastwards for 150 metres to Piazza Maggiore, and of Via Sant'Agostino, which shadows another intact section of the walls as it climbs to the fourth of Castelluccio's active churches, Sant'Agostino. The town museum, the Museo Civico, is to be found a short distance beyond Sant'Agostino, and from the museum it's a brief walk north to the last of the gates, the Porta di San Zeno. A public garden overlooks the Porta di San Zeno and the nearby Porta di Volterra; at the top of the garden there's a terrace that gives a superb view of the countryside to the north of Castelluccio, with Volterra visible in the distance, on a fine day.

1.9

The restaurant of the Ottocento is not, this evening, a relaxing place for a woman on her own; Claire tries to concentrate on her book, but is repeatedly distracted by glances from other tables – from families, couples, groups of men. In the corner of the room, sitting with three friends, is a lean-faced man of fifty – he has an air of failed marriage, but clearly still fancies himself – who smiles at her three times, perhaps with interest, perhaps with commiseration. A child – a boy of nine or ten – stares at her as though she has green skin and antennae. Within an hour she has finished her meal, but she stays at the table for ten minutes more, doggedly reading, taking sips from her glass of water. It's not yet ten o'clock. She decides to go for a stroll.

On Corso Garibaldi a teenaged boy, sitting on a scooter, is talking to a lad on crutches, who is holding the hand of a girl who's talking on her phone. There's nobody else on the street. She passes the café on the corner of Piazza Maggiore; a man is standing at the bar, staring into a glass of wine; he's the only customer. The façade of the church on Piazza Maggiore glows under a floodlight that's bolted into the pavement at the foot of the steps; a figure of Christ, above the main door, grimaces into the light; a bat skims the wall of the church repeatedly. Claire watches the aerobatics of the bat, thinking mostly about her uncle: he fits with what little her parents had told her; there is something stagey about him as well, and almost seedy. She remembers, around the time of her grandmother's funeral, her father referring to his brother as a big child, and her mother adding: a big child who thinks he's a great man. He had thought he was a great man from about the age of twelve, her father said: Gideon had signed the drawings he did at school, ostentatiously, in rehearsal for his inevitable years of fame. In a drawer in the living room there was a small drawing of their mother, done when Gideon was fourteen, and the signature in the bottom corner was the same as it is now: a G and a W strung on a line, with a couple of posts – the double 'l' – at the far end. It was a very good drawing; astounding for a fourteen-year-old.

She asks herself: Why have I come here? She was curious, above all – curious about the uncle, the well-known artist, whose name had come to be unmentionable at home. She has never known anyone famous, nor any artists. And she is in need of a holiday: she had thought it would do her good to see some places she had never visited before. It was a risk, coming here, but doing something bold might be good for her, she'd thought.

She has never taken much of a risk with anything before; she wishes she had done, though she can't think, offhand, of any occasions on which a risky decision might have made a difference. Nevertheless, she is feeling a sort of unspecified regret, as well as a regret that has a clear location: she should have gone somewhere else; Gideon is dislikeable and he has no interest in her. Tomorrow, perhaps, she will give him what she has to give him and then she'll leave, maybe for Siena, maybe for Florence, if she can find a place to stay.

Wandering without paying attention to where she's going, she has arrived at another church, unlit, and a gate in the town walls. She passes through it, and finds a panorama of dark hills, speckled with house lights and streaked by headlights flashing through trees. The town at her back is as quiet as the countryside; she hears an owl, but the cry comes from behind her, from the houses. Not as tired as she wants to be, she meanders along the alley that flanks the church and arrives at a courtyard in which a TV set grumbles in a room above her head. Looking up, she sees a square of deep indigo sky, with a dozen fat stars in it; and there is the owl again. She goes on, down an even narrower alleyway, which turns one way and then the other before opening onto a street she does not recognise. She turns left, sure that this is the way back to the main street, and instead sees the town walls in front of her; she follows the walls, and in a minute is back at the gate; she wouldn't have thought it possible to lose one's bearings in so small a space. For a few minutes more she looks towards the hills; the quietness is beginning to make her drowsy.

She walks back along Corso Diaz and sees, silhouetted against the floodlight of Piazza Maggiore, Robert hurrying across the road. She stops until he has gone, then hurries herself, concerned that she may come across Gideon between here and the hotel. But she gets back to the hotel without seeing anyone other than the waiter in the empty café, and the boy with the crutches and his girlfriend, who are kissing on a doorstep.

In her room she takes from her case the interview with Gideon that she had printed from a website the night before she left. She reads a paragraph or two.

1.10

Teresa Monelli, née Emidia, was born in Castelluccio and has lived here for most of her thirty-six years. She works for Gianluigi Tranfaglia's property agency, in an office in Palazzo Campani; she has been there for almost four years, which is too long.

At the university of Florence she studied architecture, as did her husband, Vito. They married shortly after graduation; their daughter, Renata, now thirteen, was born a few months later, and Teresa stayed at home to raise her to school age, while Vito worked all hours at an architectural practice in Siena, his home town. They lived in Castelluccio, three streets away from her parents, who helped out with Renata whenever necessary; Vito would call on his parents in Siena two or three times each week, after work. Though home and office were some distance apart, and often he did not get back to Teresa and Renata until late in the evening, Vito was happy in Castelluccio, or seemed to be. He liked the scale of the place, its modest fabric, its setting. They had a plan: within ten years Vito would set up his own office, with Teresa, and they would gather their clients from the Castelluccio area, where properties were regularly bought by outsiders who needed an architect to improve their new residence or holiday home. Vito and Teresa cultivated the goodwill of Gianluigi Tranfaglia, and were soon rewarded: as a freelance project, Vito designed a music studio for Albert Guldager, the composer, whose house outside Radicóndoli had been bought through the Tranfaglia agency.

Other commissions came Vito's way: he rebuilt a farmhouse at Mensano and another near Monteguidi. Ahead of schedule, he opened his own office in Siena, where he planned the conversion of a dilapidated villa into a hotel. On the back of this project, he was commissioned to produce an extension for the Ottocento in Castelluccio. The council consulted him with regard to the possibility of finding a new use for the Teatro Gaetano. Thanks in large part to the recommendations of Gianluigi Tranfaglia, private clients were in more than sufficient supply: he restored and rebuilt a farm and its outbuildings at Paganina; a Roman couple bought a derelict house in Castelluccio, on Piazza San Lorenzo, and hired him to turn the husk into a hi-tech dwelling, no expense spared; he was entrusted with the conversion of the old candle factory in Via Santa Maria; and he designed a house near San Dalmazio, built on land that had once been an orchard, for a wealthy Dutch woman, divorced, called Carice van Kapelleveen, who had made a lot of money as a fund manager in London and now, disenchanted with city life, had decided that she would withdraw to the depths of Tuscany and get closer to nature, while maintaining a healthy revenue stream by marshalling the investments of a select roster of clients. Whether or not Carice van Kapelleveen succeeded in getting closer to nature is not known; she did, however, succeed in getting closer to the architect of her dream house. Vito came home one night and informed his wife that he had to leave; so unsuspecting was Teresa that she thought for a moment that he was talking about a business trip.

That was five years ago. Since then, she has had just two relationships of any significance: a two-month fling with a cousin of Gianluigi Tranfaglia, which was never going to amount to anything but made her feel better about herself for a while; and now she's with Robert, who is much more like Vito in many ways – tender, calm, and a little melancholic. Maybe he's too calm at times. It's one o'clock and he is asleep. She looks at him. He always sleeps deeply, and his face is as composed as a face on a coin. He seems to have no dreams.

Through the open window the cry of the owl comes in, and she recalls the first time she spoke to Robert. She had left Gianluigi and his family an hour earlier, and had sat for a while by the Porta di Siena, looking at whatever was there, not wanting to go back to the apartment; Renata was with her father for the weekend. She walked through the sleeping town; a man was smoking a cigar on Piazza del Mercato; on the Corso there was only a cat, sauntering down the middle of the road. Walking past the gardens, she saw someone standing under a tree, gazing up. She recognised him as the painter's assistant: she had never spoken to him, but had often seen him, nearly always on his own. He had never seemed unfriendly, but she'd had the impression that he was happy to be left alone, which she quite liked, even if Gianluigi, who'd spoken to him once or twice, had described him as 'very English', which was not intended as a compliment. He was, said Gianluigi, a man who wouldn't talk to you unless you said something to him first, so she was surprised when, as if she'd asked him what he was looking at, he pointed into the branches and told her to look: and there was the owl, staring at him.

She's awake for another hour, and sometimes the call of the owl is so faint she's not sure if she's hearing it or remembering it.

I.11

Gideon, in his studio, regards his self-portrait. The picture is progressing slowly: the disc of canvas is almost bare, with only part of a table painted, and the outline of a picture on the wall in the background, behind the orbits of pencil-marks that will become his face. Every year he commits himself to this exercise in self-scrutiny, and never before has it proceeded so haltingly. Previously it has always been a pleasure, this self-scouring; it has brought a satisfaction akin to what he imagines the satisfaction of confession must be. The disappearance of Ilaria, he decides, is the explanation for his slowness: to look at himself, into himself, with absolute honesty he must concentrate, and concentration in these circumstances is too difficult. When he tries to study his face, he evades himself. Glancing aside, he sees his reflection in the black glass of the window, and what he glimpses is a man who is in no mood to be examined.

He takes a sketchbook from a shelf. It opens on a drawing of Ilaria leaning against a wall, arms folded over her breasts, sullen; the lower half of her body is a flimsy outline. The date, on the reverse, is seven months past; he cannot recall if the expression was one he'd asked her to assume, or if this had been one of her truculent days. On the opposite side of the room, near the head of the stairs, is the place where she had stood to be drawn; he looks across at that area of blank wall, and the air in front of it seems to be charged with her absence, as if she has disappeared from it just an instant before.

He opens the window and silence comes in, then the hum of a car on the road outside the walls. A voice calls across Piazza del Mercato. Shutters scrape against a sill. A crate of empty bottles is being placed on the pavement below. Another *Buona notte*. Normally they help him to work, these sounds of the town falling into sleep. He hears the cry of the owl. His niece has the air of someone who has come in judgement; she is like her father, he can tell – minds that think in monochromes and right-angles. He must work.

For a few minutes he inspects the still life: he applies a spot of Terre Verte to the head of the lizard; he stops. With this painting there is nothing to think about: in his mind he can see it, finished. All he has to do is allow his hand and eyes to complete it, but tonight there is a great torpor in him. It occurs to him that he might go for a coffee at the Corso – it will be open for another half-hour. He goes over to the self-portrait again, like a doctor making a round of the wards. The picture on the wall behind his head might be better as a window, and the angle of the head is wrong, too aggressive. With a pencil he makes adjustments. The owl cries again. Usually it comforts him, like the soft chiming of a clock; now it seems to deride his lack of resolution.

The spot of paint that he has added to the lizard is superfluous; with a knife he teases it off. In an hour he completes the tail. This picture is boring him, but his boredom is an irrelevance: art is servitude to reality, and servitude is wearying. Before going to bed he makes a sketch, in charcoal, of the spotlit tower. It is a poor piece of work; he tears it up.

1.12

Had he lived one hundred years earlier, Muzio Bonvalori might have been assigned a place in Dante's *Inferno*, immersed to the brows in the seventh circle's river of boiling blood, beside Ezzelino da Romano and Obizzo d'Este. He was perhaps a lesser monster than these two, and a person of lesser significance to the history of his country, but he was indubitably a man of habitual and extravagant violence, and a deserving candidate for damnation.

Ercole Bonvalori, his father, had two sons and two daughters by his wife, Maria. A third son, the youngest, Muzio, was illegitimate: it is believed that his mother was a cook in the kitchens of the Rocca Nuova. Muzio was for many years his father's favourite: he was a beautiful child, with hair as curly as a lamb's and the colour of new brass; and he was intelligent, too – he could read and write at an age at which his siblings had been able to utter only syllables, and he quickly learned to play the dulcimer with a dexterity that astonished his tutors. He grew into a prodigiously well-developed child, but at around the age of ten he began to show signs of an unnatural cruelty. One afternoon his mother found him, in his chamber, squeezing the body of a songbird in his fist, like a lemon; blood trickled through his fingers; he had cut the wings off the creature. At the age of twelve he slew with one stroke of his sword a horse that had thrown him.

His father, in the last years of his life, as Muzio was later to boast, would often lament that Muzio's mind was diseased. One incident in particular became as well known in Castelluccio as a folk tale: on Muzio's orders, a man who had stolen food from the larders of the Rocca Nuova was kept in a cell without food for many days before being nailed into a wooden cask; a small hole was bored into its lid – not to give air to the captive, but so that the curious Muzio might observe the soul of the miscreant escaping at the moment of his death.

Ercole Bonvalori died in 1420, and his two legitimate sons were dead within one year – poisoned, it was rumoured, by their half-brother. The younger of their sisters became pregnant; she was unmarried, and the child she bore had hair the colour of brass. Maria, Ercole's wife, died soon after this grandchild's birth; everyone knew that she had died of shame and grief. Muzio's wife, Lucia, a beautiful and pious young woman, was subjected daily to his brutalities. Little more than a year after her marriage to him, she lamented to her family that she had been treated like a dog since the day she had become his wife. Whenever Muzio was displeased with her, she was made to perform the most menial of duties, and to sleep on the bare stone floor. At twenty-one, driven to the brink of madness by the things she had endured and witnessed, she abandoned their twin daughters and fled to a convent in Siena, where she died, her health broken, only three years later. Muzio married again: his second wife died after giving birth to their first son, and was said to have welcomed her death with joy. The child died on the same day. Muzio mourned him to excess; he spent weeks on end alone; a servant who disturbed him in his weeping was struck in the eye with a blade. Before long, however, Muzio had married for a third time; his new wife soon fled, and nothing more is known of her. Many saw these misfortunes as punishment for Muzio's innumerable sins, but Muzio Bonvalori, contemptuous of judgement, continued to inflict miseries of every description on his birthplace.

For more than twenty years, without respite, Muzio brought suffering to the innocent people of Castelluccio. There was not a man or woman who did not live in fear of him. Given to proclaiming that he was *the enemy of God and of compassion*, Muzio was a drunkard, a thief, a blasphemer, a murderer, a violator of women. He was reputed to have deflowered both of his daughters, and to have tortured men solely for the pleasure it gave him.

The grass below the walls of the Rocca Nuova was said to grow so thickly because of the quantity of blood that had flowed into the soil. It seemed that the soul of Muzio seethed in a perpetual fury; when his anger was at its most demented pitch, the whites of his eyes would turn black. A chronicler of the time describes him as *a devil in exile*.

But then, on the eve of the forty-third anniversary of his birth, Muzio Bonvalori was changed. A servant whose name was either Marta or Margareta, recently taken into the Rocca Nuova, one morning caught the eye of her master, who later that day assaulted her. A stable-lad, a boy called Lodovico di Pietro, hearing her screams, ran into the chamber in which the attack was occurring and threw himself between the woman and her assailant. Enraged, Muzio Bonvalori pursued the boy into a room on the uppermost floor of the tower, and there drew his sword. Retreating in terror, the child stumbled, fell backwards, and tumbled from the window. But Lodovico did not die, because as he toppled from the window he called out the name of Saint Zeno, and at that instant, at 3pm on the afternoon of August 22nd, 1443, an angel appeared in a golden whirlwind above the walls of Castelluccio and flew into the courtyard of the Rocca Nuova to catch Lodovico di Pietro and place him on the ground, as softly as a landing dove. And then the angel flew upward into the room in which Muzio Bonvalori stood aghast, and a light brighter than the sun was seen to blaze from the window from which Lodovico had fallen.

Muzio Bonvalori emerged from that room transformed: in all but his physical features, he was a different man. He lived for another twenty-seven years, and in that time he was constant in his care for the people on whom he had hitherto inflicted such misery. For the welfare of the poorest, he founded the Ceppo dei Poveri, which distributed alms to the distressed. No citizen died unattended by a priest. In times of bad harvest, the granaries of the Rocca Nuova were thrown open. Muzio paid for the building of the Cappella Bonvalori in the church of San Giovanni Battista and for the altarpiece depicting Saint Bernardino. He commissioned a copy of the Gospels, and another of *The Golden Legend* and he read them continuously from first light to last. The man who had for so many years been impervious to any sentiment of pity was seen to weep like a child at the thought of the pains of the martyrs. On his deathbed, in his final hours of consciousness, though reduced by illness to little more than a breathing skeleton, he recited the vision of Saint John on Patmos as perfectly as if the text had been inscribed onto the bedsheet he was clutching.

2

2.1

THE MANAGER COMES OUT of the office as she drops the key on the counter. He introduces himself as Maurizio, and gives her a handshake; his hand retains hers for a good five seconds longer than is necessary. He is a good-looking man: fiftyish, slim, hands slender and manicured, bold blue eyes, hair swept back into thick curls behind the ears, handsomely veined with grey. The shirt – white with sky-blue stripes – is pristine; he wears a heavy black-faced watch. 'Very pleased to meet you,' he says, maintaining eye contact. 'You are, I believe, the niece of Mr Westfall, our great artist,' he goes on.

She's not sure if sarcasm is intended – it may be nothing more than an effect of the accent. 'I am,' she confirms. 'How did you know?'

The innocence of the question amuses him. 'Mr Bancourt,' he explains. 'We are friends.'

'Oh,' she says.

This response appears to be charming. 'Yes,' he says, 'we are friends for many years. You have met him, yes?'

'I have,' she answers.

'Yes,' says Maurizio, gratified. 'Yes. Of course. Good.' He glances to the side, through the window, as an old woman hobbles by, carrying a bag that makes her tilt twenty degrees to the left; watching her pass, he smiles again, as if the old lady were a relative going about her daily routine. 'You are going to the exhibition?' he resumes.

'Gideon's?'

'Of course,' says Maurizio. 'You know where it is?' he asks, as a formality.

'I do, yes.'

'It is very good,' he says, his face now appropriately serious. 'Very beautiful.'

'I'm sure it is,' she says.

'He is a master.'

'Indeed.'

'You are going now?' he asks; there's a possibility that he's going to volunteer to accompany her.

'This morning, yes, but not right away,' she answers, hoping to give the impression that an experience as serious as the Master's exhibition should not be rushed. 'I'll wander for a while first. Explore,' she says, making a meandering motion with her hand.

Maurizio watches her hand as if her gesture were one of extraordinary elegance. 'That will not take a long time,' he says, in a tone of apology. 'But it is a nice town, for people who do not want big lights and activity all the time. I like it. I hope you will like it as well.'

'I think I shall,' she says, with a glance at the door.

'You must go,' says Maurizio, imposing another handshake, but brief.

Less than ten minutes later, having sauntered the whole length of the main street and doubled halfway back, she is in the entrance hall of the Palazzo Comunale, where a black cardboard arrow, attached to a poster bearing her uncle's name and the image of a painting of a stone wall, directs her up the staircase. At the head of the stairs a second arrow diverts her into a long vaulted room, past a table and unoccupied chair. To the left, beyond the doorway, five laminated sheets of card are attached to the wall: texts in Italian, English, French, German and Spanish, each with a photo of a brooding Gideon in the top right-hand corner. She scans the English page, and reads that Gideon Westfall regards himself as 'the medium of the image' . . . that in his portraits he strives to capture what he calls 'the third person, that volatile product of the fusion between the spirit of the sitter and the spirit of the painter' . . . that he reveres, 'in no particular order', Raphael, van Eyck, Ingres, Morandi, Poussin, Piero della Francesca. Someone called Angelica Martinuzzi believes that Westfall 'meets the enormous demands of his concepts with certainty and conviction'.

The pictures are hung on tall partitions that make a maze in the middle of the space. Facing the door, alone, is a self-portrait, a drawing, in which Gideon – though much younger than he is now – presents himself to the public much as he presented himself to her: challengingly, confident of his charisma. Round the corner she comes upon a line of pictures – sketches in pencil and charcoal and oil paint – of a small chapel that appears to be situated in the middle of fields of grass, and to have been abandoned. The sketches, the labels inform her, are all from the same year, 2008, and several are almost identical: slight changes in the shape of the shadows or in the tone of yellow that he's used for the walls are all that differentiates them. At the end of the line hangs a finished painting of the chapel, in which every little element – sprigs of weed; crumbs of stone; flaking paint on the door – has been raised to a more than natural focus. It strikes her as the sort of thing that photography has made redundant, but it's accomplished, very. The sky behind the building, cloudless, has a dozen different shades of blue in it.

A similar sequence faces the chapel pictures: here the subject is a flight of stone steps with an arch of brick above it. It's the same idea: a run of sketches, then the final item, which is again remarkably precise, unquestionably fine, but finicky. Drawings come next – highly worked pencil drawings, all of them, and all are of women, naked: women from the front, women from the back, women lying down, women standing up, women sitting down, women looking straight at you, women looking winsomely askance. She knows what a woman looks like unclothed. But the following section is full of women too: small paintings, in which the figures are finished but have areas of roughly applied paint all around them, as if the artist had been testing out colours for the background and then given up. She is on the point of giving up herself, but she feels that she is under an obligation, so she works her way along the queue of nudes. The labels all follow the same form: *Nude Study (June 2005)*, *Nude Study (August 1992)*, *Nude Study (May 2001)* and so on. There's more than twenty years between the first and the last, but you could swap the dates around and it would make no difference; this doesn't seem right – shouldn't artists, like everyone else, develop with time? She stops at *Nude Study (September 1999)*. This is a beautiful young woman; the body is delectable; there is skill here, immense skill; but the picture could have been made by Gideon in 2009, as far as she can judge; it might have been made in 1899, come to that.

She is no longer alone in the hall. At the far end, a large painting of a pile of fruit and books is being scrutinised by a man who's more interesting to look at than any of the pictures: he's tall, gaunt, around Maurizio's age or a little older, with close-cropped white hair and a nose like you might see on a cartoon of a Roman emperor, on which is perched a pair of expensive-looking glasses, rimless. The general demeanour is academic, but the suit – blue, linen – and the immaculate white shirt have the look of designer clothing, and he's carrying a stylish briefcase. On the way out, she stops at the fruit and books; the man has moved on, to a small painting of a monk in his cell. He glances at the picture she's looking at, then at her, and he cocks an eyebrow as she passes, seeming to have intuited that she too has her doubts.

2.2

The Palazzo Communale of Castelluccio was built in 1232 as the Palazzo del Podestà, alongside the church of San Giovanni Battista, from which it was, and remains, separated by the width of a street. The market square, in the shadow of the Rocca, had previously been Castelluccio's centre of gravity; now a shift began, and by the close of the thirteenth century the open area in front of the Palazzo del Podestà and San Giovanni Battista had acquired its current name, Piazza Maggiore.

An almost cubic building, with walls of undressed grey stone that are punctuated irregularly with plain windows of various sizes, the Palazzo del Podestà is of no great architectural distinction, but the Piazza Maggiore façade is enlivened by the coats of arms – forty-one in total – of various men who held the post of *podestà*. The most decorative of these coats of arms are the eight glazed terracotta shields from the sixteenth century, but the largest (and the oldest) is a limestone disc on which two griffons support a spear above a barely legible inscription that reads: *Ugo Bonvalori, MCCCLX.*

In addition to the *podestà*, the town's governing council and the courts of justice were also based here. Nowadays, the building functions as the seat of the mayor and the offices of the local government, and only one part is regularly open to the public: the Sala dei Quaranta, once the meeting hall of the forty-strong Great Council. Unlike many other rooms in the Palazzo del Podestà, it was left almost unaltered by the wide-scale refurbishment that followed Unification; redecorated in the early sixteenth century, after Castelluccio had fallen under Florentine control, the walls of the Sala dei Quaranta are painted with maps of the major towns of Florence's territory; some of the furniture is from the same period.

Other sections of the Palazzo del Podestà are occasionally accessible to visitors, notably the small chapel below the Sala dei Quaranta, which dates from the thirteenth century, and the prisons, which are located two floors below the chapel. One cell still has an array of fifteenth-century locks and bolts on its massive oak door, and its walls are covered with prisoners' graffiti. A large drawing, scratched into the stone with a nail, shows a man remonstrating with a devil; the name Daniele is visible above the man's head.

2.3

Claire rings the entryphone at 1pm precisely and Gideon answers. He's standing at the head of the stairs, beaming, sleeves rolled up, a kitchen knife in one hand and a couple of fat tomatoes in the other. 'Come in,' he says, stepping aside so she can precede him into the apartment. He sounds like a company boss welcoming a candidate for her second interview. 'That way,' he directs her, jabbing the knife in the direction of an open door, which turns out to be the door to a kitchen that's more like a section of corridor equipped with a sink and cooker and fridge than a proper kitchen. But there's a glass door at the opposite end of the room, and on the other side of it there's a wide terrace, with a table and two chairs. Plates and glasses are in place on the table; a bottle of white wine and a bottle of water are standing in a glass bowl of half-melted ice cubes. An awning, winched out from the kitchen wall, keeps the terrace in shade.

The view, in other circumstances, would immediately soothe: old red roofs in the foreground, the town walls beyond, and a procession of dusty green hills in the distance. Leaning on the railing, she can see, down to her right, a segment of Piazza del Mercato, its paving stones as bright as frost in the sunlight. Gideon puts a glass of water in her hand and points out the village of Mensano, and Cásole d'Elsa again.

'So, sleep well?' he asks, sitting down. With a grandiose wave of an arm he invites her to take the vacant chair.

'Very well, thank you,' she answers.

'Good. Good,' he says. He indicates the spread: a bowl of olives; slices of tomato; peppers; artichoke hearts; thick discs of moist mozzarella in dark green oil; a plate of other cheeses; ham and three kinds of salami; soft rolls. 'I don't mind what I eat,' he says, 'as long as it's always the same thing. Habit – the key to success.' This does not seem to be intended as a joke. 'Please, help yourself,' he says. 'The ham is exquisite. And the salami—.'

'I'm a vegetarian,' she tells him. At this he raises an eyebrow and smiles quizzically, as if not eating the corpses of animals were a studied peculiarity, like eating only foodstuffs that are yellow or start with the letter V. 'Oh well,' he says. 'The cheeses are fine too. You do eat cheese?'

'I do.'

'OK,' he sighs, hugely relieved. 'Well, tuck in.'

As he waits for her, he makes his fingers rise and fall in waves on the tabletop, as if playing a keyboard. His hands are stiff, he explains; he's been drawing all morning. A pianist must practise his scales; an artist must draw; drawing, as Ingres said, is seven-eighths of what makes up painting. 'And what about you?' he asks. 'What did you do with your morning?'

'Strolled around. Got my bearings.'

'OK,' he responds, encouraging her to go on; it is taken for granted, she can tell, that she's been to the town hall.

'And I looked at the exhibition.'

'OK. And what did you think?'

'Interesting. A lot to take in,' she says. 'I'll have to go back.'

'First impressions?'

'Interesting,' she repeats, but with a more considered inflection.

'Go on.'

But she doesn't have much more to say. She makes some observations – inane, she knows – about the pictures of the chapel, their precision and the quality of the light. These remarks seem to satisfy him – or not to irritate, at least. As first impressions, it seems, they will pass. He tells her about the

x

z

w

v

u

t

s

r

q

p

o

n

m

l

k

j

i

h

g

f

e

d

c

b

a

A

B

C

D

E

F

G

H

I

J

K

L

M

N

O

P

Q

R

S

T

U

JONATHAN BUCKLEY

chapel: what it is, where it is, how he found it. He talks as if it had been the building's ultimate destiny to be discovered by Gideon Westfall.

A raised voice from the street interrupts their conversation. A man can be seen on Piazza del Mercato, apparently haranguing someone who is out of view. 'What's he saying?' she asks.

'I'm not absolutely sure,' he answers. 'I think he's arguing about a car.' It's not an argument; ten seconds later the man smiles and raises a hand, departing with: '*Ciao Marco. Ciao ciao.*' Gideon does a mock-embarrassed cringe. His Italian, he admits, is deficient – shockingly so, for a man who's lived here for so long. But Max Beerbohm – 'You know Max Beerbohm?' he asks, and has the good grace to betray only the slightest dismay at her ignorance – lived in Italy for more than forty-five years, and in all that time he hardly learned a word of the language. 'I'm not that bad. Not quite,' he says, beguiled by his own incorrigibility.

Coming to Italy, he tells her, was a 'test of solitude'. The insularity of Castelluccio had been a significant part of its appeal, but he hadn't been sure that he was equipped for such isolation.

'But when you walk down the street a dozen people say hello,' she points out.

It took a long time to reach that stage, he answers, and even now he's not really integrated into the town, certainly not as much as Robert, and even Robert can never become a native. 'If you can't trace your roots back to the Etruscans,' he says, 'you're an interloper. That's the attitude round here.' He is an exile, he tells her. England, the English art scene, the 'art racket' had become inimical to him; he had felt obliged to leave.

'Well,' she says, 'it's a comfortable kind of exile.'

Surveying the hills with a philosophical gravitas, Gideon agrees that it is.

Claire reaches into her bag. 'I have things for you,' she says. 'This is the sketchbook I mentioned in my email. And I came across some pictures of you and my father, when you were boys. I had copies made. I thought you might like them.'

She seems hopeful that the gift will please. 'Thank you,' he says, and he puts the sketchbook and the wallet of prints on the floor, beside his chair. Her eyes twitch, as though struck by specks of grit.

'Aren't you going to look at them?' she asks.

'Later,' he says. 'We're talking. It wouldn't be very interesting, watching me looking at old photos.'

He smiles, but there is a coldness that the smile does not obscure, the coldness of a man who has detected a trap and is refusing to fall for it. He looks at her and blinks, and there is something so smug in that blink, so domineering, that she is instantly angry. 'You know,' she says, making every effort to speak evenly, 'the last year of my mother's life was horrible. Really horrible. Indescribable. She knew she was dying, and we knew she was dying, and my father was in despair—'

'Of course. And I'm very sorry—'

'Let me finish. He wrote to you, telling you she wasn't going to pull through. You remember that?'

There is contempt in the question; she could be addressing a man she believes to be feigning feeble-mindedness. 'Yes, I remember,' he replies.

'And you replied. Remember?'

'I do.'

'I can remember it as well. A single sheet of paper; a few lines.' She can see that he's recalling it; he may actually be having a moment of guilt.

'It was more than a few lines,' he states.

'One piece of paper. One side of writing.'

'You read it?'

'No, I didn't read it. I saw it, and I saw it go into the bin.' To this, there is no discernible reaction.

'But he told you what I'd written?'

'No. It was never mentioned again.'

'Do you want me to tell you what I wrote?' he asks, as if offering a trivial favour.

'No. I think I can imagine.'

'I doubt it.'

'I think I can.'

'So you just want me to know that it was thrown in the bin?'

'No,' she says.

'I have taken note of the information. I'm sorry your father reacted as he did. Did you ask him why he threw it away?'

'No,' she replies. 'Of course not.'

She looks up at the sky, to arrest the tears that are forming. 'I don't know what else I can say,' he says.

Gideon is gazing at her; the expression, it appears, is an attempt at empathetic sadness; the wisdom of his gaze, he seems to think, should be enough to console her. 'I suppose I want to understand,' she says.

'Understand what?'

'What happened with you and my father, mainly.'

'Nothing happened.'

'That can't be true. How did things get to be so bad between you?'

'We didn't like each other. As I'm sure he told you.'

'Yes, he did.'

'Well then.'

'But you were brothers,' she objects, as if their antipathy were a conundrum as perplexing as God's permission of suffering.

'A biological fact, but nothing more than that. We were never close. Never.'

'That's not true,' she says. 'I know that's not true.'

'Sorry, but it is.'

'The photos suggest otherwise.'

'What photos?'

'The ones I've just given you.'

He glances at the ground, and for a moment it seems that he's going to take a look. Instead, he purses his lips, then says: 'Photographs aren't necessarily true.'

'I think these are. You'll see.' He smiles, indulging a baseless but endearing optimism. 'And he said you used to get along fine, when you were kids,' she adds.

'Not as I recall,' he says. 'We were on diverging paths from the start. Further and further apart with every year. In the end the gap became too wide,' he says, ploughing the air with separating hands. 'That's all.'

'But it wasn't a gap, was it? We're not talking about a gap. Something had happened before that letter. Afterwards, your name was banned. But even before it, he didn't want to talk about you.'

He looks away; perusing the roofs, he smiles as if in bitter-sweet recollection. 'Not much more I can say,' he says, then he turns towards her again, and leans closer, hands pressed together, prayer-like, with the fingertips to his lips. He squints at her, as if peering through a slit. 'I am not the bad guy,' he tells her. 'Your father didn't like me, and I didn't like him. The older we got, the more we disliked each other. There were arguments. I said things I shouldn't have said, I'm sure. And things were said to me. But it doesn't matter. Blood is sometimes thinner than water, that's all there is to it.'

'OK,' she says.

'Do you believe me?'

'Yes,' she answers.

Gravely he looks at her; she does not believe him, he knows. But he smiles, and replenishes her wine and his water, and slumps back in his chair. Gazing into the sky, he breathes out deeply, consigning the topic of his brother to the air. 'What plans for the afternoon?' he asks.

'Nothing in particular,' she says.

He lists for her the sights of Castelluccio, such as they are; he offers her the use of his car.

'Perhaps another day,' she says.

'But you'll join us tonight, yes?' he says, rubbing his hands to signify that this conversation is reaching its conclusion.

'Us?'

'Robert's easy company,' he says. 'It'll be more relaxed with him along. You might find me a bit too gristly on my own. Robert will make me more palatable. He's a very nice chap.'

'I'm sure he is.'

He checks his watch again. 'A table is booked for 8.15, so we'll call for you at ten past.' This is later than she would prefer, but the arrangement, clearly, is not negotiable. 'And now,' he concludes, standing up, 'I must get back to work.' It's as if she's a guest who hasn't noticed that everyone else has left.

He escorts her into the kitchen, leaving the sketchbook and the photos beside the chair. 'So,' he says at the door, 'am I what you expected?'

'I didn't expect anything,' she replies.

He smiles at what he pretends to be her slyness, and almost shoves her out onto the landing.

2.4

On the Tuscan flank of the Apennine mountains there are three distinct areas of isolated upland, which – like other similarly de-tached outcrops – are classified as Anti-Apennines: the Chianti hills, Monte Amiata and the Colline Metallifere. Castelluccio (pop. 5,300) is located on the northern edge of the Colline Metallifere, a little over twenty kilometres to the north of Montieri; it is not to be confused with the hamlet of the same name in the south-ernmost part of Tuscany, near Scansano, nor with another tiny Castelluccio, more properly known as Castelluccio di Pienza, which is situated not far from Chianciano Terme.

Encompassing the *comuni* of Montieri, Monterotondo Maríttimo, Massa Maríttima, Follónica, Gavorrano, Scarlino and Roccastrada, the Colline Metallifere rise to a maximum altitude of 1,059 metres at Le Cornate di Gerfalco, a short distance to the northwest of Montieri. Since the Etruscan era these hills have been mined for metals: iron, copper, silver, lead, nickel, zinc and mercury have all been extracted here, and the area is also rich in deposits of alum, gypsum and borax. The Parco Nazionale Tecnologico e Archeologico delle Colline Metallifere Grossetane has been instituted to conserve and promote the mining heritage of the Colline Metallifere.

The name of the small town of Montieri is derived from Mons Aeris, meaning Copper Mountain. The Etruscans and the Romans dug mines here, and the castle of Montieri, which dates back to the eleventh century, was as much a factory as a defensive structure, enclosing as it did a mint for the production of silver and copper coins: in Via delle Fonderie you can see the remains of some eleventh-century foundries. More conspicuous remnants of Montieri's industrial history are to be found outside the town, in the valley of the Merse, where there are several disused mines, such as the Campiano pyrite mine, which closed in the mid-1990s. The valley is best known, however, for Le Roste, huge red mounds of scoriae which are heaped beside the main road from Massa Maríttima to Siena.

Monterotondo Maríttimo, to the west of Montieri, is dominated by the cooling tower of its power station, which generates electricity from the steam produced by the stratum of hot granite that lies beneath the town; the area named Le Biancane, on the north side of Monterotondo, is renowned for its boracic fumaroles and springs. The geothermal field of this area is known as the Larderello geothermal field, after the nearby town of that name, around which several craters have been created by volcanic activity; the largest of these, some 250 metres in diameter and now filled by a lake known as Lago Vecchienna, was formed by a phreatic eruption that was described in 1282 in Restoro d'Arezzo's *Della composizione del mondo con le sue cascioni* (On the Composition of the World, with its Reasons), the first scientific book to be written in vernacular Italian. Geothermic power generation was pioneered at Larderello, which was given its name in 1846, in honour of the French businessman and engineer François de Larderel, whose factory – built to extract boric acid from volcanic mud – formed the nucleus of Larderello. Steam is

expelled from the earth here at temperatures as high as 220 °C
(396 °F). Using a steam vent to drive a small turbine, electricity
was first generated at Larderello on July 4th, 1904, in an experi-
ment conducted by Prince Piero Ginori Conti; enough power was
produced to brighten four light bulbs (or five, according to some
sources). Seven years later, the world's first geothermal power
plant was built in Larderello's Valle del Diavolo, or Devil's Valley,
so called because of the sulphurous fumes that seep from it. Until
1958, when a similar plant was inaugurated in New Zealand, this
was the only such facility in the world.

2.5

Returning from Fausto Nerini's workshop, Robert passes the
alimentari on Corso Diaz. Giovanni Cabrera is outside, lounging
against the wall; in one hand he has a cigarette, and in the other
he's holding one of his crutches, with which he's jabbing at a lad
who's brandishing a flagpole at him. Alessandra Nerini is there
too, standing on the other side of the shop window, arms folded,
gazing down the street with wearied eyes. Giovanni's father
comes out, to take a couple of boxes from the van that's parked
opposite; the van drives off, and Alessandra lifts a hand a few
inches off her forearm, by way of a wave to the driver. Noticing
Robert, Giovanni assumes a sneer and lowers the crutch; the lad
with the flagpole turns, to see what's changed the mood.
   'Have you heard anything?' Robert calls to Giovanni.
   Giovanni shakes his head.
   'You?' asks Alessandra.
   'Nothing,' Robert answers.
   The lad with the flag, as if this has nothing to do with him,
grimaces at the sky.
   Once Robert has passed the shop, Giovanni mutters some-
thing, at which Alessandra laughs. Robert glances back, and sees
the flagpole flung up, and the flag opening out, revealing a saffron
oval and the boar of Saint Zeno, scarlet, in the centre of it.

2.6

The most famous Saint Zeno, patron saint of anglers, babies and the city of Verona, born circa 300 AD, is not the Saint Zeno who is celebrated in Castelluccio. Neither is Castelluccio's Saint Zeno the Saint Zeno who became the bishop of Gaza and is thought to have died in 400 AD, having survived the persecutions ordered by Julian the Apostate, which had claimed the lives of three of this Zeno's cousins: Eusebius, Nestabus and another Zeno. And he is not the earliest Saint Zeno, who was beheaded in Carthage in the middle of the third century. According to the Roman Martyrology, no fewer than 10,204 Christians, having been forced to work on the construction of the Baths of Diocletian (c. 300–305 AD), were slaughtered in a single massacre, at the commencement of what has come to be known as the Great Persecution of Diocletian; a Saint Zeno was prominent among this vast company of martyrs. This Saint Zeno is not the Saint Zeno of Castelluccio, who is also not the Saint Zeno who was martyred at Nicomedia with his two sons, Concordius and Theodore, nor the Saint Zeno whose jaw was smashed prior to his decapitation, as punishment for having laughed as Diocletian offered a sacrifice to the god Ceres.

Tradition has established the salient points of the life of Castelluccio's Saint Zeno, starting with his birth in the environs of the village that would become Castelluccio, in either 330 or 340 AD. His father was a miller, and Zeno grew up beside a stream that has come to be identified with the stream that skirts the north side of the town. His parents were not Christians, but when the boy was six or seven years of age he encountered a peripatetic holy man, by whom he was converted to the Christian faith. Manifesting a depth of piety that was remarkable in one so young, Zeno soon brought about the conversion of his family and of many others in the vicinity of the village. At the age of ten he performed his first miracle: the upper floor of his father's mill collapsed, crushing Zeno's mother beneath it; the child raised the fallen beams with his bare hands and revived his lifeless mother, whose body was found to be unscathed. Some time soon afterwards, Zeno drove demons out of the body of a boar that they had maddened to a terrible ferocity; the beast was thereafter as mild as a foal, and would not be separated from his saviour. In 360, all accounts of Zeno's life agree, he went to Arezzo, where he witnessed a miracle that was effected by the bishop of Arezzo, the future Saint Donatus: having picked up the scattered fragments of the glass cup that had been smashed by pagan assailants as he conducted Mass, Donatus fused the pieces with the touch of his hands and proceeded to replenish the glass with wine, which did not leak from it, even though a hole remained in its base. No fewer than seventy-nine conversions have been attributed to the miracle of the broken cup.

A month later, Donatus was arrested by Quadratian, the prefect of Arezzo. He was beheaded on August 7th, 362, one year before the end of the reign of Julian the Apostate, who as a boy had been educated into Christianity by a Roman priest, in the same class as the future Saint Donatus. When Donatus had arrived in Arezzo he had preached the Christian faith with a monk named Hilarian, whose martyrdom occurred in the month preceding that of Donatus. Zeno, who appears to have been a close associate of Hilarian, was beheaded in a meadow outside Arezzo on August 20th, 362. As it lay in the grass, his severed head uttered the words *Credo in unum Deum / Patrem omnipotentem, / Factorem cæli et terræ, / Visibilium omnium et invisibilium* – the first four lines of the Nicene Creed, which had been adopted in 325 at the First Council of Nicaea. At the moment of Zeno's death, furthermore, the stream at his birthplace ran red from bank to bank.

Zeno's body was thrown into a ditch, but in 1263 his bones rose to the surface of the earth, in the middle of the wood that had grown on the site of his execution; they were discovered when a man came across a pig that was kneeling, as if in prayer, with a thighbone held reverently between its teeth. The relics were brought back to Castelluccio, where they were placed in a sarcophagus in the crypt of the church of San Giovanni Battista. In Castelluccio,

August 20th is still celebrated as the feast day of Saint Zeno, though the Vatican removed his feast from the General Calendar in 1969, in accordance with the ruling contained in Chapter Five of the *Constitution on the Sacred Liturgy*, promulgated by Pope Paul VI on December 4th, 1963: *Lest the feasts of the saints should take precedence over the feasts which commemorate the very mysteries of salvation, many of them should be left to be celebrated by a particular Church or nation or family of religious; only those should be extended to the universal Church which commemorate saints who are truly of universal importance.*

2.7

In the last hour Gideon has improved only the tiniest portion of the still life. His progress is rarely fast – fastidiousness is one of his defining qualities. He never makes an unconsidered mark. Today, however, he is sagged in front of the painting like an old widower on the bar stool he's occupied every evening since his wife died. When at work, his eyes are usually in constant motion, taking the picture's measure, as if it were a living thing, and potentially dangerous. Today he stares for minutes at a time, in what one might take to be a state of profound ennui. Recently his concentration has been erratic; this is the worst day yet. This morning he achieved almost nothing: a drawing of a loaf of bread, half-erased. Now, yet again, he changes his brush; he applies it to the palette, brings it to the face of the painting, pauses, withdraws, stares. He has spoken no more than a dozen words all afternoon.

At four o'clock he takes his customary coffee. Robert places the cup on the table nearest to the easel. Gideon looks at it, frowning, as though momentarily confused by its arrival. Then, inspecting the tip of his brush, he mutters: 'I have a very bad feeling.'

'About what?' asks Robert.

'Ilaria. Something bad has happened. I can sense it.' Last month he sensed that Luisa Fava's mother was going to die before the end of the day; she is still alive. He has sensed her demise four times to date, and twice has been struck by a premonition of a

major road accident involving Carlo Pacetti's son, Ennio, who
has yet to be involved in an accident of any kind.

'Nothing bad has happened. I'm sure of it,' says Robert.

Gideon finishes his coffee in a single draught, like an invalid
accepting a bitter but necessary dose. 'You can't be sure,' he says.

'She packed a bag. Ergo she hasn't been waylaid or abducted.'

'You've heard she packed a bag. You don't know.'

'Well—'

'Anyway, even if she did take a bag, that doesn't mean she
can't have come to harm.'

'True. But it makes it less likely.'

'Perhaps. But the bag is just a rumour.'

'I'll bet you she's gone off with a boyfriend. Someone the parents know nothing about.'

'No,' states Gideon, softly but immediately, dismissing the
notion as unworthy of consideration.

'It's the obvious explanation.'

'No,' he repeats. 'I would have known. She would have said.'
With narrowed eyes, he gazes into the picture as if it's a window
and he's looking out at somebody who has unaccountably let
him down.

'But that would have implicated you,' Robert points out.
'Perhaps she didn't want to do that.'

'She would have told me,' he states, with quiet finality. He
straightens his back, picks up a fresh brush, works it on the
palette and raises it, charged with viridian. Having scrutinised
a corner of the canvas, he strokes on the paint. 'Anyway – lunch
went well,' he remarks.

'Glad to hear it.'

'But she appears to be in a rather fragile state of mind,' he
says. 'We need to tread carefully.'

'We?'

Gideon pulls back the brush; he makes a huff of begrudging
amusement, as if in reaction to something he's seen in the picture. 'Sorry?' he says.

'I said "We?"'

'We what?'

'You said: "We need to tread carefully."'

'Did I?'

'You did.'

'Oh,' he says, moving his face to within a few inches of the canvas. 'I meant "I".' With the tip of the brush's handle he ticks a tiny cut into the paint. He studies the mark he has made, then makes another. For the rest of the afternoon he works in silence.

2.8

Robert, waiting in the foyer, is examining a yellowed poster, framed, which the manager has propped against the desk. It's an advertisement for something called *Come le foglie* – 'Like the leaves', Robert translates for her. It was a play produced at the theatre across the road, in 1919, he explains, indicating the date.

'I think I will put it here,' Maurizio says to her, gesturing at a wall, as if her judgement might be of influence.

'Very nice,' she says, though she has no opinion.

Gideon is outside, standing in the doorway of the theatre. The blue suit is perhaps a courtesy to her, or an attempt at ingratiation: she is to note that an effort has been made. Beneath the suit, however, he is wearing a white shirt that might have been found in a heap at the bottom of the wardrobe, and his moccasins are scuffed: such is the artist's disdain for conventionality. 'Good evening,' he says, with a smile that proposes that she should join him in forgetting any disharmony that might have marred their earlier conversation.

It takes three minutes to stroll to the restaurant: they cross Piazza Maggiore, then halfway along Corso Diaz turn left, into a narrow street that runs into Piazzetta Danti, a square that's the size of a tennis court. The Antica Farmacia occupies one side of this piazzetta, where three tables have been set on the pavement. A German couple has taken one; a Dutch family the second; Gideon is taking possession of the third as a call from inside the restaurant confirms that it has indeed been reserved for him.

Menus are brought by a waitress; consulting nobody, Gideon orders a bottle of Brunello. 'This is very special,' he informs her, as the waitress – introduced as Marta – gingerly draws the cork. He pours two full glasses; for himself he pours a much smaller amount, and a tumbler of water.

An older and much larger woman appears. Gideon leaps from his seat to hug her. 'And this lovely lady,' he announces, 'is Cecilia. Cecilia is the brains of the operation. And this,' he says to Cecilia, 'is my niece.' You would have thought he'd been the most attentive of uncles since the day of her birth, and Cecilia's smile says that she has heard a lot of good things about the niece. Uncertain of the form – is a cheek-kiss appropriate? – Claire half-rises from her chair, to have her hand sandwiched by Cecilia's wide, soft palms, and as this is happening her husband, Giacomo, comes out from the kitchen. He is clutching a huge knife, and has the look of a man who is just about managing to keep chaos at bay. To Gideon he dispenses a comradely pat on the shoulder; to Robert, similar; he is introduced to Claire and shakes her hand crisply; he doesn't smile.

In Claire's eyes there's a tremble of amusement at the contrast between the slow and pillowy and pink-faced Cecilia and her fraught, swarthy, quick and tiny husband. Thirty seconds after arriving, Giacomo has returned to the battle in the kitchen.

The owners of the Antica Farmacia are, says Gideon, the best double-act in town. 'After us,' he corrects himself, to Robert. Claire is assiduously reading the menu. She shouldn't feel constrained by what's listed there, Gideon tells her: Giacomo can rustle up whatever she would like.

He summons Cecilia, and makes a great show of explaining that his niece, incredible though it may seem, does not eat meat.

'My husband will make you something good,' Cecilia assures her.

'It'll be wonderful,' guarantees Gideon. He proceeds to extol the talents of Giacomo; he professes envy of him, because Gideon has no aptitude for cookery whatsoever. And he takes no pleasure in it, which is why, for the past ten years or more, he has come to this restaurant almost every night it's been open. Claire asks how he came to be living in Castelluccio, so he tells her about his tour of France and Italy, and the day on which, in an unseasonal downpour, he drove into Castelluccio and decided to take refuge in the hotel. The next morning, a Sunday, he was presented with this vision of a place in which he sensed he would be able to work, a town that was peaceful and moderate in the best sense: not too large and not too small; nice-looking but not so nice-looking as to attract the hordes; amid terrain that was pleasing to the eye but not spectacular. Six months later, in winter, he flew back to see it at a time when it would be at its least appealing, and this second visit was a confirmation of that first impression. 'I wanted to change my life,' he tells her, 'and I knew that this was where I would change it.'

'And you?' says Claire, to Robert.

'I was part of the package,' he answers.

'OK,' says Claire, after a moment's hesitation, which provokes too loud a laugh from Gideon.

'He recruited me at the Tate,' says Robert, and Gideon promptly takes over, to recite the story of how his assistant came to join him: Gideon heckling the lecturer at the Jackson Pollock painting; the full and frank exchange of views; Robert, working as a guard, starting a conversation once the lecturer and his audience had departed; the discovery of shared opinions; the dead-end situation of Robert, the disenchanted former student of art; the offer of employment, days later. 'God bless Pollock. He brought us together,' he chuckles. 'Do you know Pollock?'

'Not really, no,' says Claire.

'Terrible man,' he says. He gives her the truth about Jackson Pollock: 'The Great I Am,' he proclaims, fists clenched, eyes directed heavenward. 'The hero who released the unconscious.

Through his supposedly spontaneous dribbles and spatters the essence of ourselves is speaking. That's the idea. But the essence turns out to have a liking for pretty patterns: a dash of yellow up here to balance the dash of yellow down there, a flick of blue there, to fill up this little vacancy. This isn't the voice of the depths – it's decoration. Pollock is a decorative artist.' And so on and so forth. Ninety percent of the talking has been done by Gideon by the time Claire gets her main course – fried zucchini, marinaded and, as promised, delicious.

Not until the food has been finished does Claire – in answer to a question from Robert – have a chance to say something about the job she has recently left, in the advice centre. After half a dozen sentences Gideon is glancing at his watch. Claire is trying to think of the right word for something when Gideon interrupts with: 'Sorry, but I have to go.' To Claire, who is blinking as though Gideon has just broken wind explosively, he adds, by way of explanation: 'Inspiration is for amateurs. Professionals go to work.' He gives a fold of banknotes to Robert, and to Claire he says: 'In the evenings, you're my guest.' With that, he leaves.

Claire, still blinking in amazement, says: 'I know I'm not Oscar Wilde, but I didn't think I was that boring.'

'He has his routines,' says Robert. He gives her the details: from 7am to 9am Gideon walks; he is in his studio from 9am to 1pm, drawing; he stops for an hour at lunchtime; from 2pm to 6pm he is in the studio, painting; from 6pm to 8pm he reads or takes a second walk or listens to music; he eats at 8.15pm, here, six nights out of seven, twice a week with Robert, usually Monday and Thursday; and from 10pm to midnight he paints.

'Yes, but—' Claire starts.

'And nothing short of his own funeral will break the schedule.'

2.9

At some point in the coming decade Giacomo and Cecilia Stornello will retire from the Antica Farmacia, and when they quit the restaurant will pass out of the family, or perhaps it will close: their son, Giorgio, is an officer in the Guardia Costiera, and their daughter, Gelsomina, married a man from Cesena and will never come back to Castelluccio. The Antica Farmacia, which ceased to be a pharmacy in the 1910s and first became a restaurant in the following decade, was acquired in 1957 by Giacomo's father, Gaspare, who had been an army cook during the war, and worked in various restaurants all over Tuscany prior to becoming his own boss. Giacomo took over from his father in 1982, five years after marrying Cecilia, who worked for her parents in the *alimentari* that they ran in Via dei Falcucci, which closed in 1992, not long after the supermarket opened on the Siena road. Cecilia's maternal great-grandmother, Violetta, had been the last cook of the Palazzo Campani, and Violetta's eldest daughter, Marietta, had worked alongside her from the age of fourteen until the death of Paolo Campani in 1920. In the dining room of the Antica Farmacia, below a shelf of majolica jars that once contained the pharmacy's materials, you can see a photograph of Violetta and Marietta with Paolo Campani, in the kitchen of the palazzo.

Both Giacomo and Cecilia were born in Castelluccio and they intend to die here. The love they have for the town is akin to the love they have for their parents. In late July and early August, and at the end of the year, when the Antica Farmacia is closed, Giacomo goes away for a day or two, to visit his sisters in Empoli. Otherwise, he and his wife never leave the town, except to go walking in the valley. When they were younger, they sometimes went abroad for their summer break, usually to Spain or Greece. Since the spring of 1998, however, Cecilia has not been out of sight of Castelluccio, because of what happened on their holiday in Cavalese.

One winter, when Cecilia was nine years old, her parents took her to visit her aunt and uncle in Trento, and the uncle took her up into the Val di Fiemme, to go skiing. She had never enjoyed anything as much as she enjoyed this: it was easier than riding a bike for her, and a hundred times more exciting. From then on, young Cecilia went to Trento every winter for a week of skiing, a custom that was maintained after she had married Giacomo, even though Giacomo lacked her sense of balance, and even cracked an ankle on their sixth trip, after which he contented himself with hiking in the snow, and watching his wife, always dressed in bright blue, flying down the slopes like a bead of ink down a marble wall.

On the morning of Monday, January 12th, 1998, Cecilia took the cable-car at Cavalese, in the Val di Fiemme; Giacomo, Giorgio and Gelsomina had decided to spend the day in Trento. Cecilia had ridden the cable-car many times; the height made Giacomo queasy, but for her it was no more unsettling than a ride on a bus. On this occasion, however, as her gondola approached the station at the summit, the cable stopped moving. For two hours it was stuck, and midway through those two hours a wind arose. High above the snow, the gondola rocked and creaked. Among the sixteen people trapped with Cecilia were two young girls, who were soon crying; one of them had a fit of screaming, and her mother almost had to smother her to keep her quiet. A woman vomited when something on the roof of the gondola made a loud groaning noise, like steel beginning to fail. Snow was now falling, and within minutes they were cut off from the sight of the summit and of the ground below them. It was then that Cecilia began to panic. Every sound from overhead was the sound of the cable starting to come apart; the gondola shook in the wind and she lost all strength from her legs; her face hit the metal floor, and she felt that she was still falling. When the gondola was at last hauled into the station she was shaking as if she'd been left naked in the snow for an hour; she gulped for air as though struggling to stay above quicksand. A doctor had to come up the mountain to escort her down.

Every night, for weeks, she had nightmares: she was being buried alive in snow; she was floating up into space entombed in a bubble of white glass; she was falling into a bottomless crevasse. Previously ever-cheerful, Cecilia became depressed: her memory of things that had happened more than a year or so ago became unavailable to her; she felt that her mind had been damaged, that a part of herself had been destroyed in the space of those two hours of captivity and terror. And when, a month after her ordeal, the disaster happened with the Cavalese cable-car and twenty people were killed, her depression worsened. At every moment she was conscious that everyone she loved might die in an instant; she felt at times that she was in some way responsible for the disaster at Cavalese, as if she had colluded with fate to kill the twenty innocents instead of herself. Her doctor gave her drugs to reduce her anxiety, which they did, but she was even less like herself with the tablets than she had been without them, so she threw them away and became so depressed that she could not get out of bed.

By April she had begun to recover. In May she and Giacomo went to Siena one afternoon. She enjoyed herself, but then Giacomo walked off to buy some film and the moment she lost sight of him she became strange: suddenly she did not recognise where she was; the crowd seemed to have some sinister purpose, as if they had conspired to remove her husband from her; the ground felt as if it were shifting; it tipped her over. In June, in Volterra, she was in the toilet of a restaurant when suddenly, with no warning, she could not breathe properly, and was convinced she was in a cellar that had no stairs. This was the last time Cecilia ventured beyond the environs of Castelluccio.

She is wholly at ease only within the town walls, but can go out onto the hills as long as she does not lose sight of the Torre del Saraceno. The peak of Le Cornate is the farthest she has travelled since 1998. For most of the time, she is happy to be confined to Castelluccio. She would like to see more of the world, but it's a small wish, not a strong desire: we all have unfulfilled wishes, she says, and perhaps, anyway, she will one day go abroad again. In Castelluccio she has everything she needs for a good life. If God were to grant her one wish, for herself, it wouldn't be for her anxiety to be cured: instead, she would like to be the weight she was when she was half her present age. In the dining room of the Antica Farmacia, around the pictures of Violetta, Marietta and Gaspare are arrayed photos of Giacomo and Cecilia, one for every year that they have owned their restaurant, and in each successive picture Cecilia is a little plumper than in its predecessor, while Giacomo remains the same, except for the hair. But Giacomo loves her. He has never been unfaithful, as she once announced to Gideon and Robert, engulfing her husband in an embrace. It was as a reward for his virtue, she explained, that she allowed him to employ such pretty waitresses.

2.10

There are seven shops in the section of Corso Diaz that they walk along, and in the windows of five of them the poster for Gideon's exhibition is displayed. 'He's the first famous citizen of Castelluccio for a hundred years,' Robert tells her.

'Is he famous? Really famous?' asks Claire; the question seems to be a genuine request for information.

'In certain circles,' he answers. 'They're not going to raise a statue of him when he's gone, but a lot of people know of him.'

'And is it important to him, being famous?'

'Well, that's not why he does it, if that's what you're asking.'

'It wasn't. But is it important to him that he's well known?'

'He doesn't dislike it. He wants to be respected, but not necessarily by a lot of people.'

She nods, apparently making slight modifications to her view of her uncle, and says nothing more for a while. As they pass the Caffè del Corso she announces, with no evidence of regret: 'We're not hitting it off. Gideon and I. We haven't started well.'

'He said he'd enjoyed talking to you.'

'He was being diplomatic.'

'Gideon is no diplomat.'

'He thinks I'm a dullard,' she states, cheerfully enough.

'Not the impression he gave me.'

For the first time since leaving the restaurant she looks at him directly; it's a sustained examining look, to ascertain if the source of the untruth is himself or Gideon. 'And I think he's a bit too full of himself,' she says.

'You don't get far without self-confidence in Gideon's line of work. He knows who he is.'

'Nice way of putting it.'

'Anyway, you were getting along fine this evening, it seemed to me.'

'Three was company. Two would have been a crowd,' she says. Then she asks: 'Does he ever talk about his brother?'

'No,' he says.

This appears to be the truth, but she says: 'Really?'

'Never said a word.'

'When my mother died, he sent my father a letter. My father couldn't bear to have his name mentioned after that. He ever mention that?'

'No.'

'But you knew he had a brother?'

'Not until we heard from you.'

'Then what did he say?'

'About your father?'

'Him or me.'

'Nothing much.'

'He must have said something.'

'What Gideon doesn't want to talk about he doesn't talk about.'

Again she looks at him. 'OK,' she says, as if permitting him to leave after questioning.

They have arrived at Piazza del Mercato. It's a shame, he says, that she won't be in Castelluccio for the festival. He tells her about the parade, in which Gideon will be taking part, and about the high point of the festivities: the Angel and the Falling Boy. 'The boy slides down a wire, from the top of the Torre del Saraceno, and the Angel comes down from the campanile of the Redentore,' he explains, his hands describing their convergence. 'That's what Marta will be doing. Marta the waitress. She's this year's Angel.'

'Brave girl,' she comments, then his phone rings – it's Teresa, wanting to know where he is. 'Good night,' mimes Claire, walking off.

2.11

Gideon is in his studio and the photos that Claire brought are downstairs, on a shelf, with the sketchbook; he has scanned the sketches, but the wallet of photographs remains unopened. For the past twenty minutes he has merely been fiddling; the presence of those unseen pictures has become a distraction, at first intermittent, now unignorable, like the whine of a mosquito. He wipes his brush and goes down to the living room.

In the first photograph, taken in Victoria Park, some time in the autumn (judging by the trees), in 1954 or 1955 (judging by the size of the boys), young Gideon has a ball between his feet, apparently attempting to get past his brother, who is leaning onto a shoulder as though to crush him into the ground; nothing is to be read into this, he knows. The next has them sitting on a dry-stone wall, grinning at the camera, each wearing voluminous shorts, crepe-soled sandals and an open-necked shirt with sleeves rolled, white for David, dark for Gideon; David, approximately ten years old, has his left arm around Gideon, and seems to be pulling him close; nothing is to be read into this either. Gideon lingers slightly longer on this one, but only to try to recall where the picture was taken; he cannot. A third photograph: perhaps two years later, outside the shop; the windows are smeared with suds; each boy holds a water-charged sponge; Gideon is laughing in the direction of David, who glares with what was probably mock fury, but might not have been.

A couple of weeks later, after Claire has left, Gideon will tell his assistant that he tried, he really did try, to summon some fondness for the boy in the white shirt, but he could feel nothing: not affection, not resentment, not sadness – absolutely nothing. The image of the other boy, young Gideon, likewise stirred nothing more than a disinterested and tepid curiosity. 'This isn't me,' he said. 'It's a child with the same name.' He proposes an analogy with a wave travelling across a sea: it retains something of its form throughout its journey, but the substance of the water at point A is not the same as at point M. The analogy, he admits, is imprecise.

Only one photograph in the batch of half a dozen touches him: his mother with her sons, on a bench somewhere, one on each side of her, holding a hand. Looking at his mother's face, he will say, it was impossible not see a sadness in her half-smile, a sadness for a life unfulfilled, and for the discord between her children. He will show the picture to Robert, who sees a plump woman in a tight floral dress, her face expressing tenderness and exhaustion.

The sketchbook has already been scanned, but now he inspects it again. It's a miscellany of drawings, spanning more than a year, starting with portraits, in pencil, of two of his contemporaries at Camberwell: one looks a little like Vanessa Redgrave, and her name, he's nearly sure, was Rosie something; the other one vaguely resembles Ringo Starr, and he can remember nothing about him. There's a street view, drawn in Nunhead; it is of no interest. A spread is filled with studies of his own left hand; an unidentifiable dog lies on grass, belly to the ground, head held up heraldically. A page of glass bottles – a good drawing, this – is obviously a pastiche of Morandi; he would have dated the start of his interest in Morandi a few years later than this, but the evidence suggests otherwise. Two pages later, there's a sketch of Lorraine's torso, to which he reacts – he'll tell Robert, much later – with mild surprise at how comely she had been, and some displeasure at the awkwardness of the draughtsmanship.

This is the body of the last woman who could be called his lover: not the last woman he loved, nor the last, perhaps, to love him – but the last with whom he experienced complete intimacy. Yet the drawing does not move him, not in the slightest. The photograph of his mother moves him, as does one page of the sketchbook: a portrait in profile – meticulous but incomplete – of Martin Calloway, to whom he owes so much. Some of the lines are hesitant and fidgety, perhaps betraying nervousness; the shading lacks precision. Nevertheless, much of the man has been truthfully portrayed: the dignity, the intelligence, the honest consciousness of his own worth. For many minutes Gideon examines the profiled head. He cannot recall the names of his fellows students, but he can hear Martin Calloway's voice, the whisper of authority: 'Truth, not novelty,' he instructs.

2.12

A precociously gifted draughtsman, Gideon Westfall always knew that art was his vocation. The fulfilment of that vocation, however, was frustrated rather than advanced by his experiences at art college in the early 1970s. 'We weren't studying,' he says. 'We were receiving indoctrination. I was naïve. I had expected to be taught how to paint and how to draw. Instead, we were recruits to a cause. Picasso was the horizon. Beyond him lay the wastelands of history. That was the attitude,' he says. Desperate for a deeper knowledge, he would study the masters at the National Gallery, making copies of the artists he revered, and still reveres. 'I was self-taught,' he says, 'and self-taught is never good enough.'

Shortly before leaving college, he happened upon an essay by Martin Calloway: "On the Education of Painters". It made a huge impression. To this day, he knows by heart whole paragraphs of Calloway's plea for a return to the time-honoured system of studio apprenticeship. '"If our civilization is to maintain the art of painting as a vital part of its culture,"' he recites, '"we must revive the method by which nearly every painter of importance was trained."' Calloway's definition of the values that underpinned his work also struck a chord: 'Everything I do proceeds from a belief in order and in wholeness,' wrote Calloway. 'For hundreds of years our artists spoke a language that everyone could understand. After two world wars, that language has become imperilled. We are in a latter-day Babel, and my mission is to play a part in building a road out it.'

Keen to play a part in that mission, Westfall approached Calloway, asking if he would consider taking him as a pupil. He was invited to visit Calloway's atelier in Windsor; having presented a portfolio, he was offered a place on the spot. Ruthlessly self-critical, Westfall has destroyed all of the work that so quickly persuaded Calloway to take him under his wing. 'With Martin Calloway, I began again, from the beginning,' he says. He is unstinting in his praise for his mentor. 'You could put Martin Calloway in front of any painting in the National Gallery and he could talk to you for an hour about how it was made,' says Westfall. 'His understanding of materials was matchless. And his eye was infallible. Before I went to him, I didn't know how to look. To really look,' he tells me.

He's angry that a man of such talent and integrity should be so neglected. Martin Calloway died two years ago, and no public gallery placed a bid when the contents of his studio were auctioned. 'It is all one can do to not despair, living in a world in which a person who pickles animals is lauded as a major artist, while a master such as Calloway is spurned,' he fumes. The state of art education in Britain appals him. The colleges have become production lines, he complains, turning out young people whose only talent is for self-promotion. 'There's no instruction, no direction,' he says. 'Self-expression rules the roost, but at that age you have nothing to say unless you're Raphael, and you get a Raphael once in a blue moon. A young person should be learning the language, not just babbling.' The situation was almost as bad when he was at art school, he says. 'Digging a hole in the ground is not art,' he states. 'Cutting grass is not art. Throwing piles of felt into the corner of a room is not art. But these were things we were expected to take seriously.' So-called conceptualism, for Westfall, is the great plague of contemporary art. 'Blindingly obvious notions – I cannot call them ideas – are presented as if they were flashes of genius.' He has no time for abstract art, either. 'Abstraction is a pathology of the twentieth century,' he declares. 'Expressive abstraction is the apotheosis of narcissism; and geometric abstraction – call it what you will – is like asking us to accept a grammar book as literature.'

. . . To some, Gideon Westfall is a reactionary. He rejects the accusation. 'My work,' he says 'goes against the grain of modernist orthodoxies, of course, and in that respect it might be said to be provocative. But I am not working in reaction to those orthodoxies. To me they are an irrelevance. I believe in the value of tradition, which is something we are nowadays encouraged to disavow. I have one foot in this world and one in the past.'

The same is true of Italy, he goes on, which is why he has settled there. 'The Italians have a respect for tradition which the British have lost, or thrown away. Italians are conservatives, in the best sense of the word. Which is not to say that they are resistant to modernity. Far from it. This is the land of Michelangelo and also the land of Ferrari. They have the best of both worlds: craftsmen whose skills have been passed from generation to generation, and people working on the leading edge of technology. They also have some very dodgy politicians, and execrable TV, but that's another story.' His home is a large apartment beside a medieval tower. The climate suits him; the light, as he puts it, is sustenance. He cannot envisage ever returning to England . . .

Unlike his mentor, he does not have pupils: he employs a single assistant. 'Martin Calloway showed me what a teacher should be. He was a generous man and a great tutor. But I haven't his patience or his kindness. I have to work alone.' He has few close friends, he says. The sociability of Italians is something he enjoys, but he observes it from the outside. 'An artist should never be entirely at home,' he says.

We have been talking for an hour, and it's now 2pm in Italy – time for Westfall to return to the studio. I ask him what's on his easel at the moment. His work, he tells me, has been taking a new tangent of late: he is making studies for a *Last Supper*. It will be philosophical rather than dramatic in conception – he has in mind something akin to the *Sacraments* of Poussin, but he cannot say more than that. He's never happy talking about his work. The work should speak for itself, he believes. 'Artists talk too much nowadays,' he adds.

Tomorrow he is driving to Sansepolcro, to study Piero's *Resurrection*. 'To some of us, the Renaissance is still news,' he says. 'True art never ceases to be news.'

From: Quentin Scammell, "Gideon Westfall: radical traditionalist", *Painting Today*, vol 25, no. 3, April 2001.

 3

3.1

CROSSING PIAZZA MAGGIORE, Robert sees a woman in jeans and a white shirt taking a photo of the square, then he realises that she's Claire. The lens is pointing in his direction, but she doesn't see him until he waves to her; she reacts with a start, and lowers the camera. 'I think I might have wandered into your shot,' he tells her; they take a look, and there he is, on the edge of the picture, arm partly raised. 'How are you this morning?' he asks.

'Very well,' she says. She looks rested and relaxed, and the casual way she holds the camera – at her side, fingers encircling the lens – is suggestive of competence. The white shirt suits her, and there's a good perfume too: a pleasant musky scent that has bergamot in it, and perhaps violets, and vanilla.

'What does the day hold?' he asks.

'Gideon rang the hotel – we're having lunch,' she says, with a flexing of an eyebrow.

'Give it time,' he says.

She raises her face and momentarily closes her eyes in the sunlight. 'And where are you off to?' she asks, as though accusing him of playing truant.

Before starting work, he explains, he has a coffee in the Corso, then he walks to the Santa Maria gate and back.

'Every day?'

'Most days.'

She smiles at this. 'Gideon and his schedule. You and your ritual,' she comments.

'Habit might be a better word,' he says.

She has been reminded of her ex-husband – his need to have all doors and drawers shut perfectly, which was once an endearing quirk, and later an irritant.

'You're welcome to join me,' says Robert. Claire looks around the square, as if assessing whether it might offer something better than a stroll to the Santa Maria gate.

She's about to answer that she'll stay here for a while when a chubby bald man, bespectacled, in a rumpled black suit, making a detour across the square, comes towards them. He shakes Robert's hand, says something that has the word *maestro* in it, and Robert introduces Mr Lanese, director of the Museo Civico of Castelluccio, to the maestro's niece. Mr Lanese removes his glasses before squeezing her palm with fingers as soft as chamois; in English he professes to be delighted, and observes a resemblance to Mr Westfall. But he must hurry, he apologises, as if to say that nothing could have pleased him more than to linger with them.

'A very nice chap,' remarks Robert ruefully, as soon as Mr Lanese is out of earshot. 'He deserves better.'

'Better than what?'

'Being in charge of the most boring museum in Italy. You should give it a look. It's terrible. Like a Renaissance degree show, but worse. Anyway, I mustn't dally. Coming?' he asks, and she goes with him.

Before they have reached the end of Corso Diaz at least ten people have greeted Robert. Three have stopped for a quick word. 'Tell me,' she says, after the third has left them, 'do you know absolutely everybody in this town?'

'A small place,' he answers. 'And we've been here a long time. Everybody knows Gideon, and I'm his representative on earth.'

'I couldn't stand it.'

'What, being his representative?'

'Living in a tiny town. Everyone knowing your business.'

'Oh, they know your face,' he says, 'but not necessarily much more than that.'

As they arrive at Santa Maria dei Carmini a stout woman, of Gideon's age or thereabouts, comes out of the church and, seeing Robert, smiles as a woman might do on encountering a favourite nephew. '*Ciao* Roberto,' she calls across the square, and performs a mime – which involves turning a key in a door – to explain why she's not stopping.

'This is ridiculous,' Claire says.

'Her name's Luisa,' he tells her. 'A pal of Gideon's. She has a shop, near the hotel. The window full of industrial-strength knickers and bras.'

'She seems to like you.'

'She likes Gideon. And vice versa.'

'You're telling me she's his girlfriend?'

He laughs at the idea; he is watching Luisa, waiting for her to disappear into Corso Diaz, as if this conversation cannot be continued until she has gone. 'Got a minute?' he asks. 'I'll show you something, in here.' He leads her into the church, where he stops at the entrance to the sacristy, below a life-sized Virgin, a bearded man and a pair of angels, all made of white plaster. 'Right,' he begins. 'You need to understand what's going on here.' He proceeds to explain that this tableau represents the mo-ment at which, on July 16, 1251, in Cambridge, the Virgin Mary appeared to St Simon Stock, the vicar-general of the Carmelites, and placed the scapular – 'that rectangle of cloth with strings attached' – in his hands, with the words: *This shall be a sign of grace for you and for all Carmelites: whoever dies clothed in this shall not suffer eternal fire.* 'That's what it says, on the ribbon the angels are holding,' he tells her.

She is facing the figures, but her eyes don't seem to be looking. 'Am I boring you?' he asks.

'Not at all,' Claire replies. 'Really. I'm interested. It's bonkers.'

'Well,' he continues, 'several years ago, one Sunday morning, the left arm of St Simon fell off and crashed to the floor. You can see where it's been repaired,' he says, pointing to a thick grey seam above the elbow. 'The arm landed here, where Luisa had been standing only a minute earlier. She'd been standing right on this spot, talking to the priest. If the arm had come away sixty seconds earlier, she would have been killed. And the thing is, Luisa wears the scapular. Which of course explains why she survived. The scapular of St Simon Stock saved her from his arm. Celestial vigilance; no casualties.'

'You believe that?' she asks.

'No. Of course not.'

'Just checking.' After a few more seconds have passed, she smiles.

'What?' he asks.

'Like I said,' she replies. 'Life in a small town. We pass an old lady in the street, and you have a story about her. Everybody knows everybody.'

'Coincidence. We happened to see Luisa, but I couldn't tell you anything about anyone else we've seen this morning. Hardly a thing.'

'Ah, "hardly,"' she says. 'A lot of leeway there.'

Robert has to get to work; he leaves her in the church. For a moment or two she regards the broken-armed saint, though it's not of much interest. When she comes out, the movement of a lizard on the wall makes her jump, and her pulse races, for longer than it should, as though she's just climbed a dozen flights of stairs.

3.2

The Common Wall Lizard (*Podarcis muralis*), which is widespread in Mediterranean Europe, was first described in 1768 by the Austrian naturalist Josephus Nicolaus Laurenti (1735–1805). Of the various subspecies that have been classified, several are native to Italy, including *Podarcis muralis breviceps*, *Podarcis muralis nigriventris*, *Podarcis muralis bruggemani*, *Podarcis muralis cerbolensis* and *Podarcis muralis maculiventris*, which was identified in 1838 by Charles-Lucien Bonaparte, Prince of Musignano and Canino, and nephew of Napoleon Bonaparte. The lizard that has startled Claire is a female *Podarcis muralis nigriventris*. Being three years old, this specimen is approaching the midpoint of the average life span for the subspecies; measuring 135mm from nose to tail-tip, it is of moderate size for a creature that rarely exceeds 190mm in length. Purely insectivorous, *Podarcis muralis nigriventris* is prey to birds, snakes, scorpions, spiders, cats and various other mammals.

3.3

It's a Saturday, so when his father closes the shop Giovanni Cabrera will have a meal with his parents, then he'll meet Alessandra and they'll see who's around at the Torre, and at ten or eleven they'll pile into Ivo's Lancia and they'll drive to a club on the coast, or maybe they'll go to Florence. If they go to Florence they'll clear their heads in the morning with a walk by the river, and have a smoke on the Trìnita bridge, with the water sliding underneath them, then they'll drive back, fast, with the hills changing colour all around.

It was Alessandra who told him what Ilaria was doing. And after he'd split with Ilaria he was down by the stream with Ivo one evening, shooting cans with the air rifle, and Alessandra had turned up and said she'd just seen Ilaria with the Englishman, the younger one, and although it didn't matter any more this made him miss a can or two, which made Alessandra laugh. A few days later she came down to the stream again, and this time he shot ten cans in a row, including one that Ivo balanced on the palm of an outstretched hand. That night Alessandra came with him to the cypress trees, where he often goes when the sky is clear, because the trees screen out every bit of light from the town, so with his binoculars he can see thousands of stars. An astronomer is what he would be in a perfect world, but what he'll do instead is run the shop when his father packs it in. He has wanted to be an astronomer ever since the day at school, ten years ago, when the class was shown a film about Mount Palomar, but later he'd realised that he wasn't smart enough to do that kind of thing for a living, though he was smart enough to do it as a hobby. So he would have sat by the trees with Alessandra and showed her which constellation was which, and explained how the stars were formed and how far they were, and what that meant: that this speck of light started its flight through space when there were dinosaurs walking where Castelluccio now was. He would have told her, as it would seem he tells every girl he brings here, about the signal that came from the direction of Sagittarius on August 15th, 1977: the 37-second pulse that made an astronomer called Jerry Ehman write "Wow!" on the printout at Ohio State University's radio telescope. It's an exciting story, and it makes a girl move closer. And soon Giovanni and Alessandra were going up the hill nearly every night, even though Alessandra's father doesn't like him, and neither does her mother.

It was Alessandra's best friend Bernarda who told her what Ilaria was doing. Bernarda, like Alessandra, was in the same class as Ilaria, and for a few months, unlike Alessandra, had been her friend, until Ilaria became too much of a drag, always moaning or talking about the things she was going to do to get famous. They had gone riding together a few times, and for a while they were both in the group that used to hang out at the Torre. It was at the Torre that Ilaria got to know Giovanni. There was a shoot-'em-up game in the bar, and one night Giovanni made the highest score ever. They took a liking to each other, though they didn't see eye to eye about Castelluccio. 'This place will drive me insane,' she told him, raking her hair back in despair. 'I like it,' he said. His mother was born here; his father was born here; three of his grandparents were born here. 'I belong here,' he said. 'There is nothing to do,' she said. He had to agree, but he found it hard to imagine living anywhere else. 'Castelluccio is my shell,' he told her. 'I am not a tortoise,' said Ilaria. For her, Castelluccio was a cage, and she couldn't stand living with her father and mother; her father made her work like a slave. When they went up to the cypresses, she was like a girl on leave from prison. When she fired the air rifle, she seemed to be settling a score. Ilaria was sexy as hell, even when she was going around as if she had her own private thundercloud hanging over her head. They argued, usually at the weekend, when her father wouldn't let her go with them in the car. He'd no more let her go clubbing in Florence than he'd let her have heroin for breakfast, she said. On one occasion, after Ilaria had stayed out until midnight, he ambushed Giovanni on the street and swore at him for getting his daughter drunk. So Giovanni would have to go to Florence without her, every other week or so, and the following day she wouldn't speak to him, or she'd arrange to meet him and not turn up, or shriek at him for an hour non-stop, as mad as her father.

It was Viviana who told Bernarda about Ilaria and the painter. Viviana left the Torre late one Saturday night and saw Ilaria opening the gate that led to the apartments. As soon as he heard this, Giovanni confronted his girlfriend. 'Why were you going in there?' he demanded. 'What business is it of yours?' answered Ilaria. She wanted to know if he'd had a good time in Florence. He asked her again what she'd been doing, and this time she replied, with no hesitation, as if he'd merely asked what she'd had to eat that evening: 'I am a model.' You could see the information working its way into the depths of Giovanni's mind, she said, like a tiny drop of coffee trickling into a sugar cube. 'You take off your clothes?' he asked; he could not have been more bewildered if she'd just told him that she was in fact a man. 'That is what models do,' she told him. 'He says I'm good,' she went on, 'and he pays me. He says good models are hard to find.' She showed him the envelope with the notes in it. 'What exactly is he paying you for?' Giovanni enquired. She was going to slap him, she said, but as her hand moved upward it changed its shape and she punched him instead, on the ear. Then he slapped her, right in the middle of Via Sant'Agostino, in broad daylight, and that was the end of that, more or less. Within a week, all of her friends and all of his knew what Ilaria was doing. One afternoon she stormed into the shop and emptied a carton of milk over him. And that really was the end of that.

The following week, Giovanni was on his way back from Volterra, on his Vespa, when he saw Ilaria walking along the road with the painter's assistant. They were walking close to each other, and he could tell by the smile on Ilaria's face and the smile she was getting back from him that something was going on. He rode past as if he hadn't noticed them, but a few days later he went up to the stables to have it out with her. 'So, what's happening?' he asked. Nothing was happening, she told him, and if something was happening it wouldn't be any of his business, would it? Voices were raised. 'Are you fucking him?' Giovanni shouted. 'Maybe I am and maybe I'm not,' Ilaria shouted. Her father appeared, and Giovanni kick-started the Vespa.

Giovanni rode through the Porta di Santa Maria at speed, at precisely the same instant as a lizard, crawling up the wall beside the gate, was spotted by a cat that had been taking the sun on the pavement on the opposite side of the gate. The cat sprinted across the road, into the path of angry Giovanni, who was not quite as attentive as he should have been. He swerved too sharply, skidded, and fell. Some skin was scoured from one forearm, a hip was heavily bruised, and a shin was cracked, so

now he can't take his place in the parade, because you can't hurl
a flag and catch it when you're on crutches.

34

Following Via Sant'Agostino, Claire passes a nice-looking
building called L'Antica Cereria, which seems to contain apartments or maybe offices, and comes to a narrow street that cuts
back towards Corso Diaz. She takes it, and after twenty yards
the street widens out, in front of an old house that has a crum-
bly piece of stone – perhaps a coat of arms – stuck between the
ground-floor and first-floor windows. It looks like a solidified
sponge; she can make out the tail of what might have been
a dolphin. Sunlight is on the top of the building; the bronze-
coloured guttering glows; she can hear applause on a TV set
– and then, for no discernible reason, Joe appears in her head,
and suddenly she's remembering that evening, arriving home
from work to find him at the kitchen table, waiting for her, obviously, with his face pre-set in Remorse mode. 'We need to talk':
she can hear him saying it, and it's funny now, usually – as if
he'd rehearsed for his big moment by memorising lines from a
terrible film. And she can see him: the anguished clamping of
hands to brow; the watery-eyed protestations of self-loathing;
the woebegone stare. There's still a sting in the memory, but no
longer any great sense of loss. She is not thinking about him,
yet he is in her mind, like a phrase from a stupid tune that she
can't get out of her head. To chase him out, she starts looking for
things that would make a picture.

She crosses Corso Diaz, saunters back to Santa Maria, frames
a shot of the façade, thinks better of it, then goes through the
gate. On the outside of the town wall, *ILARIA TI AMO* has been
sprayed in scarlet paint; the script is angular and quite elegant;
she takes a photo. She returns to Piazza Santa Maria, and this
time goes right, into Via Santa Maria. Halfway along, she finds
a lane: she walks up it, and within a few seconds she becomes

aware of a sound, a pulsing clatter with a hiss in it, which is coming from somewhere in front of her. The lane makes a right-angled turn to the left, and at this angle she finds the source of the noise: a door is open, and through it she sees a large room and a printing press. It's an old contraption, black, the size of a small car, and a man in blue overalls is standing beside it, with his back to her, watching sheets of yellow paper rolling through fast-spinning drums. To the right of the door is a small barred window, which allows her to look for longer, unseen. One whole side of the room is taken up by a machine that looks like a vast white cupboard with a computer attached to it; a young woman is sitting at it, tapping at the keyboard, and then Claire notices that, to the side of the young woman, cards are being ejected into racks at a remarkable rate. And in a corner, surrounded by packets of paper, an older woman is taping the wrapping of a brick-sized parcel; a shoulder is hunched to hold the phone into which she's shouting. The man keeps patting the printing machine, as if it were an animal. He gathers a printed yellow sheet, plucking it with a quick pinch of thumb and forefinger; he presses a button and the drums wind down; he turns, inspecting the sheet, and she sees who he is – he's the man with the flattened nose. Feeling conspicuous now that the din has stopped, she moves away from the window.

After two or three twists of the street, she emerges by another gate, on the square that has the memorial with the full-breasted angel on top of it. When she frames it in the viewfinder it looks good, the bright bronze against the clear blue sky. She takes half a dozen shots and deletes four of them. That done, she glances to her right, where an old man in a denim shirt, arms crossed, scowls at the monument, at her, and at the monument again, as if at a loss to understand why anyone would point a camera at it. He shrugs; the scowl softens into an expression of barely interested bafflement, which promptly melts away. He says something to her; to judge by the tone of it, it's a piece of information. All she can do is smile, which brings the scowl back. He points at the inscription on the base of the monument and says something else, before going on his way, limping slightly, not waiting for a response.

3.5

Castelluccio's war memorial stands on the edge of Piazza della Libertà, by the town's southern gate. Fronted by an area of grass, the monument comprises a limestone block, set against a curving brick wall; the block measures 2.5 metres by 2.5 metres by 1.5 metres, with the names of the dead listed on the front face, a high relief of crossed flags on one of the two smaller faces, and a relief of a laurel wreath on the other. The names are carved in Roman-style lettering on a slab of Carrara marble which is attached to the block by four bronze rivets. The inscription is as follows:

RIDORDA I SVOI FIGLI MORTI PER LA PATRIA 1915–18

TENENTE: PERELLO GIOVANNI
CAP MAGG: BASTIANELLI UGO
CAPORALE: MANNI EVARISTO
SOLD: BALDINI VINCENZO
BEVACQUA RINALDO
D'ALESSANDRO MICHELE
FACCHINI GIOVANNI
GIZZI PASQUALE
JOVENE TOMMASO
MARTINI PAOLO
PACETTI ENNIO
RICCIUTO VALERIO
SILVESTRINI AMATO
TASSINO UMBERTO

The monument is surmounted by a winged female figure in bronze, representing the Spirit of the Italian Nation. She was created by the Florentine sculptor Giovanni Vela (1880–1953), and is one of six identical statues cast by Vela and his assistants in the early 1930s. Brandishing a spear in her left hand and a *tricolore* in her right, she bears an often-noted resemblance to the central figure in Eugène Delacroix's *La Liberté guidant le peuple*.

Vela's winged woman was acquired by Castelluccio after the rejection of the work submitted in 1930 by Achille de Marinis, the artist who had been originally commissioned to design the memorial. Achille de Marinis was triply qualified for the task: he was a local man, having been born in the nearby village of San Dalmazio in 1896; he was a talented sculptor, who had studied with no less a master than Ettore Ferrari; and he had fought in the war. He was wounded on September 9th, 1917, on the slopes of San Gabriele, during the Eleventh Battle of the Isonzo, within an hour of the death of Ennio Pacetti, with whom he was acquainted, and who died but a hundred metres from the spot where de Marinis was shot. Umberto Tassino died on the same mountain, at 2pm the following day.

As first conceived by de Marinis, the limestone block was to support a life-sized figure of a soldier, lying on his back, with a coat covering much of his body. He was perhaps dead, perhaps alive but exhausted, and his eyes were to be open to the heavens. The face was to be expressive of 'nobility and suffering', said the sculptor, but the commissioning committee, upon being shown the plaster maquette in the studio that de Marinis occupied in Via Santa Maria, saw too much suffering and too little nobility. In the words of one committee member, it was deemed inappropriate that the town should commemorate its fallen warriors with an image of 'a cadaver on a slab'. Three months later, de Marinis presented a second version, representing a soldier seated against a shattered tree trunk, clutching his rifle across his chest, gazing into the distance with a look of, to quote the artist, 'indomitable resolution in the face of great hardships'. Again the committee was not satisfied. 'The man appears dazed,' was one complaint. 'Why is he sitting?' was another, and: 'We wish to mark a victory, not a defeat.' Costanza Pacetti, the young widow of Ennio, protested that the seated soldier was an 'unpatriotic' concept. De Marinis was given one last opportunity: the soldier must stand, he was told, and he must be heroic. He duly gave the committee a standing figure, a man who 'has endured all, and will not be beaten.' Costanza Pacetti was no more impressed by the risen soldier than she had been by his seated predecessor. 'He seems to be starving, and he has the face of a lunatic,' she remarked to a local journalist. Others thought that the soldier looked like a man in shock, or a deserter facing a firing squad.

While the committee was discussing what should now be done, the chairman came to hear that a cast of Vela's *Spirit*, which had been acclaimed in the towns in which it had already been unveiled, could be obtained at a reasonable price. Achille de Marinis withdrew to Rome, where rumours regarding his political sympathies soon began to spread: he was said to be a communist. His critics felt vindicated when, a year after the debacle of Castelluccio, de Marinis left Italy for London. He became an art teacher in Nottingham, where he died in 1972. For most of his life he had continued to work, on a modest scale; small figures and portraits of his wife and daughter, mostly in clay, comprised the bulk of his output. He achieved something of a reputation as a designer of sports trophies, and was given one substantial public commission: a statue of St Michael, ten feet high, which was affixed to the entrance wall of a shopping precinct in the West Midlands from 1964 until the redevelopment of the site in 1995.

3.6

At ten minutes past ten Robert is at his workbench, constructing a frame, when his phone rings: it's Eliana Tranfaglia, from the Palazzo Comunale. There has been, she tells him, an incident: one of the pictures has been ruined – well, not ruined entirely, but damaged, defaced. 'Can you come, right away?' she asks;

she sounds like a woman informing her brother that a parent is near death.

Robert passes the news on to Gideon. He wipes the excess paint from his brushes, puts them in their rightful places, washes his hands, unhurriedly dries them, while scrutinising the painting he has been forced to abandon. 'Let's go,' he says, like a sheriff prepared for a showdown.

Eliana Tranfaglia is awaiting them at the top of the stairs, hands clasped. Never the jolliest of women, today she has a face of fierce severity; her outfit – dark grey skirt, crisp white blouse, burgundy ceramic brooch worn on the left breast like a decoration for her years of service to the community – could not be more appropriate to the occasion. She escorts them swiftly to the site of the outrage: a corner of the room, in the angle of two of the display panels. The picture in question is a study, in oil on canvas, of a young woman seated on a wooden stool, naked in a vertical shaft of sunlight, with a glass pitcher of water at her feet; the word *MERDA* has been written with a marker pen in block capitals that run from edge to edge, obliterating the torso.

'When did this happen?' Robert asks.

It must have been yesterday afternoon, late yesterday afternoon, she tells him, because it was noticed this morning, when the hall was unlocked, or very shortly afterwards. They had a visitor almost as soon as the doors were opened, and he drew their attention to it.

Gideon has a word with Robert, to ascertain that he has understood what Signora Tranfaglia has said, before suggesting to her that this man was likely to have been the culprit.

'It was a Dutch man. A tourist. He did not do it, I know that for sure,' she answers. 'He was very shocked.' She goes on to tell Robert that the criminal act must have been perpetrated at the end of the day, because otherwise a visitor would have seen the damage and reported it.

Above the display panels, bolted into the wall, a CCTV camera is aimed in their direction. Gideon's gaze, which for a few seconds has been scanning the room, as if in search of someone who might address this situation with greater adequacy than Signora Tranfaglia, latches onto the camera. He jabs a forefinger at it, directing Signora Tranfaglia's attention to this crucial instrument, which appears to have slipped her mind. She looks at the camera, then at Gideon; from her eyes he knows what she's about to say. She says it, at some length.

'It doesn't work. Right?' Gideon mutters to Robert.

'In a nutshell.'

Gideon rolls his eyes – it's his 'God, what a country' expression. The cameras and alarms were installed by a firm owned by Alberto Granchello; Alberto Granchello's brother, Stefano, is an accountant in the town hall; these two facts are not unrelated.

The camera is being repaired, Signora Tranfaglia informs them. She does a face of weary resignation, and performs a gesture – arms outspread, as if to present to him a thing of shoddy construction – that is intended to elicit sympathy for her unending struggle with the incompetent. No sympathy is forthcoming. Gideon stares at her, and does not release her from his attention until her expression has modulated into something that suggests acceptance of at least a morsel of responsibility.

Talking to her through Robert, Gideon wants to know who was on duty at the end of the afternoon, and how they could not have observed what was going on. 'It was done at the end of the day,' he continues, before Robert has finished translating. 'There can't have been many people in here. Talk to the person who was at the desk. Let's get some descriptions.'

Signora Tranfaglia replies that she has already spoken to the girl who was on duty in the afternoon, and she saw only three people, and these were people that she knew, local people, who could not have done it.

At this point Gideon's temper begins to unravel. 'Well, the bloody picture didn't write *MERDA* across itself, did it?' he shouts. Then, in Italian, to Signora Tranfaglia: 'One of those three people did it.'

She hesitates, and glances out of the window, before replying: 'There is another possibility.'

'You're going to tell me it was the invisible man?' says Gideon, and then, understanding what she means, he puts a hand over his eyes. 'Oh God, don't tell me,' he moans. 'The girl left the room. That's it, isn't it? I entrust them with fifty pictures, and they can't even be bothered to look after them.'

For five minutes, Signora Tranfaglia confirms, there was nobody at the desk. 'Five minutes at most,' she tells Gideon.

'Oh well, that's all right then,' he yells. 'Five minutes. What could possibly go wrong in five minutes? Nothing. Five minutes don't matter. A part-time guard can do the job just fine. Forgive me for having made a fuss. I understand now.'

She tells Robert that he need not translate. With frigid dignity, she informs Mr Westfall that the girl was required to attend to something urgently, and that she left the desk right at the end of the day, when it was entirely reasonable to expect that there would be no more visitors, because if there are only five minutes left before the exhibition closes, nobody will arrive. 'You cannot see an exhibition in five minutes,' she says.

Gideon listens to this reply; a stony composure takes possession of his face. In a grinding monotone he answers, in English: 'No. You cannot see an exhibition in five minutes. You're right, Signora Tranfaglia. Some bastard can march in here, past your untenanted desk, and scrawl all over one of my pictures in five minutes, but you cannot see an exhibition in five minutes. You are quite correct.'

Robert tells Signora Tranfaglia that Mr Westfall is very angry. Signora Tranfaglia says that she understands. After a few moments of silent fuming, during which he has glared at Signora Tranfaglia, then at the defaced painting, then again at Signora Tranfaglia, Gideon, switching to Italian, says: 'There was nobody here for five minutes, at the very end of the day. Yes?'

'Five minutes, that is correct,' she answers.

'And in that time, somebody came in here.'

'That is the only explanation, yes.'

'In that case,' he says to Robert, 'could you point out to Signora Tranfaglia that there are cameras at the entrance to the building and on the staircase, and that it should therefore be quite straightforward to get a shot of whoever entered the hall at the end of the afternoon. Unless none of the cameras in this building are working. And as soon as I have uttered these words, of course, I have a feeling of great foreboding. But be a good chap and put it to her anyway, would you?'

Robert conveys Gideon's suggestion to Signora Tranfaglia. At some length, with eloquent non-verbal expressions of exasperation and excuse, she explains the situation. 'The cameras aren't working,' Robert confirms.

'No,' murmurs Gideon, 'of course they're not. Why ever should they be? It's only the town sodding hall, after all. The cameras are for decoration.' The look he is directing at the area of wall in front of him suggests that he is seeing there a person who will receive a fist in the face if he or she utters one word more.

'It is a computer problem,' Signora Tranfaglia tells Robert again, the implication being that he will understand what such a problem might entail, whereas the artist cannot.

Gideon repeats her words, exaggerating the helplessness.

'Nothing is to be gained by this discourtesy,' says Signora Tranfaglia to Robert.

'She understands why you're angry,' says Robert.

'Bravo,' says Gideon, and he claps his hands three times, lethargically. 'This is unbelievable' he mumbles to no one. 'Absolutely unbelievable.' He goes over to the window, and looks out at the war memorial; Carlo is down there. He turns and regards the form of Signora Tranfaglia, as if she's not the curator of his exhibition but an item of furniture that doesn't belong here. 'OK,' he decides, addressing Robert, 'could you tell her that things have to change, as of today. There must be someone at the desk, all the time, and someone sitting there,' – he points to the opposite corner – 'so they can keep an eye on everything.'

'I will see what is possible,' says Signora Tranfaglia, in English.

'No,' says Gideon, to Robert. 'It will be done or I will remove my works from this exhibition.' He walks out.

Signora Tranfaglia remains with Robert while he removes the picture from the panel. She is sorry, so sorry, she tells him. But it could have happened anyway, even if six people had been on guard. If somebody wants to do something like this, you cannot stop them.

'But you can deter them,' says Robert, 'Or you can catch them.'

'Yes, that is true,' she admits. 'He is so rude, though,' she says, and she starts to whimper.

Robert tilts the picture in the light to inspect the surface of it. 'I can repair it,' he tells her. Her gratitude is profuse, like that of a mother who has just been told that the surgeon can save her child's life.

3.7

Gideon Westfall is 'technically as accomplished a painter as any currently at work in Britain'; his *Self-Portrait with Skull*, for example, might bear comparison, 'as a demonstration of painterly expertise, with the work of Zurbarán' [*The Sunday Telegraph*, January 24th, 1988]. But it has been remarked that his paintings are the products of a mind that has been 'disabled by nostalgia' [*Artworld*, June 1991]; some regard his portraits as 'ingratiating' and 'superficial' [*The Guardian*, March 9th, 1990]; the adjective 'sedulous' has been applied to his work [*The Daily Telegraph*, January 4th, 1984]. He has been called 'an embalmer of the visual' [*Panopticon*, May 1990]. Westfall's integrity, however, has not been questioned. 'If only it were possible to believe', wrote James Hannaher [*Ark*, December 1987], 'that this stuff about truth and beauty is a pose, [that] the anachronism is a pretence ... But there is no irony here.'

3.8

Gideon is waiting for her on the steps. He smiles, doffs his hat, makes a gift-offering gesture with both hands, and says: 'I thought lunch at the Corso might be an idea. Something light. A roll, a coffee, a cake. What do you think?'

It takes her a moment to understand why Gideon, the creature of habit who eats the same lunch every day, is making this proposal: if they are in a public place, with people sitting close, he'll be safe from further interrogation. 'Fine with me,' she says, as she has to.

'Glorious day,' he observes, flourishing a hand upwards.

'Beautiful,' she agrees. In a few minutes they will be at the café, so she asks straight away: 'Did you look at the photos?'

'I did,' he answers. 'Yes. Thank you.'

'And?'

'And what?' he asks, quite sunnily.

'Did they make you reconsider?'

'No, I can't say that they did,' he says. 'But it was interesting. I'd forgotten them.' He does not look at her; it's as if they were hikers, forging a path through undergrowth, with no time or energy to waste on chit-chat.

'And perhaps forgotten what they show?'

'Claire,' he says, 'I think we covered this topic yesterday.'

'We broached it, yes.'

'Well, I'm afraid I don't have anything more to say on the subject. You appear to think that I'm hiding something. You think I'm hiding something and that I'm the villain of the piece.'

'No. But—'

He stops. 'Listen,' he says, quietly. 'My brother and I were incompatible. This, believe it or not, is a fairly common phenomenon. There is no story here,' he tells her, with calm condescension. 'Cain and Abel are at one end of the spectrum, the Horatii are at the other. David and Gideon Westfall are around midway, a little nearer the Cain and Abel end, some way short of everyday humdrum brotherly affection. That's how it was. I was often unpleasant to him, he was often unpleasant to me; for most of the time we lived in a state of reciprocal indifference.' And now he smiles, satisfied at having concluded the matter with eloquence. 'Shall we?' he suggests, bowing slightly and waving a hand in the direction of the Caffè del Corso.

Outside the café only one of the tables is unoccupied, and it's next to a group of noisy Englishwomen, two of whom are flirting ponderously with the scarlet-waistcoated waiter. But it's a hot day, and the tables are in a shady angle, and there's more to see on the street than inside, says Gideon, so they sit down. The waiter, his arm released by the most excitable of the gang, turns and sees Gideon, whose hand he shakes with vigour. He is introduced to Claire, and waits like a servant of the *maestro* to take their order.

She is expecting a change of subject, but as soon as the waiter has gone indoors Gideon has more to say about his brother. David, he tells her, was the brainy one, the one who excelled academically, the first of the family to go to university. His brother was not greatly burdened by self-doubt, says Gideon, who confesses that some might indeed say the same of him. They were both ambitious, both worked hard. But there was a difference: Gideon had respect for his brother's achievements, whereas David did not: art was not an intellectual activity, and it was not work. 'He had no interest in what I was doing. None whatever,' says Gideon, and the resentment could not be more blatant. David's tendency to self-righteousness, it had to be said, became more pronounced as he got older: medics were the chosen people; artists were mere hobbyists, who sometimes mistook their hobby for a vocation. 'He saw art and science as opposites,' Gideon regretfully informs her. 'But art is a science too.' Neither was fair to the other. They saw each other as caricatures. But it was an irreducible fact that they were mismatched. If they hadn't known better, they'd have thought they were from different parents.

After the food has been brought, Gideon resumes his mono-logue, at first somewhat more conciliatory in tone. Her father was right to regard himself as the more intelligent sibling, if by intelligence one means excellence in the acquisition and deployment of knowledge that can readily be calibrated, he tells her. David was of the opinion that his brother didn't have what it took to be a doctor, and he was correct in this as well. 'He had the right stuff,' says Gideon, 'and I didn't.' A doctor, Gideon proclaims, requires a certain coldness of heart, a capacity for detachment. David had this faculty, this imperturbable clarity, whereas Gideon – he admits with a rueful aversion of the eyes – did not. 'I would have made the most dangerous doctor on earth,' says Gideon – because he has an excess of empathy, of compassion. He admired his brother, he tells her. He didn't much like him, but he could admire him. David always had a splinter of ice in his soul, and this was crucial to his success. It made him hard to love, but it made him very good at what he did.

'I had no difficulty loving him,' says Claire.

'Different situation,' responds Gideon, smiling sympathetically. 'Entirely different.'

'I don't recognise the person you're describing,' she says.

'Well you wouldn't, would you?' he says, and seems to think that this settles the matter.

'And my mother loved him.'

'Of course,' he says, as a forty-something man in a dark suit and white shirt and maroon tie – a town hall bureaucrat if ever she saw one – spots Gideon from fifty yards off and waves to him. Of course, this is another reason for choosing to sit outside – it allows him to demonstrate his standing in the town. 'That was a real meeting of minds,' he tells her. She thinks she detects a grain of sarcasm in the magnanimity; she has something to say, but he sees that she's about to speak and he raises a hand to prevent her.

'Enough, enough,' he says, frowning, as though rebuking himself rather than her. 'Let's enjoy our lunch, and this beautiful day.' As he says this, he casts an acerbic glance at the gaggle of women, who are now taking snaps of themselves with the waiter. Their chatter becomes so loud, he actually grinds his teeth. Raising his voice, as if against a gale, he tells her that, to be perfectly honest, he's not terribly interested in the past – or rather, in his own past. He is prone to nostalgia, as is everyone, but his nostalgia is not for his own life – it's for a more distant past, a Golden Age that perhaps never existed. He is, he declares loudly, like a snake; he sheds his skin each year. 'My paintings are my cast-off skin,' he says, then gives a half-impressed nod, as if this notion had never occurred to him before.

This afternoon she is going to take a walk in the valley; Gideon suggests a route; the waiter brings him a piece of paper, so that he can sketch a map for her. Then it's time for work. They are at the hotel, about to part, when Gideon, observing a woman emerging from the Palazzo Campani, raises a forefinger and says: 'One minute'. He jogs up the street to catch up with the woman, his belly moving like a vast rubber water bottle. The woman and Gideon exchange kisses; she is wearing huge sunglasses and a cerise V-neck top that reveals much of a finely formed chest; the hair – auburn, of country-singer volume – gleams like wet wood. Gideon comes back, evidently pleased. There'll be a fourth at the table tonight – Teresa, Robert's 'lady friend'. The words are accompanied by an expression that says a treat is in store; it is taken for granted that Claire will be there.

3.9

Until quite recently one could buy, in the sacristy of Santa Maria dei Carmini, a postcard that showed an image (a print by an unnamed artist) of a nun named Suor Veronica, who entered Castelluccio's Carmelite convent in 1697, died there in 1709, and thereafter became the object of much local devotion. On the reverse of the card, a tightly printed text celebrated the piety of this remarkable woman, who, as Teresa Campani, on January 30th, 1697, took the habit of the Carmel and the name of Sister Veronica, and eighteen months later, at the age of nineteen, after an episode of near-fatal ill-health, professed before the Lord her perpetual vows of chastity, poverty and obedience.

At midnight on January 1st, 1700, Suor Veronica experienced a vision of the crucified Christ, and awoke in an ecstasy, proclaiming that her soul had become suffused with the blood of Our Lord. It was to be the first of many such visions. They came to her as she slept, and in her sleep Suor Veronica would give voice to what she was seeing and hearing. Suor Veronica was by nature a modest and quietly spoken young woman, but the voice in which she recounted these visions was sonorous and strong, and the words she spoke were of great power. Throughout the night, two sisters would sit with her while she slept, to record her speech, and often they would fill many pages with the words she unconsciously dictated. Suor Veronica spoke of becoming, through her pure love, the spouse of Christ, and of sharing with him the sufferings of the cross. She would come awake writhing and wailing with His pain, and rend the sheets of her cot in agony, but the pain would pass quickly from her and her whole being would be imbued with the radiance of grace. In her ecstasies she spoke often of the blood of Christ: in her vision of September 9th, 1701, for example, she saw the people of Castelluccio in a fall of rain that was the sacred blood. To return to God, she told her sisters, self-love must be annihilated through humility. 'Humility is the gateway to grace' – these are words she spoke on the night of her last vision, April 5th, 1709. 'The soul must do nothing, will nothing, and comprehend everything. To transcend all created forms, we must make ourselves completely dead in God.' She foresaw with perfect serenity the day of her death: Tuesday, April 9th, 1709. Despite the weakness of her body, she passed the preceding day in prayerful ecstasy, standing upright in her cell from dawn until darkness. At midnight, precisely as she had seen, she died in her sleep, whispering the name of our Lord; at the moment of her death a powerful joy pervaded the convent.

Teresa Campani was the youngest daughter of Pierpaolo Campani and his wife Giuditta. By 1697, the year in which Teresa entered the convent, the fortunes of the Campani family had been in decline for some time. Investments in Florence had produced no profit; businesses in which the Campani had an interest had foundered; harvests had failed; it was rumoured that when the frivolous duchess, Marguerite Louise d'Orléans, decamped to Paris in 1675, she owed a considerable amount of money to agents of the Campani, for wall hangings and Chinese porcelains and perfumed jars from Peru. It was said that nobody had seen the melancholy Grand Duke Cosimo III smile in public; the same was true of the beleaguered head of the Campani. In 1691 he sold the family's house in Florence and a villa that he owned near Volterra. He now devoted himself to the cultivation of his estates around Castelluccio. In 1692, when Pierpaolo Campani's first daughter, Anna Maria, was married, her husband received a substantial dowry, as did the husband of her sister, Chiara, the following year. Their brothers – Michele, Paolo and Tullio – were not without funds. The last child, Teresa, however, was unmarriageable: there was now no surplus in the Campani coffers, and the girl, besides, was timid, plain and morose, and her health was poor. She was placed in the convent of Santa Maria dei Carmini.

Her most frequent visitor was Tullio, the brother closest to her in age. In his journal he made observations on his conversations with his sister, and on her conversations with other members of the family. This journal was discovered in 1979, when a research student, at work in the archives of the Palazzo Comunale, came upon sheets of Tullio's writing interleaved between the pages of a ledger of accounts relating to the revenues of the Campani estate in the year 1702. Some suspected forgery. Why was it, they asked, that nowhere in the copious correspondence preserved by the Campani family – a hoard that includes many letters composed by Tullio himself, and scores by Anna Maria and Chiara – there is not so much as a single mention of the 'facts' recorded in the supposed journal of Tullio Campani? As far as anyone was aware, no document in all of Castelluccio offered the slightest corroboration of these 'facts'. Unconvinced by those who argued that it was entirely understandable that the Campani should have kept secret some of the things of which Tullio wrote, the sceptics nominated a culprit: Paolo Campani, a Freemason, and widely known to have been a man of troublesome temperament. Paolo Campani, it was suggested, had written the journal himself, and secreted it amid the family's papers, knowing that sooner or later, after his death, it would be found.

The theory that the journal was an act of posthumous sabotage was refuted, to the satisfaction of nearly everyone, by archivist Cinzia Zappalorto, who matched the script of the journal to letters known to have been written by Tullio's hand; she produced, furthermore, evidence to show that the paper of Tullio's journal was fabricated around 1700. There are many in Castelluccio, however, for whom the journal of Tullio Campani is a libel against the blessed Suor Veronica. For them, Tullio himself was the saboteur – for whatever reason (and plentiful reasons can be proposed), he had simply lied about her.

The earliest visit described by Tullio took place in the summer of 1699. He found his sister, at first, to be in good spirits. She joked about one of the novices, an empty-headed girl who had absconded while on a pilgrimage to Rome. She spoke with respect and affection of the Mother Prioress. There were many admirable women here, she told her brother. But as Tullio was preparing to leave, Suor Veronica's face seemed to darken. Some days, she confessed, she watched the shadows creeping up the walls of her cell and it was as though she were watching the rising of floodwater. From time to time she had terrible dreams of murder and torture; her dreams, she said, were 'full of blood'.

Pierpaolo and Giuditta Campani also went to the convent that summer, soon after Tullio. Their daughter greeted them coolly, and was taciturn throughout. 'I live a life of prayer,' she said to them. 'I have nothing to tell you. Each day is the same as the one that came before and the one that will come after.' It would seem that her relationship with her parents – especially with her

father – was never to be warm again. Indeed, she would sometimes say nothing to her father after greeting him, addressing
herself solely to her mother, and then in the fewest words possible. In 1701 she requested that they should not visit her again,
and they seem to have complied with her wish.

Her visions of Christ are first mentioned by Tullio in an entry
written on July 23rd, 1700. She had dreamed that she was asleep
at a table, in a ruined house, and He had awoken her and showed
her the wounds in His hands and His side, and an extraordinary
happiness had overwhelmed her. A little of this happiness had
remained with her, but not for long, when she had awoken in
her cell, 'as water adheres to us after bathing'. When she was
read the words she had uttered in the course of the night, it was
as if they were words she had heard many years ago. 'She wept,
silently, in anguish for the loss of the bliss of her vision,' wrote
Tullio.

To her sisters, it seems, she said nothing of these experiences.
Anna Maria and Chiara came to the convent at Easter every year,
and usually Suor Veronica wanted to talk about their lives in
Florence, where both now lived. Sometimes they found her melancholic, sometimes she was excitable and laughed in a manner
that disturbed them; they attributed the fluctuations of her spirit
to her illness. Anna Maria and Chiara would pass an hour with
her, and their sister always wept when they had to leave.

With Michele and Paolo, similarly, Suor Veronica never talked
of the things she saw in her sleep. Michele's conversations with
his sister were as perfunctory as his father's. She rarely spoke
except when asked a question, and her replies were as terse as
she could make them without insult. She stated that she was
contented with her life. 'I am satisfied,' she would answer, again
and again: 'I am satisfied,' as if the word had no meaning. It was
always Christmas when Michele went to the convent; he would
shiver as he spoke to her, but she sat on the other side of the
grille, apparently insensible of the cold, making him feel like a
great sinner before a statue of Our Lady. In 1706 she told him he

need no longer trouble himself with her; she had said the same to Paolo, earlier that year. Paolo too described his sister as a statue with a censorious gaze, and complained of her silence.

But to Tullio she talked at length about the experiences she was having. 'I am happy when I sleep, and only when I sleep,' she told him. 'In my dreams it seems that there is only myself and God in all the world.' She described to him dreams in which, like Saint Thomas, she had placed her fingers in Christ's side. She had taken His body from the cross, and in the instant His weight had fallen upon her she had become as light as a bee. With her own eyes she had seen the bestial faces of Calvary; in her flesh she had taken the pain of the thorns and the flail. And with the pain she had known a joy that was beyond all speech, a joy in which she seemed to dissolve like incense smoke in air, and which disappeared on waking. 'I am in God in the night,' she told him. 'but he is not with me now, as I talk to you. He abandons me in the daylight.' In order to sleep more deeply, she worked as hard as her body would allow. In the hours between prayers she sewed surplices and tended the convent's orchard and garden, in all weathers. She washed clothes, repaired linen and sawed wood to exhaust herself. Often she would go without food, because her visions were most intense when she had starved her body. She had a vision every night now, she told Tullio on October 3rd, 1707, but in the mornings she might have no memory of what had happened to her; instead, she would awaken into a sense of being in a mist of delight, or rather of being herself a mist of delight, and from this mist her everyday self, the dismal Suor Veronica, would begin to take form for another day. Each morning, the nuns who had sat beside her bed would read to her the words that had come from her mouth. The words never sounded like her own: they were the words of a scholar, or a preacher. Sometimes the words were Latin: in her sleep she spoke Latin with greater mastery than she read it when awake. On February 17th, 1708, she told Tullio, in tones of wonder, that two weeks previously she had spoken in sentences that the sisters had been unable to understand, and so had written down as approximations to the sounds that they had heard. Upon waking, Suor Veronica was shown the syllables, and she had been unable to make sense of them. The pages were sent to Siena, where the text was understood to be the confession of Suor Veronica's soul in the German language, a tongue of which she was not aware of possessing the slightest knowledge.

This was to be Tullio's penultimate conversation with his sister. In August he found her very sickly, with 'a face as pale as milk . . . and eyes like pewter'. She told him that she was too tired to talk, and that she would soon be leaving 'this holy prison'. In December they met for the last time. Tullio wrote: 'Teresa was proud and full of argument.' (In Tullio's journal she is nearly always Teresa rather than Suor Veronica.) She quoted to him the lines by Ciro di Pers, a poet of whom he was most fond, on the sorry fate of man and the vanity of our lives, which are but passing shadows, and then laughed wildly. She shrieked with laughter after instructing him: 'Deny your desires and you will find what your heart longs for.' Tullio believed that disease had made his sister almost mad. Flecks of blood sprang from her lips as she cursed the Campani and declared that she had seen a vision of her father in hell. Her skin had become mottled, like some reptile's, and her eyes were 'full of black fire'. She told Tullio that of her family he alone was the one she had loved, then she ordered him not to visit her again. Nevertheless, he presented himself at the convent in February and again in March, but he was not admitted. On Friday, April 12th, 1709, he wrote in his journal: 'The Mother Prioress told me that Suor Veronica lay in her cell for two whole days, uncovered, and in all that time not one fly alighted on the body.'

3.10

Robert and Gideon are at the table with Teresa, who introduces herself immediately, extending a bare and beautiful arm, which is circled above the wrist by a broad band of silver, embossed with grapes and tiny birds. Claire takes the offered hand: the fingers are cool and long, and the nails have a shapeliness that can be achieved only through daily maintenance. Everything – the hands, the exquisitely low-key make-up, the enviable hair – suggests a woman for whom the day begins with a long session at the mirror. The face is not remarkable, except for the finish of it – and the eyes, which are large and the colour of mahogany. Looking at the skin around the eyes, Claire can tell that she must be thirty-five or thereabouts; otherwise, she could be taken for seven or eight years younger. The dusty pink V-neck, top-grade cotton, well filled, offsets the complexion perfectly.

'You have come to Castelluccio to see our grand Gideon?' Teresa enquires, with an adoring PA's smile for Gideon. The teeth, of course, are marble-white.

Gideon raises his hands in self-deprecation. 'She is here to see her uncle,' he corrects her. 'And our fine little town, of course.'

'And what do you think?' asks Teresa. 'Of our fine little town.' The question is asked with such keenness, she could be discussing something that Claire might buy from her.

'It's a pretty place.'

'It is,' says Teresa. 'But you are from London, yes?'

'That's right.'

'So this is like toy town for you. Ten thousand Castelluccios make one London.'

The smile is powerful, but there is perhaps a fleck of defensiveness in the tone of voice. 'I like it,' says Claire.

'A good time to be here,' says Teresa. 'In winter it is dead. We push the Pause button on our life. But this is a good time. The best time.' Then she turns to say something to Robert, in Italian, to which Robert shakes his head and Teresa cries 'No,' in a quiet wail of incredulity. 'He says you are not here for the festa,' she complains to Claire.

'She has to leave on Thursday,' Gideon sadly confirms.

Teresa presents a pout of frustration. 'It is the best day of our year,' she tells Claire.

'So I've heard,' Claire answers. 'But my flight is on Thursday.'

Marta distributes the menus; Teresa scans hers in ten seconds and orders at once. 'You must come another year,' she goes on. 'It is fun, you must believe me. Great fun. Tell her,' she orders Robert, tapping the back of his hand.

'It is fun. Great fun,' Robert repeats, as though reading from a card, at which Teresa rolls her eyes, for Claire's benefit. Robert lifts her hand and kisses it; she reciprocates. 'You arrived when?' she asks.

'This is my third evening.'

'So already you have seen everything.'

'I'm taking my time.'

'What did you see today?' asks Teresa, emitting an implausibly bright interest.

'I went for a walk,' Claire answers. She describes the loop she followed up and down the valley, at which Teresa's eyes widen with every sentence.

'That is very far,' says Teresa, fanning her face at the effort involved. She tells a story about how, when she was a girl, on a hot day in August, she decided to walk to Mensano. 'I don't remember why. I did some crazy things,' she says, putting a finger pistol to her temple. Because she didn't take enough water, she fainted in the heat. She was meant to be home for lunch, but hours went by with no sign of her, and her mother was praying to Beata Veronica for her safe return. 'You have been to the museum?' she asks, interrupting herself.

'Not yet. Saving it,' Claire answers, with a glance at Robert, which makes Veronica pause momentarily and cock an eyebrow.

'There is a picture in the museum, of children. One of the girls is called Teresa. My mother loved her face, so I am called Teresa.' Flattening her hands, crossed, on her chest, she lets out a percussive high laugh. 'Is it possible to believe? You name your daughter for a dead girl in a painting? I love my mother, but what a thing to do. A film star, OK. Not a dead girl in a painting.'

'A dead nun,' adds Robert.

'That's right. The girl became a nun. So when her Teresa didn't come home my mother prayed to the other Teresa who became the nun Veronica. And I was found, safe and OK, of course. Because of the nun.' She spreads her beautiful hands like wings at the side of her face, illustrating the wackiness of her mother's logic.

Marta returns with the starters, imposing a break. The moment the last plate is down, Teresa is talking again. She wants to know what Claire does in London. Claire tells her: she has been helping people who have money troubles, and problems with their landlords, mostly.

Before responding, Teresa consults Robert. 'Useful,' she comments, instantaneously in earnest. 'But it is not very interesting?' she suggests.

'It can be. Not always. But more than sometimes.' She tells Teresa about a recent case – the tenants of a top-floor flat who were in dispute with their landlord and came home one evening to find he'd removed the staircase and chucked their possessions out of the kitchen window.

Though she looks appropriately appalled, Teresa appears not to be listening closely; rather, she seems to be reading Claire's face and gestures, taking note of every little movement, as if trying to work something out. 'My job is not very interesting also,' she remarks when the story is finished; her eyes are now directed at her hands, which are cutting up her food with surgical delicacy. 'I sell houses. To Germans and Dutch people. Some Italians too.' She holds up a semi-disc of salami on a fork and examines it as though it might be a mistake to eat it. 'I studied architecture. Michelangelo, Palladio, Bernini, Borromeo, Nervi – I studied them. I understand them.' The perfect teeth snap onto the meat. 'Now what do I do? I sell empty farms to men from Munich. But that is the world. In Italy there is no work. You do what you can,' she says, and she fans the fingers of her free hand upwards, letting her dreams fly away. 'But it is funny, no? We are in the same business, at different ends,' she proposes, with a smile of sisterly complicity.

Claire is about to say that she will be starting a new job soon, but Teresa turns to Gideon, with: 'Robert told me about the picture. It's so terrible.' The eyes are suddenly tight with indignation. 'Who would do such a thing?' she demands.

Gideon has been content to cede centre stage to vivacious Teresa; looking on with amusement, gratitude, maybe even affection, he has contributed nothing but an aura of good humour for the past ten minutes or so; now he takes over. 'I can think of many people who would do such a thing,' he answers. 'I am not sure that any of them would travel all the way to Castelluccio to make their point, but our vandal is far from the first to abuse my work. Not the first to abuse it in those terms either. I once had a critic tell me I was shit. To my face. At a private viewing. I suppose I should have applauded his frankness. At least he didn't scrawl it on the canvas. But he was a bilious little toad' – Robert whispers the translation in Teresa's ear; the insult evidently pleases her – 'by the name of James Hannaher. A failed painter – so many critics are. "A pile of anachronistic shit" is what he called my work. Delightful phrase.' He glances at Claire, and a smile develops. 'You're thinking *I see his point*, aren't you?' he says. Smacking his brow in revelation, he roars, attracting the attention of diners on the far side of the room: 'Oh my God – it was you, was it?' Then he laughs and puts an arm round her shoulder – seizing rather than hugging her. Teresa's brow contracts for a moment, as if there's something puzzling in Claire's discomfiture.

And now Gideon delivers his thoughts on being an anachronism, a topic on which he has often held forth. Robert interjects from time to time, usually to qualify a point, and Teresa interrupts occasionally with expressions of fervent agreement, but in essence it's a monologue, for Claire's benefit, and it lasts until his meal is finished. 'The idea of anachronism is enormously interesting, and less straightforward than most people think,' he begins. Having never had a thought on the subject, Claire nods noncommittally. 'We think of the Renaissance as a period of resurgence, of innovation, of invention,' Gideon tells the company, gesturing as if addressing twenty. There follows a brief disquisition on the etymology and history of the word 'Renaissance'. 'And we are not wrong to think of it in this way,' he goes on. 'It was indeed a time of unprecedented progress (if we may be permitted to use so unfashionable a noun), an epoch in which the foundations of modernity (in its best sense) were laid. Yet the Renaissance – as I will continue to refer to it, despite the objections of modish scholars – was also a period in which the most advanced artists and thinkers were always looking backwards, defining themselves by reference to the ancients: it was a period, in other words, in which anachronism was a good thing.' The mother tongue of the great architects of the Renaissance, he exlains, with a gesture of acknowledgement to Teresa, was the architecture of imperial Rome. Throughout the history of western civilisation, radicalism and classicism have been intertwined. Poussin, Ingres, Canova and David are cited, plus several others. Gideon is glad to align himself with such artists – philosophically they are in the same camp, in which past and present and future are indivisible, whereas for ignoramuses such as Hannaher the three concepts have to be put in three separate boxes for ease of use. Consider this as well: two hundred years from now, perhaps, what seems to some of our contemporaries to be merely a throwback to a dead tradition may be seen by the artists of the twenty-third century as a vital continuation of that tradition, while much of our so-called modern art will be revealed as a dead-end digression. And one last question: is Gideon dismissed as a crank simply because he is just one man, working alone, beyond the pale of the Art World? If there were a thousand Gideon Westfalls, working in London or New York, with galleries and critics to promote them, wouldn't they constitute a group, a movement, and therefore be taken seriously by the self-appointed arbiters of value? Instead of being an anachronism, wouldn't he be a neo-Neoclassicist or something like that? Doesn't it all come down to a question of numbers and influence?

'But the value of art is not a matter of statistics and geography,' he declaims, and he would certainly go on, if it were not for the fact that his watch is showing 9.50pm. As if summoned, he stands up; he pulls banknotes from his jacket and passes the cash to Robert; Teresa, unperturbed at the abruptness of Gideon's departure, raises a straight arm at an angle of forty-five degrees, and Gideon and takes her slack-wristed hand to plant a kiss on the back of it. He departs.

'That's a party piece,' Robert tells Claire. 'He has several. The decline of the art schools – that's a good one. The decline in our understanding of materials – another favourite. The decline of drawing – I'd be surprised if you don't get that one at some point.'

Teresa seems to have been exhausted by the performance, and the eye movements are suggesting strongly that she would rather have Robert to herself now. But when Claire says goodnight, Teresa springs up from her seat to clasp her. 'It was so good to meet you,' she says, with every appearance of sincerity, while holding Claire's hands in hers and pressing them lightly, as though to transmit encouragement.

3.11

Too weary to continue the confrontation with himself, Gideon turns aside from the mirror; his gaze, listless, slides from canvas to table to floor to canvas, before coming to rest on the charcoal drawing of Ilaria that's pegged to a board by the door of Robert's work room. It was made just two days before she disappeared, and he wonders now, not for the first time, if that session will turn out to have been the last; it will.

He studies it from this distance, the distance from which he would study the girl herself. It has force, he judges, and a simplicity, a robustness, that this body, this young person, had demanded of him. The images that she made him create had a vigour that had seemed to promise a new direction for his work – not a

wholly new direction, but, as it were, a fresh path across familiar terrain, an opening of new vistas, new challenges. He closes
his eyes and sees her again in this room, between poses, sitting
on a stool, eating an orange, as fully at ease as she would have
been clothed. Of all the models he has worked with, Ilaria was
the only true innocent: there was no vanity to her, no coquettish-
ness. 'Stand there,' he would tell her, and she would move into the
light and install herself in it, immediately finding the position that
was required and at once seeming fixed in it, as though she had
placed her body in an invisible mould. Her face, as he worked,
had the tranquility of someone in a deep daydream; they worked
in silence; once they had begun, she never needed to talk. Looking
towards the stairs, he can hear her heavy footfall; he sees her with
the orange, giving all her attention to the pleasure of it, as intent as
someone reading a book. Closing his eyes again, he sees the tone
of her skin, the muscles of her arm; he sees and hears Ilaria's father
in the doorway, raging, while Robert, hands in pockets, calmly
translated the insults: *He says that people like you belong in prison . . .
He takes exception to what you have done . . . Your attitude towards the
family unit is to be deplored in the strongest possible terms.*

He replaces Ilaria's father with the night he came face to face
with her, in the alley by San Lorenzo: a door opened, and there she
was, fiddling with the neck of her shirt, hair awry. She was fifteen
years old. Since the time of the painting of the dead horse, a good
four years earlier, they might have exchanged a dozen hellos, little
more than that. He hadn't as much as laid eyes on her for several
weeks; but now, as he glanced into the doorway, she struck him
with a look that established in a moment a true intimacy: the look
– a glare, with a hint of smile – told him to say nothing to anyone
about what he was seeing, while letting him know that she knew
that he could be trusted, and that he did not disapprove.

But another two years had to pass, two years of nothing more
than a smile in the street, perhaps a 'How are you?', answered
without stopping. Then, at last, the fulfilment: outside the Porta
di Santa Maria, he saw her sitting on the ground against a wall,

Coke can in one hand and cigarette in the other, in a grubby white vest and ripped jeans, the very image of disgruntlement. She stood up and approached him, but did not stop as they passed: rather, she slowed a little, angled herself towards him in mid-stride, and stated that she would like to come to the studio. Which she did, that night. She was still in the same outfit. A picture of Laura Ottaviano was hanging in the living room. Arms crossed, she regarded it; a shrug signified that she was begrudgingly impressed. 'You can paint me,' she said. 'Do you want to paint me? If you pay me, you can paint me.'

'I would have to speak to your family,' he said.

'I am old enough,' she answered.

'But I would want them to know,' he said. 'I'd be happier if they knew.'

'I would not be happy,' she said. Before he could reply, she had removed the vest; the jeans came off, then everything. Arms by her side, as though for medical assessment, she stood naked in the centre of the room. Smoothly, as if on a slow-moving wheel, she turned full circle. 'Yes or no?' she asked.

He showed her the studio; she surveyed the room in the manner of a tenant accepting accommodation that was barely up to the acceptable standard. A fee was agreed without discussion, and a time for the first session. Ten minutes after ringing the bell, she was leaving. 'This place is not alive,' she said at the end, standing at this window, scattering contempt over all of Castelluccio with a sweep of her arm.

He looks at his face in the mirror: the life has gone out of him; he is sick of himself.

3.12

'She is nice,' says Teresa to Robert's reflection in the bathroom mirror. 'Not exciting, but she has a nice face. But sad. And sad clothes. Terrible clothes. Does she have no money? The job she has – maybe the pay is bad.'

'She has enough. Her father died last year. She got some money from him.'

'What was he?'

'A doctor.'

'OK,' says Teresa, wiping her cheek. 'So that is why she is sad. Because of her father.'

'I don't know that she's sad.'

She fixes him with a frown of incredulity. 'She is very sad, Robert. Anyone can see that.' She releases the cotton-wool ball from the grip of thumb and forefinger, held high over the bin; it falls precisely into the centre. 'And she is scared of Gideon,' she says, before scooping cold water onto her face.

'I'd say she finds him a bit overwhelming.'

She shrugs, then reaches for the towel. Having dabbed her face, she leans towards the glass, to examine first the left eye, then the right. 'She doesn't like him, I think,' she says, pressing a forefinger to a cheekbone.

'It's a strange situation. They've only just met. Gideon is a strong character. It can take time to adjust.'

'She is a nervous woman,' says Teresa.

'Possibly.'

'And I think also she does not like me very much. I scare her too, a little.'

'I don't know why you say that.'

'I had a feeling,' she says, with another shrug. Taking her toothbrush, she says: 'But not frightened of you. Oh no, not frightened of you at all.' Her face in the mirror gives him a mock-annoyed smirk. 'She likes you, I can tell. Certainly.'

A couple of months ago, in the same room, with Teresa looking at him in the mirror, she had said exactly the same thing, about Ilaria Senesi, after catching a glimpse of them in the Caffè del Corso – and that was nonsense too. But at least in the case of Ilaria she had half-believed it.

'Don't be silly,' he says, as he'd answered before.

'Not silly,' she replies, through a mouthful of foam.

He goes into the bedroom; he hears the shutters of the Sant'Agostino bar come down; it's another ten minutes before Teresa comes in – she had an email to send, she explains. 'You know I'm right,' she says, getting into bed.

'About what?'

'Your lady from London. She likes you.'

'I'm a likeable person.'

She is wearing one of her white La Perla vests; her shoulders gleam; he kisses her on the collar bone, and she rakes his hair lightly. She kisses the crown of his head, then reaches for the light on her side. 'I am very tired,' she says, but she isn't. She has to be in Siena by eight, to collect Renata, she tells him, because Vito has emailed to say he has an appointment in Florence at ten. 'On a Sunday. Unbelievable,' she says, forcing exasperation into her voice. 'There will be an argument,' she sighs.

Half an hour later she is still awake; she lies with her face towards the window, motionless; she's breathing deeply, but she's awake.

At two o'clock Robert gets out of bed. He opens a window. Castelluccio is silent; above the roofs there are hundreds of motes of light, each one an inconceivable and perpetual explosion, at distances that he cannot imagine. Back in the bedroom, he crouches to gaze at Teresa's face, and again a flash of the horror makes him catch his breath: he sees the bones in which her eyes are nestled, the skull like the fruit of death inside its rind of skin and muscle. He kisses her shoulder, twice, keeping his lips on her skin the second time; she murmurs a syllable, but doesn't stir.

 **4**

4.1

THIS MORNING'S ROUTE is the one they most often take: south
from Castelluccio, climbing to Montieri and over the saddle
between the peaks of Le Cornate and Poggio di Montieri,
then on to the main road and north through Castelnuovo and
Larderello, before turning for San Dalmazio and home. The
morning is perfect: a cloudless sky; the air mild and faintly
perfumed with the scent of moist soil; tracts of pallid sunlight
on the slopes. As they ride past Montingégnoli the first bell of
the morning starts to ring across the valley from Radicóndoli.
They are always near Montingégnoli when the church bell in
Radicóndoli starts to ring, and it is a peculiarly satisfying sound,
both for the tone of the clanging in the quietness, and for the
fact that the sound always happens at this point, when they
are on this portion of the road. For a moment or two, while the

bell is ringing, no time has passed since they were last here: this Sunday and the previous Sunday are the same. And there will be other repetitions of pleasure in the course of the morning, episodes that he anticipates barely consciously, as he might anticipate moments in a piece of music or a film that he knows well and invariably enjoys: the clouds of vapour rising through the bushes at Travale; a stand of chestnut trees near Montieri, arrayed like a copse in a picture by Claude Lorrain; the light on the cooling towers at Larderello; the tang of the sulphuric air. From time to time he thinks of Teresa, and repels the notion that they are tiring of each other. For minutes at a stretch his mind is wholly passive. He hears the whirr of chains and cogs; there is a bird – a warbler; there is another bell; a gunshot. They are on the steepest part of the incline, riding into warmer air, and Fausto Nerini passes him, as he always does on this stretch of road, with a slap on the back for the laggards. *'Forza, ragazzi,'* Fausto urges, and the group closes up behind him.

As they are going through Castelnuovo, Maurizio Ianni comes alongside, swigging from his water bottle. 'OK?' shouts Maurizio. 'OK,' he answers; it's the first thing he's said for an hour. In a line they swerve onto the San Dalmazio road, where they quickly gather speed; he sways through a curve, cutting close to the verge, then loses his nerve and applies the brakes, just as he passes the white wooden cross beside the road, where the partisans were ambushed. As often happens, a sense of his triviality arises from the sight of the cross: he is ludicrous – they are all ludicrous, this gang of middle-aged men on their expensive bikes, dressed up like professionals. But the embarrassment is gone in seconds, because they are at the long left-hander where the tarmac is new and slick, and bang on cue Maurizio sweeps to the front, to show them he's feeling as fresh after ninety kilometres as after nine, and to make sure he reaches the Porta di Volterra first, as usual.

4.2

On June 1st, 1994, the former Albergo Belvedere, Castelluccio's only hotel, having been closed for refurbishment since the previous January, was re-opened as the Ottocento, with genuine nineteenth-century furniture in all rooms, sepia photographs of the village circa 1900 in the corridors and dining rooms, and a large photo-portrait of Silvio Ubaldino – once the owner of the Belvedere, and founder of the Caffè del Corso – on display in the reception area, opposite a watercolour of the Torrione at the resort town of San Benedetto del Tronto, the birthplace of the hotel's new owner, Maurizio Ianni, then aged just thirty-eight.

As a schoolboy Maurizio had made up his mind that he would become his own boss by the time he was thirty. His father was a waiter at a restaurant in San Benedetto and his mother cleaned hotel rooms; they had no money, and there was only one day in the week when the family had the chance to spend any time together. Maurizio could not and would not live like this, he decided. He left school as soon as he could, and found a job in a club on Viale Trieste; he moved to another club, for more money; every year he moved on to a better club, and before long he was managing one of the best places on the coast, in Grottamare. Like his parents, he was working like a slave, but Maurizio's slavery was part of a plan, and would come to an end in the near future. And it did come to an end: not yet thirty, he opened a club of his own, Barbarossa, on Viale Trieste, within sight of the spot where his working life had begun, a little over a decade earlier.

He'd worked like a demon for ten years, and had saved much of what he earned, but the Barbarossa was a large and stylish and expensive operation, and there was some gossip about the means by which Maurizio Ianni acquired the capital necessary to set it up. He talked of a backer, a 'man with vision', who advanced him a loan at a highly favourable rate, but nobody knew the visionary's name. This anonymous patron also helped Ianni with the finance for his second club, Barbanera, which opened two years after Barbarossa, ninety kilometres to the north, near Ancona. In 1992, in the course of the trial of a man called Fedele Cisternino on charges of extortion, photographs were shown to the court in which the accused was to be seen drinking with one of his alleged victims, at a party held on the occasion of Mr Cisternino's fortieth birthday, at the Barbanera; it was also alleged by the prosecutors, and vehemently denied by the defence, that Mr Cisternino was an associate of some extremely unsavoury characters in Bari. Was it entirely coincidental, some asked, that the shady Mr Cisternino should have chosen the Barbanera as the venue for the celebration of this significant date in his life? And was it purely by chance that a club called Blu, located within a few kilometres of Barbanera, suffered a decline in its popularity in the wake of two outbreaks of food poisoning in the space of six months? It was hard not to wonder, especially when it emerged that the former classmate of Maurizio Ianni who became the manager of the Barbarossa in 1992 had been working in the kitchen of the Blu during the period in question.

Publicity for the Barbarossa and Barbanera boasted that they had the best DJs and the best sound systems south of Rimini, and a lot of people agreed: the Barbarossa was voted the hottest club in the province of Ascoli Piceno three years in a row, and in 1992 it came first in a poll to find the top night-spot in the entire region of Marche. They were 'cash factories', to quote Maurizio, and in 1993 he sold them for a 'magnificent sum', to a company registered in Bitonto, the so-called 'City of Olives', eighteen kilometres west of Bari.

He had become bored with the club scene, he says, and had long been dreaming of a hotel that he would own, a modest but refined establishment, with a restaurant; one of the things that motivated him, he'll admit, was a need to redress the hardships that his parents had endured. As with his previous ventures, he did his research thoroughly: he identified a corner of Tuscany that was ripe for the development of its tourist infrastructure, and found within it an investment that was perfect – the Belvedere. It was not too large and not too small; it had history (you must have history) but was in fair condition; it could be acquired cheaply, and refreshed for not too great an outlay.

So he bought the Belvedere, and invited his brother, Orsino, to come and work for him. His brother, a year younger than Maurizio, was in Milan, still learning to be a chef. Maurizio doesn't often speak of his brother: they had a big falling-out, many years ago, he'll tell you, and Orsino is stubborn: he won't let bygones be bygones, and he won't admit to himself that he's never going to be the sort of guy whose food gets reviewed in the best magazines. Orsino works hard, of course, and he's a good enough cook, but he's not got that spark, and he doesn't have what it takes to be a boss. 'One day,' says Maurizio, 'he'll see sense and he'll come to Castelluccio.' Usually he makes it sound like an act of fraternal charity, but sometimes you sense the pleasure of retribution in his voice. And of course some people, such as Carlo Pacetti, have ideas about the falling-out of the brothers back in San Benedetto del Tronto, ideas which overlap with the gossip about the Barbarossa and the Barbanera. All Maurizio will say is that Orsino was never a clubbing kind of guy; and Maurizio doesn't blame him for that; Maurizio wasn't a clubbing kind of guy for long.

Maurizio Ianni is not to everybody's taste, even if few are as hostile towards him as Carlo Pacetti, for whom the boss of the Ottocento is a man of no principles other than the love of money, and the embodiment of so much of what is wrong with the country today. You will hear it said that when Maurizio Ianni is talking to you it's impossible to resist the feeling that he's try-ing to work out if this conversation might in some way be of advantage to himself; when Ianni does a favour for someone it's always with an eye to the reward. He is charming, it must be admitted, but many would agree with Gideon's jibe, that Ianni 'vents his charm on you'. Others, though, think that Maurizio Ianni should be the mayor of Castelluccio, because he, more than any other person, is keeping the town alive. And none would accuse Maurizio Ianni of idleness. Almost every hour of the day – Sunday mornings excepted – is devoted to the various Ianni enterprises: the Ottocento hotel, the Cereria apartments, his restaurant in Mensano, and his latest project, the conversion of a farm on the outskirts of Monteguidi into a five-star hotel complex, complete with pool, spa and fitness centre. 'One day they'll rename this Ianniland,' he has told his fellow cyclists, saluting the valley with a raised arm.

When he was in San Benedetto, making his money and a name for himself, he never had time for a serious relationship, and he doesn't have much time now. There have been some lady friends since he's been in Castelluccio, but it seems that all of these affairs were short-lived. He is on his own at the moment, and he knows that he may be heading for a lonely old age. But he will have no regrets, he says; at the age of sixty, or earlier, he will sell up and retire to a villa with a view of the sea, in Liguria; he has never had any desire to pass on his business to an heir – that is a feudal way of doing things, he'll tell you, whereas he is a man of the twenty-first century.

Maurizio is fond of characterising himself as someone who lives, as he puts it, in 'the world as it is'. And yet, though it would appear to many that Mr Ianni conducts his life in a manner that accords more closely to the lessons of *Il Principe* than to the Gospels, he attends Mass regularly, in the church of the Redentore. Every Sunday, just before noon, after his ride, you'll see him ascending the steps, alone, in Prada suit and silk tie, with the bearing of a businessman on his way into a meeting with a potential partner, expecting success. He is an intelligent man, and is aware that certain of his fellow citizens would accuse him of hypocrisy. The accusation is rebutted with ease: 'I am a realist,' says Maurizio. 'I leave it to the priests to tell me about the world as it should be, and of the life that is to come, or so I hope.' And should there be a life to come, he is confident that he will be permitted to partake of it: he has done good work, he would suggest; he has ameliorated, albeit in a small way, and for a small space of time, the lives of a considerable number of people. Furthermore, though he would not pretend that his faith has always been steadfast, he has never succumbed to despair, and – as Father Fabris and the orphans of Vietnam could attest – he has been diligent in his observation of the third of the Theological Virtues.

'Your boss and myself, we are alike in many ways,' he has remarked to Robert on occasion. 'We both give pleasure to people: his pleasures are expensive but long-lasting, mine are more affordable and more trivial. But we both change the world a little.' He is joking, but not entirely. And he is exaggerating only a little when he refers to himself as the town's other artist. After Mass he will take a stroll around the town, slowly, pausing to greet and to survey, like a man who imagines himself a potentate on a tour of his domain. For a moment he will linger, always, outside the Teatro Gaetano. He dreams of owning it, he confesses. He can see the derelict theatre transformed: the auditorium is a dining room, as spectacular as any in Italy; music is played on the stage, to enrich the experience of eating here; backstage are the kitchens; and on the upper floors there are rooms as luxurious as any you can pay for in Florence. But Castelluccio, he fears, is too small for his dream.

4.3

Six days out of seven, Gideon has only Trim for company on his morning walk, but Sundays are different: barring severely inclement weather or some other special circumstance, he takes his walk with Carlo Pacetti. They meet outside the Pacetti garage and stroll outside the walls, anticlockwise, invariably, past the Porta di Volterra and the Porta di San Zeno, before entering the town at its western gate, the Porta di Santa Maria. The conversation is sporadic: Gideon is no linguist, and Carlo Pacetti's English – acquired chiefly through his son, Ennio, who studied the language at school and has always preferred American rock bands to Italian – is only a little less rudimentary. One man speaks a mixture of Italian and cracked English, the other cannot produce more than a couple of sentences of Italian without resorting to English to clarify his obscurities, but they understand each other. They understand each other, as each would tell you, at a level that is deeper than speech. They are true companions in spirit, their alliance being founded upon the respect of master mechanic for master artist, and vice versa. 'We are men of another age,' as both have more than once remarked, an age in which artist and artisan were of the same blood.

A minute into the walk, Carlo Pacetti will ask about the work that Gideon has done in the week since last they were together. 'Anything I can see?' he will ask. This morning Gideon's response is: 'Not yet; soon, I hope.' Carlo nods, and leaves it at that; one might mistake them for an artist and his agent. At the Porta di Volterra they halt to admire the view; a grass-scented breeze moves over them, and Carlo takes three gluttonous breaths; Gideon, standing at his side, does likewise. Then the cyclists appear, swerving through the gateway, led by Maurizio Ianni. 'Superman arrives,' Carlo remarks, taking his friend by the arm as they cross the road. He's heard that Ianni has had to bring his prices down to fill the hotel; but the credit crunch has been good for Ennio, because people think they can't afford a new car so they're keeping the old one going as long as possible. Ennio's wife – she's usually 'Ennio's wife', rather than 'Silvia' – has just bought a smartphone that doesn't work properly; this amuses him, as it does Gideon.

The daughter-in-law and her ludicrous phone are worth a minute or two, then Carlo divulges that he's heard something else about Ianni: that he had offered Ilaria Senesi a job at the Ottocento a few weeks before she disappeared.

'Seems unlikely,' says Gideon. 'Where did you hear that?'

'Customer of Ennio's,' answers Carlo.

'News to me. Can't imagine it.'

'I can,' says Carlo, grabbing a phantom female bottom with both hands. Carlo has a theory: the girl had got herself pregnant by Ianni and has gone off to get something done about it.

'No,' says Gideon.

'Not impossible,' suggests Carlo.

'Totally impossible,' Gideon tells him.

His companion shrugs, and they walk towards the Porta di Santa Maria, in silence. Carlo's face undergoes a few small contractions, as if he's listening to a more thorough criticism of his theory, and not being convinced by it. As they reach the gate he has to speak: he cannot comprehend why Gideon should feel such an attachment to that worthless girl.

'She was an excellent model,' Gideon tells him.

'She's ignorant.'

'She is not ignorant. She might not be a reader—'

'She's stupid.'

'—but she has a natural intelligence.'

'Intelligence my arse,' Carlo guffaws.

'A natural intelligence,' Gideon repeats. He endeavours to draw a comparison between Ilaria and the young, unschooled Pau'ura of Paul Gauguin.

'This is not Tahiti,' Carlo points out.

'I know. But still—'

'Let's be honest, *maestro*. She has a body, and that's all that needs to be said. Your Pora, or whatever her name is—'

'Pau'ura.'

'Right. Well, I'm sure she had a nice body too. And that's OK. An artist needs nice bodies. I understand. But let's not talk about intelligence. Ilaria knows a few things about horses. That's her limit.'

'No, Carlo. You're wrong,' says Gideon. He tells his friend that he accepts that Ilaria might not make a good impression on people who don't really know her, that she might appear – how can he put it? – somewhat crude, but he had come to know her well, and she had surprised him with some of the things she had said. 'And she has a good eye,' he goes on. 'She has an instinct—'

Carlo puts a hand on his arm to interrupt him; they have reached the piazza in front of Santa Maria dei Carmini, and people are going into the church. 'There's your Luisa,' he says, seeing Luisa Fava entering the piazza from Corso Diaz. Luisa, seeing Gideon, waves to him, and they go to meet her.

Falling back a pace or two, to allow Gideon and Luisa to talk freely, Carlo finds himself standing in the way of a man who is taking a picture of Santa Maria dei Carmini; his wife or girl-friend, standing beside him, gives Carlo a little cringe of apology. Certain that they are English – which means, much more likely than not, that they'll know fewer than twenty words of Italian – Carlo addresses them; to ensure incomprehension, he speaks rapidly. This, he tells them, is the famous church of the Blessed Lady of the Underwear, one of the most remarkable sights in Castelluccio. The woman smiles, but her eyes are panicky. 'I'm sorry,' the man says, in Italian, 'but—'. This would appear to be the extent of his vocabulary. Carlo gives them more informa-tion, again in Italian: this magnificent monument was built to celebrate the appearance of Our Lady to an English monk called Simon the Simple, he explains; Our Lady appeared to Simon in a huge red cloud, surrounded by cherubs, and gave him a bra to wear, a special holy bra, which he gratefully accepted and wore for the rest of his life. The woman looks as if she's been given a lemon and been obliged by courtesy to chew it. '*Mi scusi,*' she begins, whereupon Carlo, with a gracious smile, raises a hand to exempt her from saying more. He shakes their hands to send them on their way, as Gideon and Luisa part.

'Now why did you have to do that?' asks Gideon, who has overheard and comprehended some of Carlo's nonsense.

'To make their visit a little more interesting,' says Carlo.

'They had no idea what you were on about,' says Gideon, nodding in the direction of the couple, who are walking hand in hand towards the Corso; the man shakes his head very slightly, as if taking care not to give offence to the lunatic behind them.

'No harm done, in that case,' says Carlo.

'You're a bad man, Mr Pacetti,' Gideon tells him.

Carlo takes his arm once more, and they resume their circuit of the town, heading for the Caffè del Corso.

4.4

The Carmelite order traces its origins to a loose community of hermits who are said to have dwelt on Mount Carmel, in succession to the prophets of ancient Israel. The written history of the Carmelites, however, begins in the first decade of the thirteenth century, when the hermits of Mount Carmel were given a Rule of Life by Albert Avogadro, the patriarch of Jerusalem. Later in that century, with the Saracen conquest of the Holy Land, the Carmelites moved westward into Europe, where they continued as an order of friars, priests and lay brothers until 1452, when the Second Order, of nuns, was founded by the Prior General, John Soreth. The number of Carmelite convents soon increased rapidly, thanks in large part to the example of the Duchess of Brittany, the Blessed Frances d'Amboise (1427–85), who founded and then withdrew to a convent at Vannes. Before the close of the century new convents had been established in France, Italy and Spain. In 1562, in the wake of the Council of Trent, Saint Teresa of Ávila instituted a reform of the conventual order, and in 1568, with Saint John of the Cross, she founded the first convent of the Discalced Carmelites, in Duruelo. Instituted as an autonomous order in 1593, the Discalced Carmelites lived in accord with the original Rule of St Albert, devoting themselves to silence, solitude, prayer and contemplation. 'What more do you want, O soul!' wrote Saint John of the Cross. 'And what else do you search for outside, when within yourself you possess your riches, delights, satisfactions, fullness and kingdom – your Beloved whom you desire and seek?'

The Discalced Carmelite convent of Santa Maria dei Carmini in Castelluccio was founded in 1598. The convent was disbanded in 1873, and many of the conventual buildings were demolished or converted to other functions, but the church, a small and plain structure, consecrated in 1607, is still in use. On the façade, a niche above the door is occupied by a statue of Elijah (c.1650), carved by a pupil of Alessandro Algardi. Elijah is honoured as the founder of the Carmelite order, because it was on Mount Carmel that the prophet proved to his people that Yahweh, not Baal, was the true God of Israel, by offering a sacrifice to Yahweh. As related in chapter eighteen of the First Book of Kings: *the fire of the Lord fell, and consumed the burnt sacrifice . . . And when all the people saw it, they fell on their faces: and they said, The Lord he is the God; the Lord, he is the God.* Elijah is shown brandishing a fiery sword: *the sword of the spirit, which is the Word of God* (Carmelite Rule no. 19). Below the statue is the Carmelite crest, in which the fiery sword is again prominent, framed by a garland bearing the words *Zelo zelatus sum pro Domino Deo exercituum* (I am on fire with zeal for the Lord God of hosts [First Book of Kings 19:10]) and twelve stars, representing the Virgin Mary, Mother of God, the *woman clothed in the sun, with the moon under her feet and on her head a crown of twelve stars* (Apocalypse 12:1). The crown from which the sword rises is a symbol of the Kingdom of God, and the peaked brown shape in the shield beneath the crown is an image of Mount Carmel. The white star in the centre of the mountain represents both Mary and the beginnings of the Order on Mount Carmel, while the brown stars that flank it stand for Elijah and Elisha, and for the expansion of the Order to the west and east.

Images of Virginity and Humility, by the sculptor of the figure of Elijah, stand to the left and right of the high altar, respectively. The high altarpiece, *Our Lady of Mount Carmel with Simon Stock, Angelus of Jerusalem, Mary Magdalene de'Pazzi and Teresa of Ávila*, painted in 1664 by Girolamo Bonanno, was removed to Paris some time around 1810; its present whereabouts are unknown. At the foot of the altar steps, a large inscribed stone, decorated with a dolphin above the inscription and a worm-filled skull below, marks the resting place of Jacopo dal Borgo (1570–1647), a benefactor of the church. On the left side of the church hangs an anonymous and badly preserved *St John of the Cross at Prayer*, which dates from the middle of the seventeenth century; the only other painting of any note, Marco Spinosi's *Vision of Antonia d'Astonac* (1761), is to be seen in the sacristy. The doorway to the sacristy is surmounted by a large stucco tableau, *The Virgin Presenting the Scapular to St Simon Stock*, created in 1753 by the brothers Gianantonio and Giandomenico Colombini.

4.5

Crossing Piazza del Mercato, Gideon sees Claire on the bench by the loggia. She is holding a book open, but her eyes are trained at a spot on the ground. When Trim presents himself to her, she looks up.

Smiling as if delighted to find her here, Gideon comes over. 'What are you reading?' he enquires. She shows him the cover: a biography of John F. Kennedy. 'Good?' he asks.

'As far as I can tell. I'm learning things.'

'Well, that's always good,' he says.

A bottle of water stands on the bench; she takes a sip, and closes the book on her lap, keeping her place with a finger.

'What are you going to do today?' he asks.

'Might give the museum a look.'

'Closed on Sundays,' he tells her. 'You're more than welcome to take my car, if you'd like to get out. Sunday is soporific round here.'

'I can handle soporific.'

'And it's going to be a boiler,' he goes on. 'Hotter than yesterday.' She nods.

Trim is sitting at his feet. He ruffles the dog's ears, and then, looking up as if struck by an idea, he says: 'Perhaps you'd like to see the studio?'

With narrowed eyes she gazes across the sun-blanched paving of the piazza. A solitary pigeon is crossing it on foot. 'I'd like that,' she answers.

Misunderstanding, she closes the book and picks up the bottle. Quickly, with a glance at his watch, he clarifies: 'Some time after twelve? After twelve and before one.'

She squints at the pigeon, smiling at her error. 'Sure,' she answers.

At ten past twelve she knocks on his door. Without a word he leads her through the living room and up the wooden staircase to the attic studio. It's a long room, white-walled, with thick beams of rough timber spanning the walls; there's a window at each end, and half a dozen skylights have been cut into the roof; at the far end, two large tables are piled with paper, tubes, pots, brushes; three easels, each holding a picture, stand directly below skylights; against the walls, dozens of canvases have been propped, most with the painted surface facing inwards; an arm-chair stands by the nearer window, and there's a skull on the wall behind it, a large skull with tusks; there's an old chaise longue too, and a bench beside a wide steel sink, below shelves on which are ranged plastic pots filled with powders, dozens of them, and each a different colour; the air smells of linseed oil and warmed wood.

'Nice. Very nice,' she says. She glances at Gideon, and is given an approving half-smile, as if she's passed the first part of a test he's devised for her. She moves towards the nearest easel; Gideon takes a couple of steps in the same direction, like a security guard in a gallery. She looks up, at a rectangle of blue sky. 'A beautiful room,' she says.

'Thank you,' he says. His smile is transmitting an amused sympathy for her nervousness.

'What's through there?' she asks, pointing to a door she's just noticed, near to the two large tables.

'Robert's den,' he answers.

Clearly, she is expected to pass some comment on the picture that's on the easel in front of her. It's in tones of grey, mostly, and what it shows is not quite clear until she's within a yard of it: an array of cogs and other pieces of small machinery, with some fruit, and flowers, and, in the foreground, a dappled green lizard – other than a rose and a fig, the only episode of colour in the picture.

'I have to tell you,' she says, 'I don't know much about art.'

'But you know what you like,' he adds, and he emits a laugh that's loud but empty, as if he's quoting someone else's laughter.

'Well, yes.'

'So there's no difficulty. I don't paint for people who know much about art.' At this she frowns, uncertain as to whether he's joking, and whether it's at her expense. 'I'm perfectly serious,' he goes on. 'Don't take offence. If you take offence you've misunderstood me. Anyone with eyes that function and a mind that isn't cluttered with prejudices can tell if a painting is true. So simply look, and tell me if what you see gives you pleasure. But not this one – it's nowhere near being finished. How about that one, over there?' he suggests, indicating the easel on the other side of the room.

The second picture represents an expanse of old wall that has a wide opening cut into it, within which, mostly obscured by shadow, a man in blue overalls is bent over the exposed engine of a jet-black car.

She puts her face close to the canvas, as if her judgement will be decided by the fidelity with which the artist has rendered the texture of the wall. 'I recognise this place, don't I?' she says.

'Quite possibly.'

'It's outside the town, isn't it?'

'That's right,' he says, in a tone that says: 'But now tell me what you think.'

For a few seconds more she examines the painted wall; she looks closely at the figure in the shadows. 'It's very realistic,' she comments.

He smiles at this, as one might smile at a foreigner who has selected a word that's not quite the right one.

She resumes her scrutiny of the details. In the foreground there is a strip of gravelly road, more sketchily painted than the wall. 'Is it finished?' she asks.

'Almost.'

A sprig of weed emerges from a crack in the wall, at the edge of the picture. She is giving this her attention, when her gaze slides off, to hit a drawing which lies on a board, at an angle, on the nearer table. It is an image of a young woman, naked, with her arms extended and raised in a curve, as though supporting a large and invisible ball. 'May I?' asks Claire, pointing to the table, now moving towards it.

'Of course,' says Gideon. He does not follow her; arms folded, he awaits her reaction.

'Who's this?' she enquires.

'A model. A figure. It doesn't matter who she is.' This is said, it seems, not as a rebuke but as a redirection.

The young woman is stocky, small-breasted, and has a firm-looking little pod of a belly. The face is as solemn and symmetrical as a statue on a tomb. One thigh is talking more weight than the other, and the muscles of it are thick and smooth. 'She's quite something,' says Claire.

'Do you mean "She's quite something" or "It's quite something"?'

'Both, I suppose,' she says. The areas of shading – in the armpit, under the breast, in the crotch, on the thigh – are webs constructed of hundreds of sharp, light pencil-strokes. 'Both,' she states. Now she notices, on the floor, leaning against the wall, a board with a drawing of a nude woman pinned to it; and on the table, on top of a stack of books, there's another one – a young woman seated on the arm of the chaise longue with her feet on the floor, her head incomplete, her body all pale grey tones except for the triangle of deep black hair.

'Same model?' she asks, indicating the stack.

'It is.'

'And that one?

'Yes.'

'Quite a specimen.'

'Remarkable,' he agrees. He comes to the table, picks up the drawing from the pile of books, regards it for a few seconds, and hands it to Claire. A minute later, having said nothing, she hands it back. 'I know what you're thinking,' he tells her.

'I doubt it,' she replies.

'You're thinking something along the lines of: dirty old man.'

'Actually, I wasn't.'

'I think you were,' he insists, with a grin.

'Well, if that's what you think.'

He gives her a slightly wounded look, a look that's intended to winkle out an admission. 'It's OK,' he says. 'Better artists have had to face that accusation. Do you know how old Ingres was when he painted *The Turkish Bath*? He was in his eighties. In his eighties, and he was still painting naked ladies. What are we to make of that?' he asks, cocking an eyebrow. 'An unquenchable appetite for life? An unquenchable appetite for art, for beauty? Pathological lechery? Which is it?'

'All of the above?'

'Maybe, maybe,' he says. 'But let me quote you the words of a great Italian. "The movements of the soul are shown by the movements of the body," he wrote. So a study of the human figure, if it's to have validity, must also be a study of the soul, not merely of the flesh. It must be expressive. There must be an idea.'

'OK,' she says slowly, having noticed another half-dozen nudes in various parts of the room, some stocky, but not all. She nips at her lower lip. 'And the idea here would be what, exactly? Other than the obvious.'

'The obvious being—?'

'That this girl has a nice face, and doesn't believe in shaving.'

Gideon emits a laugh that is like the crack of a thick dry stick; there is no merriment in his eyes. 'All true, all true,' he says. 'But there's more, I'd say. I hope.'

She looks at the drawing that's resting on the floor, at the girl with her arms raised, at the drawing on the book pile, and then, with the demeanour of a woman at an identity parade, at all three once more. 'Men don't have souls. Is that the idea?' she eventually asks.

'I beg your pardon?'

'Well, you said – or your great Italian said – that the body shows the soul, or something like that. But I don't see anything except women's bodies. Very nice bodies, but all female. So am I to conclude that only women have souls? Young women in particular.'

'No,' he says, 'that's not what I'm saying.'

'So where are the men? And the older women.'

'There are some men, I assure you.'

'But not as many, I'd guess. Nowhere near as many.'

'That would be true,' he says. 'But women are more beautiful.'

'Not to everyone.'

'There are certain proportions, certain shapes, that please the eye. We don't know why this should be, but that's how it is. You've heard of the Fibonacci Sequence?'

'Not until now.'

'It's a sequence of numbers: 0, 1, 1, 2, 3, 5, 8, 13, 21 and so on. You see the pattern? Add two succeeding numbers and you get the one that follows. Zero plus one is one; one plus one is two; one plus two is three; and so on. From this sequence you derive the Golden Section and the Golden Spiral. Harmony in music is derived from these numbers, and harmony in art, in architecture. You find Fibonacci numbers all over the place in nature – in the spirals of pine cones, pineapples, seashells. Most daisies have 34, 55 or 89 petals. It's astonishing how many correspondences there are. I'll bore you on the subject some other time. The crucial point is: there are rules that govern the forms that give pleasure, rules that we didn't make up.'

'So you like naked girls because of the maths?'

'The female form is proportioned to please.'

'Up to the age of thirty.'

'Beauty is youth, youth beauty,' he recites, appearing to find the line immensely witty.

'And what has Fibowhatsit got to do with souls? That's what it was supposed to be about, wasn't it? The soul of the pretty girl.'

'Yes. And you asked me where the older women were. So let me show you something. Come on,' he says, and with a hook of an index finger he commands the doubter to follow him to a cabinet by the staircase. Bending slowly, he opens a drawer and teases from it a large sheet of thick, ragged-edged paper. 'Behold,' he announces, 'the senior Venus.' The woman in this drawing sits squarely on a chair, face-on, and she is not young: the calves are wide and tubular; the knees are like soft buns, and the thighs overhang the seat of the chair; the breasts, pressed by folded arms, cover much of the torso; thick pleats of flesh encompass the midriff, but the flesh looks hard and its indentations deliberate, as if cut in stone. There is no face: the head consists only of an outline, and a mouth, belligerently set. This woman, says Gideon, had come to hate her own body. 'Do you know what she said to me once?' he asks. 'She said: "I can't use a mirror any more." Isn't that saddening?' But this was an admirable woman, a beautiful woman, and for years he had wanted to draw her. In the end she'd consented, and she'd been able to see at least something of her beauty on this sheet of paper. 'She's a powerful piece of womanhood, don't you think?' he asks. He doesn't wait for an answer. Critics have accused him, he tells her, of idealising people in his work. 'I take it as a compliment. Of course I idealise. That is the purpose of art, of my art. To elevate. To ennoble, if you like.' He makes no apology for this. He makes no apology for believing in the importance of the concept of beauty. Nowadays we revere glamour, and glamour is not the same thing as beauty. 'This,' he says, brandishing the drawing of the big woman, 'is a naked portrait, but a portrait suffused with the Ideal. Do you understand what I mean?'

'Not entirely clear, no,' she says.

He exhales and regards the roof-beams, readying himself for another bout of education, but at that moment Robert comes up the stairs, carrying a loaf of bread.

'Enter Roberto,' Gideon announces. And then, to Claire: 'I thought we might go for a picnic. Acceptable?'

4.6

In Gideon's car – an ancient butter-coloured Mercedes that's in museum-quality condition – they drive up to Gerfalco. There's a perfect picnic spot just below the village, says Gideon, and he leads the way, leaving Robert to carry the food and drink in three plastic bags. The perfect spot is a curving slope of grass with a screen of trees behind it – a natural belvedere, giving a long and wide view to the north. There's a tree stump on the slope, on which Gideon – taking charge – arranges the plastic beakers (one each for wine, one each for water), having first given Trim his dish of meat scraps and biscuits, and his water bowl. Onto heavy plastic plates he distributes portions of three different cheeses, plus ham for himself and Robert; there are three fat peaches; he cuts wedges of thick-crusted bread with a horn-handled knife; he has brought a salad and a little bottle of dressing, a recipe devised by Mrs Fava, of which the crucial ingredients are honey and coarse-grained mustard.

'See our tower?' says Robert, pointing into the far distance.

'Where?' she asks, then she sees it: like a stalk of slightly darker straw sticking up from a bale. The distant hills in the heat resemble clouds of thick smoke; villages look like scattered chips of stone; in the foreground, when you look closely, there is every shade of green, from almost black to silvery jade.

Gideon removes his Panama prior to taking off his jacket, then his shirt. His belly is creamy silicone and he has breasts that make her think of puppies' muzzles. Noticing her glance, he regards his torso; with the fingertips of both hands he lifts a belt of fat and lets it fall. He smiles, as though impressed by the rebound. 'I sing the body electric,' he chortles, and does it again; the quivering extends from waist to armpit. She offers him her sun lotion. 'Very kind,' he says; he squirts too much of it into a palm and slathers it on; he applies it to his face as though splashing his skin with water. 'Don't worry,' he says to her, laughing, 'the back can fend for itself.' He replaces the hat on his head, puts the plate on his thighs; he eats, appreciatively surveying the land below.

Prim in his spotless white polo shirt and jeans, and his neat soft moccasins, Robert sits higher up the slope, crossed-legged, paperback in hand. 'What are you reading?' she asks him.

'*On the Eve*,' he answers, showing her the cover.

'He loves his gloomy Russians,' Gideon tells her.

'Turgenev is not a gloomy Russian,' Robert corrects him.

'Well, I haven't heard much in the way of laughter,' Gideon replies. Ignored by Robert, he asks Claire: 'Have you read Turgenev?'

'I haven't,' she says. 'To tell you the truth, I don't read novels.'

'Never?'

'Afraid not.'

'Really?' he responds, in a shriek of delight. 'You don't read novels? Neither do I,' he announces, hands outspread as if inviting her to rush over for a hug. 'Why not, in your case?'

'I don't know. I never have.'

'But you read a lot.'

'I don't know about a lot.'

'And what do you read?'

'Biographies. And history. Some history.'

'So no time for make-believe, is that it?' he suggests, approvingly. It seems to be a jibe aimed at Robert, but Robert continues to read, as unperturbed as a deaf man.

'I wouldn't put it like that,' she says. 'It's just I've never been able to lose myself in a story, I suppose. Perhaps I don't have the imagination. I don't know.'

'I know what you mean about losing yourself,' says Gideon. 'You do have to give yourself up to a novel.'

'Bollocks,' murmurs Robert, turning a page.

'No, you do,' says Gideon. 'You have to give yourself up.'

'No more than you do when you're listening to Bach,' says Robert quietly; he gives the impression that he's had to make this point a hundred times before.

'Not quite the same thing,' says Gideon, in a similar tone. And then, to Claire: 'But when you were growing up, you didn't read stories then?'

'Not really.'

'Your parents didn't read to you?'

'Oh yes, when I was small. But that was different.'

'Yes. Of course,' he says. He turns away and gazes towards Castelluccio, in a way that suggests reminiscence. After a minute he says to her: 'And have you got JFK with you now?'

'I have,' she says, opening her bag to show him.

'Well, I'll let you get on with it,' he says, as if apologising for detaining her; he takes from his jacket a sketchbook and pencils.

For almost an hour nothing is said, except 'Thank you,' as her glass is replenished. Then Gideon closes the sketchbook, with sufficient firmness to ensure that they take note.

'Can I see?' she asks.

He angles the sketchbook towards her, and turns four or five pages. Trees cover the pages – sketches of individual trees, with just two or three lines for each trunk, a smear of graphite or a flock of tiny ticks for foliage.

She is impressed, both by the exactitude and by the productivity, but she says: 'You don't paint many landscapes. I looked at the website, and there weren't many landscapes. Which strikes me as strange. Living here, I mean. With all this.'

'I don't paint any landscapes,' he says, and she sees Robert smile into his book. 'If by "landscape" you mean a transposition of the terrain. An image of what's in front of us. Is that what you mean?'

'Well, yes. I suppose so.'

'In that case, I don't paint landscapes.' The tone is that of a teacher – a complacent one – shepherding a student towards greater precision.

'I swear I've seen one or two,' she says.

'No, I'm afraid not,' Gideon insists.

'But there are landscapes in your paintings,' she counters. 'I've seen them.'

'But there's always something else. The land isn't the subject. I don't have anything to say about it, and it doesn't have anything to say to me. I'm a humanist. That's my subject – humanity. The meaning of it. Landscape on its own doesn't mean anything.'

'Unless you're Cézanne,' Robert interjects, barely opening his mouth; his eyes stay trained on the page.

'But you do paint it,' Claire persists. 'You've painted this landscape. I recognise these hills. This one, and that one over there,' she tells him, pointing to Poggio di Montieri.

'Ah, yes,' answers Gideon, 'but what about the rest of the scene? The hills are on the horizon, but what's in the foreground?' He seems to be expecting her to recall a particular painting photographically. 'It's made up. I'm not trying to reproduce what's here. The hills are an element. These trees' – batting the sketchbook with the back of a hand – 'might be other elements. I combine them, in my own way. I invent. Each element is real, but when I put them together I make something that's ideal. Do you see? I eliminate the accidents. That's what Poussin did. Lorrain. The artists I admire. They observed; they recorded; and then they invented. Paintings that merely show you what's there are a waste of time and material. They are redundant, superfluous, tautologous. Nature is not the standard of art; art is the standard of nature.'

Robert gives her a look over the top of his book: a raising of the eyes and a sympathetic pursing of the lips. Half turning in Robert's direction, Gideon calls out: 'I hope you're getting all this down, Boswell.'

'Not missing a word,' Robert responds, reading.

'That doesn't make sense to me,' says Claire. 'People have accidents. Hills and fields don't. A hill can't be an accident.'

'In the context of a work of art, it can,' says Gideon, with a smile for her naivety. Sweat, coloured by sun lotion, is coursing down his belly like droplets of melting wax. 'Of course, there is an order here,' he goes on, indicating the hills. 'There's a profound order. When you look, you see it. The shape of ferns, the shape of branches on a tree, the branches of your lungs. River systems. They follow the same patterns. Fibonacci we've talked about. But Mandelbrot too – you know him?'

'No.'

'Well, when you get home, look him up, and follow the trail. Fractals and so on. Fascinating. So there is an order, as you say.'

'That's not quite what I meant.'

'OK, but there is an order. The problem is, however, that the order is not readily apparent. Things get in the way. It's my task, or part of my task, to make it apparent, and I make it apparent by changing what strikes my eye. I invent in order to be true. I misrepresent what appears in order to represent what is really there. Do you see?'

Robert has put down his book and is looking up at the sky; his cheeks puff out, and he exhales with a pop.

'I think so,' she says, but all she's thinking is that she wishes he'd put his shirt back on.

'I'm going for a walk,' says Robert.

'And may be some time,' adds Gideon, self-amused.

'Anyone care to join me? I'm going up to the ridge.'

'You joke,' says Gideon. 'It would kill me. Or is that the idea?'

'Claire?' asks Robert. 'Trim?' The dog regards him, but does not move from Gideon's side.

As soon as she and Robert are out of range, she mutters: 'Bloody hell.'

'I don't know what you mean,' says Robert, straight-faced.

'He doesn't half go on, doesn't he? Was there any need for the lecture? That was something about nothing, wasn't it? Or have I missed the point?'

'I wouldn't say it was something about nothing. But he does go overboard sometimes.'

'You can say that again.'

'And what Gideon knows about fractals could be written on a blade of grass,' says Robert. He indicates a path that rises steeply through trees. 'That way OK with you?' he asks.

Nothing more is said about Gideon on the walk up to the ridge. Robert walks quickly, a few paces ahead, glancing back occasionally to check that she's keeping up, which she is, apparently with ease; concentrating on where her feet are falling, she has a surging sort of stride, as if pushing her way through entanglements.

At the ridge there are dozens of loose rocks; she sits on one and wipes her brow with a forearm; he sits on another, five or six yards away. 'Great view,' she says; she takes a swig from the water bottle and passes it to him. He names the villages they can see, and points out the puffs of vapour rising from the borax fumaroles – the *soffioni* – at Travale; perhaps, he suggests, they could take a look at them tomorrow or the day after. 'Maybe,' she answers; in the sunlight she can't make out what he's pointing to. He starts telling her about the geology of the area, but soon stops himself. 'Too many lectures for one day,' he says.

'Not at all,' she replies, but she doesn't ask him to continue. She closes her eyes, and smiles as a breeze reaches the hill. For another five minutes they sit in silence, then, out of the corner of his eye, he sees her wipe her brow again and he looks at her and sees that she's whisking what may be a tear from under an eye.

'You OK?' he asks.

'Fine,' she responds.

'Shall we go back?'

'In a minute,' she says, and a minute later they return to Gideon, with Claire leading the way.

Gideon is asleep beside the tree stump, with his face in its shadow; his mouth is ajar, and one hand is crumpling the crown of his Panama, which rests on the summit of his belly. He resembles a vast meringue.

Taking care not to wake him, Claire retrieves her book and settles herself higher up the slope, equidistant from Robert and Gideon. She is reading about the New Hampshire primary when Gideon, without moving a limb, calls out: 'Claire?' He sounds like a man calling into a cave for someone who might have strayed into it.

The surprise almost makes her drop the book. 'Jesus Christ,' she protests. 'We thought you were asleep.'

'Oh no,' he says, still recumbent, hand on hat, eyes closed. 'Rehearsing, not sleeping,' he says.

'Rehearsing for what?' she asks, seeing that Robert isn't going to.

'I fancy the idea of being left here when I finally expire. You know, like the parsees. Towers of silence and all that. Providing sustenance for buzzards and whatever other wildlife happens to drop by. Eco-friendly and philosophically sound. Better than hiding the process from view, I say. *Denn alles Fleisch es ist wie Gras*,' he burbles to himself, smiling blindly skywards.

Robert sighs; he starts to gather the plates and beakers into the carrier bags. To Claire he says: 'What he really wants is a damned great marble mausoleum. Carrara stone. "Gideon Westfall" in finest neo-Roman lettering.'

'But all I'll get will be a slot in the local cemetery. A drawer with a little lid on it.'

'And a rose brought weekly by faithful Carlo.'

'I should hope so.'

'I'll put in an appearance as well,' says Robert.

'Thank you.'

'Might arrange a job-share with Luisa.'

'I am grateful,' says Gideon. 'And let's not forget our loyal Trim,' he adds, and his hand goes out to the dog's head, which nudges the hand to invite stroking. 'Every day in the grave-yard, in broken-hearted attendance. The Greyfriars Bobby of Castelluccio.' Gideon smiles broadly and opens his eyes. He sits up, presses the dog's head lightly in his hands, bestows a kiss on its brow. Then he looks at Claire, with an expression of sudden seriousness. 'Siena,' he says to her, hands thrust towards her in a gift-offering gesture. 'I need to spend some time with a painting in Siena. I'm going tomorrow. Lunchtime. I thought you might like to come too. Not to see the painting, necessarily. Might not be your kind of thing. But to spend an afternoon there. I won't lecture you, I promise. And if you want to explore on your own, that's fine. Think about it. No obligation.' He stands up, slowly, like an inflatable figure being pumped full of gas. He puts on his shirt, buttons it, brushes off the scraps of grass, with the air of a man who has accomplished something.

4.7

Daniele da Montieri, otherwise known as Il Beccafico, was born in 1428, probably in the village of Gerfalco, in the *comune* of Montieri. The earliest written record of his life states that he is the third and youngest son of Piero, a worker in the Montieri silver mines. A brother, Marco, died in the mines in 1441 or 1442; of the other brother we know nothing, and neither do we know anything of Daniele's mother, other than that she bade farewell to him on the second day of July in the year 1444 and never saw him again in this life.

Many years later, when Daniele was imprisoned in the Palazzo del Podestà, it was noted that he had suffered for many years from a 'debility of the limbs'. This condition may explain why, instead of joining his father in the mines, he became an apprentice to a dyer. He was working for this dyer when, in the summer of 1444, the painter Giovanni di Paolo d'Agnolo came to Montieri, in connection with a commission for the church of San Giacomo. It was outside San Giacomo that the painter had an encounter with Daniele that made a deep impression on him: the boy, having been presented to the artist by the dyer, proceeded to demonstrate an unusual talent, by inscribing on a wall, with a stick of charcoal, a perfect circle, a perfect square and a perfect equilateral triangle. He also, in conversation with the artist, demonstrated a remarkable knowledge of pigments and other aspects of the painter's craft. Giovanni di Paolo d'Agnolo informed the boy's father that he would have employment for Daniele in his workshop in Siena, and it was soon agreed that, a month later, Piero would send his youngest son to the city.

The misadventure on the road to Siena is the second episode in the known life of Il Beccafico. He travelled in the company of a cousin – a saddler by trade – and a mason from Gerfalco. Each carried little more than a bundle of clothes and the food and drink he would need for the journey, but the boy was also carrying two coins, which his mother had given him and sewn into his cloak, along with a coin that belonged to his cousin. By sunset they had reached the hill of Poggio ai Massi, where they passed the night. At dawn they set off, and an hour later two men rode up to them. One dismounted, sword in hand, and asked the three travellers to display their property. The bundles were opened on the ground: nothing of any value was revealed. The swordsman searched the shabby trio for purses, and found none. He made them hold out their hands: there was not even a ring to steal. His companion called them a pitiful crew, and signalled to the swordsman that he should remount. As he did so, the robber looked at Daniele, who had not spoken since the horsemen had appeared, and saw something that made him approach the boy again. He ordered Daniele to open his mouth; grasping his jaw roughly, he peered in. 'You have something,' the man said, and Daniele, who had been told by his mother repeatedly that he should always tell the truth, answered that he had three coins, of little worth, sewn into the neck of his cloak. The robber removed the cloak and felt around the collar. He examined his face, as though to determine if this were a fool or a brave young man, then returned the cloak to him, with the coins still inside. He commended the boy for his honesty and wished him well.

The robbers rode away, but when they had ridden no more than two hundred paces the three travellers, gathering their scattered belongings, could see that a disagreement had arisen between the pair. The riders halted to continue their dispute, then the one who had stayed in the saddle turned round and came back. He stopped by Daniele, held out a hand for the cloak, ripped its collar to spill the coins into his palm, and returned it to the boy, without a word. Daniele was beaten by his cousin, for being the most stupid creature in Christendom, and left to continue to Siena alone. So severe had been the beating, the journey took him three more days instead of one.

After this incident, we have no trace of Daniele until 1452, when Giovanni di Paolo d'Agnolo and his assistants were at work on the frescoes of the Loggia del Mercato in Castelluccio. By this time, it seems, Daniele had become proficient in the depiction of architecture and furniture, and accordingly he was entrusted with substantial parts of the scene in which St Nicholas appears to the prefect Ablavius. However, his employment on the loggia did not last long: only a small portion of the frescoes had been completed when Daniele was dismissed for 'drunkenness and brawling'. We have no details of his misdemeanours on this occasion, but this episode might mark the origin of his reputation as a man whose temper was as short as his capacity for wine was long.

Despite his ejection from the workshop of Giovanni di Paolo d'Agnolo, Daniele evidently decided that he could make a living for himself as a painter. He acquired rooms on Castelluccio's Piazza San Lorenzo, and found employment here and in the surrounding towns, albeit painting houses more often than pictures. But he did receive commissions for works of art, notably from the church of Santissimo Redentore, for which, in 1453, he painted an image of the sufferings of Job. Amid the foliage of this picture one can see a small bird, a species of warbler known as a *beccafico*. In most of his paintings he included a *beccafico*: in effect, it was his signature. Il Beccafico – 'the fig-eater' – became the artist's nickname, but the nickname seems to have preceded his use of this motif. There are various explanations for it: he had an inordinate appetite for the fruit; there were times when his poverty was such that he ate nothing except what could be scavenged from the fields and orchards around Castelluccio; when he had money, he would treat himself to a dish of songbirds; or he kept a warbler, caged, in his studio, in tribute to Saint Francis, to whom he professed a particular devotion.

Images of Saint Francis became something of a speciality for him, as were battle scenes and depictions of courtly life, based on fables and poetry. By the end of the 1450s, though still living amid squalor in his rooms on Piazza San Lorenzo, Il Beccafico was successful enough to employ an assistant of his own, a boy called Luca, whose mother was a slave in the household of Domenico Vielmi – grandson of the more famous Domenico Vielmi – and whose father, everyone knew, was his mother's master. Luca's testimony to the magistrates of Castelluccio is a principal source for the life of Daniele da Montieri. The boy reports that his employer is capable of kindness, has never struck him and is often in a good humour, particularly after two or three measures of wine. But two or three measures, it seems, were rarely enough for Il Beccafico, who would regularly drink so much that he would collapse in the street. When he had money for good food he would eat until his stomach threw out what it had been forced to consume, whereupon the glutton would immediately commence to refill it. He had fits, during which he would froth at the mouth and break whatever objects were to hand. It was only for money that he painted religious pictures, he told Luca more than once. He despised the people who bought his work, both for their ignorance and their miserliness. To earn a crust he had to paint the walls and doors of rich men's houses, and this lowly labour caused him much bitterness.

In the winter of 1460, Il Beccafico became embroiled in a dispute with a merchant in Grosseto, who had ordered from him a painting of a marvel that he had seen in the town: a mermaid displayed on a bed of ice and seaweed. Il Beccafico had seen the mermaid too, in Massa Maríttima, where he had made a drawing of it. He painted an image that matched precisely in colour and in form what he had seen, but when the painting was delivered the Grosseto merchant said that it was not a true image, and would pay nothing for it. Eventually he paid half of what had been agreed, which was insufficient, as Daniele complained to Luca, to recompense him for the cost of the pigments.

Within a matter of weeks he was at odds with his former master, Giovanni di Paolo d'Agnolo. According to Luca, what happened was as follows. One morning a servant from the Rocca came to Il Beccafico's studio to inform him that the lord of Castelluccio, Muzio Bonvalori, having spent several days in the company of a friar who had followed Saint Bernardino all over Italy and heard many of his sermons, was minded to have a portrait of the preaching saint, and also a depiction of the martyrdom of Saint Zeno. The servant had been ordered to establish how soon the artist would be able to start work on these paintings. 'Immediately,' replied Daniele, who had long desired, more than anything else, to produce a picture for the Rocca. The servant departed, telling Daniele to await instructions. Daniele waited, and waited, until one day he saw, riding up to the gates of the castle, none other than Giovanni di Paolo d'Agnolo. He ran up to him. Giovanni made it clear that he did not wish to talk, but Daniele would not be refused, and thus learned that Giovanni had come to Castelluccio to paint for the lord a scene showing Saint Bernardino preaching in Siena. Furious, Daniele threw a stone that struck Giovanni on the thigh as he went through the gate. A guard seized him, and he was taken into an ante-room of the Rocca, where he railed at length against Giovanni di Paolo d'Agnolo, before being expelled with a warning, delivered on behalf of Muzio Bonvalori, that if he were ever to repeat abroad his complaints against the honourable Giovanni, or to offer him violence, his punishment would be swift and severe.

His final disagreement was with Domenico Vielmi, who in 1463 commissioned Il Beccafico to decorate a pair of walnut *cassoni* with scenes from the tales of Boccaccio. It was agreed that he should complete the decoration of the first *cassone* before commencing work on the second, and the subject of the first should be the story of Griselda. In October the panels were finished, and the *cassone* was sent to the Vielmi house. It came back later the same day, with a letter from Vielmi, in which he stated that if Daniele wished to be paid the work would have to be redone. The client complained that it was not possible to read these scenes as the tale of Griselda, because the lady looked quite different from one scene to the next. Not only that, it was impossible to tell which woman was the queen and which were her maids, and they all looked more like upright corpses than living women. Daniele repainted the panels. Again his work was rejected: his colours, Vielmi complained, were of inferior quality, and appeared to have been mixed with mud. Griselda's expression, furthermore, was that of a half-wit. The commission was withdrawn.

Daniele immediately dismissed Luca, accusing him of conspiring with Vielmi to ruin him. Three days later, before morning Mass, he was apprehended in the act of removing from Santissimo Redentore the picture of Job that he had painted for the church. He had been promised, he complained vociferously, that he would be given more work for the Redentore, and this promise had been broken by the very men who set themselves up as exemplars of God's law. And those dishonest men were fat and sleek, as Domenico Vielmi was fat and sleek, whereas he was enfeebled by hunger, and he would surely die soon, because there was nobody in this town who would pay him fairly for his labours, which was all he asked of them.

He was imprisoned in the Palazzo del Podestà, where he claimed to have visions. The Virgin appeared to him, he told his gaoler. She had appeared to him before, which was why he had taken his picture from the church. She had told him to bring his painting to her: he was to place it in the trunk of a particular oak tree near Gerfalco; he would recognise the tree because it was as wide as a horse's body is long, and had leaves the colour of emeralds. Some days he would lament for hours on end that he had never been able to afford *azzurro trasmarino*, and that if only he had been able to use *azzurro trasmarino* his life would have been different. His face decayed into a mask of pustules: Job had been in his cell many times, he said, and he had caught the disease from him. One morning he said that he had passed the night in conversation with Saint Francis; he asked for paper and quills and ink, then spent all of that day writing. He died some time before the following dawn. Most of what he had written was illegible, but what could be read was an indictment of his fraudulent and hypocritical patrons: he cursed Domenico Vielmi and Giovanni di Paolo d'Agnolo and the man from Grosseto and all the liars who had blighted his life. They deserved, he wrote, to 'die like pigs, and be forgotten as soon as they are in the ground.' For five years afterwards, it was said, the voice of Daniele da Montieri could be heard crying out from the prisons of the Palazzo del Podestà.

4.8

Gideon shuffles into the room, heavy as an insomniac at four in the morning. He doesn't speak; standing at his shoulder, he watches as Robert works a cotton bud on the E of *MERDA*.

'If you don't mind,' says Robert, having tolerated a full minute's surveillance.

'Sorry,' says Gideon, stepping back to the doorway.

Robert dips a fresh cotton bud; he brings the lamp closer to the surface of the picture, and swivels the magnifying glass.

'How is she?' Gideon asks.

'Coming along nicely. Four or five hours should do it.'

'Excellent. Thank you.'

'Don't mention it.'

Gideon stays by the door. A sigh is emitted, then he says: 'She was a strange one, wasn't she?'

'Who?'

'Our French girl,' says Gideon. 'The philosophy student. What was her name?'

'Laure,' Robert answers, teasing the ink from Laure's shoulder.

'That's it. My God, she was a strange one.'

'She was.'

'Don't think I understood a word she said,' says Gideon. 'Lovely neck, though.'

'Indeed,' says Robert, waiting for the question he knows is coming next.

'What do you make of our guest?'

'Nice enough,' he answers.

A pause precedes the second inevitable question: 'When you went for your walk up the hill, did she talk about me?'

'Not much.'

'Really?'

'Really. She's not a talker.'

'But she must have said something.'

'Gideon, I'm trying to work.'

'Of course. Sorry,' he says. He doesn't leave.

Robert rotates the cotton bud, to lift another small smear of ink from the pale body of Laure.

'Very like her father,' says Gideon. 'Same cast of mind,' he says, with chopping gestures of the hand: six chops, as if hewing a cube out of solid air. 'Lacks poetry.'

'I wouldn't know.'

'Looks more like her mother, though. A plainer version. The eyes are very similar.'

Robert, lowering the lens to inspect the surface, responds with a vague hum to signify that he has heard.

And Gideon proceeds to tell him that Lorraine had been a physiotherapist; that she'd once had dreams of being a dancer, but injury had put paid to that – though he'd always doubted that she would have been prepared for the sacrifices that an artist has to make.

Robert murmurs another non-word.

'Good-looking woman,' he goes on. 'Lorraine, I mean. But more of a sense of humour wouldn't have gone amiss. Rather like her daughter in that respect as well. But decent people, both of them. Somewhat pedestrian, but decent. Very decent.'

'Indeed,' says Robert.

Gideon approaches the table; he halts at arm's length from Robert's back. 'It's extremely good of you to give up your time like this.'

'Cometh the hour . . .'

'I do appreciate it. Take a day off in lieu, won't you?'

'I shall. Don't you worry.'

Gideon leans over his shoulder. 'Fine job,' he says.

'I try my best,' says Robert. 'Now sod off.'

And Gideon tells him, yet again, that he can imagine him, 'once I've gone', working as a restorer, back in London; which is indeed what will happen. 'A lot of demand for a chap with your skills and knowledge,' he says.

'If you use that phrase once more between now and Christmas, I shall be obliged to harm you,' says Robert.

'Which phrase?' says Gideon, affecting innocence.

'"Once I've gone".'

'Oh. I—'

'Back to work, Gideon.'

4.9

Torquato Tasso at Sant'Onofrio
Oil on canvas; 30cm x 17cm
1996
Private Collection, London

In November, 1594, Torquato Tasso arrived in Rome, at the invitation of Pope Clement VIII and his nephew, Cardinal Pietro Aldobrandini, in order to be crowned on the Capitol with a garland of laurels, as Petrarch had been crowned. He was exhausted and his health was poor; at the age of fifty, he was an old man. Eight years earlier he had been released from the madhouse of St Anna in Ferrara, where he had been imprisoned since 1579; after his release he had wandered all over Italy, to Mantua, Bologna, Loreto, Naples, Rome, Florence, back to Rome, Mantua again,

Florence again, Rome again, Naples, Rome, Naples. The great poet was querulous, melancholic, argumentative, vain, suspicious, violent. He had patrons, or potential patrons, in every city, and all found him insupportable. With his coronation on the Capitol, however, and with a pension bestowed by Pope Clement, it appeared that Tasso's final years would be a period of acclaim and comfort.

The coronation did not happen. Cardinal Aldobrandini fell ill, and the ceremony was postponed until the end of April, 1595. On the night of April 1st, in a storm, Tasso presented himself to the prior of the convent of Sant'Onofrio al Gianicolo, and announced that he had come to die there. He died on April 25th. The work for which he is chiefly remembered, *Gerusalemme Liberata*, had been completed twenty years earlier; during the intervening two decades he had written *Gerusalemme Conquistata*, a revision of his masterpiece, in which the fantastical elements of his original poem were suppressed in the interests of Catholic orthodoxy; he had also written *Le sette giornate del mondo creato*, an equally lifeless blank-verse retelling of Genesis.

Torquato Tasso at Sant'Onofrio was painted as a preparation for a larger picture, which was commissioned by Stanley Pavel, a property developer and client of Milton Jeremies, who intended to donate the finished work to the Museo Tassiano, the small collection of Tasso manuscripts and editions now housed in the cloister of Sant'Onofrio. Pavel's wife, Meriel, had been diagnosed with breast cancer in 1991; a period of remission followed surgery and chemotherapy, but in 1994 a tumour appeared in a lymph node, and further surgery was necessary; the following year, in February, an aggressive tumour was found, and this time the prognosis was hopeless. Meriel Pavel rapidly declined: it was expected that she would die in June. But then, inexplicably, the tumour ceased to grow; it shrank; by October it had disappeared. Every day, since the February diagnosis, Mrs Pavel's brother, a friar of the American order of the Franciscan Friars of the Atonement, had prayed for the restitution of his sister's health, and to Meriel Pavel it now appeared that there might be some connection between her remarkable recovery and her brother's prayers. Her husband accordingly decided that he would make a donation to the Friars of the Atonement; her brother – a student of Italian literature before entering the monastery – proposed a gift for the Sant'Onofrio convent, his order's only community in Europe. Gideon Westfall was commissioned to deliver a picture of Tasso by the end of 1996, but in August of that year Meriel Pavel died of cancer; the planned picture was cancelled.

Torquato Tasso at Sant'Onofrio should be regarded as a highly finished sketch. It shows the poet reading, seated on the bare stone floor, dressed in a Franciscan habit; in the doorway stands a young friar, bearing a loaf and glass of water, but Tasso, immersed in the study of a book, seems oblivious of him. The cell is dark, lit only by a thin shaft of light into which the poet turns the book; the light falls from a small high window, with blossom visible beyond it. The model for the poet was a homeless man whom the artist had encountered by the ruined Badìa in Volterra; he had served a sentence for manslaughter in Volterra prison, and had remained in the town ever since his release. The attendant friar is Robert Bancourt.

Robert Bancourt appears in a number of other pictures by Gideon Westfall, notably: *The Travellers* (1999), in which he is one of five passengers in a train compartment, looking out at a deserted country station and the scorched grassland beyond it; *Porta di Siena, May, 2001*, in which he is the man seated on the bench, reading a newspaper; and *The Last Supper* (2003), where he provides the figure of Thaddeus. In addition to scores of pencil sketches, there is also an oil-tempera portrait of Robert Bancourt, painted by Gideon Westfall in 2007 and given to his assistant's parents to mark their fortieth wedding anniversary, and to provide a means of supplementing their pensions, should necessity arise. It shows him under a skylight, at a workbench on which are ranged various pigments in jars, along with some of the implements of his craft: a set of scales, a mixer, a glass cylinder, a slab of marble, a half-filled bottle of white wine. In one hand he is holding an egg, which he is about to break into a porcelain dish. Though the picture would fetch a considerable sum, and the money would be useful, the Bancourts still own the painting.

'It's exactly how we see him,' said Mrs Bancourt, when the artist handed the painting to her, by which she meant not only that the features of his face had been caught as precisely as any photo could have caught them, but that they were imbued with the affection of a parent's gaze. 'But a family,' replied Gideon, 'is one of the many things – perhaps the most important thing – that the artist must deny himself if he is to achieve everything of which he is capable.' And he proceeded to list for her the child-less greats: Raphael, Ingres, Michelangelo, Titian, et cetera, et cetera. 'What about Picasso? He had children, didn't he?' asked Mr Bancourt. 'Precisely,' answered Gideon.

4.10

Having given up much of the day to the picnic, Gideon needs to do a long shift tonight, and thus, with apologies to Claire, he leaves the Antica Farmacia less than an hour after sitting down. 'I'll call for you at the hotel, 12.30,' he says on leaving, with a grin for the prospect of the pleasure that lies in store for her tomorrow.

It is, Robert says, an extraordinary occurrence, for Gideon to deviate from his schedule twice in two days. And he cannot recall the last time Gideon asked someone to accompany him on a trip.

'Other than you,' she replies.

'Well, yes. Not counting me. But that's business.'

'Always business?' she asks.

'Nearly always,' he answers.

'But you're not just an assistant, are you? You're friends,' she says. 'That's the impression I get, anyway.'

'Perhaps "companion" rather than "friend",' says Robert.

'And is that what he pays you for? To be a companion?'

'No,' says Robert. 'I'm paid to be his assistant.'

'I'm sorry. That sounded rude. I was curious about the job description, that's all.'

'We get along well. It's become a part of my role, I suppose.'

She asks him what exactly his role entails, and he explains: he mixes paints, buys materials, prepares canvases, acts as an intermediary with clients, maintains the website, answers emails and letters, pays bills, deals with whatever bureaucracy has to be dealt with, occasionally walks the dog. 'Thank you,' he says, as Marta puts the coffees on the table. 'Anyway,' he goes on, 'things are improving, aren't they? With you and Gideon.'

'He wants me to like him,' she says. She takes a sip and asks: 'Does he pay well?'

'Not sure what the going rate might be,' Robert answers.

'OK. But do you feel you're decently paid?' she asks, as if she were a union representative who's been asked to take up his case.

'Well, I'm still here,' he answers, then adds: 'Yes, I'm decently paid. More than decently. He's a good employer.'

'And is he a good artist, do you think?' she asks, and it seems to be a plain enquiry, a straightforward question of classification.

'He's very gifted,' Robert replies.

'Are you answering the question or avoiding it?'

'I'm not avoiding it. He's an unusually gifted painter.'

'That's what you believe?'

'Yes. That's what I believe.'

'It's an impressive website,' she tells him.

'Thank you.'

'But I find it a bit odd.'

'In what way?'

'Well, the shopfront aspect of it.'

'It's what you have to do. You can't sell yourself short in this business.'

'Is that how he sees it? A business?'

'A business is what it is. We have to sell.'

'Van Gogh didn't sell, did he?' she points out.

'Name another,' he challenges. He downs his coffee in one. 'Gideon can paint anything he sees,' he goes on. 'And he's genuine. He's an interesting man, and I'm happy to work for him.'

She stirs and nods, as if provisionally accepting a response that contains a dozen ambiguities, then she tells him that she was five years old before she even knew that her father had a brother. Her grandmother had let the cat out of the bag – she can't recall precisely the circumstances, but suddenly she knew that she had an uncle, and that the brothers weren't like other brothers she knew. When she'd asked her father about her uncle he'd said much the same thing – they did not speak to each other, and had not spoken to each other for many years. Some time after this, perhaps a year or two, her mother told her that they had tried to repair bridges, but Gideon wasn't having it. Uncle and niece came face to face just once, at the funeral of her grandmother. The brothers shook hands outside the church: Gideon was wearing a black hat, and a black cloak that fastened at the throat with a silver chain; each of the brothers, she thought at the time, looked like defeated soldiers, surrendering. Gideon spoke not a word to his niece. He sat on the other side of the aisle, at the near end of the pew, and nodded to her as the coffin went past. They went back to the house and she'd thought Gideon would be there, but he wasn't, and nobody mentioned him. 'He didn't come to my mother's funeral,' she tells him. 'So that was the last I saw of him, until now,' she concludes, smiling, as if this fact were strange and slightly saddening but of no real importance. 'Shall we go?'

They stroll along Corso Diaz and onto Piazza Maggiore, where they see Carlo Pacetti, in conversation with a couple of his pals from the Sant'Agostino bar. Carlo raises a stick in surly salute, as Robert veers right, taking them into the road that separates San Giovanni Battista and the Palazzo Comunale. 'Gideon's number one pal,' says Robert.

'Which one?'

'Denim shirt guy, with stick.'

'I saw him yesterday,' she says. 'He spoke to me. I had no idea what he was saying. Didn't strike me as the friendliest man in town.'

Robert laughs at this. The grumpy old man, he tells her, is Carlo Pacetti, formerly the proprietor of the garage by the Porta di Siena, father of the current proprietor. 'And a great huntsman,' he goes on. 'That's where the boar's skull came from. A token of the hunter's esteem.'

They have arrived at Piazza della Libertà – this is where she saw the old man yesterday, she tells Robert.

'Ah, I see,' he says. He strides over to the monument and beckons her to follow. 'That's his grandfather,' he tells her, indicating the name. 'And his father was killed by partisans in the last war, so this rankles mightily,' he says, pointing to the wall plaque that lists the dead of the Second World War, but features no Pacetti.

He waits while she reads the names. 'And now I'm going for a swim,' he says. There's a pool in a friend's house, a couple of hundred yards past the walls, he explains; the garden can be seen from the town gate. They cross to the Porta di Massa, where he points towards a lane that slopes away in front of them, under feeble yellow lights. 'He's away for the rest of the month and I've got a key. So any time you fancy a dip, just say. You're welcome to use it,' he says. He can see what she's thinking, and knows that she'll decline.

'Thank you for the offer,' she replies. 'But I'll walk for a bit longer.'

'Well, whenever,' he says. 'Goodnight.'

'Goodnight,' she says.

4.11

She goes out through the gate once Robert is out of sight. There's a bench against the town wall; she sits there for a while and looks, thought-free, at the night sky. She is in two minds about tomorrow's excursion. She hears Gideon say 'The artists I admire', as if his admiration were some sort of posthumous award. She hears him bickering with Robert, then a vision of Gideon in his ridiculous hat, pontificating, is before her. She gets up, as though to leave him there.

She walks down the lane, under the yellow lights. A moth as fat as a cotton reel almost collides with her face; bats are dancing between the lamps; it's so quiet, she can hear the whisper of their wings as they pass overhead. From the other side of a high hedge there comes a quiet and rhythmic splashing. She carries on, down the slope, past the last of the houses. Here the road swerves left; around the corner it levels out and becomes gritty. About a hundred yards away stands another house, with high green gates of solid metal, spotlit. On her right it's open land, dashed with house lights. Before she reaches the gates she stops to look over the fields. A car is creeping up a slope, perhaps a mile distant; the headlights fade and brighten through the roadside bushes; the sound of the car does not reach her. The flashing light of a plane is moving through the stars. She tries to describe Gideon, then realises what she's doing: she is addressing an imaginary audience, and that audience is her father. She will never see his face again, she tells herself, and at this moment the idea is new again. It often comes to her like this. This afternoon it struck her: looking down from the summit of the hill, she had for an instant imagined she would be able to tell him about what she was seeing. It's like living in a darkened room and whenever her eyes have adjusted to the darkness it deepens again and is wholly black, but her eyes get used to it and she starts to see once more, then the darkness intensifies again and so it goes on. Her situation is ordinary: people outlive their parents, generally. But the idea that she is now doing something that he will never know about is unbearable.

For many minutes she stands in the road, until a sound brings her back. Behind her, enclosing the garden of the green-gated house, there is a chain-mesh fence, and something is making the mesh vibrate. A scratching noise is coming from the base of the fence, about ten yards off; it could be a dog. She waits, then something dark, half a disc, is waddling across the road, and a rustling sound is coming from it. Cautiously she moves closer: the thing is about to go into the long grass when she sees what it is – a porcupine. The surprise of it makes her smile.

4.12

The crested porcupine (*Hystrix cristata*) is a species of rodent of the *Hystricidae* family, and is one of eight species of the *Hystrix* genus of Old World porcupines; it was classified by Linnaeus in 1758, in the tenth edition of his *Systema Naturae*. Native to North Africa, sub-Saharan Africa, Sicily and mainland Italy, it is to be found in a variety of habitats, from shrubland and forests to dry rocky areas. It inhabits caves, crevices, holes, or burrows that the animal digs for itself; burrow systems are often extensive, and are typically occupied by an adult male and female plus several offspring. Though it has been widely asserted that *Hystrix cristata* was introduced into Italy from Africa by the Romans, as a game animal, fossil evidence indicates a presence in Europe in the Upper Pleistocene period.

An adult crested porcupine weighs 10–30kg (22–66lbs) and is 60–95cm (24–38in) long, excluding the small tail. The head, neck, shoulders, limbs and underside of the body are covered with dark brown or black bristles; the head, nape, and back are also covered with quills; sturdier quills, which can reach a length of some 45cm, grow on the back half of the body. Pliny the Elder and Aristotle both believed that these thicker quills were used as projectiles, and Marco Polo wrote: *When hunted with dogs, several of them will gather and huddle close, shooting their quills at the dogs*. This notion is fanciful. When disturbed, the porcupine will at first raise its quills to increase its apparent size; it may then stamp its feet – the larger quills, being hollow and thin-walled, produce a hissing rattle when agitated. As a last resort, the animal will charge backwards, to stab its assailants. This tactic has been known to kill lions, hyenas and humans.

Hystrix cristata is monogamous, nocturnal and mainly herbivorous, with a predilection for roots and tubers, but it will also eat insects and carrion. Though legally protected in Italy since 1974, they are nonetheless often killed by farmers because of the damage the animals can do to cultivated crops. They are sometimes poached for food as well; porcupine meatballs are the most popular dish.

5

5.1

IN THE INTERNET POINT of the Ottocento, preparing for the afternoon, Claire reads an interview with Gideon at www.master-softhereal.com. *I lack the gift of faith, but the spiritual chaos of our time arouses in me a sense of rebellion,* she reads. *Everywhere I see the triumph of No over Yes,* Gideon informs us. He simply wants *to show people how to see . . . only the visual image can do this – words cannot . . . I do not entirely trust words.* He also says that *it's an error to suppose that originality is merely a matter of inspiration,* and that he doesn't suffer for his art – *I have no patience with the cult of the suffering artist. I paint. That is my job. I paint what I see. You don't have to suffer to see and you don't have to suffer to paint.* At www.livingmasters. com he tells an interviewer that the *internet is a supernova of drivel . . . it reduces everything to mere 'content' . . . art, 'celebrity' gossip, TV programmes, computer games, football – it's all of equal value. It's all just 'stuff'.* She reads that he's *never happy talking about his work,* which makes her laugh. *I have no time for so-called conceptual art; the concept is where an artist starts, not where he finishes,* she reads. And *all strong art contains a strong element of the banal.*

The laugh has attracted the attention of Maurizio Ianni, who comes over, his smile charged to the maximum. 'Good morning,' he says, adjusting a cuff link as the eyes perform a rapid scan of the computer screen. 'You are reading about our Mr Westfall?'

'I am.'

'It must be interesting, to have an uncle who is so famous.'

'It is,' she replies.

People come to see him from all over the world, he tells her; a lot of Americans; last year, a man from Japan and his wife. 'They stayed here,' he tells her, as though movie stars were the subject.

'Of course,' she says.

He tries another tack: 'I heard about the picture,' he says. 'It is terrible. Barbaric. The picture is ruined, I was told.'

'Damaged. Not ruined.'

'I heard ruined.'

'No. Robert says he can clean it.'

'It wasn't—?' Maurizio mimes a knife-slash; he appears to relish the idea.

'No. Someone wrote on it, that's all. But Robert can repair it.'

'That is good news,' says Maurizio.

'It is,' she says, closing the website.

'I will leave you to your work,' says Maurizio, with a courtier's bow. He takes a backward step, then halts, clearly having something to say that can no longer be held back. 'That perfume,' he says, jiggling his fingers in mid-air as if dabbling them in a stream of fragrance. 'It is a personal question, forgive me. But if you don't mind—'

'Après l'Ondée,' she tells him.

'I don't know it. It's very nice.'

'Thank you,' she says.

'Enjoy your day.'

'I will,' she says, with perhaps too tart a smile.

She returns to the exhibition, and is the only person there, other than the young man at the entrance, who follows her around, at a distance of six or seven pictures, as if worried that she may whip out a can of spray paint at any moment. She takes a look at the painting of the chapel. *The concept is where an artist starts* she silently recites, but she's damned if she could say what the concept of this picture might be – it's a nice scene, just as these are nice-looking young women, but where's the concept in finding an attractive girl attractive? *Strong art contains a strong element of the banal.* Well, she can see the banality all right, but the strength eludes her. She moves along, to the painting of the flight of steps and the arch; this morning she can't even bring herself to commend the brushwork. The young man is pretending to be fascinated by a drawing. 'You don't have to watch me,' she tells him. 'I'm harmless.' He blushes as bright as a radish, but follows her back to the desk, on which there's a comic book, open at a page that seems to depict a half-naked nun in a gondola.

She walks along Corso Diaz and turns into Via Ridolfi, for no reason other than that she has not walked down it before; she crosses Via Sant'Agostino, then enters a street called Via dei Tintori. Above a door there is a plaque, badly worn, with a skull and crossed bones above an inscription:

QUI IL IX GIUGNO DEL MCC[illegible]
È MORTO ANT[illegible]
[illegible]ITTIMA DELLA P[illegible].

A woman's voice calls out; a dozen doorways along, in front of a curtain of coloured metallic chains, three elderly women are sitting on wicker chairs, peeling vegetables, each with a bowl of water at her feet. The women talk without pause, dropping spirals of white peel into the water; one of the women has a laugh like a wooden rattle; another has an extraordinary nose, like Charles de Gaulle. Six months from now Claire will not be able to recall with any clarity more than three or four of the pictures in Gideon's exhibition, but the image of the three women with bowls at their feet, though it means nothing, will be almost as clear as it is now.

5.2

As implacable as nightfall, the plague descended on Castelluccio a little over a week after it had struck Volterra: on June 9th, 1348, a widow by the name of Antonella Vecchioni, a resident of Via dei Tintori, was found to have died in her bed. Much of her flesh was the colour of charcoal. On June 10th two more blackened corpses were discovered; on June 12th another death was registered; on June 17th the pestilence took no fewer than seven citizens of Castelluccio, one of whom was discovered at daybreak, at his own door, his face on the step as if death had struck him down but moments before he could find refuge. By the first week of July, dozens were dying every day. So numerous were the dead, and so great the terror of contagion, that people died alone, unshriven, with no family to attend them. The dead lay in their beds for days, to be discovered only when the stench reached the street. Many abandoned the town for the countryside, where it seemed for several weeks that every hollow and ditch had a person living in it, like the hermits of the Egyptian desert. Reasoning that separation would increase their chances of survival, husbands abandoned wives and women surrendered their children: every morning an infant would be found at the doors of the Palazzo del Podestà.

For the first few weeks of the epidemic, many of the sick were taken to the town's hospital, to be tended by friars from Sant'Agostino. In the latter part of July, when Castelluccio was at its worst extremity, this hospital was closed: most of the friars were now dead, as was the physician who had been employed by the councillors of Castelluccio. The town's other doctor had departed for his brother's home on the coast. People who possessed not the slightest particle of medical knowledge had set up stalls in the market, selling cures of no efficacy. One of them was beaten to the brink of death by a citizen who was deranged with grief at the loss of his family. But barely anyone was to be seen in the streets. In some parts of the town, the only living things to be seen in the lanes were animals that had strayed from farms that were now untenanted. One man, venturing from his house, came across a pig that was eating the body of a young woman to whom the man had spoken not two days before. In the graveyards within the walls, bodies had been covered with nothing more than skim of soil; by the end of July these graveyards were full and there were no priests to perform the offices of the dead, so a trench had been dug outside the walls, to which bodies were borne in carts. The dying were pulled from their beds while the last remnant of life was still in them, and left on the threshold for the *becchini* to carry them away. And the *becchini* of Castelluccio were monstrous men: they threatened to drag the sick away unless they were paid to leave them be, and demanded favours of womenfolk in return for disposing of their husbands' remains. At the Porta San Zeno, one of the *becchini* was stabbed to death by the son of a violated woman.

The relics of Saint Zeno were removed from their shrine and rinsed in holy water. A procession made its way through every street and alley of Castelluccio, reciting prayers to Saint Zeno and Saint Sebastian, and sprinkling the water on the doors of the houses. The blessing brought no respite. Some citizens, in a frenzy of penitence, then burned their most valued possessions in a bonfire on Piazza Maggiore; on the same night, a sodomite was attacked and killed. Some thirty people, from families that had remained untainted, withdrew to a building that until recently had been a tannery – the air there, still noisome, was thought to be repellent to the plague-bearing air. Throughout the day, half of their number prayed without pause; at night, the others prayed; twenty of them survived. Others, however, in despair or defiance of death, gave themselves over to carousing and fornication. On the first Sunday of August, a great company of these desperate revellers – some in their finest clothes, others almost naked, all bearing flowers or spices to cleanse the air they breathed – made its way through the town, playing flutes and drums and pipes so loudly it was as if they thought they might revive the dead with their cacophony.

The last victim of the Black Death in Castelluccio was buried on August 23rd, having died on the feast of Saint Zeno. Between one third and a half of the population of Castelluccio had been killed, and many families had been extinguished entirely. Of the Caraceni, previously one of the wealthiest families in Castelluccio, only one young man and his grandmother were left alive. In 1350, in response to Pope Clement's declaration of a Holy Year, young Giovanni Caraceni travelled to Rome, only to die there, almost certainly of the plague. But one Castelluccio clan escaped unscathed: the Falcucci family, who had withdrawn to their palazzo, by the Siena gate, two days after the death of Antonella Vecchioni, having filled their larders and sealed all doors and windows. They emerged, every one of them, on September 1st, and the following day they attended the ceremony at which the people of Castelluccio committed themselves to the construction of a new church, in thanks for their deliverance.

5.3

Niccolò Turone has sent an email telling Mr Bancourt that he would be very grateful if the *maestro* could give him a firm date for the delivery of his picture, because Niccolò Turone's brother and his wife will be arriving from Canada in October for a two-week vacation and they would be very disappointed if they were unable to see it. Also in this morning's in-box is an email from Max Jelinek, the entire text of which is: *Great – we have a deal – let's talk dates*. This is a reply to a message from Robert, who, having discussed with his employer Mr Jelinek's request that he should simply ask Mr Westfall to name his price for painting a portrait of Mr Jelinek's wife, had responded with a fee that exceeded by some margin the maximum amount that the artist had ever been paid for a comparable commission.

JONATHAN BUCKLEY

'I can't believe it,' moans Gideon. 'I thought he'd tell us to bugger off. How do you get to be a successful businessman if you don't recognise overcharging when you see it?'

'The customer is always right,' Robert reminds him. 'So what shall I tell him?'

'We're committed now, aren't we?'

'I think we are.'

'Christ,' mutters Gideon, wiping his hands slowly down his face. 'What did he have in mind? December, was it?'

'November.'

'OK. Let's get it over with. Tell him November would be unutterably wonderful.'

'And what about Turone?'

Gideon is standing at the easel that has Niccolò Turone's still life on it. He looks at the painting as if it were a pat of diarrhoea smeared on a wall. 'End of this month,' he says. 'He'll have it by the end of the month. Guaranteed.'

Robert goes into his room to write the replies and open the morning's post. When he comes back, Gideon is seated at the easel, holding a brush that's charged with steel-grey paint. It seems that he hasn't added a single stroke to the picture, and Gideon's expression is one that has on occasion been followed by a furious swipe of a brush or palette knife across the canvas. On the other hand, this is a commission, and the deadline is nearing, so the risk of an outburst is low.

With the demeanour of a chess player making a move that can only delay defeat, Gideon places the brush on the table; he summons Trim, to give the dog a self-consoling stroke. And here it comes: 'A hundred years from now, this will be gathering dust in an attic somewhere, if I'm lucky.'

'A hundred years from now there won't be an I to be lucky,' Robert responds.

'But in the great scheme of things—'

'Sod the great scheme of things. One day the planet will be burnt to a cinder. But here we are, and you have work to do for a client who's paid you. Like in the good old days when art-ists were artisans and they weren't squeamish about working to commission. Before the era of the Great I Am, et cetera.'

Pretending not to recognise his own words, Gideon turns his doleful eyes to the doleful eyes of Trim.

'Just get on with it, Gideon. Stop moping. Unless you want me to quit.'

Gideon smiles at the dog, brought back to sense but not out of melancholia. 'Check the contract. It says till death do us part,' he jokes, then he picks up the brush, gingerly, as if it were a filament of glass.

There is no more talk for the rest of the morning, and by the end of the session he has completed the largest steel cog; the pit-ted surface of the steel is painted with such finesse that when Robert looks at it a taste of metal appears on his tongue.

'Time for Claire,' Gideon announces, refreshed, it appears.

5.4

Myrto Jelinek
Oil-tempera on canvas, 100cm x 66cm
2011
Collection of Max and Myrto Jelinek

The portrait of Myrto Jelinek, delivered in March, 2011, is the last portrait that Gideon Westfall completed.

Portraiture was always crucial to his livelihood, and his work in this genre was particularly popular in the USA. As late as 1995 he was telling an interviewer that portraits were 'absolutely cen-tral' to his work. Velázquez and Ingres were artists he revered primarily, he said, because of their 'unsurpassable mastery' as portraitists. He ruminated on the 'two-way flow of influence between artist and subject', a relationship that made portraiture a 'uniquely rewarding endeavour.' Comparing the richness of

the painted portrait with what he saw as the 'impoverished im-
mediacy' of the photograph, he said: 'With a photograph you
know everything you're going to know about the person in the
first two seconds. In a successful painting the character emerges
in time, as one looks at it, just as the character emerged in time as
the artist observed the subject. Time is the essence of the painted
portrait.'

But time was becoming problematic for him: a portrait for
an American client, though remunerative, might require a long
absence from Castelluccio. The travelling made him weary, and
his temperament was not suited to American cities – being in
Manhattan, he complained, was like being shouted at all day.
And he was becoming tired of the people he was being asked to
portray. 'I've had enough of being a face-painter to the rich,' he
said, on returning from a two-week commission in Houston. 'If
I could afford it,' he said, 'I'd never do another one.' But a year
after Houston he was back in New York, to paint the forty-year-
old ex-model wife of an eighty-year-old property developer. She
insisted that she be depicted in a manner that respresented her
artistic leanings – a piano in the background, ballet shoes strewn
on the floor, and a volume of poetry, French, in her hand. One
morning she appeared in a Gainsborough-esque hat, and it took
an hour to convince her that this accessory should be discarded;
her make-up was drastically different from day to day; on the
fifth day she had her hair cut short, and dyed. 'It's just a tiny bit
shorter', she assured him skittishly, as if she thought he might be
flirted out of believing the evidence of his own eyes. He did not
complete the portrait, and on returning to Italy he announced
that he would not be travelling again; if necessity compelled him
to do another portrait for money, it would have to be done in
Castelluccio.

Myrto Jelinek came to Castelluccio in December 2010, with her
husband, and again the following February, alone. Expectations,
based on emailed photographs, were not high, and the first sitting was not an unalloyed success, partly because Mrs Jelinek's

facial muscles had been even more extensively decommissioned by injections and incisions than the photograph had suggested, but chiefly because Max – a voluble, pugnacious and shrivelled little chap, about a foot shorter than his wife – remained in attendance throughout, as if he thought Gideon or his sidekick might get up to something if he were to leave his wife with them, though at regular intervals he interjected comments on his wife's attractiveness, apparently unconvinced that the painter had yet appreciated what a gem he was dealing with here. From time to time Max would creep round the easel to assess what progress had been made. On his fifth or sixth inspection, Myrto's embarrassment shifted into exasperation: 'For crying out loud, Max,' she snapped, 'let the man do his job.' Max resumed his seat, and limited himself to asking Gideon questions about 'the art business', until instructed by his wife to shut up. The next day, she came to the studio unaccompanied; Max, she explained, had been persuaded to make a nuisance of himself in Siena.

Unencumbered by her garrulous husband, Myrto Jelinek was a most enjoyable subject: sardonic, self-aware, frank, intelligent. 'I am sixty-two years old,' she told Gideon, 'and I'm finding it hard to accept that reality. Same for Max. He's sixty-eight, and he finds that tough, but me being sixty-two is tougher. I used to be a doll,' she said, with a laugh that left her eyebrows and everything northward entirely unmoved. 'The boobs have been done as well,' she told him, cupping her chest in a parody of kittenish self-delight. 'I'm on my third pair,' she said. 'You have to downsize when you reach a certain age, otherwise you look fucking absurd, like coconuts on a surfboard.' She didn't know if the surgery was more for Max's sake than for hers, but what she did know was that the last bit of face-work was a tuck too far. She showed him the scars behind the ears, and what happened when she tried to open her mouth really wide. 'I can't scream,' she complained. 'And a woman has to be able to scream.' Litigation was being discussed. One of her friends – a trustee of the same charities that Myrto supported, 'in lieu of meaningful work' – was suing her doctor after being left with an eyelid that she couldn't control, 'so guys on the street think she's a mad old woman giving them the come-on.' In the end, said Myrto, you always go too far; you never know where the limit is until you've passed it. 'But if you think I'm overdone – you should see some of my girlfriends. *The Mummy Returns*,' she said, settling back into the pose that Gideon had chosen for her. Keeping still, as she said, was not a problem.

Max's idea, said Myrto, was that this portrait would capture forever what was left of her looks, and maybe put back a bit of what had been lost. Gideon obliged, employing a few euphemisms in the delineation of her face, heightening the palette to put a slightly fuller bloom on the skin. But when Max saw the finished item, he was not at all pleased. The eyes were all wrong, he protested, phoning Castelluccio on the day he took delivery of the picture. Myrto had beautiful eyes, eyes that were full of life, but this picture made her look like she'd just come back from a funeral and was about to start an argument with someone. 'My wife is a positive person, Mr Westfall, and what I'm seeing here is not a positive person.' Myrto, on the other hand, was more than happy with her portrait, as she informed him in a letter sent too late for Gideon to read it. But although she liked the picture very much, her husband had refused to hang it in their New York apartment; instead, it had been installed in a room in their summer house in Connecticut, and Max had commissioned another portrait from a more compliant artist. 'I couldn't relate to him at all,' she wrote. 'You look at this thing, and it's like he's never met me. He's made me into a woman from the House of Wax. Max thinks it's great.'

5.5

Of course he knows the perfect place to park, a quiet street that's only twenty minutes' walk from the Campo, and of course he knows a terrific *alimentari* where they can get the most wonderful sandwiches made to order, and some fruit as well; and he knows just the spot where they can sit in the shade to eat, with a lovely view of the city. And it's all as good as he promised. They sit on a stone bench, under a pine, breathing air that's scented with resin and hot stone and dust. The city is stacked up in front of them in a pattern of biscuit-coloured walls and pink-red roofs, with the tower of the cathedral at its summit.

Gideon passes her the last of the huge sweet grapes; he removes his Panama to fan his face. 'Right,' he says, placing the empty water bottles and wrappers in the carrier bag, 'I'm off for my rendezvous with Mister Buoninsegna. You must not feel obliged to accompany me. I would like you to see it. It's one of the greatest things in all of Italy. But you may have other preferences. We could—'

'No,' she interrupts. 'I'll come with you.'

'Righty-ho,' he declares, rising with a groan at the stiffness of his knees. '*Andiamo, cara.*'

They walk side by side along the shadowed sides of the streets, slowly. 'I see no reason to rush, do you?' he says. And: 'Strolling is the gastronomy of the eye.' Inevitably, he begins to proffer opinions. Halting in front of a clothes shop, he urges her to regard its sign, and those of the shops to left and right: one in florid script, gold on black glass; one in stark letters of stainless steel; one a name written in a single continuous strand of neon tubing. 'This is why I love this country,' he declaims. 'The British high street – nothing but brands. Transplant a street from Coventry to Hull – nobody could tell the difference. Here it's about people. There's variety, individuality, the human scale. Family businesses. The family is the focus, not the company. Not the corporation.' He appears not to notice the irony of what he's saying. Yet his pomposity today is less objectionable than it has been; the quotient of geniality is higher.

When she stops to take a photo he saunters ahead and waits for her, examining a detail of a building or reading a poster, encouraging her to take her time. He points out something she may like to take a picture of: a terracotta emblem of this part of the city – the *Tartuca*, the turtle. In another street he shows her a small stone panther above a door: 'We've just crossed the border, into the *contrada* of the panther,' he tells her, then he lists the other districts: the goose, the caterpillar, the dragon, the unicorn, the porcupine. 'Social cohesion, that's what it's all about,' he says. 'Cohesion through rivalry.' He tells her about the shenanigans of the Palio – the parties, the fights, the horses being taken into church for blessing before the race. 'Lunacy. Sheer lunacy. But glorious,' he sighs.

Passing a shop window full of kettles, pots and other household stuff, he puts a hand out. Standing at the edge of the window, he squints inside. 'Look here,' he says, crouching a little, to point through a gap in the display at the woman who is standing at the counter, her back towards them. 'See her? Laura, her name is. Laura Ottaviano. Daughter of the owner. You've seen a picture of her, in the exhibition. Reclining figure, back view. But just wait until she turns round,' he murmurs, like the presenter of a nature programme on TV, peering through the fronds at a timid creature. The woman turns. 'Isn't she remarkable?' he whispers, and she really is: pale eyes, a helmet of straight black hair, beautifully curved nose, shapely full-lipped mouth, long arms and legs, dark-skinned, with a dancer's slender muscles; she's extraordinary.

They walk on. 'Robert discovered her,' says Gideon. 'He spotted her, and he thought she was a possibility.'

'As a model?'

'As a model, yes.'

'Well, she's beautiful. Anyone can see that.'

'But there's more to it than beauty. To model you need more. To model well. Some women are beautiful but you know they won't work. There has to be reciprocity. Like love. Looks aren't everything.' His smile, she supposes, is meant to be vaguely rogueish; it does not suit him; sententiousness is more his style.

'So Robert saw this gorgeous shop assistant and said to you: "I reckon this one will reciprocate." Is that it?'

'He said he thought I should see her, so I did, and I agreed with him.'

'And then?'

'And then he approached her.'

'Not you?'

'Not me, no,' he answers. 'I tend not to make the right impression.' A guffaw follows. 'Mind you, Robert's getting a bit too long in the tooth for it now. Rebuff rate has been going up, this past year or two.' He explains the procedure: when a potential model has been identified, Robert introduces himself as the artist's assistant; he says a few words regarding the eminence of the artist; he makes a gift of postcards of a variety of works by the artist – portraits, still lifes, figure studies; finally, he produces a business card. 'He doesn't ask for an answer – he merely begins the process. Some say No, immediately. A lot say No. More than used to.' He grimaces, as if he were talking about an aspect of his bodily decline. 'But if she says "I'll think about it", Robert can tell if this will become a refusal or a Yes, and if it's a Yes, how long it will take to get there. If he says "She'll phone tomorrow", she will phone tomorrow. If he says "She'll phone next week", she will phone next week. It's uncanny. He's always right. The recruitment of Laura required two visits. Robert predicted she'd agree after another talk. He wasn't going to take No for an answer. No, I don't mean that. We always take No for an answer. I mean, he'd have been disappointed if she'd said No. He was smitten, though she wasn't the most fascinating girl. Immensely vain – reasonably enough – and a little dull.'

'So looks were everything, after all,' Claire proposes.

The taunt is ignored. 'She didn't have a great deal to offer,' he says, as if Ms Ottaviano and he had signed a contract which she had somehow breached. 'Robert was greatly impressed, however,' he goes on. 'They had a brief fling – and I do mean brief. He has a weakness for pretty faces, and Laura does have an exceptionally pretty face.'

'She does,' she agrees. There follows, as though taking issue with something she's said, a disquisition on the illogicality of what he alleges to be a widespread prejudice against the beautiful: some people resent it, he tells her, on the grounds that beauty is an unearned quality. It's gratuitous, an unfair advantage, like being born into a rich family. Yet we esteem the virtuosity of musicians, the prowess of athletes, the brilliance of scientists – they are gifted, we say. 'So some gifts are good and some bad,' he concludes. 'It doesn't make sense, does it?'

She is not inclined to debate the issue, and they walk in silence for the whole length of a street. He is breathing heavily, as they go up a rise towards the cathedral, but suddenly he asks: 'What did you make of Teresa?'

'I liked her,' she answers.

He looks askance at her, and gives her a mischievous smirk. 'Neither do I,' he says. This is intended to elicit more honesty, but she says nothing. 'It's not going to last much longer,' he goes. 'I'm sure of it.'

'That's a shame,' she remarks. Her soft-heartedness amuses him; he gives her a small and patronising smile. Fortunately, they are now at the cathedral square; the steps are completely covered with people and the doorway is jammed.

But the museum will be quiet, he tells her, and he leads her to the museum entrance. Inside, he takes her immediately to Mister Buoninsegna, leading the way in a sort of solemn hurry. They enter the room of the great painting. He presents it to her, arm extended: 'her majesty the *Maestà*'. Clearly, she is required to be dumbfounded, but she isn't. It's a sizeable and beautiful object, without question. Her spirits, however, are not rising to the occasion. And perhaps that's what's wrong: the encounter has been turned into an occasion. It would have been better to come across the picture on her own, rather than like this.

'What do you think?' asks Gideon.

'Amazing,' she says.

She is aware that he is looking at her; she keeps her eyes on the picture until he looks away. Saying nothing, he sits down; he removes his hat, places it on his lap, and rests his hands on it; he looks like a man in church. Paralysed with astonishment, his gaze is locked onto the figures of Mary and Jesus, as if the picture were a pane of glass and the holy Mother and Child were sitting on the other side of it. Yet he's seen this picture dozens of times before, so this must be a pretence for her benefit. Without being asked, he identifies the figures in the foreground: they are Siena's patron saints – Ansanus, Savinus, Crescentius, Victor. When the painting was first installed in the cathedral, he tells her, the whole city came to a standstill: shops were closed, and a vast procession, headed by the bishop and the city's governors, accompanied the *Maestà* from the Campo to the church, as every bell in the city rang out. She nods, and it appears that this is enough for him. For five minutes more she remains there, out of politeness to Gideon and politeness to the painting, then she goes off to explore the rest of the museum. She doesn't say anything as she leaves, and neither does Gideon.

Half an hour later, she returns to the room of the *Maestà*. Gideon is still there, hands on hat, straight-backed, staring. If this is a simulacrum of concentration, he's going to inordinate lengths to sustain it. She stands to the side, just close enough for her presence to be registered in the edge of his vision, and he does not move. He genuinely doesn't know that she's there: she looks at him, and for a moment she feels envious. When she sits beside him he turns to her and says, as if resuming a conversation that had been broken off only a minute ago: 'Did you go out on the wall?'

'What wall?' she answers.

'The Facciatone,' he says. 'It would have been the new facade of the cathedral, had the building been enlarged as planned. Highest point in the city. Marvellous view. I'll show you.'

He leads her through the museum to a room in which a queue is forming; they join it, and ten minutes later they are conducted out onto the wall. It's terrifying: a narrow walkway with an inadequate parapet, and a very long drop to the street on each side. Gideon sets out, hands in pocket, as though walking along the corridor of his apartment rather than along a pavement that's above the roofs and barely wider than a plank; after half a dozen paces he realises that she's not following; he returns for her, hand outstretched. His expression isn't cajoling; it isn't sympathetic; it isn't in any way mocking, though she knows she must look stupid, clutching the wall; in fact, there is no expression on his face and he doesn't look at her as he offers the hand to hold. Walking across the wall, his gesture says, is simply something that has to be done; his hand, when she seizes it, is as strong as stone. At the midway point of the wall he pulls her closer, clamping her arm to his side. 'OK?' he asks.

'Never better,' she answers.

'We're perfectly safe,' he tells her. 'We'll go inside in a minute. But you can't come to Siena and not see this.' He points out the various landmarks; when he turns round to face the cathedral, he puts an arm across her back, and for an instant she is reminded of her father, the way he would put a hand on her back as they prepared to cross a road together, even when she was a teenager. In single file, Gideon leading, one hand held back for her to grasp, they creep towards the exit; as soon as they are indoors, the hand is disengaged like a lock. Gideon announces that he intends to spend another hour in the museum.

They reconvene at six o'clock, on the Campo. On the drive back to Castelluccio, after they have passed a dead animal on the road, he tells a story, about his Uncle Martin – not a real uncle, he explains, but a relative on his father's side; he was never entirely clear what the connection was. 'Uncle Martin lived near Croydon,' he tells her, 'and he owned an old Bentley, a fantastic old thing, with fragrant leather seats and a huge wooden steering wheel. One day he took us for a spin in the countryside, David and myself,' he goes on, with – for the first time – a vestige of affection in his pronunciation of the name. 'We never forgot it. A Sunday afternoon; roads quiet; sunny; woodland and meadows; and all these rabbits dashing across the tarmac. And every time a rabbit ran out, Uncle Martin would swerve to avoid them, and the big old Bentley would swing across the road.' He mimics this experience of his boyhood, swaying happily from side to side as they descend towards Castelluccio. 'But years later, after Uncle Martin had died, my father told me one evening that Uncle Martin had been – and here I quote – "the most miserable sod in Britain". His exact words. "Not an ounce of kindness in him," said my father. So I told him that wasn't true – he'd been kind to the rabbits. And my father laughed his head off: Uncle Martin hadn't been trying to avoid the rabbits – he'd been trying to hit them.' He smiles delightedly at her, and shakes his head in wonderment at the naivety of his young self.

5.6

Filling her glass, he beams at Claire and says: 'We had a good time, didn't we?'

'A nice afternoon,' she agrees.

'What did you do?' asks Robert.

'We did the wall,' Gideon answers.

Claire sets her face in a rictus of terror.

'Exhilarating,' Robert sympathises.

'And we paid our respects to the *Maestà*,' Gideon goes on, giving Claire her cue with a look.

'We did,' she says.

'A beautiful thing,' says Robert.

'Very,' she says.

Gideon, she can tell from the way he's looking at the water as it fills his glass, is not going to let her get away with so feeble an answer, but Robert rescues her with: 'And what else did you see?'

'We saw Laura Ottaviano,' says Gideon with glee.

'Always worth seeing,' Robert responds, ignoring the jibe. 'You went to the cathedral, I suppose?' he says to Claire.

'Too busy,' she says.

'Packed,' Gideon confirms.

'So I went into the old hospital.'

'Santa Maria della Scala,' says Gideon, as if it were important that she should give the place its full name.

'Then the Palazzo Pubblico. I didn't have enough time to see it properly, but I saw the knight on horseback.'

'Guidoriccio da Foligno,' Gideon clarifies.

'Guidoriccio da Fogliano,' says Robert, exaggerating the correction.

'And the other *Maestà*,' says Gideon.

'Indeed,' says Claire.

Soon Gideon is expatiating on the other *Maestà*, a monologue that modulates into a lecture on aspects of the iconography of Christian art of the late medieval period. A variety of eloquent gestures are demonstrated, culminating in an impersonation of the Virgin in Simone Martini's *Annunciation*, which involves delicate hands crossed fearfully on the chest and a sudden backward slide in his chair. The chair legs shriek on the floor tiles; Claire starts at the sound; and Gideon, affecting to be concerned that his performance – enthusiastic to the point of campness – has alarmed her, puts a hand on her shoulder for a split second. She glances at the hand, then at Robert, who raises an eyebrow by a millimetre or less, with a similarly brief and barely measurable uplift of one corner of his mouth.

And a few minutes later, interrupting himself, he touches the back of her hand lightly, making the minimum contact, to say to her: 'You should take a look at Volterra – shouldn't she, Roberto? Strange place – very distinctive atmosphere. Louring. Tell her about Volterra, Robert.' He is standing up now, because he has to say hello to someone at another table: it's Luisa Fava, with her son and daughter-in-law.

Robert duly tells her a few things about Volterra, but she's distracted by Gideon, who is directing some exuberant bonhomie at the young man and his wife. The former, though his mother seems enchanted, has the demeanour – as Claire remarks – of a man who has been cornered by an untalented busker. With a kiss of the hand for Luisa, Gideon returns. It's not yet nine-thirty, but he must get back to work now, he explains, to make up for lost time. 'Take my car tomorrow,' he tells Claire. 'Call round for the keys, before nine.' Money is handed to Robert, and – with a detour to hug Cecilia – he departs.

5.7

Within a few weeks of taking up residence in Castelluccio, Gideon had established his routine: every morning, whatever the weather, he would set off for a walk shortly after seven o'clock, and shortly before nine o'clock he would return. One cool Wednesday morning in the May of his first year in Castelluccio, he strolled out through the Porta di Volterra in sunshine, prepared for the forecasted rain: he wore a loden cloak that a German client had sent him as a Christmas gift the previous December, and carried a Piganiol shepherd's umbrella, another gift, with wooden ribs that no gust could buckle. The sky duly blackened, but with unforeseen suddenness; the rain, predicted to be heavy by midday, was torrential by the time Gideon approached the Porta di Siena; and a strong and cold wind had arisen – a wind powerful enough to evert the flimsy umbrella being clutched by the old lady who had taken shelter against the wall of the town gate, with a wicker basket full of food at her feet. Chiefly by means of mime, Gideon proposed that he should carry the basket home for her, and that she should walk beside him, in the shelter of his mighty umbrella, after swapping her saturated coat for his impermeable loden cloak. She assented; he took the sopping coat and draped his cloak over her shoulders, fastening the chain at the neck; approvingly she stroked the cloth. Threading a narrow but by no means feeble arm under his, she regarded the inundation with a huge smile, seemingly delighted by the adventure of crossing the town in this deluge. Already Gideon had taken a liking to her: she was a lively old character, and handsome. The thin nose and sunken cheeks gave her face the severity of a portrait of a Roman matron, yet mischief seemed to lurk in the large grey-yellow eyes. '*Andiamo*?' she chivvied him, delivering a nudge to the ribs; and then, in a voice that could have come from Cheltenham – 'Shall we go? I live in Via Sant'Agostino.'

Thus did Gideon make the acquaintance of Elisabetta Perello, on whom he had at once made as favourable an impression as she had on him. Well-mannered, awkward, and – underneath the Bavarian cloak – rather ill-kempt, Gideon conformed to her image of the quintessential Englishman, and Elisabetta Perello was, as soon became apparent, as ardent an Anglophile as one could hope to find. Her husband, who had died only a year earlier, and whose portrait – a sepia image of a young man in uniform, his face asserting a high consciousness of duty through the set of the jaw, the clarity of the gaze, the marmoreal fixity of the lips – Gideon noted and praised on entering the living room of Elisabetta's apartment, had served alongside English soldiers and had come to admire the qualities that he had observed in many of them: they were great stoics and comedians, Marco had said, and as brave as the ancient Greeks.

Elisabetta invited Gideon to wait until the rain – now clattering on the road with a noise like ball bearings in a drainpipe – had passed. She made tea for him (Twinings English Breakfast), and by the time he left, an hour later, he had learned the salient facts of Marco's career and Elisabetta's life. Her Marco had fought with the Corpo Italiano di Liberazione on the Gustav Line, and then, with the Cremona Gruppo di Combattimento, had been attached to the British V Corps in the battle of Rimini. Rimini was Elisabetta's city, and it was near Rimini, after the fighting was done, that she had met Marco: she was in a ditch, with her two brothers, removing the serviceable parts from a German motorbike, and Marco jumped in to lend them a hand.

She told him she had a boyfriend, and he gave her a smile and said he might have to do something about that. He shook hands with her brothers, and away he went, back to Castelluccio. Many months later, on a Sunday afternoon, there was a knock on the door and there was Marco, on his motorbike, with flowers in his hand. He had ridden more than two hundred kilometres to see her, so she had to talk to him, he said. So they went for a walk with one of her brothers as chaperon, and three hours later Marco rode back to Castelluccio, saying he would like to talk to Elisabetta again very soon. He kept coming back: every two or three weeks he would set off from Castelluccio after Sunday morning Mass, and they would go for a walk, eventually without any brother, and in the end she said she would marry him.

They set up home in Castelluccio, living for the first year with his parents. The Perello family had been in Castelluccio for many generations, and Marco's father had a shop on Piazza Santa Maria dei Carmini selling hardware and household goods, a shop that Marco's grandfather had opened. Marco would have liked to teach English for a living: he had learned some of the language while he was in the Cremona group, and after the war had applied himself with diligence to making himself proficient. Courting Elisabetta, he would recite to her, as they walked along the shore at Rimini, dozens of lines of poetry – mostly Shakespeare – which, he later confessed, he did not entirely comprehend; and Elisabetta was appropriately impressed, though the English language sounded to her, at the time, like the grumbling of Marco's motorbike in neutral. Teaching English, however, was not a possibility: the family business had to be run, and Marco was happy enough to work for his father.

At this point in the story, Gideon let it be known that he too was the son of shopkeepers. Elisabetta, charmed by this affinity between her Marco and the Englishman, enquired as to how, in that case, he came to be living here, and Gideon answered in such a way as to emphasise not the unattractiveness, to him, of a career in shopkeeping, but the irresistible allure of Italy for someone in his line of work; and thus he revealed his vocation to Elisabetta with a modesty that further beguiled her.

'I did wonder,' said Elisabetta, indicating the spots of paint on the lower reaches of his corduroys. If ever he felt the need to invest in a new wardrobe, she told him, he should visit her daughter

Luisa and her son-in-law Aurelio, who owned the clothes shop on the Corso; she'd make sure he received a discount, she promised, and Aurelio, the son and grandson of tailors, would make sure that the fit was perfect. She was as good as her word. One week later, Gideon presented himself to Aurelio Fava, whose greeting suggested that his mother-in-law had made him out to be a man of immense reputation. A summer jacket and linen trousers were purchased at a much reduced price, and altered for a minimal charge. And Gideon was introduced to the plump and serene Luisa, who bore no immediately discernible resemblance to her mother but was no less to Gideon's liking, and in turn was as beguiled by the cheery and dishevelled artist as her mother had been. Thereafter, nearly every item of clothing bought by Gideon was acquired from Aurelio and Luisa.

And so Elisabetta Perello became, in the space of an hour, his second friend in Castelluccio, and Luisa and Aurelio Fava, in the time it took to be measured properly for the first time in his life and to buy his jacket and trousers, became the third and fourth.

That Gideon Westfall was an artist, and an artist of some repute, was, Gideon would tell you, of much less significance to Luisa and Aurelio Fava than it was to Carlo Pacetti, his first friend. As Luisa and Aurelio saw it, being an artist was an interesting profession; it was very unusual, they appreciated, for people such as themselves to befriend, or be befriended by, a painter whose work was known all over the world. They knew next to nothing about art, but they could see that Gideon was an expert, and they respected him for it. Aurelio, who could cut for you a suit that would hang almost weightlessly on your body and would last so long your son could wear it, was an expert too. He spoke to Gideon as an equal, as did his wife. The Favas liked Gideon because he was Gideon – 'he is good company,' said Luisa. 'He entertains us. He is very alive.'

It was only with Luisa and Aurelio, Gideon would sometimes say, that he ever experienced envy: only the Favas ever made him regret that his choice of life had made marriage an impossibility. No arguments appeared to mar their relationship: they were naturally and perfectly attuned to each other. They were both, remarked Gideon, 'paragons of common sense and decency', and were always absolutely straight with him: if they didn't like a particular painting, or didn't understand the point of it, they would tell him so, without apology or embarrassment. Even-tempered without being dull, they were an undemonstratively affectionate couple, and amiable towards almost everybody. The sole citizen of Castelluccio whom they admitted to disliking was, unfortunately, Carlo Pacetti: Lauro Pacetti, said Aurelio, had been a horrible individual, whose politics stank to high heaven and whose character was just as rank, as had been demonstrated in an incident – never explicated – in which he had in some way grievously insulted a young woman, unnamed, of the Perello family; and whenever Aurelio observed Lauro's son, he had to confess, what he saw was Lauro with a mask on his face. Lino Pacetti had been a mean-spirited husk of a man too, just like his nephew: other people in Castelluccio had given food and clothing to POWs on the run, despite the risk of imprisonment or worse, but not Lino Pacetti – if payment was involved, he would have done business with the devil himself, but if cash wasn't involved, Lino wouldn't lift a finger, even if Saint Francis himself came to his door. So Aurelio regarded Gideon's friendship with Carlo Pacetti as an aspect of his life that had to be ignored, like a weakness for alcohol, just as Luisa, for her part, said nothing more about Ilaria Senesi, after warning him that there was trouble in that family, because the wife, more than once, had appeared at the market with bruises all over her arm, covered badly with make-up.

Gideon's first dog, the black mongrel, was acquired through a friend of Luisa and Aurelio: it was Aurelio's opinion that Gideon would benefit from the company of a dog on his morning walk, because a dog establishes a connection with nature, and its companionship is an aid to thought. Had the idea been proposed by anyone other than Aurelio, said Gideon, he might not have entertained it for more than five seconds, but he allowed himself to be persuaded by the tailor, and has never regretted it: all three of his dogs came to him through Aurelio and Luisa. Once Trim the black mongrel had been trained, it would accompany its master on evening strolls with Aurelio and Luisa. Sometimes, on a Sunday, they would all go for a drive in Gideon's Mercedes, to some hill or woodland where Aurelio would look for butterflies; once they even drove across Italy on a Saturday night so that they could spend the next day in the Majella national park, searching – successfully, as it turned out – for the elusive *Parnassius Apollo*. While Aurelio – a decade older than his wife, but slighter by far, and nimbler – dashed back and forth in pursuit of his butterflies, Gideon and Luisa would follow at their own pace, often in agreeable silence, and if not in silence then in conversation that was never about art or anything profound. Trivialities that from anyone else would have bored him never bored him when it was Luisa who was talking: they were the currency of an intimacy that was unique to this relationship. Through Luisa, he once remarked, the mundane was distilled. When he walked with her, he said, his mind received, as though transmitted by radiation, a sense of extraordinary well-being, of tranquility. He thinks she is more a Buddhist than a Catholic, and he loves her, he admits, as he has loved no one since his mother. More than anyone else he has ever met, Luisa Fava is imperturbable; she appears to live in almost perpetual harmony with herself and with the people among whom she lives – almost perpetual, because of course there were episodes of tension with a daughter who came to despair of ever finding a real job in Italy (she became a project manager on the other side of the world, in Shanghai) and a son whose adolescence was blighted by an awareness that he lacked both the intellect and the application of his sister (he works for a bank in Arezzo).

Luisa has accommodated without show the sadness of the loss of her father, the loss of Aurelio, the absence of her daughter, and the long decline of Elisabetta. It has been nearly two years since Elisabetta last left her bed unaided. Since her health began to fail, she has lived in what was once her granddaughter's bedroom, in the house on Via dei Giardini. Gideon is one of the friends who has a key to the house, so he can let himself in, and he calls on Elisabetta regularly. Often, now, she's asleep when he arrives. The window in her room is kept open all day if the weather is fine, so she can hear the sounds of the town going about its business, and the birds and the leaves in the park across the street. When she dreams in the daytime, she tells him, leaves are often rustling in her dreams, and when the leaves are rustling she sees Marco. Gideon reads to her: she has a predilection for the novels of Graham Greene, and Gideon's voice, she tells him, suits their sentences perfectly. Always she falls asleep while he is reading, and she falls asleep whenever they listen to music, which they do in the course of most of his visits, because she cannot operate the buttons on the CD player any longer and therefore has to rely on her guests. *Il barbiere di Siviglia* was her Marco's favourite piece of music in the world, so, as often as not, it's *Il barbiere di Siviglia* that she requests, with apologies, because she knows that Gideon doesn't share Marco's enthusiasm for Rossini, even if she doesn't know that Rossini is akin to torture for Gideon, and he turns the music off as soon as he's sure that Elisabetta is asleep. He has tried to make her like Bach, and she has liked some of it, but not the Masses or the cantatas – not much of it at all, in fact. It's too German for her, she confessed, in a voice that's now like the slithery rasp of parchment. In the summer she occasionally hears German being spoken in the park: she is sure they are nice people, but the sound of that language still makes her shudder, after all these years. To her ears, it's the language of slaughter.

With Gideon she sometimes talks about her death: she talks of it without fear, because she knows that she will see her Marco one day soon, just as her daughter will one day see Aurelio. Listening to Rossini, she closes her eyes and smiles like an effigy on a tombstone. She has allowed Gideon to draw her while she listens, eyes closed, smiling, on the brink of bliss. Elisabetta has been dying for so long, he says, she has almost become a saint.

He has painted Luisa's portrait twice and drawn her many times, more often than anyone other than himself and Robert. Once he suggested that she and Aurelio might model as Mr and Mrs Blake, sitting under their tree, naked as Adam and Eve. They were amused by the idea, but could not be persuaded.

5.8

'I think he's relieved it went so well,' says Robert, as they are strolling along on Corso Diaz.

'So he was expecting a day of interrogation?' she asks.

'Something like that.'

'I haven't come here to hold him to account,' she says. 'Well, not only for that.'

'What else?'

'Curiosity.'

'Curious about the horrible uncle?'

'About the artist uncle.'

'I don't understand why you waited so long.'

'It wasn't possible before.'

'Your father wouldn't have allowed it?'

'Not a question of allowing.'

'It would have been like defecting to the enemy. Is that it?'

'Not that extreme. But something along those lines.'

'And as far as you're concerned, Gideon's to blame?'

'He behaved appallingly when my mother died,' she reminds him. 'Before that, too. He was dreadful.'

'You know that for a fact?'

'I do. He was obnoxious.'

'Or so you were told.'

'He was obnoxious,' she states, halting to face him. 'Arrogant, rude and selfish.'

He raises his hands; unamused, she nods acceptance of the surrender. 'But you enjoyed your afternoon with him,' he proposes.

'I enjoyed Siena. Gideon was OK.'

'Not arrogant or rude.'

'No,' she agrees.

On Piazza Maggiore three boys are kicking a football around; one of them – a lad of about ten or eleven – bends forward sharply, arms out like wings, to catch the ball on the back of his neck. 'Your parents still alive?' she asks, waiting to see if the boy will do another trick.

'They are.'

'Get along with them?'

'Fine.'

'Where's home?' she asks

'If you mean where are the parents – Bristol.'

'Thought I could hear an accent,' she says, moving on. 'Think you'll ever go back?'

'To Bristol? No.'

'To England?'

'Who knows? One day.'

'But not any time soon.'

'Doubt it.'

'You're happy here.'

'I'm content,' he says.

She stops again, and she looks around the square – at the town hall, San Giovanni Battista, the lights in the apartments, the footballing boys, the Caffè del Corso – as if trying, and not entirely failing, to imagine how this may account for his contentment. With a nod towards the café she announces: 'I fancy a nightcap. Care to join me?'

'I'm expected,' he apologises.

Inside, there are two couples at the tables and two men at the bar. 'A woman dropping in for a drink on her own – will this be controversial?' she asks.

'It will be noticed.'

She raises her eyebrows, shakes her head, smiles to herself. '*Buona notte*,' she says, and she strides into the café as if she has an appointment with one of the customers. '*Buona sera*,' she calls to Giosuè, on her way to a table.

5.9

In 1895 the businessman Silvio Ubaldino – who had made his fortune from an aniseed-based liqueur produced in his distillery outside Volterra, and in 1893 had acquired Castelluccio's hotel, the Belvedere – bought the vacant property at Corso Garibaldi 2–4, previously the offices of an insurance company. Less than six months later, on January 1st, 1896, the Caffè Ubaldino welcomed its first customers. Luxuriously furnished and decorated in the Liberty style, it quickly established itself as the most fashionable café in the region.

The Caffè del Corso – as it has been named since 1922 – retains many of its original features. The façade is plain: the old black mirrored sign above the door is the only adornment of the exterior's cream-coloured plaster. The interior, however, is opulent, with its dark wooden panels, stained-glass partitions, brass bar fittings, marble-topped counters and small round marble-topped tables. A number of television and film productions have used the Caffè del Corso as a location.

Around the cash desk are displayed autographed photos of various celebrities, among them Tito Gobbi, Vittorio Pozzo, Umberto Saba and John Huston. The original gold and black glass sign of the Caffè Ubaldino is now affixed to the back wall, above a drawing in red chalk of Arrigo Pepe, the celebrated marksman of Castelluccio, and a crossbow that is said to have been used by him. In the corner farthest from the door, Domenico Scattolin's pastel portrait of Tommaso Galli, the manager of the Teatro Gaetano, hangs over the table at which Galli habitually sat. It was Galli's custom to take his lunch here; frequently he would also call at the Caffè Ubaldino after the evening's performance, either alone or with members of the cast. Every Wednesday night he would be joined by Paolo Campani, with whom he would play cards until late. Galli would sometimes entertain the customers by playing the mandolin, which is why he's depicted holding this instrument, a gift from Paolo Campani.

5.10

It is midnight, and again Gideon has not worked well. The still life is a chore; the self-portrait is inert. The sketchbook from Claire is out of sight, on a shelf in the corner of the room. It crosses his mind, not for the first time, that it might be expedient to return it to her: she would be less hostile, perhaps, if he did; it has some monetary value. There are other considerations, however, and now – needing to do something – he decides that these must prevail. Page by page he examines his apprentice work. The drawing of the view from his window is inept; with a scalpel he excises it and cuts it into slivers. The array of hands is better, much better – the modelling is good; he removes it and sets it aside. The students, whoever they might have been, can be destroyed without qualms. His portrait of Martin Scammell is also of poor quality, but cannot be thrown away, and the sketch of himself has some documentary value, and so is saved. The dog has almost no merit; the sketch of Lorraine is deplorable, and has to be destroyed. He stuffs the scraps in a pocket and summons Trim.

They walk to the Giardini Pubblici, where there's a rubbish bin. Trim takes a dip in the park's pool. It's a pleasantly warm night, and Gideon feels some relief at having acted decisively; he thinks he may paint a night scene soon, but has no clear conception of what it might be. Empty-headed, he sits on the bench, watching the bats crossing against the moon. When he leaves the park, the moon is far from where it had been when he arrived. He has seen nobody since coming out of the building, but a young couple are crossing Piazza del Mercato. The young woman is tilting her head to her boyfriend's shoulder – she is not tall, and the short skirt reveals powerful legs. It's Ilaria, he realises, and the shock makes him stop. It is not Ilaria.

5.11

The Lagotto Romagnolo, or Italian Water Dog, is a small to medium-sized dog, around 41–48cm (16–19in) in height and 11–16kg (24–35lb) in weight, with a dense and curly coat that might be solid off-white, solid brown, solid orange, brown roan or white with brown or orange markings. Thought by some to be the ancestor of all breeds of water dog, the Lagotto is recorded as being used in the marshes of Romagna as far back as the seventh century BC; its name derives from *Cán lagót*, meaning 'hairy wetland dog' in the region's dialect. For centuries the Lagotto was employed in hunting waterfowl, aiding the hunter by springing the birds and chasing them into nets; when guns were introduced, the dogs became retrievers. A remarkably hardy animal, the Lagotto can remain in water for hours at a time, as its two-layered coat is water-resistant; webbing between the toes makes it a strong swimmer. The draining of the Romagna marshland in the latter part of the nineteenth century brought about a change in the Lagotto's role: as the flocks of waterfowl dwindled, the dogs were increasingly used as truffle-hunters, a task for which their agility and scenting ability made them particularly suitable. At the same time, the Lagotto was being cross-bred in order to pass on its qualities to other hunting breeds, and by the 1970s this dilution had all but eliminated the pure Lagotto. Thanks to the efforts of various Romagnolo breeders, however, the Lagotto was saved from extinction. No other pure-bred dog is recognised as a specialised truffle-hunter.

Mantegna placed a Lagotto in the frescoes he painted for Ludovico Gonzaga in the Camera degli Sposi of Mantua's Castel San Giorgio: the animal is standing behind Ludovico's white-stockinged legs, in the scene depicting the encounter between the marquis and his second son, Cardinal Francesco. A magnificent Lagotto can also be seen in a painting by Guercino (or his workshop), in which the dog is flanked by Guercino and a woman who may be the artist's older sister, or his mother, or someone else.

Trim, Gideon Westfall's brown roan Lagotto Romagnolo, is the third dog he has owned since moving to Italy. The first, a black mongrel, which disappeared after a year's residence with Gideon, was also called Trim, as was its successor, an indolent Spinone Italiano that eventually suffered from so many ailments that it had to be destroyed. George Stubbs, in 1783, painted a dog named Trim, accompanied by an unnamed horse; this Trim had earned commemoration by saving the life of a Mr G.W. Ricketts, a Jamaican plantation owner, who, awoken by the dog's barking, had found one of his slaves looming over his bed, knife in hand. In 1816 Ingres drew a pencil portrait of a Mademoiselle Thévenin and her pet dog, Trim.

5.12

Teresa says: 'Why do you have to be with them every evening? Last night you were with them, tonight you are with them.'

'But it was better if I didn't come over right away. That's what you said. And—'

'Yes, I know what I said. Renata is in a difficult mood. That's how it is. But I'm not asking why weren't you here. I'm asking why you need to be with them all the time.'

'I don't need to be. I was invited,' he says. 'It's only for a few days. She'll soon be gone.'

'Every day she's here, you have to keep them company? Why? If she goes with him to Siena, she can't be scared of him any more.'

'She was never scared of him. If anything, he's scared of her.'

'That's stupid. She isn't scary to anybody.'

'Families aren't his thing.'

'That is ridiculous,' Teresa pronounces. 'Where did he come from? A test tube? He comes from a family. A family is everybody's thing.'

'He says he doesn't know how to talk to her.'

'That is stupid too. They spent an afternoon together. He knows how to speak to her by now.'

'He's worried she'll have seen too much of him. He's afraid of boring her.'

'I can understand that,' she says. 'But she can always say "No". She does not have to see him every evening. She's a big girl.'

'Perhaps she feels she can't.'

'Aha,' says Teresa. 'Because she's scared of him.'

'Not scared. Obliged, maybe.'

'It is ridiculous,' says Teresa, lobbing her jeans into the laundry basket as if thereby casting out all thoughts of Gideon.

He kisses her neck; she puts a palm briefly to his cheek. 'He asks you to be there, and you say "Yes sir",' she tells him.

'If you want me to say "No" tomorrow, I'll say "No". It's not a big deal.' he says.

'You should do something for yourself, Robert,' she says, lifting the sheet. 'This situation is not good. When he does this' – she raises her chin haughtily and snaps her fingers – 'you run. You are forty years old. It is not good to be a servant when you are forty.'

'I'm not a servant.'

'You are a servant,' she states. She kneels on the pillow, facing him. 'You could be an artist,' she says, aiming a hand at his drawing of her, on the wall beside the door, urging him to face the evidence.

'I'm not good enough,' he tells her.

'Yes, you are good. You could be good.'

'Every art school in Europe has students who are better than me.'

'There are worse artists who make a living from their work.'

'I have nothing to say,' he answers.

'An artist does not have something to say. A writer says something. A painter paints.'

They've had this conversation before; they both know they are quoting themselves. 'You need drive to make a living from it,' says Robert, 'and I don't have it.'

'He's made you lose it.'

'I like working for Gideon,' he says. 'It's a good job.'

'It would be better if you did not work for him,' she says, stroking his back. 'Think about it, Robert.'

'I have thought about it.'

'Think about it some more. Please.'

He says he will think about it. They read for a while, then Teresa turns out the light and within a minute she's asleep.

6

6.1

WHEN ROBERT GOES into the kitchen Renata is there, looking out of the window, earphones plugged in, iPod tucked into the waistband of her pyjamas. The earphones are leaking something he recognises: Marracash, he thinks. It's a small kitchen; his reflection is on the glass right in front of her; it's not possible, despite the music, for her to be unaware that he's behind her, but she does not move. He takes a carton of juice from the fridge; he lets the door close loudly, and still she looks out of the window, from which there's nothing to see except some sky and the windows of the apartments on the other side of the alley. He puts a glass on the table, fills it, puts the carton back in the fridge. As he's leaving the kitchen Renata at last turns round; at least she doesn't feign surprise at seeing him.

'Good morning, Renata,' he says. 'How are you?' The girl has never warmed to him, but occasionally she has seemed to take some pleasure from practising her English with him. Now, leaving the earphones in place, she just raises a thumb, and returns her gaze to the windows across the street. In her hand she has a peeled orange, at which she noisily sucks. 'Catch you later,' he says.

She unplugs one ear. 'What?' she asks; the syllable has a trans-atlantic sound.

'How are you?' he says.

Renata shrugs, looking over his shoulder. 'OK,' she says. 'Good.'

She replaces the earpiece, lifts the iPod and starts scrolling.

'See you later,' he says, raising the glass as if to toast her.

'Yes. For sure. OK. See you,' she responds, and for an instant a smirk appears.

Teresa is awake when he returns to the bedroom; she lies curled on her side, eyes closed, with the clock in one hand. 'You're up early,' she murmurs. 'Renata's out of bed?' she asks.

'She is,' he answers, bending down to kiss her.

'You're going?' she asks, opening an eye.

'See you tonight,' he says, putting on his shoes.

'Have fun,' she sighs. She raises a hand, takes his, and pulls him onto the bed; she presses her face into his neck, then groans and rolls over. 'I'm so tired,' she moans. She's never a quick starter in the morning, but she is not, he suspects, as drowsy as she's making out.

'Get up,' he says, tugging the duvet, and she swats his hand, smiling, eyes shut.

Two minutes later he's on Piazza Maggiore, where the sacristan of San Giovanni Battista is positioning a ladder to the side of the door. Above him, an A.C. Milan scarf dangles from the head of the Baptist, and a burst plastic football is stuck behind the kneeling Christ. In the middle of the square, Maurizio Ianni is watching the sacristan's tentative ascent. 'The scarf is a nice touch,' he remarks to Robert. The sacristan, nervous on the upper rungs, extends a hand towards the football; he withdraws it; slow as a slender loris, he raises himself by a rung. 'Is your visitor enjoying her stay?' asks Maurizio.

'She is,' Robert replies.

Again the sacristan fails to seize the ball. Shaking his head, Maurizio says: 'You would not think they are related. A different kind of character, no? She is a bit—' and he brings both fists clenched to his chest, as his face tightens.

'A bit, maybe,' says Robert.

'I would say she is a lonely person,' Maurizio goes on; he applauds briefly, the ball having now been extracted.

'I don't think so.'

The lack of agreement makes Maurizio pause for a moment. 'She could make more of herself,' he says, then chuckles. 'Why do English women act as if they are ashamed of their bodies? English style, it is a mystery.'

'We're a very subtle people, Maurizio,' says Robert.

The sacristan, balancing on one foot, moves a hand towards the end of the scarf; the hand comes to a halt a few inches short. 'The old man's going to kill himself,' says Maurizio. Robert jogs towards the ladder, with Maurizio yelling: 'Hold on! The English are coming!'

6.2

A church existed in Castelluccio prior to the tenth century, when the town was destroyed by marauding Hungarians in the course of the war between Berengario I and Adalberto, the Margrave of Tuscany. It is commonly assumed that this church was located on the spot now occupied by San Giovanni Battista, the oldest building in Castelluccio, but all that can be said for certain is that the basilica of San Giovanni Battista stands on the site of earlier structures: excavations of the crypt in the 1980s discovered, at a depth of 85 centimetres, the remains of a brick pavement, which has been dated to the early years of the Ottonian period (936–1056). Beneath the pavement were found portions of *cocciopesto*, a compound of lime mortar and crushed pottery, much used by the Romans.

The construction of San Giovanni Battista commenced around 1160, and fragments of ancient buildings were utilised by its builders: the beading around the central door, for example, is almost two thousand years old, and the capitals of the second and third columns on the left side of the nave are Roman too. Progress was not rapid. When the church was consecrated, in 1210, the exterior was completely unadorned. By 1348, when the Black Death ravaged the town, only the lower part of the façade had been completed. It remains unfinished to this day: from the ground to the cornice that traverses the building, the pilasters, walls and arches are patterned with white and black marble; above, and along the sides of the church, the grey stone walls are bare. Between 1500 and 1700 no fewer than fifteen architects submitted plans for the completion of the façade of San Giovanni Battista, but nothing was added until the early 1880s, when the statues were installed above the doors. Created by the Sienese sculptor Maurizio Puppa, they depict St Mary and St Elizabeth with the infant Jesus and the infant St John (over the left-hand door), the baptism of Christ (central door) and the beheading of St John (the right-hand door).

The interior has changed little since the thirteenth century. The only significant addition to the original basilica is the Cappella Bonvalori, on the right; it was built in 1470 with money donated by Muzio Bonvalori, who is buried here with several generations of his family, including his parents and grandparents, whose bodies he transferred to San Giovanni Battista from the church of San Lorenzo. The chapel's altarpiece, *The Madonna and Child with Saints John the Baptist and Zeno*, painted by Giovanni di Paolo d'Agnolo in 1472 and poorly restored in the nineteenth century, is the only notable painting in the main body of the church.

The crypt, below the raised choir and presbytery, is the resting place of Saint Zeno, whose relics lie in the stone sarcophagus beneath the altar. The sarcophagus is a Roman coffin: chisel marks at each end show where carvings have been removed. Fragments of Roman decorative stonework are set into the walls behind the altar.

A magnificent pulpit, made some time around 1210, is the most notable feature of the raised area. It is thought that the large plates of porphyry that cover two sides of the pulpit were brought back from Constantinople by a Castelluccio man who had fought with the Venetians in the Fourth Crusade. In the sacristy, which is entered from the choir, you can see a sequence of paintings by Girolamo Bonanno. Painted in 1670, the three scenes are: *The Miracle of Lodovico di Piero*; *Saint Zeno Exorcises the Boar*; and *The Death of Saint Zeno*, in which the artist has conflated two different incidents – the city walls and towers are those of Arezzo, but the blood-red stream on the left is the stream below Castelluccio. Bonanno has included a self-portrait in the midst of the crowd of people astonished by the speech of the saint's severed head – he is the figure in the golden cap, with his hands clasped in prayer.

Many members of the Campani family are entombed in the right aisle. The most conspicuous monument is that of Pierpaolo Campani (1770–1853), which takes the form of a bust of the deceased on a plinth of Carrara marble; into the plinth is carved a weeping woman, who rests her cheek against the inscription: *La moglie e i figli inconsolabili*. Pierpaolo's grandson, Paolo, the last of the Campani, is buried under the slab of black granite that lies beside the third column of the nave.

6.3

The Avelignese horse is a very close relative of the Haflinger, which takes its name from the village of Hafling (in Italian, Avelengo), which lies at an altitude of 1,300 metres above sea level, ten kilometres outside the spa town of Merano (in German, Meran), in the province of Bolzano/Bozen, in the Italian region Trentino-Alto Adige, or Südtirol. For a Haflinger or Avelignese to be considered

a pure-bred, its ancestry must be traceable to the breed's foundation stallion, an animal named 249 Folie, which was born in 1874
in Sluderno/Schluderns, seventy kilometres west of Avelengo/
Haflinger. The dam of 249 Folie was a native Tyrolean mare, and
its sire was a half-Arabian stallion called 133 El-Bedavi XXII, the
great-great-grandson of El-Bedavi, an Arab stallion that had been
imported for the Hungarian State Stud of Babolna. Prior to the
mating of 249 Folie's parents, however, there was already a strain
of Arab blood in the horses of South Tyrol, but there is no agreement as to how this mixture came about. Some have argued that
it can be attributed to horses brought to the region by Ostrogoths
who settled there in the middle of the sixth century, having been
driven north by the Byzantine army. An alternative explanation
is that the interbreeding began with a single stallion, given by
the Holy Roman Emperor Louis IV to his son, Margrave Louis
of Brandenburg, on the occasion of the Margrave's marriage to
Princess Margarete Maultasch of the Tyrol in 1342.

Avelignese horses are not large (13.2–15 hands, 54–60 inches,
140–150 cm; weight 800–1000 pounds, 365–455 kilos) but are
muscular and hardy. They are also long-lived, often reaching
an age in excess of thirty years. They were originally bred for
use in agriculture and as pack horses and are still used for these
purposes today, but are also popular for recreation and sport.
Descriptions of the breed invariably refer to the good nature of
the Avelignese, its adaptability, dependability, tenacity, elegance
and energy. The father of 249 Folie was a gold bay stallion, and
its dam was a chestnut mare; all pure-bred Avelignese have a
chestnut coat, with a pale golden colour being preponderant;
the mane and tail are always white or flaxen. The Avelignese is
nowadays Italy's most populous breed of horse.

6.4

Gideon's walk this morning takes him along the periphery of the
Senesi farm, and there, under the trees at the bottom of the slope,

stand two of the horses. The sight of them is always satisfying: their golden coats, the thick white manes, the stillness of them, their mass. One of them stands in profile with its left forehoof delicately crooked, head erect, immobile. The other, grazing, advances slowly out of the shade, and stops as soon as it has fully entered the sunlight; it continues assiduously to crop the grass, then raises its muzzle from the ground, in a movement of hydraulic smoothness, and turns its head to face the man who is looking at it from the edge of the field. But for a quiver in its hindquarters, the animal is perfectly motionless; it seems to be possessed by a deep and simple thought.

'They are mysterious creatures,' he had once remarked to Ilaria, as he now recalls. To which she had responded, with the brusqueness of a country girl correcting a fool from the city: 'They do what you tell them to do. Nothing is happening in their heads. Rocks for brains,' she said, rapping her brow. And now he sees her beside the horse, clearly enough to draw her. He sees her as he saw her for the first time: the horse in the sunlight is the same horse, with the scar on its pastern. She was in jeans and a filthy red T-shirt, barefoot, brushing the horse's neck; she noticed him, nodded to him as a busy adult might, and carried on; and he watched her run to the house – a stocky little sprite, outrunning the dog that had joined her. And when he came to paint the group of children, she proved to be – as he believes he had instantly seen she would be – a most unusual child. Five minutes was as long a time as any of the others could manage to pose; it was a game for them, whereas for Ilaria it was not a game, and she would sit for as long as it took. And the way her face changed for the pose was extraordinary – it took on an expression of serious threat, as though in some sort of ritual display; it was not quite play-acting. Shown the finished picture, with the dead horse in their midst, the other children had pulled faces. Not Ilaria: she regarded it gravely, and didn't speak; her eyes said that she didn't understand, but would in time, she knew, work it out.

The vision of Ilaria has gone. He holds out a hand to entice the horse to approach, but it does not move. It lowers its head to the grass, at which moment he sees, on the track beyond the trees, a tractor with her father aboard. 'Home, boy,' he whispers to Trim.

6.5

Landscape with Dead Horse
Oil-tempera on canvas; 75cm x 105cm
2004
Private Collection, Stuttgart

The stand of cypress trees in the middle distance of *Landscape with Dead Horse* is a landmark on the north side of Castelluccio; other components of the territory – such as the profile of Le Cornate – are also clearly identifiable, but they have been combined to form a terrain that exists only in this painting. The figure of the horse, an Avelignese, is derived from a photograph of an animal that had been struck by lightning in Montana, and from studies of the small herd kept at the Senesi farm. An avowed admirer of the work of George Stubbs, Gideon Westfall made hundreds of studies of horses during his years in Italy, filling no fewer than thirty sketchbooks with drawings of them. Horses are present in several other Westfall paintings, such as the first portrait of Jane Jeremies (1994), in which she stands beside Coriolan, her grey Holsteiner, and *Grape Harvest* (2001), Westfall's homage to Stubbs' *The Reapers*. The latter, shown at an exhibition in Milan in 2002, prompted a local journalist, in the course of an interview conducted at the private viewing, to observe that whereas horses are to be seen in many of Westfall's pictures, cars are notably absent, as are lorries, vans, scooters – all forms of motorised transport, in fact. The interviewer found this to be something of an oddity, in the work of a self-professed humanist, because traffic is an ineradicable aspect of human activity, is it not? 'The car,' replied the artist 'is an invention of modernity, whereas the horse has for centuries been a companion to man, a workmate and a rebuke. The horse has been a maker of history.'

Landscape with Dead Horse was bought in 2004 by a Stuttgart industrialist, a man with a reputation as a collector of German paintings of the 1920s. In correspondence with Gideon Westfall, this collector compared *Landscape with Dead Horse* with certain works by Franz Radziwill in particular, discerning common qualities of *precision, tranquillity and menace*. In 2007 the picture was loaned to an exhibition in Koblenz entitled *Memento Mori*, where it was singled out for praise, not solely for the virtuosity of the brushwork, but for its *uncanny atmosphere*. The five children seated on a grassy mound at the centre of the painting, facing the viewer with an *innocent insolence*, seemingly undisturbed by the stiff-legged corpse that lies on its side at the foot of the mound, were thought to be a remarkable invention, as was the scene's *discordant light*, with an oily dark sky overhanging a meadow that appears to be lit by a fierce midday sun. Balthus was cited as a forebear.

It should be noted too that *Landscape with Dead Horse* is the first picture by Gideon Westfall in which Ilaria Senesi appears: she is the second child from the left, holding the small axe.

6.6

They are walking to the car when Gideon suddenly says, two seconds after making a remark on the weather: 'I do understand, you know. I understand how you're feeling.'

Assuming that he's referring to her feelings about himself, she doesn't speak.

'When the second parent goes, it's terrible,' he goes on. 'Especially if it's the one to whom you were closer.'

'I don't know if we were closer,' she answers. 'I had more time with him. That's the difference.'

'OK,' he concedes. 'The one with whom you had the longer relationship. I know it's very hard.'

'It is,' she says, not meeting his gaze.

'I think about my parents every day,' he says. 'Particularly my mother. We were close.'

This is peculiar, she thinks, because it was a fact within her family that Gideon and her grandmother hardly ever saw each other after she moved back to Cheshire. 'You'd think she'd gone to live in Greenland,' she remembers her father saying. She says nothing, but Gideon seems to intuit what she's thinking: he didn't see as much of her as he would have wished, he says, but they spoke on the phone two or four times each week. This does not accord with what she'd been led to believe. And she recalls another comment: that Gideon carried on as though being the son of shopkeepers was a misfortune from which he was determined to extricate himself.

'I owe her a great deal,' he goes on. It saddens him, though, that it was only in the last years of her life, when she was on her own, that she had time to devote to herself, to develop interests, to develop aspects of herself that had lain dormant for so long. 'Do you know, as far as I'm aware she had never read a book from beginning to end before she reached her sixties? Isn't that incredible? Then she discovered that she loved Dickens. I think she read his complete works,' he tells her, as if giving his mother a pat on the head. But she could have done so much more, he says with regret. For a woman of her generation, of her social class, education was something that stopped on the day she left school, he informs her.

Claire's image of her grandmother Rita is faint and incoherent: she often seemed a fussy woman, a little too prompt to complain, and something of a snob as well; but she was generous, and affectionate – though sometimes, through these demonstrations of affection, a certain coldness could be glimpsed, or if not a coldness then a preference for being left alone. She doesn't know. She reminds herself that she knew Rita only for a few years, and who knows what she misunderstood or misperceived as a child, or has forgotten since?

'I owe her a great deal,' Gideon repeats. 'Above all, she impressed upon me the importance of hard work.'

This much, at least, tallies with what she remembers – Rita never had much sympathy when her mother complained about the hours that doctors had to work.

'I must have been in quite a state the last time you saw me,' Gideon supposes.

'Not as I recall,' she answers.

They are at the Porta Siena, and here Gideon halts. His gaze roams over the hills and fixes on a point at which there is nothing notable to be seen; he appears to be willing himself into being upset. Narrowing his eyes, still staring at the horizon, he says: 'You were wearing a dark indigo coat and thick black tights. And new black shoes. You were hobbling by the time the burial was done.'

'I don't remember,' she lies.

'But you were very demure. You conducted yourself admirably, with great maturity,' he says, making her understand that such a compliment, from him, is to be valued. 'The car's parked over there,' he says, pointing into the shade of the trees on the opposite side of the road. He takes the keys from his pocket, and is about to say something else when his name is called, and here's his number one pal, hastening from the garage.

Gideon does the introductions: 'This is my niece, and this is my good friend Carlo Pacetti, master mechanic and prize curmudgeon.' Hands are shaken, then the prize curmudgeon, betraying no reaction to being thus described, takes a step back, smiling as if the niece is something in a shop window, perhaps remembering their previous encounter, or entertained by the exactness of the correlation between what he's now seeing and the description that Gideon has given him.

'Welcome,' he says. She thanks him. 'You like our town?' She does, she tells him. He nods; this is as it should be. Then he asks, as if to verify a rumour that she's a resident of Ulan Bator: 'You are vegetarian?'

'I am,' she answers.

Mr Pacetti smiles amiably, uncomprehendingly. He jabs a thumb at his friend. 'He says you—' and he turns to Gieon to say something in Italian.

'You speak your mind,' Gideon translates, almost bashfully.

'You don't like his paintings,' Mr Pacetti tells her, scowling as you'd scowl, half in jest, at a misbehaving child.

'That's not true,' she says.

Mr Pacetti regards her gravely, then laughs, as an overalled man comes out of the garage, a phone in one hand and a wrench in the other, and shouts in their direction. 'My son,' explains Mr Pacetti. 'I go.' Again he shakes Claire's hand; he offers a slack military salute to his friend, then limps towards his son.

Gideon leads Claire across the road. He opens the car door and starts to dip his face towards her cheek, but recollects himself.

6.7

Five days ago Carlo Pacetti placed a single flower outside the deconsecrated church of San Lorenzo, as he has done on almost every Thursday morning since his mother left Castelluccio; Thursday is the day of the week on which his father was killed.

The problem with Italy today, Carlo Pacetti will readily tell you, is that the people distrust the law and they distrust each other. They are irresponsible, and little better than children. His great-uncle Lino and his grandmother had been contemptuous of those whose allegiance to the cause had faltered as soon as the bombs began to fall: 'They care only for themselves, not for Italy,' Lino would say. This attitude, according to Carlo, prevails again today. Success is everything, and only the cunning, the masters of *furbizia*, can succeed – witness, as evidence, the success of Maurizio Ianni.

One evening, in the bar on Piazza Sant'Agostino, Maurizio Ianni confronted Carlo Pacetti, demanding that he apologise publicly for a lie that Carlo had broadcast in the bar the previous evening. 'And what lie would that be?' Carlo enquired. This disingenuousness further enraged Maurizio Ianni, who began to talk of proceedings for slander. 'That should be interesting,' commented Carlo, because he didn't think there was a single person in Castelluccio who did not believe that the mistress of a certain local politician had on a number of occasions been accommodated free of charge in Ianni's hotel, and he was furthermore certain that when he had remarked that many people in Castelluccio were of the view that there might be a connection between this largesse and the ease with which Ianni had obtained permission to disfigure the old candle factory in order to convert it into another Ianni enterprise, he had merely been stating an incontrovertible fact. Maurizio Ianni denied that anyone's mistress had received preferential treatment at the Ottocento. Carlo Pacetti said that he was grateful to be disabused of this misapprehension, and would endeavour to spread the news. The two men have not spoken to each other since.

Carlo Pacetti is renowned in Castelluccio as an inexhaustible exponent of *dietrologia*, the 'science of what lies behind'. He believes, for example, that the Freemasons are in charge of Castelluccio's town hall, and every other town hall in Italy, come to that; that Pope John Paul I was assassinated by the Jesuits; that the British secret services were responsible for the death of Princess Diana; that the CIA killed both JFK and his brother; that the US government murdered Aldo Moro; that the US government connived at the destruction of the Twin Towers; that the Bilderberg Group is the world's covert government ; and so on.

Carlo Pacetti loves slapstick, in particular the exploits of *Stanlio e Ollio*.

Like his uncle, Carlo Pacetti is something of an autodidact. The history of ancient Rome is something of an obsession for him. He claims to own more than 500 books on the subject, but there is no independent verification of this claim. Even Gideon has never been inside Carlo's apartment.

Carlo Pacetti has a problematic relationship with Silvia, his daughter-in-law. Silvia is an arch-consumerist, and exemplifies everything that is wrong with Italy today. She spends more on clothes in a year than Carlo's wife has spent in her whole life. In the past five years she has nagged Ennio into buying a new kitchen and a new bathroom and a new car. They have three TV sets, one of them as big as a dining table. Every year she buys a new phone, and she spends hours each day in pointless conversations that say little more than: 'Hello, I'm phoning you.' Carlo Pacetti will be the last man in Italy without a mobile phone.

Though some of his fellow drinkers at the Sant'Agostino bar are of the opinion that the idea of global warming is an intellectualist/communist conspiracy, Carlo Pacetti is not. 'Humanity is consuming itself to extinction, and the Italians are leading the way,' he says. The Pacetti garage, he would have you believe, is an environmentally sound enterprise, doing its bit to forestall the inevitable by keeping old cars on the road, and thereby, however infinitesimally, reducing the demand for new machines.

Carlo Pacetti thinks of himself and his son as craftsmen, struggling to make a living in a world in which car maintenance is becoming a branch of computer technology rather than a manual skill. Fausto Nerini, though his workshop is now infested with computers, is also a craftsman; he takes pride in his work, and is therefore to be respected, for all his socialist claptrap.

Carlo Pacetti has a problematic relationship with his daughter Edda, who is married to a sociology teacher called Franco, who cannot abide Carlo, and vice versa. 'This man,' Carlo has complained to Gideon, 'has no sense of humanity. He talks about people as you'd talk about apes.' Edda and Franco have two sons, who spend half their waking time playing video games, which Carlo believes to be an instrument of an Americo-Japanese plan to suppress the human spirit in the interests of capitalist enterprise.

Carlo Pacetti wears a blue shirt most days; his father wore a blue shirt most days.

Passing a half-devoured rabbit and attendant buzzard, Carlo Pacetti once said to Gideon that the 'voice of Nature is the sound of perpetual screaming'. When drunk, as he not infrequently is, Carlo Pacetti will often remark, in the course of one of his monologues , that 'Man is a sick animal'.

In the office of the Pacetti garage, before Ennio took over from his father, a heavy black glass ashtray was usually to be seen in the centre of the desk. One could stub out a cigarette in this ashtray without noticing anything unusual about it. Were one to lift it up, however, and angle it into the light, a bust of Il Duce would appear in the base. The observant might also notice, above the door, a strip of yellowed paper bearing these words, in Carlo Pacetti's careful script: '*Io rispetto i calli alle mani. Sono un titolo di nobiltà.*'

Carlo Pacetti's first love, he has confessed to Gideon, was a woman from Mensano: a widow, thirty-eight years of age, a seamstress. Carlo was twenty at the time the affair began. The woman's reputation was far from spotless: it was said that she had slept with six different men since her husband had died. One morning, as Carlo was walking back home from Mensano, a priest accosted him. The priest warned him that his relationship with this woman was widely known, that it was sinful, that he must end it forthwith. The woman was of doubtful character, said the priest. She was, in fact, little better than a prostitute, and was old enough to be his mother. Young Carlo received the priest's chastisement in silence. It was a magnificent day, already hot, though noon was hours away. When the priest was done, Carlo wiped his face with his hands; his face was damp with perspiration; the perfume of his lover's skin rose from his palms. Then calmly he replied that the priest knew nothing of life, and that if he had to make a choice between the goodness of the widow and the shrivelled virtue of the priest, he would choose the former and let his soul take its chances. He has not set foot in a church since that morning. He continued his affair with the widow for months after he had ceased to love her, out of contempt for the village gossips and the priest.

Lino Pacetti was in Grosseto on April 26th 1943, Easter Monday, when American bombers destroyed the playground in Piazza De Maria and all the children in it. From that day on Lino Pacetti despised all things American, as Carlo often professes to do.

Carlo Pacetti is an avid hunter. The animal skulls that feature in many of Gideon Westfall's still lifes were all gifts from Carlo.

Carlo Pacetti's mother, Maria, married Lauro Pacetti on her twentieth birthday, two days before Germany and Italy signed the *Patto d'Acciaio*, the Pact of Steel. Prior to his marriage, Lauro and his mother, Costanza, lived with his uncle Lino, his father's older brother, who had established a small business supplying and repairing farm equipment. Lauro was one of his employees. Maria, the daughter of a butcher from Monteguidi, was a pretty girl who loved her husband, and was afraid of him, and relied on him for everything. Anyone who remembers the young Maria will tell you this, and they will tell you that after Lauro was killed she was helpless and in a constant state of distress. It was said that for many months she spent more time at church than at home, and that it was only at Mass that she stopped weeping. After Lauro's death she went back to Monteguidi with their son, where they lived, with her parents, until 1956, the year in which she married a man called Marco Belluzzi, a carpet salesman, whose eye she had caught at the Festa di San Zeno parade in 1954. Carlo had not liked Signore Belluzzi at first: he seemed insincere and stupid, and he dressed like an American gangster. By the time of the wedding, two years later, Carlo's antipathy had matured into loathing: Marco Belluzzi was indeed an oily dimwit, and the boy took his mother's attachment to this man as an insult to the memory of his father. Disliked in return by his stepfather, Carlo returned to Castelluccio, to the apartment of Costanza Pacetti, in 1959, two years after the birth of his twin half-brothers, Michele and Mauro. His mother seemed to have forgotten his father as you might forget an old friend; Carlo, on the other hand, revered his father – or rather, having been born just four years before his father's death, he revered the idea of him. From the stories that his grandmother told him, from her half-dozen photographs of heroic Lauro, Carlo pressed the essence of his father, like the last drops of oil from olive stones. In their hearts the self-described orphan and his grandmother honoured unceasingly their two dead patriots, discerning a profound significance in the symmetry of their sacrifice: for just as the infant Carlo had lost his father to assassins in wartime, the infant Lauro had lost his father to the Austrian guns on the Isonzo. The faithless Maria was discarded. She and Marco are still alive, in their nineties, living in Siena; Carlo has seen neither of them since 1973, when they met in Monteguidi to bury Maria's father. This was also the last occasion on which he saw his semi-siblings, Michele and Mauro. The twins were the most sinister people he has ever encountered, he will tell you: flawed replicas of their father and perfect replicas of each other, they spoke always in the same tone of voice and in half-sentences, each leaving it to the other to finish his utterance. Carlo will tell you that his meeting the twins was the only occasion in his life that he has truly been frightened, apart from the time he took Gideon hunting and let him use a gun.

In his prime, Carlo Pacetti looked somewhat like an abbreviated version of Victor Mature.

When Carlo Pacetti came back to Castelluccio in 1959 his great-uncle Lino was dead and his business had long been defunct. Carlo was given a job by a man called Matteo Negri, a former classmate of Carlo's father. Matteo had remained on good terms with Lauro until what turned out to be the penultimate year of Lauro's life, when the German occupation made Matteo undergo a change of heart, for which Lauro could not forgive him. Nevertheless, Matteo retained a residue of affection for his erstwhile friend: he had known Lauro for twenty years, after all. So Matteo gave Lauro's son a job in his workshop, repairing cars and motorbikes, and the lad proved to be as talented a mechanic as his great-uncle had been, if not better: he had a feel for machines, as if they were living things that could tell him what they needed. Carlo worked for Matteo Negri until 1970, when he set up a car workshop on his own, leaving the agricultural stuff to his boss. He made a decent living, even though, twenty-five years after the war had ended, there were people in Castelluccio – turncoats and the sons of turncoats – with whom Carlo Pacetti would not do business, and vice versa. He worked long hours; Gideon Westfall is the only man he has ever met who works as many hours in a day as he used to work.

Carlo Pacetti spends an hour or two, three or four nights a week, in the Sant'Agostino bar. Once or twice a month he takes his wife, Patrizia, for a meal at their favourite restaurant, a trattoria near Mensano. Other than these evenings, their social life consists of little more than visits, more or less monthly, to her sister and her family, in Radicóndoli, the village in which the sisters were born. Piera, a shy and uncomplicated and generally happy woman, like Patrizia, is excessively devout. There's not a room in the apartment without a picture of Padre Pio, says Carlo: the shameless old fraud even watches you when you're taking a piss. But Carlo keeps his godless thoughts to himself whenever they visit Radicóndoli, out of respect for Patrizia, and for Piera too: she is a good woman, if credulous, and her husband, Stefano, a carpenter, is a good man as well, though he lets himself be pushed around too easily, and is much too content with the status quo. Stefano regards politics as a thing like the weather – it happens, and there's nothing you can do about it. Piera, like Patrizia, has no interest in politics. And Carlo will at times admit that he himself has little interest in politics nowadays, now that Italy is run by crooks, salesmen and TV producers.

In November of 2006 Carlo Pacetti achieved some local notoriety after an altercation with three Arabs who expected him to drop everything to perform emergency surgery on an Opel that had a broken water pump, no functioning shock absorbers, and a hole in the floor so big you could have put a watermelon through it. When Carlo declined to assist, the three men became aggressive, accusing Carlo of being an incompetent mechanic and a racist. Ennio, returning from his lunch break, found his father cornered by the door to the back office, with one of the men jabbing him repeatedly in the chest while screaming at him in Arabic. At this point, a police car happened to pass by. Ennio ran after it, and the three men leapt into the Opel, with suspicious alacrity; the vehicle would not start. Explaining the incident to the police officers, the trio stated that the old man had insulted them, and accused them of stealing the car. Carlo did not deny having said that it would not have surprised him to discover that the Opel was stolen. It was not stolen, but the three men – Libyans, who had come from Calabria, where they had been picking fruit for much of the summer – were not, it turned out, legally entitled to be in the country. 'I knew at once they weren't right,' Carlo told a reporter.

Carlo Pacetti's finest hour as a citizen of Castelluccio, most would agree, came on Tuesday, June 19th, 1995. He was outside the garage, fitting a tyre to a truck, when he saw Franca Alinei walking past with her daughter, four-year-old Marta. No sooner had he taken note of the wickedly attractive Signora Alinei than he observed, by the Porta di Siena, a large mongrel, slack-bellied, scrofulous, underfed. Marta was dragging a wooden duck on a string. This noisy little toy caught the dog's attention, and Carlo foresaw at once what was about to happen. He dashed from the truck as the dog dashed towards the child, who, turning, saw the dog running at her. Marta leapt to her mother's side and snatched up the duck; in the same moment the dog snapped at her hand and Carlo arrived. He struck the animal on the jaw, shocking it into releasing the child, but then it went berserk, springing at its assailant and clamping its teeth onto his leg. The battle lasted at least half a minute, until Carlo succeeded in shaking off the dog and planting a swift kick between its hind legs. He required several stitches in a hand and forearm, and many more in his right calf. 'Wounded at last,' remarked Maurizio Ianni. 'Maybe that'll make him happier.' And indeed many did observe a slight, albeit temporary, mellowing in Carlo Pacetti, after the incident with the feral dog of the Porta di Siena and the consequent gratitude of Signora Alinei and her family.

Carlo Pacetti's wife, who worships at the Redentore, has told Carlo that she will leave him if he ever again addresses a word to Father Fabris. This was after Carlo, drunk, had one evening encountered the priest on Piazza Sant'Agostino and proceeded, within earshot of the drinkers in the bar, to inform him that the history of Christianity was a history of lies, or words to that effect. He compared the philosophies espoused by Father Fabris to those espoused by *maestro* Westfall, much to the detriment of the former. 'He loves the world, but you hate it,' proclaimed Carlo. 'The artist knows that the spirit and the body cannot be separated,' he told the priest. The word *eunuco* was used, at which point one of his cronies intervened.

The Italian people, Carlo Pacetti will tell you, were until recently a 'people of the land'; now they are 'a people of the television set'. He never watches TV, except for the football and *Stanlio e Ollio*.

6.8

At ten o'clock the doorbell rings: two policemen are there; they would like to talk to Mr Westfall. Robert brings them into the studio, introduces them to Gideon, explains that Mr Westfall speaks Italian imperfectly, and offers his services as interpreter. 'This will be about the picture,' says Gideon.

'Is it about the painting?' Robert asks the policemen.

'What painting?' is the reply, from the younger of the pair.

'The painting that was vandalised,' says Robert. 'In the Palazzo Comunale.'

The younger policemen, a gum-chewer, to whom Gideon has taken an immediate and obvious dislike, says they know nothing about any picture. The missing girl is what they are interested in.

'They are not here about the picture. They want to talk about Ilaria,' Robert tells Gideon, who rolls his eyes.

'What's there to talk about? There's nothing more to say,' Gideon complains. 'Don't these people ever talk to each other?'

'He is at your disposal,' Robert translates.

'We want to check if you have heard from her,' says the other policeman, who's perhaps ten years older than his colleague; he's the one whom Gideon is addressing.

'If I'd heard from her I would have said so, wouldn't I? I'm not an idiot. I want her found as much as you,' answers Gideon.

Robert: 'He says that he has heard nothing. If he hears from her, he will report it.'

'But perhaps,' suggests the gum-chewer, 'Mr Westfall would not report it if Miss Senesi asked him not to.'

Robert: 'He is suggesting that Ilaria might have asked you not to tell anyone.'

'Why would she do that? Why would she ring me rather than her mother? She'd ring her friends for God's sake, not me. Have they spoken to her friends? Have they talked to that girl – what's her name – Bernarda? She's a friend. Have they talked to Marta? Why on earth do they imagine Ilaria would phone me and not anyone else, and ask me to keep it a secret? What's the logic in that, for Christ's sake?'

Robert conveys the essence of this response, and is informed that all of Miss Senesi's known acquaintances have been interviewed, that none has heard from her, and all have reported that her phone is unobtainable.

Gideon's behaviour is not convincing the gum-chewer that he is being wholly co-operative. 'You saw her on the day before she disappeared,' he says.

'You know this already,' answers Gideon. 'Why do I have to repeat it? Haven't you got anything better to do with your time?'

Robert: 'That is true.'

'She said nothing about leaving Castelluccio?'

'Christ Almighty. I've already been through this. No, she did not. Not a word. Nothing. *Niente.*'

'But we have been told that you were intimate,' says the older policeman.

'It depends what you mean by intimate,' replies Gideon, which Robert translates precisely.

'Intimate means intimate,' gum-chewer responds. 'We all know what intimate means.'

'If this gentleman is telling me that it is rumoured that I was having sexual relations with Miss Senesi, my answer is that I was not. I have made this abundantly clear to his colleagues. Perhaps he should have talked to them before coming here to insult me.'

Robert: 'Mr Westfall's relationship with Ilaria Senesi was entirely professional.'

Gum-chewer makes a great show of examining his surroundings; his eye alights on a nude study, and another one, and another; a smirk of some scepticism is presented to Gideon.

'I'll bet that's what her father told you. It was, wasn't it?' says Gideon. 'It might have crossed your mind that there's some malice at work there. He doesn't like me. He didn't like the fact that his daughter worked for me. As far as I can see, he didn't approve of much that Ilaria did. As you might have gathered.

Or maybe not. It's a line of inquiry that might be worth following. Rather than pestering me with gossip.' His indignation is confirming the suspicions of gum-chewer; the colleague, on the other hand, exudes well-practised neutrality.

Robert: 'Mr Westfall thinks that Miss Senesi's father may be the source of the rumour about himself and Miss Senesi. He says that Mr Senesi did not like the fact that his daughter worked for him.'

'We know,' says the older policeman. He is satisfied, for now; with a nod he signals to his colleague that they should go, but his colleague isn't leaving before he's done a little more goading.

'How often did Miss Senesi "work" for you?' he asks.

Gideon's Italian may be poor, but it's good enough to hear the stress on the verb. 'Ilaria Senesi removed her clothes for me twice a week, on average,' he answers.

Robert: 'Miss Senesi came here twice a week, on average.'

Policeman: 'For many weeks.'

'That is correct,' replies Gideon.

'That is something unusual. An intimacy, one would say.'

Gideon hears Robert's translation; his reply is a disdainful blink.

Policeman: 'She was here the day before she disappeared.'

Again Gideon stares and says nothing; gum-chewer stares back, demanding at least a word.

'I'm not going to repeat myself yet again,' he says.

Robert: 'She was.'

'Miss Senesi took clothes and money with her. She appears to have planned when she would leave. This was not a spontaneous action. And yet, though you have this special relationship, Miss Senesi nevertheless did not give you any clue that she was about to leave her home. She said nothing. This is what you want us to believe?'

Robert: 'She gave no indication that she was going to run away?'

'God give me strength. Is this chap being paid by the sentence? Is there something wrong with his hearing? Does he suffer from short-term amnesia? She said nothing. Shall I write it down for him? Tell him I have work to do, even if he doesn't.'

Robert: 'No. She said nothing.'

'She never said anything about being involved with somebody?'

'As far as I'm aware, there was no boyfriend, if that's what you mean. Not since that twerp in the *alimentari*. I assume you've talked to him?'

Robert: 'No. She mentioned no one.'

Undeterred, gum-chewer goes on: 'Miss Senesi came here regularly. Twice a week. So I assume that before she left here on the Monday you made some sort of appointment for later in the week. Is that right?'

'I expected her on the Friday,' says Gideon.

'But she did not call to say that she could not come?'

'I have not seen her or heard from her since that Monday afternoon. As I have said. Several times. Can you please tell me what is being gained by the prolongation of this discussion, for want of a better word?'

Robert: 'She has not called.'

'And when she didn't turn up, at the time you had arranged, did you try to contact her? I assume it would have been an inconvenience for you. You had "work" to do together. You would have been looking forward to it. You had plans, but then the girl is not here. A small disaster,' the gum-chewer proposes, miming a man astounded, aggrieved.

Robert: 'Did you try to ring her?'

'I did not try to ring her, for the simple reason that I don't know her number.'

This answer provokes disbelief, then amusement. Scratching a cheek, the gum-chewer again casts a look at the drawings pinned to the wall; his gaze strikes his colleague, where it lingers for an instant, before passing to Gideon. He smiles broadly. 'OK' he says, as if all of his doubts as to Gideon's innocence have now been eliminated, and he offers a hand to Gideon, as does his partner.

As he shakes Gideon's hand, the older policeman says: 'If you hear anything, speak to us.'

'*Certo*,' says Gideon.

Not until he's at the top of the stairs, having let his colleague descend first, does the senior policeman say to Robert: 'We have a sighting of her, by the way. On the Tuesday morning, walking along the road, near San Dalmazio. On her own. Calm.'

'What was that?' Gideon calls out.

'Ilaria was seen at San Dalmazio. On the Tuesday,' Robert explains.

'And? Since then?'

'A backpack was found. Yesterday,' says the policeman.

'They've found her bag,' Robert tells Gideon.

'Where?' demands Gideon.

'Volterra,' is the answer.

'And? And?'

'We are investigating,' says the policeman, hands open to emphasise the obviousness of the answer.

They are at the bottom of the steps when Gideon shouts: 'And what are they going to do about my bloody picture? Some bastard walked into the town hall in broad daylight and defaced my work. What's being done about it? Anything? Have they spoken to Senesi? He was the one who did it. Have they talked to him? Is anyone going to do anything? Eh?' The rest is mumbling.

'Mr Senesi did not damage the picture. He has not been to the exhibition,' says the older policeman, in English, before Robert can translate Gideon's shouting. Giving Robert a smile and a pat on the back, he adds, again in English: 'We can find the door. Thank you for your assistance.'

6.9

Light bangs into her eyes off the hot stone walls; a car turns and its windscreen flashes like a firework. She consults the guidebook: Volterra's art gallery is a short distance away. She follows a German family into the building and through the first few rooms; they have a guidebook that must be more detailed than hers, because on entering each room they check the page before looking around. She overtakes them and is detained by nothing for more than a minute, until she's made to stop by a large picture which, she's gratified to discover from the caption beside it, is the picture that is regarded as the museum's greatest treasure: the *Deposition* by Rosso Fiorentino. It's a weird thing: overcrowded, like a building site, with ladders all over the place and haggard old workmen shouting at each other. The figures are at awkward angles, like puppets – even the clothes look like painted wood. The faces of the women are as hard as masks; the shouting old men, on closer inspection, appear deranged; and the dead Christ appears to have a peculiar smile on his face, as if pleased with the way things are turning out. Everything in the scene seems deliberate, but she doesn't understand what's meant, and neither her book nor the caption are of any help. She sits and looks at it for five minutes more; she simply doesn't get it; for a moment she wishes Gideon were here – he might be able to explain.

Peckish and thirsty, she decides on a picnic and goes looking for a food shop, which is soon found. The guidebook shows her that if she continues along this road she'll come to the cliffs, the *balze*, over which a substantial quantity of Volterra has toppled in the course of the centuries; it's a remarkable sight, says the guide, which also mentions greenery in that part of town; all the brown stone and brown brick is slightly oppressive, as Gideon had said; she sets off. The cliffs, their clay golden in the sun, are indeed a fine sight, with the yellow-grey hills rippling away below them. Eventually she comes to a grassy avenue flanked by cypress trees, leading to a church; the perfect spot. She eats her sandwich and a peach, and lies down on the grass, amid thousands of pills of sunlight; within a minute she's asleep.

When she wakes up, a man is standing near her feet, looking at her as if trying to decipher the inscription on a tombstone.

Alarmed, she sits up, putting fingers to her throat; the man steps back, hands raised, palms towards her. A smile breaks in the depths of his beard, which is coal-black, with rivulets of grey in it, and reaches midway down his chest; his hair, grey-streaked black and lank, hangs straight from a central parting and is knitted into the beard; he looks like Rasputin. His shirt, once white, now the colour of an oyster shell, is open to the navel, exposing a pale and bony chest and whorls of damp black hair; the jeans are every shade of grey and blue; on his feet, though, he has a pair of natty lime-green trainers that seem brand new; he is wearing no socks, and his ankles are graphite coloured. He says something she can't understand and points over her shoulder; the fingernails are black and glossy and pointed, like the claws of a dog. He keeps speaking, softly, as if saddened by what he's seeing. Then she realises that he's pointing to the carrier bag, in which a peach is visible. She takes it out and offers it to him; he bends a knee to receive it, like an actor playing a courtier in obeisance to a queen; he takes it as if cradling a bubble in his palm. '*Grazie,*' he croaks, then he closes his free hand into a fist and makes a small and gentle punching gesture; the meaning of this gesture is obscure. 'Goodbye,' he says, pronouncing the English word loudly and with great formality. He walks away, down the middle of the track of grass, holding the fruit to his chest; at the point of disappearing he turns to repeat the soft mid-air punch, and swings an arm slowly to the right, as though to direct her attention towards the church at the end of the avenue.

And now she remembers coming out of a cinema with her husband, and handing a coin to a young man who looked so emaciated and crazy it seemed likely that he would eat it rather than spend it. That's all it was, a one-pound coin, but Joe proceeded to give her a lecture on the futility of giving money to beggars: 'How do you imagine he got where he is? Drugs. And what's he going to do with the cash? Buy drugs. Complete waste of time.' And so on and so on. To which she'd replied, she thinks, that it didn't matter how he got to be there; his life was worse

than theirs. 'And it'll stay worse, if people like you keep buying his drugs for him.' And more in that vein, much more. She
couldn't understand at the time why he was so angry; later it became clear that guilt explained it. This is the first time for several
days that he has as much as crossed her mind, it occurs to her.

The guidebook says there is one other museum she should not
miss: the Etruscan museum. It isn't thrilling: room after room of
funerary urns, most of them indistinguishable from the rest; one
of them – the one of which the museum seems proudest – has a
sour-faced and boggle-eyed couple on its lid; in another room
there's a skinny figure made of bronze, like a poker with a tiny
child's head on top of it and a dinky little penis stuck on the
front. Less than an hour after entering, she's back outside, in the
booming heat. But the drive is again a pleasure: the roads are as
quiet as an English countryside Sunday, and Gideon's old car is
like a big canoe on easy water.

6.10

The Antica Farmacia is closed on Tuesdays, so tonight they
have to make do with La Loggia, the restaurant on Piazza del
Mercato. It's not as good as the Farmacia, Gideon tells her, but it's
tolerable. Because it's in a prime location, and the decor is faux-
antique and cosy, it attracts whatever tourists blow through, he
explains, pointing to the window, where a sticker advertises that
La Loggia was recommended by an American travel guide three
years ago. 'There won't be a single Italian eating here tonight,
I'll bet you,' he says, holding open the door. They enter a room
in which all but three of the tables are occupied, and English is
the only language to be heard. The room is low-ceilinged, with a
terracotta floor and thick beams of black wood overhead, and old
prints of Siena on the walls, between small cast-iron sconces for
flame-shaped lightbulbs. 'Fibreglass,' whispers Gideon, rapping
a timber post, smiling at the approaching waitress, whose face is
radiant at receiving the celebrity of Castelluccio. Menus clasped

to her chest, she awaits his judgement of the relative merits of the tables on offer; he decides in favour of the one that gives a view of the piazza. 'They seem quiet,' he says, with an imperfectly discreet nod in the direction of the quartet at the adjacent table.

'Nothing much for non-carnivores, is there?' he says to Claire, setting aside the menu and summoning the waitress. 'Robert, would you mind taking charge of the negotiations?' The situation is explained by Robert; the waitress withdraws to the kitchen and returns a minute later with a proposal.

'So,' Gideon resumes, with a smack of the thighs that attracts the attention of their neighbours, 'your day. How was it? What did you do?'

Claire's account of her visit to Volterra begins with the incident at lunchtime. After one and a half sentences, Gideon interrupts.

'I know the chap in question,' he announces and proceeds to describe Claire's beggar. 'A wild man,' says Gideon. 'Calls himself *Diogene* – Diogenes. Lives in a hole in the ground. Used to, anyway. Mad as a bag of frogs, but harmless.'

'Harmless now,' Robert intervenes. 'As far as we know.'

'He did twenty years for burying a knife in some poor sod's head,' Gideon explains.

'Spanner.'

'Spanner, was it? I stand corrected. The recipient of the spanner,' he informs Claire, 'was the wife's boyfriend. The latest of several, yes?' he enquires of Robert.

'So I believe.'

'Died of his injuries a week later.'

'Something like that.'

In the course of this exchange Gideon has been the object of repeated glances of distaste from one of the women at the table alongside, as if he'd been describing the murder in all its bloody detail. Her husband too has registered his disapproval, by raising his voice by a decibel or two. In appearance it's a strikingly homogenous group: all four are thirty-ish, unrelaxed in demeanour, blandly presentable, clad in clothes that are remarkably free of any signs of wear; three of the four are wearing pastel-toned polo shirts that might have been bought from the same shop at the same time; they could have strayed out of an advertisement for a golf complex in the Algarve. Their conversation – in which an irritating episode at the foreign exchange desk of a bank in Siena is a recurring motif – stalls when the food arrives. After a *sotto voce* conference, one of the husbands – he has a springy little quiff and slot-straight parting, and is wearing a regrettable shirt: khaki, button-collar, short sleeves – is elected to take action. Up goes the right hand; fingers are snapped three times. The waitress comes over. 'Excuse me Miss, but we have a problem here,' whines the spokesman. The problem is explicated: each of the company has been brought, as ordered, a portion of home-made cake, but if one looks one will observe that two of the portions are rather less substantial than the other two. It would be appreciated if the anomaly could be corrected.

The waitress peers down at the plates. 'I think your assistance may be required,' says Gideon, and Robert duly asks if he might be of help. The waitress does not immediately answer. She has taken hold of two of the plates and is examining them, perplexed. Robert translates the customer's complaint, but the waitress has understood perfectly. With a chilly smile for Mr Quiff, and a '*Certo*,' she bears the two under-filled dishes away.

The conversation returns to Volterra. Claire remarks that she was intrigued by the stick figure in the Etruscan museum.

'The "Shadow of the Evening", so-called,' says Gideon, as if everyone who goes to the Etruscan museum says exactly what she's just said. 'The only interesting thing in there. All those bloody urns,' he moans, grasping his brow. 'Row after row of the damned things, and every one the same. Tedious buggers. No wonder the Romans wiped them out.'

'Here we go,' says Robert, filling his glass for him.

'He has a soft spot for the Etruscans,' Gideon tells Claire. 'Inexplicable.'

'They are our ancestors,' says Robert.

'They were here before us, certainly. But that doesn't in itself make them interesting, or mean that there's a connection of any significance between us and them. They are the Neanderthals of European civilisation. They lead nowhere. They are lost to us. Why don't you try telling us what the "Shadow of the Evening" is about?'

'I don't know what it's about.'

'Quite. We don't know. We look at a Roman sculpture and we know what we're looking at. We look at a Greek sculpture: we know what we're looking at. We look at your Etruscan stick-boy, and we don't have a clue. It looks modern, so we have a response, but the modernity is an illusion. We don't understand it.'

'And so it's fascinating,' responds Robert.

'I remain unfascinated,' Gideon asserts. 'The thing is a curiosity, that's all. But better than all those bloody urns, I grant you that much.'

'Some of them are beautiful. And the jewellery—'

'Sod the bloody jewellery. Who cares about earrings and bangles? Name me a great Etruscan artist. Name me a great Etruscan poet. An architect. A dramatist. Go on.'

'None that have survived.'

'Or been remembered. What does that tell you, if not a single name has been remembered?'

'It tells me the Romans did a thorough job.'

'Arse,' laughs Gideon. 'The Etruscans had it coming to them. The Volterra museum is as good as they get, and it's deadly. Am I not right?' he asks Claire.

'You have to go to Rome,' Robert tells Claire. 'The Vatican and the Villa Giulia. You haven't been there, have you?'

'No.'

'Well, you can't begin to understand the Etruscans until—'

'Life is too short, Roberto. The Etruscans are dismal bastards,' states Gideon, at which point the wife of Mr Quiff leans over and, wincing as if pained by intolerable noise, asks if he would mind keeping his voice down. Gideon blinks at her, as though her form had materialised out of nothing. 'I beg your pardon?' he asks.

'Would you mind keeping your voice down,' she repeats. 'You are talking very loudly and we are trying to have a conversation.'

'As are we,' says Gideon.

'We are in a public place,' she says.

'Thank you for reminding me,' he replies, baring his teeth in a vulpine smile. He turns back to Robert. 'You were about to bore us, I believe?'

And Robert is permitted to make his case: that our idea of the Etruscans has been skewed by the depredations of the Romans. When the Romans razed the Etruscan city of Volsinii, for example, two thousand bronze sculptures were melted down, and you only have to go to the archaeological museum in Florence to see how wonderful Etruscan bronzes could be. Funerary urns, being of no value as raw material, were simply discarded, and they now comprise the bulk of what has been recovered, which is why we tend to think of the Etruscans as a gloomy and death-obsessed people, et cetera, et cetera. He is talking about D.H. Lawrence's *Etruscan Places* – 'pure fiction and utterly daft', Gideon interjects – when the bill is delivered to the quartet's table.

Pinned to the tabletop by a forefinger, the document is examined and found to be flawed. Again the hand goes up.

'What is it now, for Christ's sake?' sighs Gideon.

'Did you say something?' the noise-sensitive woman enquires.

'Is there a problem with your bill?' asks Gideon. He is ignored; the waitress arrives.

There is indeed a problem: they have been charged much more for their bottle of wine than they should have been. A wine list is produced by the waitress; Mr Quiff indicates what he ordered, a bottle of Rosso di Montalcino; the waitress indicates what he actually ordered, a bottle of Brunello di Montalcino, three times more expensive. The waitress lifts the empty bottle from the table, shows him the name on the label, then the name on the wine list.

'We wanted this one,' states the customer, tapping the list so assertively he almost knocks it from her hand. 'This is what we ordered.'

'No, you order this,' the waitress tells him, dangling the bottle. 'You made a mistake.'

'You said Montalcino. I asked Brunello. You said yes.'

'We wanted the other one. Why did you assume that we wanted this one? There was no reason to do that.'

Robert, called upon to translate, translates the waitress's reply: 'Americans always want Brunello rather than Rosso because it is the most expensive wine on the list.'

'Please tell her that we are not paying for a wine we did not order.'

The waitress repeats that she brought them what they asked for.

The customer repeats that she did not bring them what they wanted.

The boss is now on his way to the table, but before he can reach the location of the disagreement – to which everyone in the restaurant is now attending – the wife of Mr Quiff hisses a remark to her husband that includes the phrase 'these people', and at this provocation Gideon at last erupts. 'What the hell is the matter with you?' he bellows, seizing the bottle as if he intends to use it as a truncheon. Instead he displays the label to each of the four in turn, with a finger underlining the name of the wine. 'You can read, can't you? Brunello – that's what it says. It's not in Cyrillic, for fuck's sake. Why would the girl have brought it if you didn't ask for it? She showed you the bottle and you drank it. You showed them the bottle, yes?' he asks the waitress.

Robert obtains confirmation that the bottle was shown and approved.

'OK. It was shown to you. It's been staring you in the face for the past hour, and you've drunk every drop. So pay up.'

Mr Quiff presses his lips together as if trying to crush the blood out of them. The recipient of inexcusable effrontery, he inhales deeply. 'She made a mistake,' he states. 'But if the pro-prietor agrees to divide the difference between the price of this wine and the price of the wine we ordered, I would be happy with that.'

The proprietor, examining the bill while listening to Robert's translation of the proposal, is prevented from responding by another explosion from Gideon. 'This is beyond belief,' he trum-pets. 'You people are quibbling over a few bloody euros. How much do you earn? All of you, together. How much?'

'Excuse me?' shrieks Mrs Quiff. 'Who do you think—'

'You're lawyers, aren't you? You look like lawyers.'

'Look, sir, I don't know what—' begins the other man, hitherto silent.

'And how much do you think these people earn in a year?' Gideon demands, putting a hand on the waitress's shoulder. 'Shall we ask them? My bet is it's about the same as you pay your cleaners or dog-walkers or whatever menials you employ to make your lives more easeful. And you're quibbling over a few euros. Unbelievable. You should be ashamed of yourselves.'

Mr Quiff's jaw is trembling, and his wife is staring as if Gideon has directed a mighty belch in her husband's direction. The other man, addressing Robert, says in a slow and even voice that is intended to convey the impression that it is only by the greatest effort that physical retribution is being withheld: 'You'd better take your father outside.'

'Oh lordie,' shrieks Gideon, covering his mouth with effeminate hands, 'the alpha mannequin is getting tough.' He stuffs some notes into Robert's hand and moves towards the door, muttering loudly. 'What a bunch of arseholes.' At the door he turns. 'Good people,' he proclaims, 'these indigent travellers have inadvertently consumed a bottle of wine that turns out to be rather more costly than their meagre resources will allow. If you wouldn't all mind contributing a euro or two to this worthy cause, their gratitude will be immeasurable.'

6.11

'Well, that was quite something,' Claire remarks, as soon as they are out on the piazza. 'How much of that was for show, would you say?'

'About ten percent,' says Robert.

'I'd have thought more.'

'He blows up occasionally. Two or three times a year on average. We haven't had an eruption since January, so we're overdue.'

'And what brought on the last one? Something more important than the price of a bottle of wine, I hope.'

'A buyer came to pick up a picture he'd seen on the website, then tried to haggle. Gideon went ballistic. I had to patch things up.'

'Is that part of the job?'

'From time to time,' he says. 'But it's rarely a major crisis. People expect their artists to be temperamental.'

'And Gideon is happy to oblige?'

'He has a temper. But he keeps it under control most of the time.'

'I know about the temper,' says Claire. 'From what I've heard, he never used to make much of an effort to control it.'

'We must assume, then, that he's a changed man.'

'One possibility,' she agrees.

They have reached the Corso. 'You going back to the hotel?' he asks.

'I thought I might go clubbing,' she says. Then: 'Yes, I'm going back to the hotel.'

'OK if I walk with you? Teresa's place is over by Sant'Agostino.'

'Sure,' she says.

Neither of them speaks for a minute, then Robert says: 'I knew he was about to blow.'

'Why? Because I'm here?' she asks.

'No, no,' he answers. 'There's something else going on.'

'Which is? Or are you sworn to secrecy?'

'No. But—'

'You don't have to tell. But you were the one who raised the subject.'

So he tells her that Ilaria, the daughter of a couple who run an *agriturismo* just outside the town, has gone missing, and that she had been working for Gideon. 'So he's concerned, obviously.'

'Because he thinks something has happened to her?'

'I think she's OK. She seems to have just packed her bags and left.'

'But Gideon doesn't think she's OK?'

'He's inclined to take the gloomier view. Nobody has heard a word from her; she can't be reached on her mobile. Gideon imagines the worst.'

Claire looks at him, as though peering through misted glass. 'When you say "working for", you mean she was his model, right?'

'Yes.'

'And she was modelling for him immediately before she disappeared?'

'Yes.'

'Was there an incident?'

'Between her and Gideon?'

'Yes.'

'Not that I know of.'

'But there might have been?'

'He would have said.'

'Would he?'

'Definitely.'

This prompts a wry half-smile. 'Such trust,' she comments. 'Better than most marriages. But he doesn't tell you everything, does he? I mean, you were in the dark about his brother, weren't you?'

'I don't think he was keeping me in the dark. He had nothing to say.'

'Maybe,' she says. 'Anyway, is he worried there's a connection? That she's run away because of him.'

'Not because of him directly. Perhaps because of the way some people reacted when they found out she'd been working with him. Some of her friends. Her parents.'

'How old is she?'

'Late teens.'

Her mouth makes a silent mewl of distaste. 'I see,' she says.

'A perfectly innocent relationship,' Robert states.

'A perfectly innocent relationship with a naked teenager? Or am I jumping to conclusions? She was a clothes-on model. Is that what you're going to tell me?'

'I'm not, no. But there was nothing untoward going on.'

'He never laid a hand on her.'

'Absolutely not.'

'Still, that doesn't necessarily mean that there was nothing untoward about it, does it? Staring at a naked girl isn't quite the same thing as staring at a bowl of fruit. Or are you saying that in Gideon's case it is?'

'As near to the same thing as it's possible to get, I'd say.'

She cocks her head and squints at him, as if to discern whether or not he genuinely believes this to be the case.

'There was an attachment,' he admits. 'She made him work well. But it wasn't about sex.'

'If you say so.'

'And he wouldn't have done anything to make her run away. For one thing, that wouldn't have been in his own best interests,' he says, and she appears to concede the point. 'But please,' he goes on, 'you mustn't let Gideon know that I've told you. It would embarrass him.'

'Heaven forbid,' she answers.

'No, really. He wouldn't want to discuss it.'

'Not a word,' she promises, with a sardonic tilt of an eyebrow.

'Any plans for your last day?' he asks.

'Thought I'd do the museum. Only thing left to see.'

'Want to meet for a bite at lunchtime? The Corso,' he suggests, nodding over her shoulder at the caffè.

'Sure.'

'Shall I persuade Gideon to come?'

'Up to you,' she says. Then, looking at the spotlit façade of San Giovanni Battista, she remarks: 'I do like this square.' The church and the town hall, she thinks, look best at night; the shadows give the old buildings a special aura.

And he says: 'A friend of mine used to say they were like batteries. Batteries of history.'

Her eyes show that the phrase is a bit too rich for her tastes, but she says: 'That's nice.' They arrange to meet at twelve-thirty, by the loggia. 'See you then,' she says, with a final sustained look at San Giovanni Battista.

He walks across the piazza, past the building with the new brass plate where the one that read *Antonio Zappalorto / Studio Dentistico* used to be; and for an instant he can see Signora Zappalorto, scurrying towards the door from the Palazzo Comunale.

6.12

On the Saturday preceding the 1994 Festa di San Zeno, the Teatro Gaetano was opened in the afternoon for a one-hour guided tour, given by Cinzia Zappalorto, archivist of the Palazzo Comunale. Eight people turned up for the tour: a couple from Rome, both actors, who had just happened to drive into Castelluccio that morning; a Dutch couple, staying at the Ottocento; Monica Nerini, in attendance chiefly to support her friend Cinzia, whose advice ensured the accuracy of the costumes that Monica made each year for the San Zeno pageant; the property agent Gianluigi Tranfaglia and his sister Eliana; and Robert Bancourt, who had been in Castelluccio for a year and was glad of any opportunity to learn more about the town.

Cinzia Zappalorto welcomed the group at the door of the theatre, and Robert recognised her at once: several times he had seen her crossing the piazza in the evening, scuttling from the

Palazzo Comunale, aiming for a door in the corner of the square. Her energy was unusual, as was her appearance: she was a burly little woman, a little over five feet tall, in her late fifties or early sixties, with short grey hair that looked as dense as astrakhan, invariably wearing white tennis shoes and a brightly coloured cardigan, often fuchsia, sky blue or orange.

The way Cinzia talked was in keeping with what he'd observed of her: she spoke at such speed that he missed much of what she said, but her enthusiasm was irresistible. She led them through the backstage areas, to the room that had been the office of the theatre's actor-manager, Tommaso Galli, and her voice took on a tone of reverence, as if the obscure Galli had been a figure as important to the history of stagecraft as David Garrick or Henry Irving. Standing on the stage, she directed their attention to the finer points of this masterwork of Andrea Gaetano, an architect so thoroughly forgotten that it was as though he had never existed, as she told them, with the sorrow of a loyal granddaughter. At the conclusion of the tour she told the group that she would be happy to answer any questions. Robert alone stayed, and she gave him another half-hour, clarifying with patience many of the points that his defective Italian had prevented him from fully comprehending. She would gladly have given him even more time if she hadn't had to get back home to put the finishing touches to her husband's outfit for the following day's parade.

After she had locked up the theatre, they walked together to Piazza Maggiore. It was a great pity, she said, that so few people in Castelluccio – no, not just in Castelluccio, but everywhere – have an interest in anything except what's happening to them right now. 'They miss so much,' she said, with acute dismay, like a conservationist despairing of people's disregard of their environment. Most of the citizens of Castelluccio, she complained, are content to have just a little bit of history in the air, like a whiff of incense. Jostling against him, with her urgent and bouncy gait, she conjured a stream of smoke in the air with a hand. It was so gratifying to come across someone whose attitude was different, she said. On the piazza she halted abruptly, as if suddenly remembering something she had intended to tell him.

'The dead,' she pronounced, in the manner of a teacher giving last words of advice to a departing pupil, 'emit a radiation, and this radiation can be detected if you are receptive. If you are receptive,' she went on, 'the world is richer. It is like the change from black and white to colour. This is what I believe. If you are not receptive, you see the way a dog sees. Dogs cannot distinguish between red and orange. They cannot tell the difference between yellow and green. They have a poor sense of space. But if you are receptive you see all the colours. You see in depth. For many people here,' she said, with a gesture towards the Palazzo Comunale, 'that building is part of a theatre set in which they live, a piece of furniture. But it is not a piece of furniture. It is a battery – a battery of history.' She rested a hand on his forearm. 'But I am peculiar,' she told him, adopting a doubtful scowl, as though regarding the peculiar person that was herself.

After this, whenever they passed each other in the street, she would stop to exchange a few words, but there was no conversation of any substance until the following year, when, again on the Saturday preceding the San Zeno festivities, she gave a tour of the Palazzo Comunale, from the prison cells up to the bell-chamber. As before, Monica Nerini was there, this time with her husband in tow; Robert was there; and the party was rounded out by the members of a Swiss string quartet, who were playing three Shostakovich pieces at Santa Maria dei Carmini that evening. And, as before, Robert lingered after the others had left, though this time he didn't need a recapitulation of points that had passed him by. They sat in the room in which she worked from Monday to Friday, between glass-fronted walnut bookcases that rose from floor to ceiling. On her desk was a square of paper on which was recorded the discovery on Piazza del Mercato, on a June morning in 1619, of a man who had starved to death; 'his stomach was full of grass,' read Cinzia, tracing the words with a finger. She showed him a document in which a citizen of Castelluccio denounced Giovan Antonio Ridolfi for breeding serpents in his house. 'A whole life, and this is all that remains – a denunciation, a scrap of paper, one tiny story. Body and soul boiled down to this one little blob of fact,' murmured Cinzia, gazing at the pages as if at photographs. She sometimes thought of herself as their life support machine, she told him. 'Almost gone,' she whispered, and her finger slid out over the table, flatlining, with one tiny blip at the end.

Cinzia was perhaps, she admitted, over-attuned to the frequencies of the dead. Often, as she walked through Castelluccio, she could feel the air around her change, its atmosphere thicken. 'For a moment, I am not in this century,' she told him, eyes round as an owl's. 'I actually see things, sometimes.' It was, she explained, like an after-image, when you've been looking at a picture on your computer screen then you look at a blank sheet of white paper and for an instant the picture is there, grey and watery, but nonetheless there. She had once seen a figure that was the image of Tommaso Galli outside his theatre. It was, she supposed, a form of – 'what is the word?' Together they arrived at synaesthesia, *sinestesia*. They talked for more than an hour.

In subsequent years, always around the time of the Festa di San Zeno, she led tours of Santa Maria dei Carmini, San Giovanni Battista and, once more, the theatre. She led a walking tour of the whole town. In the ballroom of Palazzo Campani she gave a talk on the Campani family; at the Palazzo Comunale she gave lectures on Giovan Antonio Ridolfi ('the most interesting man this town has ever produced'), Domenico Vielmi, the Bonvalori family, and, finally, Achille de Marinis, of whom her grandfather had been a friend and supporter. Robert attended all of them, and afterwards they would talk. Nearly twenty people – the largest audience she had ever drawn – heard her lecture on Achille de Marinis; that evening, walking home, she confided that she was about to start working on the life of Teresa Campani. This was their last conversation of any length.

Antonio Zappalorto, the first time Robert went to see him, informed him, after Robert had told him how much he'd enjoyed Signora Zappalorto's tour of the theatre, that his wife intended to write a book – an encyclopaedia of Castelluccio – when she retired. 'Her head is a magnet for facts,' he said, clamping a fist to his forehead. And, with pride and tenderness, in American-inflected English: 'My wife is an original person.'

Antonio was born in a house on Prospect Street, Paterson, New Jersey. His grandfather, a plumber, fearful of his country's future, had left Italy after the 1924 election, with his wife and two teenaged sons, the elder and smarter of whom, Vicenzo, became a dentist and in 1929 married Louise Brannigan, a secretary at the Grimshaw Brothers mill; the following year a son was born, the first of three, of whom Antonio was the last; all of them followed their father into dentistry. Louise died in 1959; in 1960 her husband returned to Italy, accompanied by Antonio, the only unmarried son, and the one who had always been the keenest audience for his grandparents' stories about life in the motherland. The brothers stayed in America, where they became, as Antonio would tell you, rich, fat and unhappy; one of them was already divorced when Vicenzo and Antonio left, and would later divorce again; the other stayed miserably married to an alcoholic until he was fifty-five, and found nobody to replace her after they had parted.

The Castelluccio to which Vicenzo returned was almost unrecognisable: the friends of his youth had changed too much, or had left, or been killed or died. With Antonio he set up a *Studio Dentistico* on Piazza Maggiore, and they did well; with the techniques they had learned in America, they quickly established a good reputation. But Vicenzo became nostalgic for America. In Castelluccio, he told his son, he felt that he was perpetually in mourning. The town was as uncomfortable as a suit that was too small. He bought a big car and every Saturday and Sunday he would drive for miles, not going anywhere in particular, just driving. He was surrounded by devious people, he complained;

in America people were honest and direct. For six months he had a relationship with the widowed daughter of Lino Pacetti, an affair that gave him some pleasure and much more guilt. Eight years after coming home, Vicenzo went back to Paterson.

Antonio, this time, did not go with him, because Antonio was making money and he liked the pace of life in Castelluccio; and – most importantly – he was now with Cinzia, a woman whose soul, as he told his father, was infused with the spirit of Castelluccio. It had been, he once told Robert, moments before applying the drill to a molar, a genuine case of love at first sight. They had met on a Thursday evening in October, in Via Santa Maria, where Cinzia was standing outside the Cereria, hand braced against the wall, breathing in a way that made Antonio wonder if this young woman might be having an asthma attack. He spoke to her. Nothing was wrong, she told him; she'd picked up a scent of beeswax a moment before, and was trying to get it back. Did he know what this building used to be? No? So she told him, then breathed deeply again. She wasn't trying to make herself seem interesting, said Antonio. The thing about the beeswax was a simple remark, as you might remark on the scent of a flower. 'I might come and see you,' she said, before he had even introduced himself. 'I have a problem with a tooth,' she said, opening wide and pointing, like a child. And she did come to see him, the very next day. That evening they went for a walk together. At the war memorial she told him that she had discovered that the Gizzi whose name was carved there was almost certainly descended from a slave who had been owned by the Campani family. Such was Cinzia's excitement at this news, he felt compelled to kiss her.

No other man in Castelluccio was much interested in Cinzia, thought Antonio, because they thought she must be a strange kind of young woman to be happy spending all day in dust and piles of old papers. 'And she was no Sophia Loren, whereas I am a second Mastroianni,' said Antonio, whose teeth were gleaming but whose face was marred by a nose that would have better suited a head twice the size of his, and whose ears were aligned almost perpendicularly to his skull, so that, as he put it, he had hearing like a bat, as long as the sound was coming from straight ahead. 'She is an odd one,' Antonio told him, 'and we complement each other well. She attends to the past, and I attend to the present and the future. Come the Day of Judgement, all my clients will be offering the Lord the finest smiles that money can buy.'

They had no children. This was the only misfortune of their lives, said Antonio; it was a major misfortune, but the only one. Cinzia and Antonio were devoted to each other; after they had retired, you never saw one without the other. And after Cinzia died, Antonio visited her at the cemetery every day. In the evenings he often ate at the Antica Farmacia, because he had never learned to cook, and he wanted company, but not for talk. His wife's sister, who had taught Giacomo and Cecilia Stornello at their *scuola elementare*, sometimes dined with him, but otherwise he ate alone. He was like a man behind glass, content with the companionship of his thoughts. On evenings when Robert was there with Gideon, he would greet them and exchange inconsequentialities, but he didn't much care for Gideon, as he once confided to Robert – the painter was too extravagant for his tastes, and he had to say that he didn't greatly care for the company that Gideon kept, meaning the idiot Pacetti, a man who could never let pass an opportunity to abuse the land of Antonio's birth.

At the Antica Farmacia he drank only water and coffee. At home, though, every night, he would drink a bottle of wine because otherwise he could not sleep, as he confessed to Robert one afternoon. 'I am very tired,' said Antonio, taking an arm. At night, he said, he often had the same dream: he was in large darkened room and a blind man was in there, with a knife, stalking him; this blind man was death, he knew, and one night death would catch him, and he would die in his sleep. As they were about to part, Antonio told him that Cinzia had amassed a lot of material for her book of Castelluccio, and he didn't know what he should do with it all. 'Her sister doesn't want it. Would you?' he asked.

'I would be honoured,' Robert answered, and Antonio pressed his hand, once, very firmly, as if closing a padlock.

Nine days later, two days before the anniversary of Cinzia's death, Antonio died in his armchair, holding a lump of chiselled obsidian, which Cinzia believed had belonged to the physician Giovan Antonio Ridolfi.

7

7.1

It's Claire's last morning in Castelluccio and she's taking a slow stroll around the town. Off Via dei Falcucci there's an alley she hasn't yet walked along; it turns out to be a cul de sac, and as she's coming back out of it Trim runs up, bringing Gideon in his wake. Waving a hand at head height, Gideon calls out: 'Hail to thee, blithe spirit.' He points towards the Corso and shouts: 'We're going shopping. Care to join the fun?'

Their destination, at which they arrive within a minute, turns out to be the butcher's shop. 'Only be a moment,' says Gideon. The window is horrible: a skinned animal hangs from a hook, blood dribbling from the tip of its nose, its eyes like buttons of jelly; below it, next to a pile of glands on a bloodied white tray, a vast lump of meat is covered with skin that's creased like the skin on a day-old cup of coffee. 'You may prefer to wait outside,' suggests Gideon, noting, with amusement, her revulsion. She crosses to the other side of the road, while Trim remains at the door, static as a garden ornament. Through the door she sees the butcher – a man of Gideon's girth, with a corona of snow-white hair – giving her uncle a mighty handshake before handing him a carrier bag, evidently heavy.

'Bones for the hound,' Gideon explains, turning towards Piazza del Mercato. 'That's Marta's father,' he goes on. 'Marta the waitress. I gave him a drawing of Marta so he keeps us supplied with bones. An arrangement that pleases us immensely, does it not?' he says to Trim, who is walking behind, maintaining a steady distance of a hand's span between his nose and the bag. 'And from time to time he lets me work in the back room. Drawing carcasses.' He gives her a glance to check her reaction, but she presents a bland face. 'Anatomy – every artist should study anatomy. Human and animal, inside and out. You have to understand what's under the surface. George Stubbs. You know George Stubbs?' he asks, knowing full well that she doesn't. 'I revere George Stubbs,' he declares, and he proceeds to tell her about the revered Mr Stubbs and his helper, Mary Spencer, who took dead horses from a local tannery and hung them from the roof-beams of their Lincolnshire farmhouse, so that Mr Stubbs could dissect the flesh and make drawings of each stage of the reduction, until nothing remained but the bones. After eighteen months of work, he had produced the most detailed artistic study of the horse that had ever been created. 'As great as anything by Leonardo da Vinci,' Gideon pronounces. 'He was renowned for his strong stomach,' he tells her. 'A high tolerance of unpleasant aromas. He once got hold of a tiger and cut that up as well.' And at this point a car's horn stops him short.

Indignant at having been beeped, he swivels to glare at the driver, and his face is instantly transformed. 'Hello!' he cries. He waves at the driver, a rather severe woman who gives him a strained smile and raises one hand from the steering wheel in salute; she mouths a word or two, but does not wind down the window. 'Agnese. A brilliant woman,' says Gideon, smiling at the car as it leaves them. The precise nature of her brilliance is not disclosed, because it's more important to be told that the brilliant Agnese was once a girlfriend of Robert's. To a certain type of Italian woman, a certain type of Englishman is immensely attractive, he informs her, like a zoologist explaining an aspect of the behaviour of his chosen species. 'The dormant volcano, if you know what I mean,' he says, with a twitch of an eyebrow. 'And Robert is an excellent fellow,' he tells her.

There follows a digression on the excellence of Robert, a man who has come to know so much about pigments, varnishes, glues and so forth, that the director of the town museum has remarked that Mr Bancourt is as knowledgeable as any restorer in Italy. 'His very words,' Gideon tells her, as proud as a father. 'And of course he's a whizz with the technology – computers, the infernet and all that. It's all too much for me, but he takes care of everything. I rely on Robert more than I rely on myself. Everything I've ever created is filed away in his head. He has a very retentive memory. I don't. Mine is quite dreadful,' he sighs.

'And women do like a man with a good memory,' she responds.

He seems to take the remark at face value. 'Well,' he says, 'he's been popular around here, I can tell you. That's one reason he stays with me. I am, it goes without saying, an exemplary employer. But the women are a factor, without question. Our Robert has a past. Oh yes,' he tells her, as though she may be in need of discouragement, then he laughs. 'Whereas I don't. No past at all, except my work. A man totally devoted to his art,' he proclaims, lowering his head and putting four fingertips to his breastbone, in a parodic gesture of willing servitude.

They have reached the loggia, and he is breathing heavily. 'Do you mind if we sit down for a minute?' he asks, lowering himself onto the bench. He tips a thick bone out of the bag for Trim, who withdraws into the shade of the seat; his gnawing makes a noise like small rocks being knocked together. 'I'll tell you something,' Gideon resumes, with the air of a man who's about to disclose a piece of information that will forever change the way she regards him. 'I have not had a relationship with a woman since I was in my twenties. Absolutely true,' he insists, as if she were expressing astonishment. 'No relationships other than friendship, and very few of those. Acquaintances more than friendships. Nothing more than that.' He is not soliciting sympathy, she'll say that much for him; it's more as if he's reporting a biographical quirk, like never having been on board an aeroplane. 'I have only one deep attachment,' he tells her.

'Robert.'

'Well, yes, there's Robert. But I meant this chap.' He bends forward to reach under the bench and put a hand on the dog's head, an action that darkens his face as if he's being throttled. 'He is a wonderful animal,' he says, stroking Trim's head. 'Wonderful, wonderful,' he repeats, sitting up; his eyes have become watery, perhaps with the effort of bending over. He joins his hands over his heart and breathes deeply.

'You OK?' she asks.

He takes two or three deep draughts of air. 'Fine, fine,' he assures her, then he's off again, talking about how we could all take a lesson from animals, because animals don't fret about the past or about the future: 'They think just enough', he says.

'We have no idea what they think,' she says. Gazing fondly down at Trim, Gideon makes no reply. 'For all we know, Trim really wishes he were a cat.'

His smile is that of an adult touched by a child's whimsy. 'I doubt that,' he answers. 'He's a simple creature. A simple and happy chap,' he says, stooping again to rub the dog's brow.

'Happy to be alive.'

'I think so.'

'But cows and pigs aren't?'

He looks at her, puzzled, then a smile appears. 'Have you ever looked a cow in the eye? Nothing there.'

'I disagree. Ever seen what goes on in an abattoir? Ever heard the noise they make? I don't think they're having fun. They know what's happening.'

'You may be right,' he concedes. 'But I don't think a cow is conscious the way a dog is conscious.'

'Conscious is conscious.'

'Well—'

'And suffering is suffering.'

He sits up, flushed puce around the eyes. 'But we're built to eat meat. We need it,' he says, with a suggestion of regret that this should be the case.

'I know some very sporty vegetarians.'

'We have incisors for a reason.'

'We inherited them.'

'Humans are not ruminants.'

'Quite. We can argue and discuss and make decisions. We can decide not be ruled by our teeth.'

He looks down at the ground, as if considering what she's said, but he's not considering it, she can tell. He raises his head and squints at the church tower. 'You see,' he says, 'this is what I need. Some more friction in my life. It would be good for me.' He shows her a grimace of a smile – an imitation of embarrassment at having confessed to such a lack, she thinks. Again he looks down, then he turns his head to glance up at her and says: 'You're very direct.' It's a compliment, but she feels as if it's been imposed on her, like a rubber stamp smacked onto her forehead. 'I do like that,' he says. 'Very much.'

A wiry little beige dog is crossing the piazza on a pink lead, galloping on tiny legs behind a woman in a searing pink dress and sunglasses that almost entirely cover her cheeks. Abandoning his fragments of bone, Trim trots across the tarmac to sniff at the miniature terrier, whose owner reacts as if the new arrival has brought a stink of sewage with it. A clap of Gideon's hands brings Trim back immediately.

'Here's a funny story, starring Trim,' announces Gideon, and he tells her about the time he took Trim for a dip in the stream one January afternoon, a couple of years ago. They have a routine: Gideon walks up the valley to a particular tree beside the

stream and then comes back along the bank, with Trim following in the water. On this occasion Gideon had descended about
a hundred metres from the tree when he realised that the dog
was no longer with him. He walked back, and saw Trim frisking
about at a bend where the stream has cut a metre-high wall in
the earth; Trim was splashing around beneath this wall of earth,
repeatedly ducking under the surface. And then the dog clambered out of the water, with a bone in its mouth – a human bone,
a tibia. The police were on the scene within the hour; a male skeleton was found in the mud, and further excavations unearthed
another two. The bones were taken to a lab for analysis. 'We had
a multiple murder on our hands, people thought,' says gleeful
Gideon. 'Or maybe remains from the war. People went missing
in this area and were never found, you know. For a week it was
the only topic of conversation. The most exciting thing to have
happened around here for decades. Then the verdict from the
scientists: no murder to solve; the skeletons had been there for
more than five hundred years. Plague victims, probably. Such a
disappointment.' He laughs, then again he's gulping down the
air, hands flattened on his chest.

'You sure you're all right?' she asks.

He nods, tight-lipped. He needs to lose weight, he says. One
day soon, if he doesn't get rid of a few kilos, he'll have a heart
attack. It doesn't seem to occur to him that a heart attack is what
killed her father, and not very long ago. But he does not look
good: he's sweating too much, and his fingers are overfilled. 'I
think we should get you back home,' she says.

'No need,' he says. 'I often get short of breath. I talk too
much and I'm too fat. It'll pass, don't you worry. I'll just stay
here for a while. You run along.' He closes his eyes and rests
his head on the back of the bench; Trim climbs up, and rests his
head on Gideon's lap; fingering the dog's fur, Gideon smiles
as if dreaming. 'You run along,' he tells her. 'We're fine,' he
says, looking at her, then he waves to someone behind her – the
broken-nosed printer. The man gives her a smile as she crosses

his path, then raises his fists, shadow-boxing, which appears to be a greeting for Gideon.

7.2

In June 2003 a public meeting was held in Castelluccio's town hall to discuss a plan, commissioned by the council from architect Vito Monelli, for the conversion of the Teatro Gaetano into a mixed-use building, with a studio for drama and music on the ground floor, restaurant premises above, and a bar with roof terrace at the top. The project was widely approved, most vigorously by Maurizio Ianni, who was no doubt already envisaging his Ristorante Gaetano, its walls adorned with posters of the great Italian stars of stage and screen. But the proposal had one vehement opponent, Fausto Nerini, who condemned it as a 'fantasy' that had less chance of being realised than he had of being elected to the papacy. And he was glad that there was no possibility, as he saw it, of raising the necessary money, because the idea of a 'performance space' for Castelluccio was absurd. The town was smaller than it had been when the theatre was built – you need an audience to keep a theatre alive, and Castelluccio no longer had an audience. Only a city could keep a theatre alive, because people watch TV nowadays, they don't go to the theatre. Houses had been demolished to build it, so why couldn't it be demolished in turn, to build something that has a function? Let's get rid of the theatre and build a centre for small businesses. Today you can run a successful business with just brains, some phone lines, some computers and a place to put them. And while we're at it, let's do something about San Lorenzo – it would make a good sports hall. Face facts: we have too many churches. We don't need San Lorenzo and we don't need a theatre. Nostalgia is the only reason for keeping them, and nostalgia will be the death of us, Fausto Nerini concluded, to no applause.

Over the centuries, Castelluccio has manufactured paper, candles and silk. Wheelwrights and tanners have had workshops here. As recently as the 1980s there was a small company in Via Sant'Agostino that constructed made-to-measure bicycle frames. Now there is only one business within the walls of Castelluccio that could be described as a manufacturer: Nerini, printers and binders, founded in 1930 by Moreno Nerini, grandfather of Fausto, at the address from which the Nerini business still operates, Via del Pozzo 7. Fausto has a single full-time employee, his wife, Monica, who supplements the family's income by taking in clothes for alteration, as her mother used to do. Monica also makes many of the costumes for the San Zeno parade, in which for several years Fausto has impersonated Muzio Bonvalori, a role allocated to him on the grounds that he is the toughest-looking individual in town.

Fausto used to be a boxer; indeed, in his late teens, he was one of the half-dozen best teenage lightweights in Tuscany. In 1978 he won six fights and lost none, and his father – though it was understood that Fausto would one day take over the presses – began to entertain the idea that his boy might be able, in the interim, to make a living out of the sport. Then, on the evening of Friday, February 16th, 1979, in Grosseto, he had a fight against an undertrained boy who looked like a muslin sack full of mozzarella, and moved like one too. The first two rounds were won by Fausto with ease. In the third round, assured of victory, with only forty seconds left, Fausto stepped back, dropped his guard and winked at his girlfriend, who was sitting beside his father. His exhausted opponent, humiliated into one last mighty effort, sprang forward with a speed of which Fausto would not have thought him capable, and with all his strength launched a fist into the face of his cocky opponent, cracking his nose and knocking him out for the first and last time. That evening, Fausto was seeing everything in triplicate, through fog. The next day, his right eye was functioning more or less properly; the left, which had taken the full force of the punch, was not. A doctor took a look at him. His advice to Mr Nerini was that another blow of such magnitude could have permanent consequences for his son's vision. He might be able to fight for many years with no further ill effects; on the other hand, his next fight might blind him. Fausto was prepared to take the risk, but his father was adamant: a blind printer would be of no use to anyone.

So Fausto retired to his father's workshop with immediate effect, and after his father's stroke, fifteen years later, he took it over completely, just as one day Fausto and Monica's son, Aldo, will take over from them, unless the experience of working in Vietnam – where he's slaving in an orphanage seven days a week, thanks to the persuasive powers of Father Fabris – turns his head permanently against home. As for their daughter, Alessandra, she doesn't know what she'll do with her life, but whatever it is, she's not going to be doing it in Castelluccio. Aldo will come back, however; they hope.

Fausto uses letterpresses and litho machines that his father and even his grandfather used, and recently he's invested in a Xerox digital press, which cost a lot of money but nowadays keeps the business afloat. The Nerini workshop produces posters and flyers for the festival of San Zeno and other events in the area; catalogues, matchbook covers and wine labels; postcards for local churches and museums, and tickets for the Museo Civico; brochures for Maurizio Ianni and menus for the Antica Farmacia and dozens of other restaurants from Volterra to Siena; reports and other documents for the town hall; and stationery for, among others, *maestro* Westfall, who, in gratitude for the quality of his products, drew the sketch that hangs in the back office, showing Fausto at the old Heidelberg Windmill machine.

Gideon will be on his way to the Nerini workshop, to collect a ream of monogrammed paper, when he dies.

7.3

After the dazzle of the street, the entrance hall of the Museo Civico is so dark that it takes several seconds to see the desk at the end of it, a desk at which sits a pretty young woman, reading a magazine in the breeze of an electric fan. The young woman looks up and regards Claire as if momentarily unable to explain why someone should be standing at the desk, holding out a five-euro note. 'One?' she asks, then from an almost empty cash-tray she takes a couple of coins, which she hands to the visitor, with a ticket and two sheets of typescript, stapled together.

Claire reads: *The town Museum is in the Town hospital and orphange (XIV–XV sec.). From the entry of the building you get in through a door which introduces a corridor covered by a voult.* In the corridor are displayed: a walnut credenza (seventeenth century), with carved panels depicting the Seven Works of Mercy; a sixteenth-century Madonna and Child, wooden, missing the right hand of the Madonna; and shelves from a pharmacy, dated 1764, laden with ceramic flasks of the same period.

The next room has a reliquary that once belonged to the church of Santa Maria dei Carmini and another that came from Sant'Agostino; each contains, in a crystal phial encased within a gilded sunburst, what appears to be a sliver of bone, but the guide doesn't specify whose bones they might have been. A second vitrine is occupied by a miscellany of tarnished metallic items and terracotta fragments, none of them labelled. *Domestic use objects, of Etruscan and Roman ages,* says the guide.

The paintings are in the third room. On the left are hung a *Madonna with Child (XV sec.)*, a *Madonna with Child in throne (XVI sec.)*, *Saint Francis receiving the stimmates (XV sec.)*, *Saint Francis preaches to the birds by Il Beccafico (c. 1460)*, and a flaking little picture *that has been identified with some doubts as a portrait of the son of Bartolo di Tura Bandini (1391–1477), famed phisician of the Spedale di Santa Maria della Scala.* Opposite, there is a wormhole-ridden panel of wood that appears to show a man hugging a small cloud, which illustrates an *episode of a folkloristic story.* The cloud picture used to belong to the *emminent Campani family,* some of whom – Pierpaolo and Giuditta, with Anna Maria, Chiara, Teresa, Michele, Paolo and Tullio – are depicted in the painting alongside.

In the centre of the room, a steel frame supports a *masterpiece by Giovanni di Paolo d'Agnolo (c.1409–c.1480)*. Created for the private chapel of Muzio Bonvalori in the Rocca Nuova, it *rappresents S. Bernardino who preaches to the contempt of terrestial things and stamps onto the mitries, symbols that he refuses the ecclesiastical power*. In it, the emaciated and marble-eyed saint aims a blazing golden plate, bearing the letters IHS, at a crowd of finely dressed folk, all kneeling; directly above the saint's head, at an altitude of approximately twenty feet, a crown is supported by a pair of angels. Visitors are instructed to note *the vivacity of colours and the particular of the characters*. One of these characters, she reads, is Muzio Bonvalori, whose shield, adorned with his coat of arms, lies on the ground beside him.

Propped on an easel in a corner of the last room is a portrait – an eighteenth-century copy of a lost original – of Giovan Antonio Ridolfi (b. Pisa, 1570; d. Castelluccio, 1636); the cheeks appear to have been rouged and the mouth enhanced with lipstick; he has the look of a man who has been embalmed and is not at all pleased by the liberties that have been taken with his body; for some reason he is holding a sprig of oak leaves. To the side of the picture, a caption describes Giovan Antonio Ridolfi as a man of great learning whose home was filled with *items of zoological and botanical interest, and objects of curiosity*. Two of these objects are on show, under the gaze of their former owner. The first is a cherry stone, mounted like a jewel between silver curlicues with a pendant pearl; no fewer than thirty-five cherubic faces have been carved onto the stone, as one can verify with the aid of the lens that has been suspended in front of it. Having counted the thirty-five faces, Claire crosses the room to inspect the second object of curiosity. No more than eight inches tall, it consists of a corkscrew pedestal that supports a perforated sphere, in which nestles a dodecahedron, also perforated, which in turn encloses a small hollow hexahedron, which contains a tiny sphere of solid ivory. The whole thing, the pamphlet informs her, was carved from a single piece of ivory, by *the famous Manfredo Settala of Milan*

(1600–1680), whose museum, comprising around 3,000 items, included coins, minerals, articles of Africa and the Americas, and scientific instruments builded by Settala himself. The thing is astonishing: the carving of it would have required the fingers of a brain surgeon and the patience of a monk. A ball inside a polyhedron inside another polyhedron inside a sphere – she can't imagine how it could have been done. And she can't imagine what its purpose might have been – merely to amaze? Already her amazement is dwindling. It must have meant something more than would a model of the Empire State Building made out of toothpicks, mustn't it? But what did it mean? The text in her hand says only that Settala was a *master of the art of ivory carving*, and that this art was practised by *no other than Rudolph II.*

One final section remains: a wall hung with ex-votoes for Saint Zeno, painted on bits of wood by grateful recipients of his supernatural aid. Various accidents are depicted, but the pictures are identical in one respect: in each scene the saint appears in the top right-hand corner, standing on a puff of cloud. Sometimes he's shown with a boar kneeling at his feet, and sometimes he's shown twice: on his cloud, and at the scene of the mishap. In one picture he's in mid-air, with arms outstretched like a diver, descending to the aid of a fat little chap who is floating face-down in a river, as plump as a beach ball. The saint supports the head of a bloodied man who lies supine behind a rearing horse; he hauls a child out of a well; he places a bale of hay beneath a toppling ladder; he causes the knife of a would-be murderer to splinter against the torso of the intended victim. Painted between 1700 and 1900, the ex-votoes are *fasinating examples of the folk art*. She goes back for another look at Settala's ivory puzzle; the amazement has gone entirely; she can get nothing more from the Museo Civico.

A different young woman, a little younger than the first, with a fuller face and longer hair and narrow-framed glasses, is perched on the edge of the desk, reading a magazine. 'Thank you,' she says when Claire puts the stapled pages back on the

desk beside her, and gives her a glance that seems a little embarrassed for the tedium that the visitor has had to endure.

7.4

In *The Man Who Knew Everything*, his two-volume biography
of the Jesuit polymath Athanasius Kircher (1601/02–1680), the
historian Maximilian Böhm cites the great Kircher's description
of Giovan Antonio Ridolfi as 'a questioning man, of immense
learning but most melancholy'. The biography has little more
to say on the subject of Ridolfi: 'the magus of Castelluccio' has,
Böhm notes, 'almost disappeared from history'. Unlike many of
the other pre-eminent collector-naturalists of his time, Ridolfi
wrote no account of his own life – or none of which we are aware
– and published no books. He is said to have delivered a series of
lectures in Bologna, but no record of these has survived. He died
before he could complete the catalogue of his collection, and the
thousands of entries that he did have time to write have now disappeared, with the exception of five pages of the catalogue of his
herbarium, which came to light in Turin in 2005. Letters written
by Ridolfi have been found in various places, but most of what
we know of him is derived from the writings of contemporaries.

Born in Pisa on January 7th, 1570, he was the second son of
Count Girolamo Ridolfi and the first son of Girolamo Ridolfi's
second wife, Agnese Donoratico. As a young man he was small
of stature, strong, and a keen horseman. His most remarkable
features, it would appear, were his eyes, which were 'lynx-like'.
His face, another writer records, was not handsome, yet 'bespoke
intelligence and audacity'. He was a studious youth. Botany was
a particular interest, so much so that his mastery of the subject
was held to be the equal of any professor's. His memory was
prodigious; to friends he was known as 'our Mithridates'.

In 1593 an incident occurred in the botanical gardens of the
University of Pisa, involving Ridolfi and two other young noble-
men. In one version of events, Ridolfi's conduct towards a certain

young woman was the occasion of the quarrel; in another, the argument arose from a point of botanical classification. Whatever the cause, offence was taken on both sides and, some days after, a second and more violent altercation ensued. In consequence, Ridolfi left Pisa in October of that year, perhaps expelled. Forty years would pass before he returned to his native city.

A sentence in a letter sent in 1607 to the Veronese botanist-physician Giovanni Pona suggests that Ridolfi travelled widely after leaving Pisa. Where precisely he travelled is unknown. For the next five years, we have but a single trace of him: in 1594 he was in Bologna, where he met and was entranced by little Antonietta Gonsalvus, daughter of Petrus Gonsalvus, the celebrated monster of Tenerife. Antonietta's manners were refined and her voice delightful, he wrote, though her face was 'as hairy as a wolf's'. While in Bologna, Ridolfi became closely acquainted with Ulisse Aldrovandi, in whose *Catalogue of men who have visited our museum* he is described as a 'man very extraordinary'. Ridolfi in turn would extol Aldrovandi as 'the most percipient reader of the book of Nature'.

Ridolfi had a villa built outside the walls of Castelluccio, and by the end of 1599 he was in residence there. No image exists of the villa, which was demolished in the early years of the nineteenth century, but we know of some of its features. Above the portal was set a large relief in stone, depicting Sisyphus and his rock. A 'speaking tube' connected the hall to Ridolfi's *studio*, enabling his manservant to announce the arrival of guests. Portraits of Aldrovandi and other scholars were the only paintings that Ridolfi owned. In addition to these portraits, the rooms were adorned with representations of Ridolfi's personal emblem: an oak tree above the motto *Descendo ut ascendam* (I descend in order to rise). Whereas the museums of collectors such as Aldrovandi, Francesco Calzolari, Ferrante Imperato, Ole Worm and Manfredo Settala are recorded in numerous engravings, there is no such depiction of Ridolfi's *studio*. From the accounts left by visitors, however, we can imagine a spacious room, windowless, in which

thousands of specimens were arrayed in cabinets, ordered by
type. A cabinet of shells and corals occupied much of one wall;
butterflies and insects filled another. In the cabinet of birds, two
parrots flanked a bird of paradise. The jaws of a colossal shark,
found on a beach near Livorno, hung above the cabinet of fishes,
in which was displayed a remora, a fish that, though no longer
than a man's leg, could attach itself to the hull of a ship and stop it
in mid-ocean, more suddenly than any anchor, as had happened
to the ship carrying Mark Antony at the battle of Actium. A
skeleton of a siren was suspended from the ceiling; a cat with
one head and two bodies could be seen beside a snake with two
heads. Ridolfi kept a live chameleon, a creature that was as much
a favourite as a specimen. 'The admirable courtier-lizard, always
at one with his place of habitation,' is how Ridolfi described
the animal. The most extensive part of Ridofi's collection was
the botanical section: he is said to have possessed a sample of
every herb that had been known to Dioscorides and Pliny. In the
centre of the room, armour and weapons were displayed, with
astrolabes and armillary spheres and telescopes. A visitor from
Germany stated that there were more than 15,000 'things' in the
museo of the esteemed Giovan Antonio Ridolfi. Others called it
a *teatro*, a *microcosmo*, a *cornucopia*, a *gazophylacium*, a 'forest of
knowledge'.

Collecting was Ridolfi's sole extravagance. His household
staff never numbered more than two: he had a cook and a
manservant, who was also his draughtsman, in which capacity
he accompanied his master on his frequent excursions into the
countryside around Castelluccio. Always in search of specimens, Ridolfi travelled extensively. In 1604 he journeyed to the
Pyrenees, an expedition that lasted six months. On his way home
he passed through Verona; from there, with Giovanni Pona, he
climbed Monte Baldo, where they gathered orchids, rhododen-
drons, heliotropes, *noli mi tangere* and *costo*. The last of these
was needed for the preparation of theriac, a universal antidote
derived from the concoction with which Mithridates the Great,

by means of frequent ingestion, had made himself invulnerable to poisons. Whereas many physicians strove to produce a compound that used the same sixty-four ingredients that Galen had used in his theriac, Ridolfi's theriac was a mixture of no fewer than one hundred ingredients, and it was deplored by several other physicians for its inclusion of 'inauthentic simples'. Matteo Picco of Siena condemned Ridolfi's 'stew of Africa, Asia, Europe and the New World.' Ridolfi planned to sail to the Indies; there is no evidence that this ambition was fulfilled.

Soon after his return from the Pyrenees he was called to Volterra to assist an apothecary in dissecting several vipers for their poison – the apothecary could not be certain of his ability to distinguish the barren vipers from the pregnant, a distinction that was of vital significance in the preparation of theriac. In the same year a dragon with bird's feet and the head of a serpent was killed in an orchard near Certaldo, and Ridolfi was asked to inspect the corpse of the beast. His opinion is not recorded. After that, it appears that he rarely travelled further than a day's walk from Castelluccio.

He had, though, many visitors and many correspondents. A physician in Bergamo wrote to thank him for the *balsamo orientale* that Ridolfi had sent him. Another doctor expressed his gratitude for sticks of Portuguese cinnamon. He exchanged letters with Johann Faber, supervisor of the papal botanical gardens, and with Federico Cesi, founder of the Accademia dei Lincei, who in 1614 sent to Castelluccio a specimen of the luminescent *lapis Bononiensis* or 'solar sponge'. From a correspondent in Florence he acquired a microscope (*occhialino*), with which he explicated to certain visitors the anatomies of flies and bees and all manner of insects. To a professor from Bari he demonstrated that the body of the lowly snail does indeed contain a heart. Another scholar, believing that birds could generate spontaneously from trees, and frogs from menses and dust, had a strong disagreement with Ridolfi and left the villa on bad terms. In 1616 the Jesuit linguist and mathematician Tommaso Casati, a friend of

Athanasius Kircher, came to Castelluccio, where he and Ridolfi debated, to an audience of scholars, the qualities of the lodestone: for Casati the magnetism of the stone was a manifestation of God's cohesive power, of the 'golden chain' that holds the world together; for Ridolfi it was proof of the wisdom of Galileo. At the debate's conclusion the two views remained unreconciled; nonetheless, Casati and Ridolfi continued their discussions by letter, amicably. A letter from Ridolfi preserves his argument that the new species being discovered every year in distant parts of the world made it impossible for any reasonable man to believe that Noah's Ark was anything other than a fable. In February 1617 he wrote to Casati: 'I am a slave of no philosopher'. And: 'Philosophy lives in the shops and the countryside'. Later that year, Casati drowned in China.

'The house of Ridolfi is a shambles,' wrote the man who believed in the spontaneous generation of birds and frogs. He mentions a tub of entrails beside Ridolfi's desk, a dog's head on a windowsill, a flayed horse. 'The air of the villa is noisome,' he wrote, and 'his *studio* is a pit of crawling things'. Ridolfi paid farmers to bring him specimens of unusual plants and insects; in this way he came to record five plants for which there was no name. He was in contact with fishermen all along the Tuscan coast, who would send him freakish fish and sea plants for his collection. At night he could be seen on the hills around the town: he had devised some sort of hat or helmet to which a small lantern was attached, and the light of it could be seen from the town walls, moving over the land like a tiny wandering star.

In Castelluccio he seems to have associated with only three men: Antonio Manetti, a lawyer; Pietro Appiani, an apothecary; and Giuliano de Solis, a physician, who occasionally consulted Ridolfi on medical matters. One such consultation occurred in 1627, when the magistrate Jacopo dal Borgo presented himself to de Solis, complaining of abdominal pains. Theriac was administered, but the symptoms worsened. Other medicines were taken; quantities of blood were drained; the man rapidly declined.

Unable to walk, he was carried to the resting place of Saint Zeno;
such was his agony, he could not speak. He was on the threshold of death when Ridolfi was brought to him. A purgative of
antimony was proposed, and taken. At once the magistrate's
body began to evacuate itself, expelling noxious matter so copiously that it did not seem possible that he could survive. But
survive he did, and though many gave thanks for his recovery
primarily to Saint Zeno, the potions of Giovan Antonio Ridolfi
were sufficiently credited for Ridolfi's aid to be more promptly
sought when, a little over a year later, a friar at the convent of
Sant'Agostino was struck down by an illness which, like the
ailment of Jacopo dal Borgo, seemed certain to bring about his
demise. The friar, Fra' Pietro Negri, was passing a bloody flux;
he could drink water but could take no food; he had a fire in his
bowels; with each passing day his flesh was dwindling. Under
Ridolfi's guidance, Giuliano de Solis prepared a compound,
which the priest consumed as a man would consume water in
the desert. As had happened with Jacopo dal Borgo, the effects
of the potion were swift, but in this instance they were terrible.
Father Negri writhed as if wolves were gnawing at his bones; he
screamed that his blood was burning, that he had become blind,
that he was already among the damned. After many hours of
atrocious suffering, Father Negri died, and it was said by those
who had witnessed his death that it would have been better for
all if Ridolfi had not interfered.

It seems that Ridolfi, never a gregarious man, now became
reclusive. He no longer attended Mass. At night his light could
still be observed, moving slowly across the fields, but during
the daylight hours he rarely left his villa. A letter written by
Giuliano de Solis two years after the death of Father Negri states
that he has not conversed with his friend for many months, and
describes him as 'a man lost in the labyrinth of phenomena'. He
also records that it was said that Ridolfi could sometimes be seen
wandering the streets of Castelluccio in the dead of night, weeping. 'But this is to be greatly doubted,' he adds. Because Ridolfi

had correspondents in Germany, he was said to have become a Protestant, or worse. Some alleged that he was an alchemist. Others thought that he had simply become mad.

To date, just three letters written by Ridolfi in his final five years have been identified. In one of these, a single page sent in 1631 to a Florentine lawyer by the name of Giuseppe Troilo, who evidently had been obliged to remain in the plague-ridden city, he wrote: 'The treatments to which you refer are without merit. There is no herb known to me that might offer protection against this pestilence, and none that has any curative power. I can counsel only solitude and prayer.' In January of the following year he sent another brief letter to Troilo, from Naples, after witnessing the eruption of Vesuvius from a fishing boat moored in the bay. The 'terrible and magnificent' explosions threw out 'clouds that rushed to immense heights in an instant', and 'flung aloft great rocks as large as palaces'. He expresses his excitement at the spectacle of the 'burning blood of the earth', the 'infinite power of nature' and its 'glorious disorder'. He also writes of suffering some ill effects, unspecified, of the 'great exertions' to which he had put himself in exploring the sulphur fields of Pozzuoli.

In the Easter week of 1634 he began what was almost certainly his last excursion from Castelluccio. Having spent a week in Pisa, to conclude some business pertaining to the estate of his brother, who had recently died, he continued onward to Milan, where he visited Manfredo Settala, the 'Archimedes of our century', in Settala's workshop in the cloister of San Nazaro. He presented Settala with one of the specimens of the wood-fossil-mineral that had been sent to him by Federico Cesi, and the two men debated at length the nature of this remarkable substance. Ridolfi was inclined to regard it as the relic of something that had once been growing from the soil, whereas Settala's view was that the object was rather an example of nature's mimicry: the 'lapidifying juices' of the earth had fashioned in stone an imitation of a living organism. Ridolfi brought a second gift: a stone that had fallen from the sky with such force that it had killed a horse. In return, Settala gave Ridolfi an object he had carved from an elephant's tusk. They also discussed Settala's design for a machine of perpetual motion, a brass contraption comprising twelve interlocking circles.

Settala's account of the visit makes reference to Ridolfi's deafness. From the last known letter in Ridolfi's hand, sent to Cesi on March 5th, 1635, it seems that he was suffering from tinnitus. He complains of a ringing in his ears, a sound so oppressive that his head has 'become a bell tower'. He is also experiencing difficulties of digestion and excretion, and has had recurrent fevers. 'I sweat like a glassblower', he writes. In the morning his bedding is so wet, 'I might have passed the night at sea.' On the night of March 10th, 1636, Giovan Antonio Ridolfi died at the house of Pietro Appiani, in Piazzetta Bandelli, having been found unconscious at his door. He had no heirs, and so his collection – 'My most dear *studio*, which has brought to me all the honour that my person has been accorded' – was broken up, with most of his specimens being dispersed to museums in Milan, Bologna, Rome and Pisa. Other than the two examples of virtuosic carving held by the Museo Civico of Castelluccio, few items can now be traced with certainty to the Villa Ridolfi. However, five books in the library of the university of Pisa bear annotations in his hand: Fabio Colonna's *Ekphrasis*, Francisco Hernandez's *Treasure of Medical Things from New Spain*, Federico Cesi's *Apiarium*, Caspar Bauhin's *Index to the Theatre of Botany* and Pier Matteo Mattioli's edition of Dioscorides' *Materials of Medicine*. He is buried in Pisa, alongside others of his family.

7.5

The noisy Englishwomen from the Caffè del Corso have camped on the edge of Piazza del Mercato, each with an easel, some facing the loggia, others directing their attention to the Redentore or the Torre del Saraceno. Gideon often goes for days without speaking to anyone except Robert; the life of the artist is incompatible with an active social life, he has always maintained, and he has never wished it were not so; nonetheless, the occasional episode of transient interaction is to be welcomed. He saunters past the easels, and initiates a conversation with the woman who is first to look up.

They are from St Albans, he discovers, and have been attending the same art class for the past five years. Last year they went away for a week in Burgundy; this year it's Tuscany. 'We've left our husbands to fend for themselves,' interjects a woman who's wearing a blue smock that she evidently takes to be the appropriate garb for a *plein air* watercolourist. 'So that's a week's worth of dirty clothes waiting for us when we get back,' adds another, at forty-five or thereabouts the youngest of the crew. 'And a binful of takeaway cartons,' adds the most attractive of the crew, a flirtatious and intense-seeming woman of about sixty, doughy about the jowls but still pretty, with shapely hands and a thick bob of blazing silver hair. They are having a terrific time, they tell him: the weather is so nice, the town is so nice, the countryside is so nice. 'And the men are so much better looking than in St Albans,' chirps smock-lady, to which others assent with a quantity of twittering laughter.

It turns out that they are staying on the Senesi farm, in the apartments in the old barn. A lovely place, is the consensus; very peaceful; but a lot of mosquitoes by the pool. And the owner is an odd little man – not as friendly as you'd expect from an Italian; and his wife seems to be a very nervous woman, but she's more hospitable than her husband, and her breakfasts are terrific, all agree.

While listening, Gideon has inspected the watercolours: they are clumsy and either vapid or lurid, and all are pointless except as a means of passing the time. The woman with the smock is unable to transpose proportions correctly; the silver-haired woman flattens everything out, and sees outbreaks of pink where there aren't any; the youngest one, at work on the Redentore, is about to apply her brush to an area of paper that should be left to dry. 'If I were you, I'd wait,' he says. He advises her to use thinner washes. 'Concentrate on the silhouette,' he tells her.

'Oh?' she responds, as if being pestered at a bus stop by a crank, albeit one who has just made a half-interesting remark.

He tells her that mass can be defined by tonal contrasts.

'So you paint?' asks the silver-haired woman.

'Yes, I do,' answers Gideon.

'Are you here on holiday too?'

'No, I live here,' he replies.

'Lucky you,' she says, an opinion seconded by all.

Then, though he tries to stop himself, he says. 'My name is Gideon Westfall.' After a delay of four of five seconds, the name achieves a reaction from one of the party: a tiny and tremulous woman who has hitherto been concentrating with apparent anguish on her labours. 'The exhibition in the town hall,' she says, with a quick glance, as though answering a quiz master. 'I haven't seen it yet,' she adds, 'but I will.' Mrs Smock hasn't seen it yet, either. 'I'll be going, of course,' she assures him, at which point, to make things worse, Luca Fabris puts in an appearance, gliding like Nosferatu up to Gideon's shoulder. Solemn as a true connoisseur, he peruses the picture of the Redentore, which its creator has just made irredeemable by dropping a blob of too dense colour onto damp paper. Father Fabris addresses the dauber: he commends her work, and the woman actually blushes. He gives Gideon a look which requests support for his praise, which Gideon, withdrawing, withholds.

7.6

Founded in thanksgiving for the town's deliverance from the Black Death, Il Santissimo Redentore – the church of the Most Sacred Redeemer – stands on the east side of Piazza del Mercato, on land that had previously been the site of a hostel used by itinerant merchants. The foundations were laid in 1360, but work seems to have come to a halt almost immediately, and to have proceeded irregularly thereafter. Though the church is not large, it was not until 1454 that it could be consecrated, and even then the exterior was far from being finished, with nothing more than the portal's marble pediment and flanking semi-columns to relieve the bare brick. At some point in the sixteenth century, the façade was covered with a thick rendering of plaster; this was the last change to be made to the exterior of the Redentore, and the unimpressive appearance of the church has been an occasion of intermittent controversy ever since. Locally the church is sometimes referred to as *Il Capannone del Redentore* – the shed of the Redeemer.

The interior is bright and austere, with tall windows of plain glass, eight columns of dark grey pietra serena on each side of the nave, and white plaster covering the walls. The painting on the high altar, *Christ Enthroned*, is by an artist named Andrea di Simone; documents in the Bonvalori archives indicate that it was commissioned by Ercole Bonvalori in 1418, but nothing is known about Andrea di Simone, nor has he been attributed with the authorship of any other work. On the back of the altarpiece there is a *Madonna and Child with Saints*, in which Ercole Bonvalori is shown on the right, with his two legitimate sons, kneeling in front of Saint George and Saint Zeno, facing his wife and daughters, whose protectors are Saint Catherine of Siena and Saint Lucy. This is the oldest painting in the Redentore. The altarpieces in the aisles are mediocre, but one of them, on the third altar on the right-hand side, is at least startling: painted in 1453 by Il Beccafico (1428–1467), it depicts a disfigured Job, writhing in anguish amid a profusion of serpent-like plants. Numerous tombs of the Falcucci family, dating from the fifteenth century to the seventeenth, are to be seen in this aisle.

The Redentore has one other arresting work of art. Should the sacristan be available, ask if you might be allowed to see *La Vecchia*. This is a sculptural altarpiece, in stucco, which was created in 1755 by Gianantonio and Giandomenico Colombini. The plague, fleeing before the figure of Christ, is personified as a naked old woman, whose nostrils and mouth are oozing worms, millipedes and other insects. For a few months the sculpture was displayed in the left transept of the church, but such was the public's revulsion that it was soon removed to a room in the base of the bell tower, where it has stayed. One other item is worth a look: in the right transept, set into the wall, there's a crystal box containing a relic of Saint Zeno – a hemp cloak that was acquired in Rome, at great cost, by Domenico Vielmi and donated to the church in August 1424, the month of his death.

7.7

The Last Supper
2003
Oil-tempera on canvas; 275cm x 365cm
Private collection, Moscow

The Last Supper, Gideon Westfall's only extant painting with an unambiguously Christian subject, is also the largest piece he ever painted.

It was not painted to a commission, but it had been the artist's intention to offer the painting as a gift to the church of the Redentore. This donation was first proposed to Father Luca Fabris by Robert Bancourt, who showed a sheaf of sketches to the priest in order to give him an idea of the general conception. Father Fabris admired the drawings; he was immensely appreciative of Mr Westfall's gesture; but it would, he said, be somewhat difficult for him to accept, as an adornment to the Redentore, a work of art by a man who was not of the faith. This objection had been anticipated, and an answer rehearsed: Guido Reni had been an inveterate gambler, but had nonetheless been hired by the Vatican; Carlo Crivelli abducted a married woman, yet was commissioned by numerous churches, as was Filippo Lippi, who was a lecher and a violator of religious vows; Veit Stoss, sculptor of the great altar of St Mary's Church in Kraków, was a forger who was branded for his deception; Leone Leoni was a man of terrible violence, yet Pius IV paid him to create a monument to

Gian Giacomo Medici, the pope's brother, in Milan's cathedral; and Caravaggio, of course, was a murderer, but does anyone think that the church of Sant'Agostino in Rome is in any way besmirched by the presence of Caravaggio's *Madonna di Loreto*? After further perusal of the sketches, Father Fabris consented to view the picture whenever it might be finished.

More than a year passed, in which time the painting underwent considerable revision. Many representations of the Last Supper depict the moment at which Christ, having broken the bread, tells his followers: *Take, eat: this is my body* (Mark 14:22). Others show the moment at which he bids his disciples to drink, saying: *This cup is the new covenant in my blood; this do ye, as oft as ye drink it, in remembrance of me* (I Corinthians 11:25). Westfall's *Last Supper* does not illustrate either of these utterances, nor does it illustrate Christ's announcement: *I say unto you, that one of you shall betray me* (John 13:21). And Christ in this painting is not delivering the sermon that is recorded in chapters fourteen to sixteen of the Gospel of St John. Westfall's Christ is not speaking: he is looking outward, rather than at any of the Apostles, and they – with one exception – are not looking at Him. Some are in conversation, some are lost in thought, some seem to be doing nothing more than looking around the room in which they are gathered. The table is bare. The betrayal has yet to be declared.

Six disciples are seated on each side of Christ, and none of them has his back to us. Other than Christ's face, however, Judas's face is the only one in full light: the rest are in shade, or obscured by hands, or have been turned away from us. Judas is seated next to Christ, and is looking at Him. A lamp hangs directly above the head of Christ, whose eyes are darkened by the shadow of his brows. He is looking in our direction, but not directly at us. What His expression conveys above all, to use the artist's own words, is a sense of *inconceivable loneliness*.

Father Luca Fabris, upon being shown the finished painting, praised its verisimilitude. One could feel the texture of the wood and breathe the air of that place, he remarked. The quality of the portraiture, he said, was astonishing: 'These are the faces of real men. One knows them, immediately.' But unfortunately, in the view of Father Luca Fabris, these faces were not the faces of Our Lord and His Apostles. Judas in particular was unacceptable: he was, to put it simply, too *simpatico*. Father Fabris (translated by Robert) reminded Mr Westfall that Dante had placed Judas in the deepest pit of the Inferno, in the claws and jaws of Satan himself. He is the vilest of the damned, and yet here, in this picture, we see a man for whom, it would appear, we are being invited to feel compassion. The artist in reply observed that without Judas there would have been no Crucifixion, and without the Crucifixion there is no redemption. Father Fabris quoted the words of Our Lord, recorded by St Mark: *It would be better for him if he had not been born.* Replied the artist: 'I do not disagree. This is what Judas is thinking, before the words have been spoken. Hence my sympathy.'

The figure of Christ was also unacceptable, Father Fabris continued. His face is not the face of Our Redeemer, he said. It has force but it lacks majesty. The painter responded that the model had been a young man he had encountered in Puglia, a young man who was all but unschooled and had suffered great hardships. He was a fighter, like Christ, and his face was expressive of a soul that was wise and – dare he say it? – profoundly good. This was, in short, the perfect face for the carpenter's son who was God in human form. Father Fabris regretted that they were not seeing the same picture. 'And Judas resembles you, a little, I think,' he added.

Father Fabris was correct in this identification: Judas Iscariot was based on studies that the artist had made of himself, some twenty years earlier. Bartholomew was a guest at the Ottocento hotel, a specialist in Etruscan pottery, from Mannheim; James, son of Alphaeus, was a nephew of a friend of Luisa Fava; a friend of Ennio Pacetti provided the figure of Andrew; Simon the Canaanite was a lorry driver, encountered at a pizzeria in Siena; Simon Peter was derived from a photograph of pilgrims at Lourdes, as was St Philip; John and his brother James were twins from Belgium, who attended the 2002 Festa di San Zeno; Thomas was a somewhat masculine Dutch woman, sketched in the Caffè del Corso; Matthew was a furniture restorer from Anghiari; and Thaddeus, whose face was almost entirely hidden, was modelled on Robert Bancourt.

Father Fabris would not take the painting. This decision was inevitable, in the opinion of Carlo Pacetti, who had told Gideon Westfall that *The Last Supper* was perhaps the finest thing he had ever created, and that Father Fabris was an imbecile. The Church was a corporation of imbeciles, he went on, gathering momentum. There is nothing more depraved than Christianity, said Carlo; it is the negation of every healthy and honest instinct; pain and misery are what keeps it alive; the Church is a death-obsessed cult which has as its banner the image of a tortured God, bleeding to death on a cross. The Christ in this *Last Supper*, he told the painter, is no sacrificial victim: he is a captain; he has come through a long battle and foresees harder battles to come. *Who is this King of glory? It is the Lord strong and mighty, the Lord mighty in battle* – this was the man that Westfall had portrayed. This painting has something to say, Carlo Pacetti told him. It is a thinking picture. But a man like Fabris does not think. He is, like all priests, a purveyor of nonsense.

One afternoon, soon after *The Last Supper* had been rejected, Carlo Pacetti, passing Father Fabris in the street, remarked that the *maestro*'s painting was much too good for the Redentore. Father Fabris began to explain that it was not a question of quality. The painting was a fine piece of work, he said, but its spirit was not in keeping with the teachings of the Church. 'The last true Christian died on the Cross,' murmured Carlo Pacetti; he wished the priest good day and went on his way.

7.8

Robert is waiting at the loggia, with a holdall between his feet. 'I have a proposal,' he says. 'A picnic by the pool. It's hot, and it's your last afternoon, and there's bugger all else to do here. Nice

pool. Shame to waste the opportunity. What do you reckon?' He
gives her a mock-chirpy grin, like an impersonation of a stall-
holder encouraging her to buy more stuff than she needs.

She points out that, nice though it may be to take a dip, she
doesn't have a swimming costume.

'Sorted,' he answers, unzipping the bag, to show a carrier
of picnic food, rolled towels, and a new one-piece, electric blue.
'Courtesy of Gideon, from Luisa's shop,' he explains, draping
the swimsuit over the holdall. 'The size will be right, I'm sure.
Gideon can take a woman's measurements in five seconds from
a range of fifty yards.'

'Interesting colour,' she observes. 'Is this his way of telling me
to lighten up?'

'He thinks it'll work well on you,' says Robert, as if merely
conveying a message.

'Does he now?' The heat is extreme; the idea of the water is
alluring. 'Gideon's not joining us?' she inquires.

'You joke,' says Robert.

They call at the hotel for her suntan lotion and book. From
the shade of the Corso they move into the blaze of Piazza della
Libertà, where the wings of the angel on the war memorial seem
to twitch in the heat. When a car drives past its tyres roll on the
road with a gluey sound. They pass through the Porta di Massa,
into air that feels even hotter, with not the slightest movement in
it. Robert, unaffected by the heat, saunters beside her. 'And how
was your morning?' he asks.

'I went to the museum.' She does not want to talk; her lungs
feel as if they are half their normal size and her legs weigh a
hundred pounds apiece.

'Enthralling, isn't it?'

'I liked the carvings,' she says. 'The ivory things.'

He has some information about Ridolfi: his plant collection;
his pickled animals and monsters; his nocturnal expeditions,
wearing his lantern-hat. It's hard to absorb any facts; her brain
has become a gas.

But they are soon at the gate of the villa. It opens onto a gravel slope, which turns tightly at an embankment of lavender and broom, onto the travertine paving that surrounds the pool. There are five white plastic sunbeds beside the water; two have canopies, and Claire drags one of these into the narrow triangle of shade which is cast by the retaining wall of the gravel slope. Robert drops the swimsuit and a towel against the wall and goes over to the other side. He's in the pool before she's finished getting the angle of the sunbed right. She watches him for a length: he swims like a man who has set himself a target before getting back to work; his stroke is inelegant and strenuous.

Having tucked the towel securely into her armpits, Claire undresses. The procedure takes some time – it's as though she imagines herself in the midst of twenty men, all eager for a peek. Eventually the towel comes off. She removes her sunglasses and stands beside the sunbed, arms outstretched, requesting a verdict. The cut of the swimsuit is matronly, but the colour does look good on her, and her legs are surprising: solid, undimpled, like a pale-flesh version of a Maillol woman. He's seen footballers with weaker legs.

Head bowed, she regards herself. 'From here, I have to say, the view is not great. Blackpool beach, 1950.'

'The colour's good.'

'It's OK, I suppose,' she says. With a finger she traces the seam of the leg, as if appraising the thing on a mannequin rather than on her own body. She sits on the sunbed to apply lotion to her face, neck, shoulders, arms, hands, legs, feet. This takes some time. At last she approaches the edge of the pool, doing springy little steps on the hot stone. He anticipates the way she'll enter the water: she'll sit on the side, dabble her feet, and slide herself in. 'How deep is it in the middle?' she asks.

'Over my head.'

She nods and immediately dives in, with as small a splash as a cormorant would make. With each pull of her arms her shoulders rise clear of the water; each kick gives her a surge; her face, swooping up from the water, is as composed as if she were performing a gentle breathing exercise. For twenty minutes she goes up and down, turning with a perfect somersault and surfacing a third of the way down the pool; she's not competing – she swims as if alone in the water – but again and again she overtakes him, though she's swimming breast-stroke and he's using front crawl.

He rests at the deep end, with his forearms on the paving and his chin on his hands, facing the hills. A minute later she stops beside him, in the same posture, leaving a good space between their elbows; her breathing is light. 'Gideon told me something this morning,' she remarks. 'He said he's not had a relationship with a woman since his twenties. A proper relationship. Is that true?'

'Wouldn't know,' he answers. 'Haven't known him that long.'

'OK. But for as long as you've known him – nothing?'

'That's right.'

'Not Luisa?'

'Definitely not Luisa.'

'He's never mentioned anyone else, from before you started working for him?'

'Never.'

'Amazing,' she says. 'He's not exactly a catch – but still, being an artist gives you a kind of glamour, doesn't it? And plenty of opportunities. Artist and model, and all that. Nice-looking women taking their kit off. Things tend to happen, I should think. But with Gideon – nothing?'

'Nothing.'

Her eyes, aimed without focus on the middle distance, seem to indicate a slight and begrudging reappraisal in Gideon's favour. 'I thought he might have been exaggerating,' she says.

Cross-legged she sits beside the sunbed, reading her biography of JFK. She holds the book open in her flattened hands, which rest on her knees, as steady as a lectern; her back and neck are straight and her shoulders level; she is perfectly, admirably still. He cannot stop himself asking: 'You do yoga, by any chance?'

'Yes,' she answers, without looking up.

'Thought so,' he says.

Nothing more is said for a quarter of an hour, then she puts the book down and stands up. 'God, this thing really is hideous,' she says, snapping a leg of the costume as she comes to the side of the pool.

'You could do without,' he suggests. 'I'll be going in a minute. You can stay for as long as you like. Just slam the gate when you go. No one can see you,' he says. 'Look around.'

She does not look around; instead she gives him a look that dismisses the suggestion, then lowers herself into the water. After a dozen sedate lengths she gets out. As he is dressing on the other side of the pool, he hears her make a hissing sound; she has dropped the towel and is picking at her hair, wincing. 'You OK?' he calls across, and in the same moment she yelps, doing a small sideways jump. She swats at the air, where now he sees three or four bees, circling above her head. 'One of the buggers has stung me,' she shouts. There's a shower built into the wall; he tells her to get under it, which she does. A flick of his towel encourages the bees to depart.

'Let me look,' he says, when she steps out of the shower. She tilts her head towards him, pointing to the spot; her scalp is reddened on the crown, and he finds two stings in there. From his wallet he takes a credit card, with which he strokes the stings out of her skin.

'You've done this before,' she says.

'Swipe, never squeeze,' he answers. 'Tweezers are the worst. They squirt the poison in.'

'Thanks for the tip,' she says.

'It would be a good idea to put some ice on this,' he tells her. 'And shampoo, to clean it up.'

She picks up her towel, and he goes over to the other side of the pool to get dressed.

Her scalp is itching, and after she has rubbed her head with the towel the itch gets worse. She sits on the sunbed. A warmth

is spreading into her face from her scalp. The sunbed feels like a
dinghy that a small wave has lifted off the sand. She dries herself,
gets her underwear on. Reaching for her dress, she sees on her
arm a blush that doesn't look like sunburn – can't be sunburn.
There are bumps in the reddened area. One side of her face now
feels sunburned too, and she has the sensation of a thumb pressing on her throat. She can't bring the dress into focus. Beginning
to panic, she calls: 'Robert – something's wrong.' Her tongue
feels much too large; the wall is lurching.

Robert holds her shoulders. Peering into her face, he says
something. The sky is changing colour; she is choking and there
is a banging somewhere, like a huge drum. She sees Robert talking into his phone; she hears him, but can't make out what he's
saying. Heat falls through her body; something has burst.

7.9

She is lying down. A woman's voice is near; the woman is holding her hand and talking to her but it isn't a woman it's Gideon
who is telling her to do something but she doesn't understand
what he's saying to her and he doesn't understand what she's
saying to him. 'Immediately,' she hears someone say. Robert is
speaking; his voice seems to be coming out of an enormous tin
box. Her skin is hot; she is trying to speak but her throat is closing and she cannot remember the words she wants. Robert has
an arm around her. The stone wall is moving, and the air is full
of grey grains. A man's face falls towards her; he has a plastic
triangle in his hand; he smothers her. Gideon is looking angrily
into her face and another man is doing something to her arm.
Her eyelashes are quivering against a milky light; the blue sky
flashes in a window above her head.

Then she is in a very bright room and Robert is talking over
her, to someone she cannot see. He talks to her, as a needle is
put in her arm. She is talking back, but from his face she knows
she is not making sense. Over and over he says the same things:

she is OK; there is nothing to worry about; she has to stay; she is OK. A woman says something to him and he is gone; Gideon has also gone.

When she wakes up Robert is there. He explains what has happened: the sting made her system shut down; her blood pressure plummeted; adrenaline and oxygen did the trick. 'Could have been a lot nastier,' he says. For some reason she puts a kiss on his hand. He writes his mobile number on a tissue. 'They're telling me to go,' he says. 'They'll kick you out in the morning, probably. I'll be here at nine.'

7.10

The Italian honey bee, *Apis mellifera ligustica*, is a sub-species of the Western honey bee (Apis mellifera), and was first described by the Italian entomologist Massimiliano Spinola (1780–1857) in his *Insectorum Liguriæ Species Novæ aut Rariores, quas in agro Ligustico nuper detexit, descripsit, et iconibus illustravit*, published in 1806. Though ill-suited to the winters of northerly latitudes, *Apis mellifera ligustica* thrives in climates ranging from the cool temperate to the subtropical. It produces a large volume of honey, and is the most widely kept honey bee in southern Europe and the Americas.

There are tens of thousands of individuals in a colony, but usually there is just one queen. The queen is the only bee to produce eggs, which are laid singly in the cells of the comb. A queen will lay either a fertilised or an unfertilised egg: fertilised eggs are laid in small worker cells, and develop into female worker bees; unfertilised eggs are laid in the considerably larger drone cells, and develop into haploid male drones. Sustained by a diet of protein-rich royal jelly (a substance secreted from glands on the heads of young workers), the queen deposits eggs continuously, laying as many as two thousand per day in spring. After three or four years, on average, the queen loses the ability to lay fertilised eggs, or can no longer produce the pheromones with which she controls the hive. At this point, the workers will create virgin queens by heavily feeding the larvae of normal workers with royal jelly, which makes them develop into sexually mature females. The ailing queen will then either be killed or will leave the hive with a swarm, to establish a new colony. Except for the mating period in the early weeks of her life (she mates once, with multiple drones, and retains the sperm for years), such a swarming would, in most instances, be the queen's first flight from the hive.

The chief function of the drones is to mate with a queen: drones are peripatetic, rarely mating with the queen of the hive that produced them, and after mating the drone will always die, because its reproductive apparatus is severed in the process. The maximum life expectancy of a drone is about ninety days. The drone has no stinger.

In an average colony of 50–80,000 bees, some two or three thousand will be drones. The rest, except for the queen, will be workers, which are non-reproducing females. For the first twenty days of its life, the worker cleans the hive, feeds the larvae, builds comb cells and stores nectar and pollen; for the rest of its life it forages for pollen and nectar. Worker bees will attack if they sense a threat to the hive. While foraging, on the other hand, they rarely sting except to repel physical contact. The stinging mechanism of the worker honey bee is a modified ovipositor, comprising a venom sac and a barbed stinger, which in turn comprises a stylus flanked by two barbed lancets. Working in opposition to each other, these lancets pull the stylus into the body of the victim by contraction, while contractions of the venom sac insert the apitoxin into the wound. When a bee stings another bee or another insect, it withdraws the stinger before the barbs can engage; if the victim has a skin, however, the barbs become inextricably burrowed in the flesh, and the bee can remove itself only by pulling away from its stinger, an action that inevitably leads to its death. The venom sac will continue to pulsate even after it has been torn from the bee's abdomen, and the injection of apitoxin can continue for several minutes. Alarm pheromones are also released as the apitoxin is being injected, which may attract other bees and incite them to attack.

For a human the sting of the honey bee is relatively mild, but in about two percent of cases the venom causes anaphylactic shock, which can be life-threatening. Queen honey bees can also sting, and the stinger of the queen, lacking barbs, can be used repeatedly; queens, however, use their venom only for killing rival queens, often before pupation has occurred.

7.11

'So she'll be out in the morning?' asks Gideon. He is at work on Turone's picture, and has not yet paused, not even at the words 'anaphylactic shock'.

'Some time tomorrow,' says Robert.

'That's good,' says Gideon, selecting another brush. 'That's good.'

'She'll miss her flight, I think,' says Robert, and Gideon nods. 'They say she should be discharged in the morning, but I doubt it'll be early enough.'

'Hmm,' comments Gideon; it's not clear whether the sound is a response to this information or to the mark he has just made.

'Did you hear what I said?'

'Oh yes,' says Gideon, applying a minuscule quantity of white to the canvas.

'Would you care to repeat it?'

'You think that she'll miss her flight,' he recites. 'You were told she should be discharged in the morning, but you doubt it'll be early enough.'

'I've spoken to Maurizio,' Robert goes on.

'OK,' says Gideon.

For a few seconds Robert watches Gideon at work; with the precision of a thief outwitting a pressure-sensitive alarm, Gideon inserts another speck of white into the image. 'The Ottocento is fully booked from tomorrow. Because of the festival.'

'Of course.'

'So she'll have to go elsewhere.'

'Understood.' He pulls back from the canvas to scrutinise it; he sniffs; the expression says he'll accept what he's done to it. A thicker brush is taken up, and he looks at Robert for a half-second. 'I can't have her here,' he says. 'You know that.'

'Well, she is your niece. And it's only—'

'The fact that she's my brother's daughter is neither here nor there.'

'OK. I thought—'

Gideon takes a steadying breath before advancing the brush. 'Have you tried any of the hotels in Cásole?' he asks.

'No, I haven't. Of course I haven't. I had to talk to you first.'

'There are some decent places in Cásole, aren't there?'

'I believe so.'

'Give them a call. I'll pay for the room. And for her flight. That goes without saying.'

'We cannot pack her off to Cásole.'

'It's not far. She can borrow my car.'

'She didn't come all this way to stay in Cásole.'

'Nice little town. What's the problem?'

'Gideon, I'm not going to take her out of hospital then dump her in a place that's miles away. Don't be ridiculous.'

'Is the Cereria full?'

'Yes, the Cereria is full.'

Affecting to see no alternative to Cásole, Gideon raises his eyebrows and sighs, nonplussed.

'I'll put her up,' says Robert, inevitably. 'If she misses the flight, I'll put her up.'

'You don't have a spare room.'

'I have a sofabed.'

'Of course,' says Gideon. 'I was forgetting.'

'Easily done.'

'But you mustn't feel that you have to.'

'God forbid,' says Robert.

'It might be the best solution, though,' says Gideon. 'I think you're right about Cásole.'

'I'm glad we agree.'

Gideon gives Robert a smile, not of thanks, but of sympathy for finding himself in a situation that has required this inconvenience of him. Returning his attention to the picture, he says: 'I'll pay the bill at Ianni's too. Tell him I'll go over there this evening and settle up, would you?'

'Aye aye, captain,' answers Robert, and here, as if finally hearing the tone, Gideon looks at him again. 'You sure you're OK with this arrangement?' he asks.

'There is no alternative.'

'No, there is an alternative, but we've agreed that it's not preferable.'

'I'm OK. It's only for a day or two.'

Already Gideon's attention has been transferred to the canvas. Arms folded, he exhales loudly and raises his gaze to the ceiling. 'Christ,' he murmurs, 'I want shot of this damned thing.' He jabs the picture lightly with a brush, as if sticking a dart into a photo of someone he cannot abide. Then he says: 'She should stay for the festival, don't you think? Shame to miss it. How would you feel about that?'

'Another day doesn't make much difference.'

'But you mustn't—'

'If she wants to stay, that'll be fine. You can reimburse me for whatever she takes from my fridge.'

'Of course.'

'I was joking,' Robert tells him, turning to go back down. He's at the top of the stairs when Gideon says, as if this is what he's been waiting to say all along: 'I would only have been in the way, if I'd come with you.'

'I don't think so,' Robert replies.

'No, I would. Chaos enough without me there,' he says, looking at him more directly than at any previous point in the conversation. He strokes the brush across the palette. 'And hospitals give me the willies,' he says, arresting the movement of his brush for a moment.

'Whereas I love them,' says Robert, descending. 'See you tomorrow.'

'Give my regards to Teresa.'

'I shall.'

'Thank you. For everything.'

'Not at all. *A domani.*'

'*A domani.*'

7.12

'But what exactly happened?' asks Teresa, lowering the volume of the TV; she turns to give her full attention to his account. 'Frightening,' she comments, with a chilled quiver of the head. 'Will you go and fetch her?'

'I will,' he answers, expecting trouble, but there – with a nod that makes no comment other than acknowledgement – the subject is finished.

'I had a good day at work,' she tells him, getting up. 'We sold a house. We actually sold a house. A big one. The villa at Pievescola. To a Belgian. A big fat Belgian with lots of cash.' She goes into the kitchen and returns with two glasses and a half-full bottle of Verdicchio. A toast is drunk to the improving fortunes of the Tranfaglia property agency.

The film that she's been watching has only half an hour left to run: it's a supernatural thriller, 'totally stupid,' she says; she tells him what the twist will be, and it turns out she's right. She apologises for being so tired the previous night.

Leaving the lights off, she opens the bedroom window and the shutters. She leans out to peg the shutter back, and the pale light of the streetlamp slides over an arm, a breast; she turns and straightens, presenting herself, arms wide, then steps forward to kiss him.

With a fingertip he relishes the sleek skin of her hip, and her gaze remains for a second where his touch has been. A smile appears to approve the form that she is making, and the form that they make together. Then, laughing, she falls onto him. She shrieks, and bites a hand to quieten herself when Renata bangs on the other side of the wall.

In the early hours of the morning he wakes up. Teresa is not there; the bathroom light is on. Ten minutes pass before she comes back. 'OK?' he asks.

'Renata was awake,' she explains.

8

8.1

IN JANUARY 1883 the town council of Castelluccio held a competition for the design of a theatre. Twelve months later it was announced that the contract had been won by the Sienese architect Andrea Gaetano, who had conceived a building which, while alluding to the Gothic architecture of his home city, and to the Palazzo Pubblico in particular, would also 'harmonise with the urban fabric of Castelluccio'. To make way for the theatre, three houses were demolished on Via del Corso, which soon after became Corso Garibaldi. On July 5th 1886 an audience of three hundred and fifty attended the inaugural presentation: *La moglie del giudice* (The Judge's Wife), written especially for the occasion by Fabio Benedetti, a playwright from Modena. Both the author and the architect were on stage to receive the acclamation of the townspeople.

The embroidered image on the stage curtain, depicting the town from an aerial perspective, was derived from a picture by Domenico Scattolin of Volterra, who also painted the ceiling fresco, showing Apollo, Orpheus and the Muses. The other notable decorative features of the horseshoe-shaped auditorium were the pairs of female figures, in painted wood, which flanked the central boxes of each of the theatre's three tiers. Carved by Maurizio Puppa, two of these figures were modelled on Puppa's wife, two on his wife's twin sister, and two on his eldest daughter. Only the last pair survived the fire that severely damaged the interior in 1931. The ceiling fresco was destroyed in the blaze, as was the curtain, and although the cast-iron framework that supported the boxes did not collapse, the structure was deemed to be unsafe, and the Teatro Civico was closed. It remained unused for the next four decades.

Restoration and consolidation was funded primarily by the film actor Filippo Beltrami, whose great-grandfather, Cesare Beltrami, had created the role of the judge in *La moglie del giudice*. Renamed the Teatro Gaetano, the theatre reopened in 1973, but in 1991 it closed again. It has remained closed ever since.

8.2

Gideon, on his way down the Corso, at the end of his morning walk with Trim, notices Giovanni Cabrera and a gaggle of his pals, outside the Teatro Gaetano, apparently looking at the door. Visible above their heads is the blond crew-cut of a thin middle-aged man in a black suit and black shirt, to whom one of the boys appears to be explaining something, until Giovanni, noticing Gideon, stubs out his cigarette on the theatre's step, whereupon, as if at a signal, Giovanni and his entourage slope off. The man in the black suit remains; he wipes his glasses with a cloth, while considering the theatre door. Gideon goes closer and sees, in scarlet spray-painted capitals, filling the entire width of the double door: *ILARIA ERA QUI.*

The man puts his glasses back on, scrutinises the graffiti again, then turns to direct at Gideon the nod of a detective greeting a colleague who's belatedly turned up at the scene of an incident that's not worth the effort of investigating. Gideon recognises the face from the festival website: he's the composer, the Danish chap.

'Ilaria was here,' the man reads aloud, as though reading a cryptic message of which he was the intended recipient.

'Or not, as the case may be,' says Gideon, to no discernible effect.

'She is a friend of those boys,' says the composer, in a drone of accentless English. 'She is missing from her home.'

'I know,' says Gideon. 'Everybody knows.'

The man looks at him again. It is clear that he has never heard of Ilaria before; it also seems possible that he doesn't know who Gideon is, though it's possible that he knows but isn't letting on. Carlo once had a pair of German students come into the garage in a disintegrating campervan; they'd driven from Berlin to Città di Castello to talk to some Italian composer who lived there, then had decided to visit the Danish composer in Radicóndoli. He wouldn't let him in; they could see him in his pool, barely fifty feet from the gate, but he wouldn't give them a minute of his time. He swims for an hour each day, even in the dead of winter, Gideon has heard. A cold fish of a man. And Luisa saw him at the market once, in Piazza del Mercato, and she said you could feel the freezing air around him.

'Do you like this building?' asks the cold fish, out of idle interest.

'I do,' says Gideon.

The man examines the façade for a few seconds, giving it a chance to reveal some mitigating qualities, then pronounces: 'I cannot care for it. Fake medievalism. Horrible.'

Gideon smiles, as you would at a manifestation of immature dogmatism.

'Nice dog,' says the composer. He crouches to cup Trim's jaw in a hand; stroking the animal's head, he looks into its eyes with the intent of a dog-show judge. 'Fine dog,' he says, with a congratulatory nod, then he walks off.

8.3

Albert Guldager was born in Copenhagen on June 18th, 1956. His father was an architect and proficient amateur pianist; his mother, a researcher with a pharmaceuticals company, played clarinet to a high standard. Albert was the youngest of four children, all of whom had musical talent. Albert, however, was exceptional: by the age of seven he was writing pieces for his parents to play, and at the age of seventeen he entered the Royal Danish Academy of Music, to study violin, piano and composition. He was marked as an outstanding student, and in 1975 won an award for his *Sonatina for Piano*.

The influence of Messiaen was conspicuous in the Sonatina and in his other student compositions. Soon after graduating, however, he immersed himself in the music of Bach and other masters of the eighteenth century, and subsequently produced a number of neo-Baroque canons and fugues of immense complexity. He played one of these fugues as an encore, after a piano recital of music by Bach, Brahms and Bartók in Odense, in July 1978; though the concert was well received, this was to be Guldager's first and last public appearance as an instrumentalist. In an interview in 1998, he would admit that he was still haunted by dreams in which he was once again sitting in the dressing room of the hall in Odense, paralysed by stage fright.

A few months after the Odense recital he married Annelise Thomsen, a cellist. He continued to write: mostly piano pieces, in which, though strict counterpoint was still employed, a distinctive voice of his own was now emerging. His official opus 1, *Piano Study 1*, was written during this happy phase of Guldager's life, a phase that came to an abrupt end on March 4th, 1981. That afternoon, walking through the district of Copenhagen in which he and Annelise were living, he passed a block of apartments on which builders were at work, on scaffolding. As he was waiting to cross the road, the scaffolding began to tremble. There was a cry from above; in the next instant, a man struck the road. 'For a minute, this man was still alive, at my feet,' Guldager recalled.

'His blood was on my clothes. It was the most terrible thing, and it changed my life. It was like a vision. For a while it made me lose my mind.'

For a long time he could not write and could not bear to touch an instrument. When at last he did return to playing, he would play chords on the piano – the same chords, repeatedly, for hours at a time. He acquired a tam-tam, a magnificent instrument which produced a sound that took almost three minutes to decay; some days he would do nothing but listen to the voice of the tam-tam. 'I left music – or music left me – for two years,' says Guldager. 'I lived in sound. I rediscovered its power, its innocence. I learned that a single sound is not a single sound. A single note, played on the piano, is not a point: it is an explosion. That is what I learned.'

His neighbours complained of the monotonous noise that came from the Guldagers' apartment. Albert and Annelise moved to the countryside, where he continued to explore 'the very heart of music'. Not long after they had left Copenhagen, the Guldagers separated. He had become interested in non-Western music, and now he travelled to India, where he remained for six months. Upon returning to Denmark, he decided that he needed to up-root himself from his homeland, to start again from scratch. In the spring of 1984 he moved to Paris, where he found himself writing with unprecedented energy. The *Three Night Pieces for Piano*, published and premiered in 1985, brought him to the attention of the musical public of Paris. Other small-scale piano pieces followed quickly, all of them characterised by slow tempi and kaleidoscopic changes in the timbre and dynamics of repeated chords. He lived – as he continues to live – frugally. For a while he taught piano and violin, privately, to a small group of young students, but though he enjoyed teaching, and all that Paris had to offer a musician, Guldager came to feel that, as he put it: 'My place is on the periphery.' So in 1987 he moved to the village of Radicóndoli, in Tuscany. 'Italy is the land of Rossini, Donizetti, Verdi, Puccini. It is a country of melody, and I am not a man of melody. I do not fit, and that is what I need,' he told his interviewer.

In the backwater of Radicóndoli he became more productive
then ever. He continued to write for piano – a series of *études*,
begun in 1989, now comprises nineteen pieces, ranging in length
from forty seconds to ten minutes – but the great majority of his
work since his departure from Paris has been for strings and
other chamber ensembles, often with percussion. The scale of
Guldager's work also changed with his move to Italy: after the
first of the études, the next three works that he completed were
his 'triptych' of three pieces for chamber orchestra, the shortest of
which, the *Second Piece for Small Orchestra*, is forty minutes long,
while the longest, *Third Piece for Small Orchestra*, lasts more than
an hour. The latter is perhaps the best known of all his works
to date, having been recorded no fewer than three times, and is
typical of his orchestral writing in the 1990s: rising above *piano*
only once in its entire duration, the *Third Piece for Small Orchestra*
is almost devoid of melodic and rhythmic incident, proceeding
instead through a succession of microtonal shadings and inflec-
tions of timbre, with several intervals of complete or near silence,
building to a subdued climax before ebbing away. The use of
quarter tones is at times redolent of Middle Eastern modes, and
the metallic mutes on some of the strings create buzzing overtones
that are similar to those of the sitar. These non-European elements
are also typical of his output at that time. His 1994 song-cycle,
Four Hölderlin Poems – which was written immediately after his
marriage to the American contralto Claudia Magris, and brought
him awards from France and Germany – owes something to
Guldager's discovery of the great Egyptian singer Uum Kulthum.
He speaks of hearing a tape of a three-song two-hour concert by
Uum Kulthum as one of the pivotal moments of his life.

The five string quartets of 1998–2000 – which resemble the *Pieces
for Small Orchestra* in their use of glissandi, innovative timbres
and episodes of silence – were followed by four string duos: one
for cello and viola, one for two violins, one for two cellos, and
one for two violas. This sequence of compositions marks another
evolutionary shift in Guldager's oeuvre. A movement towards

brevity is notable. The first quartet was an expansive work of more than an hour's duration, but each of the succeeding quartets was briefer than its predecessor: *Quartet Number Five* is a single-movement that lasts a little over fifteen minutes in performance. None of the duos is significantly longer than the last quartet, and the same is true of Guldager's subsequent works, which have also been characterised by textures that are more austere than those of the pieces written in the 1990s. The music has become more compressed, its utterances more fleeting and provisional. The role of silence has become more prominent than ever, and whereas the pieces for chamber orchestra all pivoted on a central episode (however muted), these later compositions ebb and flow without creating any sense of destination or centre. They are, as a critic of the *Süddeutsche Zeitung* expressed it, 'like excerpts from an infinite music. They lead you nowhere: they start and they end, as does life. What they offer, if you are prepared to listen acutely, is an experience of enriched time.' Many of these later pieces are imbued with what the same critic described as 'a precarious serenity'.

Acclaimed, especially in France and Germany, as one of the most significant composers at work today, Albert Guldager has published more than fifty works. The piece composed for the Festa di San Zeno in Castelluccio – scored for flute, saxophone, bassoon, violin, cello and tam-tam – is his opus 63.

8.4

Gideon is seated before his self-portrait, mixing a whorl of carmine on a palette, with the mirror set aside. He slumps on the stool as if he's been sitting there for hours; his eyes are directed towards the canvas, but seem to be seeing nothing; his hand moves in circles like a slow rotor.

'*Buongiorno,*' Robert announces from the top step.

'And good day to you, Roberto,' answers Gideon, continuing to stir.

'Claire rang an hour back,' says Robert; Gideon nods. 'They're letting her out this morning. She'll call when I can fetch her.'

'OK,' says Gideon, as if all he'd heard was a request for permission to leave.

'She can't make the flight now.'

'Of course,' says Gideon. He inserts the tip of a brush into the paint and applies a dab to the picture; he draws his head back to examine the mark he has made, and a scowl appears. 'Does she want to stay for the festival?'

'We haven't discussed it. But I think she should.'

Another speck of colour goes onto the canvas; this one is more satisfactory, it would appear. 'If you don't mind having a lodger,' he says.

'Fine with me.'

His face is close to the surface now, as he makes a quick succession of strokes, none longer than a couple of millimetres; a rose is taking shape.

'I'll suggest it,' says Robert.

Having executed another half-dozen strokes, Gideon examines this portion of the picture, squinting as if to peer through the keyhole of a jewellery box. 'Saw that Danish character this morning,' he remarks, as Robert is opening the door of his room. 'The composer. Grim individual. Can imagine him in a black gown. With a scythe.'

'So I've heard. Teresa—'

'Someone has scrawled Ilaria's name on the theatre,' Gideon goes on.

'I saw,' says Robert.

'What do you make of it?'

'Someone's idea of a joke.'

'Her idea of a joke?' Gideon asks, as if he'd be disappointed in her if it turned out to be so.

'Unlikely,' Robert answers.

At last Gideon looks at him; immediately he seems to be persuaded that it is indeed unlikely. 'It'll be that Cabrera boy,' he says. 'He was there when I went past. Admiring his handiwork, I'll bet.'

'Not impossible,' Robert agrees; seeing that Gideon has nothing more to say about it, for now, he goes into his room. When he comes out, half an hour later, Gideon is standing at one of the tables, leafing through a sketchbook.

'Who was this?' he asks, turning the book to show the face of an African man. 'There's no date on it.'

Robert comes over to the table to look at the face. 'He's the guy who was selling sunglasses in Siena. On Via di Pantaneto. From Senegal. About six foot six. Abdoulaye – was that his name?'

'Christ, I can't remember a damned thing about him.'

'He had a big piece of cardboard with the sunglasses poking through it. So he could fold it and run when the police appeared.'

Gideon rubs his forehead hopelessly. 'Completely gone. No recollection whatsoever.' For a full minute he stares at the face of the Senegalese street vendor, defeated. 'Good job I have you,' he says, 'so I can outsource my memory. Mine is going, I tell you.' He turns the pages, smiling like a simpleton in vacant-minded pleasure at what he sees there. A few minutes later, still browsing, while Robert washes a brush at the sink, he asks: 'But tell me: did you sleep with her?'

'What?'

'Did you sleep with her?'

'Who?'

'Ilaria.'

'No, I didn't.'

'OK. But what—'

'For God's sake, Gideon. I did not have sexual relations of any variety with Ilaria, as you know.'

Eyes screwed tight, pretending to inspect a drawing, Gideon murmurs an apology.

Back in his room, Robert recalls walking along the Corso with Ilaria. 'You find me attractive,' she stated, and he replied that yes, she was attractive. 'You would like to take me to bed,' she said, disregarding the people around them, as if she thought that by conducting herself as though she were talking about the weather, no one would overhear.

'No,' he replied.

'You are not telling the truth,' she told him; her face was stern, as unsexual as it was possible to be; she might have been right. 'Well, we could,' she said, as they passed the Cabrera shop and she waved at the glass, behind which Giovanni might have been watching.

'That would be a bad idea,' said Robert.

'But it could be fun,' she answered, with a moment of concentration about the eyes, as if calculating the odds of enjoyment.

'It would be a bad idea,' he repeated.

To which she answered brightly: 'OK'. And that was their only discussion of the subject. His phone rings.

'I'm off to the hospital,' he informs Gideon.

'OK,' Gideon whispers, putting the brush onto the canvas as if suturing a blood vessel in an open chest.

8.5

Self-Portrait, Castelluccio, 2010
Oil-tempera on canvas; 85cm x 85cm
Begun 2010; unfinished
Collection of Robert Bancourt

At the 1972 degree show at the Camberwell School of Art, Gideon Westfall exhibited five paintings, one of which was a self-portrait, showing the young artist seated on a bench, against a shabby white wall, under neon lights, arms crossed, facing the viewer square-on. His expression suggested a certain guardedness, and that he would rather not be sitting on this bench, being looked at. The self-portrait was intended, he later said, as the distillation of three years of disillusion. Its technical accomplishment was acknowledged by his tutors, but with little enthusiasm: it was well done, said one, but it lacked 'relevance'. A professor admitted to feeling a deep disappointment when he looked at Gideon Westfall's paintings: there was artistry here, but no art. The self-portrait was sold, to a doctor from Greenwich, on the first day of the exhibition. This was his first significant sale. Prior to the degree show, he had sold just one work: a still life, in pastels, of fossils and geological samples, bought by his art teacher at school for £2.

Self-portraits comprise a substantial portion of Gideon Westfall's output. Discounting the Camberwell picture, seven self-portraits in oil were completed in the 1970s and 1980s, of which three were sold and four destroyed by the artist, and the frequency with which he returned to this subject increased markedly following the death of his mother in 1991. After moving to Italy, two years later, he observed an annual period of intensive self-study: each year, on August 1st, his birthday, he began a new self-portrait. Some were abandoned and some discarded, but no fewer than thirteen self-portraits were completed in Castelluccio.

In addition to the twenty-one extant self-portraits, Westfall appears in several of his other works. He is sitting at an outside table in *Caffè del Corso* (2007), for example, and his face is reflected in the window in his *Portrait of Carlo Pacetti* (2005). He also appears in one of his most controversial pictures, *Epicurus in Hell* (1977), a 'philosophical fantasia', as he termed it, derived from the tenth canto of Dante's *Inferno*.

In Dante's poem the heretical followers of Epicurus – who believed that the soul was mortal, like the body – are encountered in the sixth circle of Hell, but Epicurus himself is not described. Westfall, however, shows the philosopher seated on the edge of a tombstone, in a valley of maroon soil and rocks, under a purple-black sky, addressing a figure – Dante, we must assume – of whom we see only a foot and a portion of cloak. Care-worn rather than in agony, Epicurus has the demeanour of a man who knows that he has won his argument and that his interlocutor – though he could never admit it – knows it too; behind Epicurus, each seated on his own tomb, his followers – one with the artist's face – look on with pained admiration. Westfall has given Epicurus the features of Martin Calloway, in tribute to his mentor's *insistence on the primacy of the evidence of our senses, and his disdain for fame and luxury*. The picture was included in *The New Classicism* show, where it was disparaged by one critic as *a subterranean seminar in Athenian fancy dress*; another called it *the most ludicrous painting I have seen this year*. It was sold, on the second day of the exhibition, to a businessman from Saudi Arabia.

The 2010 self-portrait, which is unique in Westfall's output in taking the form of a tondo, is unfinished; it was on an easel in his studio at the time of his death. The artist looks at us from the far side of a table which is strewn with drawings, books, pencils, brushes and other paraphernalia of his profession. One hand grasps the edge of the table; the other is pressed onto a large sheet of paper, on which a Roman ruin has been sketched. He is stooping over the table, and seems preoccupied, as if our arrival has momentarily distracted him from his work. Rose petals are scattered over an open book: an allusion to the rose petals in Lorenzo Lotto's *Portrait of a Young Man* (Venice, Accademia). The Lotto painting is freighted with other elusive symbols (letters, a hunting horn, a lizard, a ring), and the Westfall painting likewise has details that invite and confound interpretation. Light enters the scene from behind, where, through an open window, we see a tall stone tower – a taller and broader version of the Torre del Saraceno – that has a tree growing from its roof; the tree is a laurel, and the laurel, of course, was the tree into which Daphne was transformed, whereupon it became the sacred tree of Apollo, the god of light, of truth and prophecy, of medicine, of music, poetry and the arts. The window opens into a narrow street, on the opposite side of which, perched on a gutter, there is an owl, which is facing the room but has its eyes closed. In ancient Greece the owl was associated with Athena, goddess of wisdom and the arts. Is it significant, then, that the owl in this picture has been placed at a remove from the artist, and is perhaps asleep? In Rome the goddess of wisdom was given the name Minerva, whose emblem was the ever-vigilant owl, but the bird was also regarded as a harbinger of death: the cry of an owl was often taken as a warning of imminent demise, and to see an owl in daylight was a bad omen. The owl in Westfall's last self-portrait is seen in daylight.

8.6

When she wakes up she sees exactly what she saw when she awoke in the night: a woman seated on a wooden chair beside the bed opposite, holding the hand of the sleeping old woman, who must be her mother. The daughter is aged about fifty, and is dressed entirely in brown; she has a sort of shawl over her head, and her head is bowed, as if her mother's hand were a book in which she is reading the story of the life that is now coming to its close. With a thumb she repeatedly strokes the hand; otherwise, she is motionless. Her mother's mouth, always open, sometimes moves as if to close, then gapes again; her jawbone has only a film of skin to cover it; her eye sockets are huge, like two bowls with a marble in each, under tissue; her arms have not enough muscle in them to make them move; the veins might have been painted onto the skin with blue-black ink.

It is six o'clock. She wants to go back to sleep, but it's not possible to stop looking, though the dying woman and her daughter make her remember her father, watching his wife die, at her bedside every minute of that final week, talking to her in a whisper, constantly, as if she could hear and understand every word, though barely a word came back. It is unbearable, the memory of it; she is glad to have the distraction of a sudden contempt for Gideon. Her mother's life ended terribly, yet Gideon had no compassion; he should be forced to know how it ended, she tells herself; he should be forced to know what her parents endured. Then the old woman makes a faint whistling sound, and Gideon is banished.

She closes her eyes and begins to fret about missing her flight. If she can be out of the hospital by nine o'clock – nine-thirty at the latest – she should be able to get to the airport on time. At seven-thirty, as she is about to call Robert, to ask him if he can come right away, to try to speed things up, a nurse arrives, takes her temperature and blood pressure, and tells her that she will be seen by the doctor this morning, but cannot say exactly when. 'One hour, maybe a little more,' she says. Fifteen minutes later the nurse comes back. 'Two hours, perhaps a little more,' she says. She rings Robert, and asks him if he could find out about seats on the later flight; a text arrives within a couple of minutes – *No seats*; she replies that she'll let him know when she's getting out – there's no need to come yet. At eleven o'clock two doctors arrive, one grey and professorial, the other young and bright. The young one puts questions to her, in English; the senior one examines her eyes, her mouth, her back, her hands; her temperature and blood pressure are taken again. The doctors withdraw; they confer; the senior partner leaves, and the junior comes back to her. She has recovered, he tells her; and she has an allergy to bee stings. 'So you must be careful,' he says, as he shakes her hand. She calls Robert, who says he is leaving right away, and at that very moment a different nurse arrives. 'You can go,' says the nurse, with a brittle little smile, as if surprised to find that she hasn't vacated the premises already. The nurse bundles up her clothes and directs her towards the bathroom.

The bed has been stripped by the time she returns, and the nurse has gone; the woman in the shawl, still holding her mother's hand, has not once looked up. Out in the corridor, she passes the young doctor; evidently she looks lost, because he asks: 'You are waiting for somebody?' He walks with her to the junction with another corridor, which is sunlit towards the far end. 'There is a garden,' says the doctor. 'A nice place to wait. You are OK now. No worries.' He shakes her hand again. The garden is an area of grass with one flowerbed, a fig tree, three wooden benches, and a small rectangular pool, clogged with weeds. A heavily breathing man with whiskers like iron filings is sitting on one of the benches, in his pyjamas, grasping the steel stand of a drip, glowering at her as though he suspects she might try to snatch the drip away; one of the other benches is occupied by a smiling man whose eyes are shut and whose hair is covered by a thick elasticated dressing, bloodstained at the temple; the third bench is free. She sits down; the smiling man continues to smile, eyes shut; the man with the drip has redirected his gaze at the fig tree, from which is coming the twittering of a bird. The twittering is incessant, but for a minute or two it's pleasant; then it becomes as irritating as an unanswered phone. She gets up from the bench and goes over to the fig tree; the singing ceases; she peers into the leaves, and sees a plump little brown bird. As soon as she returns to the bench, the twittering resumes. The man with the drip grates his teeth in what may be meant to be a sardonic grin; the smiling man pats his dressing, eyes still closed.

8.7

Known in English as the Garden Warbler, *Sylvia borin* is a passerine songbird of the Sylviidae family, and is widespread and common in Europe and western Asia. It is primarily an insectivorous species, but also eats soft fruits, especially in the autumn months, when it requires high-energy food in preparation for its winter migration to central and southern Africa. Its name in Italian is *beccafico*, or fig-eater. Its binomial, *Sylvia borin*, was created in 1783 by the Dutch physician and naturalist Pieter Boddaert (1730/33–1795), in the table of names that he compiled to accompany the 973 hand-coloured plates produced under the supervision of Edmé-Louis Daubenton for Buffon's *Histoire naturelle des oiseaux*, which was itself a by-product of the Comte de Buffon's encyclopaedic *Histoire naturelle, générale et particulière*.

The *beccafico* is a sturdy bird, on average 13–14.5cm in length, and is visually distinguished from other warblers by the dullness of its appearance: the plumage is brown-grey, with a paler underbelly; it has no clear markings on its wings; and the face is likewise plain, though there is a faint white ring around the eye. Its typical lifespan is two years, but Garden Warblers have lived beyond fourteen years in captivity.

The song of the *Sylvia borin* is a melodiously bubbling chatter that can last as long as ten seconds, and is easily confused with that of the blackcap (*Sylvia atricapilla*), the species to which it is most closely related. Like the ortolan (*Emberiza hortulana*), the *beccafico* has long been considered a great delicacy, but the edible *beccafico* is not always a Garden Warbler – the name *beccafico* has been applied since Roman times not only to *Sylvia borin* but to a variety of small migratory birds. The ortolan – now a protected species in France, but still eaten there – is prepared by being blinded or caged in a light-proof box, fattened on millet and drowned in armagnac; the *beccafico* is rarely fattened artificially for consumption.

8.8

He sees her through the window: with her head resting on the back of the bench, she's gazing at the sky, so immersed in whatever she's thinking about that she's unaware that the gaze of the man with the drip is riveted to her chest. But when he opens the door she notices his arrival immediately and jumps to her feet so quickly that she staggers, grabbing the arm of the bench. The ogler, grasping his drip like a banner of the seriously ill, smirks maliciously, and leers at Claire's rear view as she passes. At the other bench, a man with closed eyes and a bandaged head is smiling as though watching a comedy show on the inside of his eyelids.

'How are you feeling?' he asks, holding the door open.

'A wash and a change of clothes and I'll be right as rain.' Passing a framed picture of San Gimignano, she halts for a second to look at her reflection. Raking her fingers through her hair, she says: 'I was a mess, wasn't I?'

'You were in shock.'

'Did I pass out?'

'Yes.'

'I remember the ground going wobbly. Did I say anything stupid? I think I thought I was being arrested.'

'You weren't entirely sure where you were.'

'I was babbling, wasn't I? What did I say?'

'You were concerned about your sandals.'

She looks down at her dusty footwear and shakes her head.

In the foyer he buys a bottle of water; she drinks most of it in less then a minute. 'Don't I have to sign papers or something?' she asks.

'Taken care of. The insurance is sorted. Gideon found the policy in your room.'

'I hope he's not annoyed that you've taken time off to retrieve me.'

'Of course he isn't.'

'I was joking,' she says. 'Half joking.'

'He was worried.'

'Not that worried. He wasn't here, was he? Or was he?'

'We're over there,' he says, pointing in the direction of the car.

She winds down the window; for a minute or two she looks straight ahead, impassively, hands meshed in her lap; he almost asks her what she's thinking about. 'Bugger about the flight,' she says.

'Might as well stay for the festival now,' he suggests. 'Only a few more days. Make the trip worthwhile. Bit of fun and folklore.'

'It's been worthwhile,' she states quietly, still looking ahead. 'I'm glad I met him. It's been interesting. And it's a nice little town. But I have to go tomorrow.'

'No seats tomorrow.'

'Really?'

'None tomorrow, and only one left on Saturday, which will probably have gone by the time we get back. And if you're staying till Saturday you might as well stay for the festival. Unless you absolutely have to be back in London right away, in which case we could look at flights from Rome. Flying from Pisa, there are a few seats on Sunday, but that's the big day. Plenty on Monday.'

'You've checked all the flights?'

'All from Pisa. Not Rome.'

She looks aside, considering. 'How would I get to Rome?' she asks.

'I'd drive you. It's not far. Three hours or so.'

After a pause she answers: 'I really can't afford to stay.'

'Well, you can. The hotel's taken care of.'

'What do you mean?'

'Paid. Gideon has settled the bill.'

'No,' she says. 'I can't have that.'

'He got a discount.'

'I can't let him pay.'

'It's done.'

'I'll pay him back.'

'Believe me, Claire, you can't win this one.'

She frowns, then asks: 'Has he paid for tonight as well?'

'No,' he answers. 'The hotel is booked out, so we've moved your stuff to my flat. You can stay there, until whenever.'

'Yours rather than Gideon's?'

'Nobody has ever stayed in Gideon's place. His apartment is his monastery.'

'A monastery with naked ladies.'

'Exactly.'

'You have a spare room?'

'No. But you'll have it pretty much to yourself. During the day I'll be up with Gideon most of the time. Then I'll be at Teresa's, probably. And if I'm not, there's a sofa bed.' Receiving no response, not even a glance, he goes on: 'So you can treat the place as your own, but if you want to try Rome instead, we'll do that.' She nods, then turns her face into the rush of air.

When they get to his door she looks exhausted. 'You should take a nap,' he says, and she agrees. He opens the bedroom door.

'I can take the sofa bed,' she says.

'We can argue about that later,' he replies. 'For now, take the bed. The sheets are fresh, and if you want to eat, there's plenty in the fridge.'

'Thank you,' she says, and she sits on the bed. Sweat is coursing out of her hair, and her breathing is loud.

'Are you sure you're all right?'

'Fine, thank you. Just snoozy.'

'OK. I'll get back upstairs. But if you need me, give me a call. My phone will be on.'

'Thank you,' she says, taking off her sandals. She lies down on the bed.

8.9

She is having a dream in which she is on a roof, in a town she doesn't know, and every roof except hers is packed with people, looking up at the sky in an atmosphere of patience, and from somewhere there's a banging noise, but nobody else can hear it – everyone keeps gazing at the clouds, though the banging continues and she's in a room she doesn't know, with walls as white as a hospital's walls and a lot of sunlight and her clothes on hangers on the back of a door, beyond which there is again a knocking. Her head is like a boulder and her eyelids are as thick as bacon; her watch tells her she's been asleep for four hours. She levers herself into a sitting position and swings her feet onto the floor. The floor is cool terracotta and has no clutter on it. The ceiling light is a globe of white glass; on one wall, above a shelf of books there's a shelf of identical box-files, one marked *CAMPANI*, another *RIDOLFI*; a dark chest of drawers is on the other side of the room, with a matching wardrobe; her bag is on a chair; there are no clothes lying around; the air smells faintly of cedar.

She hears another knock, then a key going into the lock, and Gideon's voice, calling: 'Hello? Hello?' When she opens the bedroom door he is standing in the hall; a vast smile appears. 'Welcome back,' he sings, loud enough to be heard in the street.

Rubbing her eyes, she says: 'I was asleep.'

'Good, good,' says Gideon, nodding sagely. 'How are you feeling? Robert said you've been given the all-clear.'

'That's right.'

'Allergic to bees, I gather.'

'So it seems.'

'Rather alarming, I have to say.' He ushers her into the living room. 'Looked like a serious situation. Well – it was a serious situation, of course. But it looked very bad. Good job the medics arrived *prontissimo*.'

'Yes.'

'They looked after you OK in the hospital?'

'Very well.'

'And Robert was on hand.'

'He was very helpful, yes.'

Gideon looks around the room, as if it were hers. 'Look—' he begins.

'I know what you're going to say,' she interrupts. 'And it doesn't matter. Robert took care of everything.'

'My Italian is dreadful. I couldn't talk to the doctors like Robert.'

'Exactly.'

'And to tell you the truth—'

'Hospitals give you the willies.'

'They do,' he confesses, with a plastic grimace at his own weakness.

'Same here,' she says, and she looks him steadily in the eye, so that he will know what she means.

His eyes show not the slightest sign that he has taken the reference. 'Dreadful places,' he says.

'Though most people in them are getting better,' she points out.

'Yes,' he concedes. 'But—'

'Many are not.'

'Quite.' Still he doesn't seem to make the connection.

'And you had work to do. I understand,' she says. From the tone and the expression, she hopes, nobody could tell if this remark was intended to cut; Gideon appears unwounded. 'You settled my bill at the hotel,' she goes on.

His hands rise, self-deprecating. 'It wasn't much,' he says.

'I'm going to pay you,' she tells him.

'No. I insist.'

'Why should you pay? Do you think you owe me something?'

And at this he at last bridles slightly. 'No, Claire,' he answers. 'I don't think I owe you something. It's a gift. A small gift. I can afford it.'

'I can afford it too,' she says. 'I've come into some money recently.'

'Well, that's good,' he says. 'But I'm paying.'

'I'll withdraw the cash and leave it here,' she says.

'No. Don't do that,' he replies. 'Please. Allow me. It's not worth arguing about. And if you leave the cash I'll post it to London and then things will get very silly. Accept it. Please,' he says, and he deflects his gaze downward, in what may be apology.

'Then I'll pay for my meals,' she proposes.

'We'll see, we'll see,' he says. 'We'll eat later, yes? All three of us. Same time, same place.'

8.10

Cecilia, effusively relieved, welcomes Claire back to the Antica Farmacia. 'Gideon told us everything,' she tells her, releasing her from a mighty embrace; she gives Gideon a sympathetic smile for the torment through which he too has passed. 'You were in good hands,' she assures Claire, patting Robert's arm. Giacomo, summoned from the kitchen, regards Claire from head to shoes and up again, as if looking for signs of damage. '*Brava,*' he pronounces, with a nod that commends her powers of recovery. He will bring a bowl of *ribollita,* which is good for strength, followed by a risotto of *porcini.* Cecilia wants to know every detail of the ordeal; Robert translates Claire's account, augmenting as necessary.

The *ribollita* arrives, and the conversation turns to Claire's departure. 'I'll try for a flight from Rome,' she says, as the bowls are being placed on the table.

'She wants to leave us,' says Gideon to Cecilia, pulling a doleful face of rejection. 'Saturday – off,' he says, making a hand take off and bank away from the tabletop.

'No,' says Cecilia, incredulous.

'Yes,' says Gideon, sorrowfully resigned.

'I have to,' Claire apologises.

'No,' states Cecilia. 'No, no, no. You must stay. It is our best day. Sunday, the big festival of Castelluccio. She knows?' she demands of Gideon.

'Oh yes, she knows,' he answers.

'You must be here. Why go on Saturday? Stay one day,' Cecilia tells Claire. 'She must stay, yes?' she urges Gideon.

'We shall endeavour to persuade her,' says Gideon.

Whereupon Cecilia says to Claire: 'I show you.' She bustles into the back room, whence she returns a minute later bearing photos, six or seven of them, all riddled with drawing-pin holes around the edges. 'This is it,' she tells Celia, putting the pictures in her hand. 'You must not miss it.'

Celia examines the pictures of the Saint Zeno's day festivities: the costumed parade, the Flight of the Angel, the Palio della Ballestra. 'Looks like fun,' she concedes, while Gideon watches her closely, as if willing her to solve a puzzle. Her attention is snagged by a figure who, by virtue of being at the front, and on horseback, dominates the shots of the parade: he's a portly gentleman, with big ears and a massive nose, wearing a gold and scarlet chequered cape and a fantastically complicated bit of headgear in the same colours.

'The town dentist,' explains Gideon.

Cecilia informs her that his name was Mr Zappalorto. With an air of wistful respect, she indicates the corner table that had been Mr Zappalorto's. 'He was so nice,' she says. Then, putting a finger on his image, she tells Claire: 'He was our Vielmi, for many years. And this year Maestro Westfall is our Vielmi.' She withdraws, leaving Gideon to continue.

'Domenico Vielmi. A local bigwig, centuries ago,' he

explains. 'Nothing to do with the story of the Falling Boy. He's an anachronism, but a decorative one. He gives someone the opportunity to dress to the nines. This year, that person is me. It is, needless to say, a great honour,' he says, pressing a hand humbly to his heart.

'So stay,' says Robert, 'and admire Gideon in all his glory.'

'Playing my part in celebrating the one significant event ever to have happened in Castelluccio.'

'Or not, as the case may be,' adds Robert.

'Indeed,' agrees Gideon. 'How can you let it pass?' he says to Claire. 'I'll be horrifically jolly,' he announces, raising his wine glass with a roistering flourish.

Whereupon Marta, obviously briefed by Cecilia, comes to the table in order to tell Claire that the show will be great, especially her contribution. 'I whizz down the wire,' she says, illustrating her descent with a long swoop of a hand, 'and I have a beautiful silver crown and silver wings and silver tights, and I get to wave my bottom at everyone. It is something you cannot forget.'

'The highlight of the day, needless to add,' comments Robert.

'Yes, of course,' says Marta brightly, departing with a curtsy.

Claire decides to stay for the festival.

8.11

Domenico Vielmi, son of Guglielmo di Girolamo, was born in the village of Mensano in 1350, and spent much of his life in Castelluccio, his mother's place of birth. In several documents he is referred to as Domenico di Guglielmo, the name by which he was generally known as a young man. Of the early life of his father, Guglielmo, little is known other than that he had three sons, of whom only Domenico survived into adulthood, and that until the early 1350s he worked for his father, Girolamo, who was a weaver. In the years immediately after the plague of 1348, however, Guglielmo became a landowner, and he appears to have increased the extent of his farmland steadily throughout the two decades that followed the epidemic. By 1370 he had become prosperous enough to invest capital with a company formed by two Florentine vintners. He soon diversified his commercial activities, moved his family to a house in Florence, and became a partner in a succession of trading companies, one of which maintained an office in Avignon, where it imported cloth from Damascus and other fine fabrics for sale primarily to the papal court.

It was while he was with this company that Domenico, having worked for partners of his father in Florence and Ibiza, began to impress his employers. 'He has acquired a name for fair dealing and perspicacity,' wrote the *fattore* of the company to Domenico's father. 'Your son has the judgement of a man of much experience,' he went on. 'He can assess at once both a man's character and the quality of his goods. He has foresight, and he can hold in his mind so many different things that another man would require a ledger to record them.' When the plague struck Avignon in 1374, and many traders deserted their offices in fear of the pestilence, he continued to work in the city, 'as if through unceasing toil he might earn God's protection.' He survived, and at the year's end his company's profits were higher than they had been in the preceding year. The next year, thanks in no small part to the diligence and shrewdness of Domenico di Guglielmo, revenue was again increased.

In 1376, with the election of Gregory IX to the papacy in Rome, the partners closed their office in Avignon and Domenico returned to Florence. Two months later, Guglielmo di Girolamo died. Father and son had been alike in more than appearance: 'he is your reflection, in mind as in body,' the Avignon *fattore* once wrote. Domenico was astute, like his father; he was a man whose word could be trusted, like his father; both were industrious, and loyal to their associates; a secret told to either man was as secure as if it had been consigned to the depths of the ocean, but they disclosed their own secrets to nobody, for, as Guglielmo once advised his son, 'to confide in a man is to turn yourself into his slave'. But in other respects Domenico and Guglielmo were dissimilar, as became most apparent as soon as Domenico, having taken possession of his inheritance, set about increasing his fortune. His father, as his letters attest, was a convivial man, whose partners were friends as well as colleagues. In all of Domenico's correspondence, on the other hand, there is barely a note of affection. In Avignon, he was said to have lived 'like an anchorite'. Back in Florence, the few hours of the day that were not devoted to commerce were spent with his mother, or alone, until he married. His wife, Simonetta, the daughter of a partner, is mentioned in none of Domenico's surviving letters that date from before their marriage, and in only two from subsequent years. Though he was often away from home on business, no letters between Domenico and his wife were found in the archive of correspondence and ledgers that came to be stored in the Palazzo Campani.

In 1379 Simonetta gave birth to their first son, Leone; a second son, Domenico, was born in 1381; the following year Simonetta died of a fever; she was twenty-five years old, and had been married to Domenico for a little less than three years. Her husband never remarried, but he had at least one other child, a daughter called Gaia, born to a slave of the same name, in Castelluccio, in 1414.

The letters of Guglielmo di Girolamo suggest a man of gentle temperament, never censorious of the weaknesses of less moderate colleagues. He loaned money to former partners who had suffered misfortune; to a relative of his wife, afflicted with poor health, he made several gifts of money. Domenico Vielmi was of a sterner, less charitable cast of mind. In 1387, for example, he formed a company with a cousin, whose alleged indolence led to disagreement and the premature dissolution of the partnership. Two years later, the company that this cousin had subsequently created with five brothers from Lucca failed when their ship was taken by pirates off the coast of Morocco. Suddenly impoverished, the cousin appealed to Domenico for assistance. Though the man had four children, and was reduced to living in two rooms no larger than a pair of carts, Domenico refused to help.

Within the year he had set up a company that provided insurance policies for sea-borne goods.

Domenico was bolder in business than his father, and by the age of forty had become much wealthier than his father had been. He traded in wheat, wood, jewellery, hides, furs and paintings. From the Black Sea and the Balkans he imported sandalwood, gall nuts, indigo, erpiment, cinnamon, cloves, nutmeg, pepper, cassia, cardamon and myrrh. And whereas his father was devout as well as cautious, and always averse to any forms of commerce that might have been incompatible with the teachings of the Church, Domenico – though always honest in his observance of contractual obligations – had none of his father's religious scruples. Not only did he offer contracts with deferred payment, thereby – in the opinion of many, and not only the priests – committing the sin of usury, he also entered into agreements with John Hawkwood, the terrible Englishman. It was said that when Hawkwood's army massacred the people of Cesena in 1377, hundreds were slaughtered with weapons that had been obtained through Domenico Vielmi. Seven years later, when Hawkwood besieged Siena, having abandoned the Pope and sold his services to Florence, it was known that Vielmi had again furnished him with arms. In the same year, soon after Hawkwood had bought the castle of Montecchio, Vielmi dined with him there. Only when Hawkwood defaulted on a debt did Vielmi cease to associate with the butcher of Cesena.

At the age of sixty, Domenico Vielmi had a house built for himself in Castelluccio, within sight of his birthplace. Two years later he put his sons in charge of the family's interests in Florence, and left the city. He was the richest citizen in Castelluccio, and his house was renowned for its size and for its garden, in which he cultivated oranges, roses and violets. Above the portal was displayed, in stone, the coat of arms that Vielmi had acquired, showing a three-masted ship with a star above its central mast. In the countryside around Castelluccio he owned wheat fields, vineyards, olive groves and ilex woods, and produce from his farms filled the larders of the Palazzo Vielmi. After many years of self-denial, he now allowed himself luxuries at the table: he drank from glasses that had been made for him in Venice; his salt was served in a silver salt cellar, in the shape of a ship, fabricated in Florence; a huge silver bowl at the centre of the table held scented water. Whenever his sons and their wives and children came to visit, he would have a magnificent meal served for them. On one occasion they ate a peacock stuffed with capon and pork and cinnamon and nutmeg; the bird's feathers were put back in place before it was brought to the table, and spirit-soaked cotton was ignited in its beak, so that it breathed fire like a dragon. Vielmi kept a menagerie in his garden, with porcupines, marmosets and peacocks. A man was employed solely to take care of the animals; he was one of six servants who worked for Domenico Vielmi; another was Gaia, who had golden hair, eyes the colour of opal, and a voice that was low and quiet and 'as pleasing as the trickle of rainwater,' as her owner wrote, in a rare instance of tenderness.

But there was a blight on his life in Castelluccio, in the form of Muzio Bonvalori. Though only a boy when Domenico Vielmi settled in the town, within a few years Muzio Bonvalori had inflicted damage on the Vielmi household. On April 3rd, 1415, one of Vielmi's servants, a girl by the name of Tina, was attacked by Muzio when, out hunting, he came upon her on a country road. Vielmi, who, several years earlier, had sold some items of Limoges enamel to the youth's father, Ercole Bonvalori, sent a letter to the Rocca in protest at the assault. That same day, a reply was delivered, in which Ercole Bonvalori expressed his regret at this occurrence, and enclosed two gold florins: one for Vielmi and one for the young woman. In September, however, Muzio offended again. Riding past San Giovanni Battista, Vielmi's stable boy was pulled from his saddle by Muzio Bonvalori, who demanded to know why the boy had presumed to give him so insulting a glance. Before any protest could be offered, a punch was delivered to the boy's face, with such force that, from that day on, he had no sense of smell. Once more, an apology was sent from the Rocca, with two gold coins.

For eighteen months there was no further trouble with Muzio Bonvalori, though the threat of it was always present whenever he was encountered. But then an incident occurred, involving Vielmi himself. One afternoon, on Piazza del Mercato, Vielmi was talking to a man whose father he had known many years before, in Mensano. It was a market day, and the square was a vast murmur of conversation, until Muzio Bonvalori appeared, trailing silence in his wake, as if a serpent were crawling through the crowd and every man was afraid to provoke it. Muzio strode up to Domenico Vielmi and the man from Mensano, pushed the latter aside, and announced that he wished to have a sword made of Toledo steel, to a specific design, and that he wished Vielmi to obtain this item for him. Vielmi informed the young lord that he now lived in retirement and was no longer a merchant. In Siena or in Florence, Vielmi went on, it would not be difficult to find traders who could procure the sword for him. But why, Muzio replied, should he go to Florence or Siena when Castelluccio was home to a man for whom the entire world was one vast market? He instructed Vielmi to present himself at the Rocca. The contempt with which this order was given made Vielmi courageous: he told the young lord that if his father were to make a request of him, he would do his best to oblige him. At this, Muzio spat in his eyes and smacked him across the face, before walking away.

A day later, Domenico became ill. He lay in bed, sweating like a blacksmith, vomiting whatever was fed to him. A physician, believing that the patient had been poisoned by the sputum of Muzio Bonvalori, administered a succession of medicines, none of which had the slightest beneficial effect. Blood was taken from an arm, and Vielmi's condition worsened. After a week he became delirious. Night after night he awoke screaming, and Gaia was always there. For three weeks she stayed at his bedside, praying, often with their daughter asleep beside her.

After his recovery he was somewhat more diligent in his religious observances than had been his wont. He received the

Eucharist every Sunday at Sant'Agostino, and presented himself for confession frequently. With a friar from Sant'Agostino he discussed the definitions and penalties of usury, and other matters of doctrine. He donated silver candlesticks to the church of Sant'Agostino, a silver reliquary to San Giovanni Battista, a pair of Pascal candles to San Lorenzo. He gave money to Santissimo Redentore. In 1419 he made a pilgrimage to Assisi, where he prayed all night in the church of San Damiano. In what spirit these things were done, we cannot be certain.

In 1420 Vielmi made two significant contributions to the civic life of Castelluccio, by funding the expansion of the hospice in the building that would in time become the Museo Civico, and the reconstruction of the loggia on Piazza del Mercato. But in the same year Ercole Bonvalori died, and Muzio Bonvalori was thereby freed from all constraint. Vielmi's servants were again insulted and assaulted. At the Porta di Siena, Gaia was knocked down by Muzio's horse. Every morning, towards midday, Domenico Vielmi would go to Piazza del Mercato to see how the work on the loggia was progressing, and it was at the loggia, in October, 1421, that he had his last confrontation with Muzio Bonvalori. The day was unseasonably cold, and Vielmi was wearing a new cloak, of blue *zetani*, from Roumania. Muzio rode up to the loggia. For a few minutes, without comment, he watched the masons at their work. Then, turning to Vielmi, he expressed admiration for the cloak. He enquired about the fabric. 'I should like one the same,' he said. 'May I buy one from you?' Vielmi repeated the words he had spoken before: he was no longer a businessman. 'In that case,' said Muzio, 'I should like to have that one.' His cloak was not for sale, replied Vielmi, whereupon Muzio unsheathed a gleaming new sword. 'Toledo steel,' he told him, and invited him to admire its edge. 'Now, I should like to have your cloak,' he said, and again Vielmi said that he would not sell it. With a laugh, Muzio Bonvalori bade the old man to consider the charity of Saint Martin, then cut the cloak from Vielmi's back and threw it over his horse's neck.

Before the year was out, one of Vielmi's farms had been razed by fire, and his emblem had been prised from the portal of his palazzo. In the spring, Domenico Vielmi left Castelluccio for Florence, where he lived out the rest of his days with his sons and their families. The house in Castelluccio was leased briefly, intermittently, but was unoccupied for most of the next two decades. The Vielmi family did not return to Castelluccio until after the repentance of Muzio Bonvalori, by which time Domenico Vielmi was in his grave.

8.12

Teresa opens the door to Robert, and there's no kiss. He follows her into the living room, where the TV is on. She sits down on the sofa and he sits beside her; he looks at her and she looks at the screen, simulating absorption in the discussion of the budget crisis. 'So, are things better or worse than we thought?' he enquires.

'Have no fear. Our government will save us,' she answers, with a quick smile.

They listen to a professor of economics berating a man from the ministry of finance, who then berates the professor of economics. When the two men begin shouting simultaneously, she says: 'So? How is she?'

'Fine. A bit tired.'

'Of course. But she's eating?' The question is toneless; she hasn't taken her eyes off the screen.

'She is.'

'Good,' says Teresa. On the TV a man is arguing that the south of the country should be left to fend for itself.

'She's going to stay for the festival,' says Robert.

'Good idea.'

The proponent of separatism is now being rebuked by the professor of economics. 'I need a glass of water,' says Robert. 'Want one?'

'No,' she says.

When he comes back into the room she's not watching the debate – her eyes are aimed over the screen, at a section of blank wall. As soon as he has sat down again, she answers the question he was about to ask: 'I was talking to Vito,' she tells him. 'While you were at the restaurant,' she says. Her gaze slides down to the TV.

'And?'

She raises a hand slowly to her mouth and presses the fingers to her lips; she closes her eyes, then drops the hand to murmur: 'I don't know what to do.'

'So something happened at the weekend,' he says. 'Are you going to tell me?'

After a plaintive glance, she answers: 'Nothing happened.'

'Really?'

'It might have happened, but it didn't,' she says, glaring at the screen to steady herself, but a tear nonetheless escapes.

He reaches across her for the remote, and turns the TV off.

She leans forward, putting her face into her hands, leaving only her mouth uncovered. Quietly she begins: 'It is so difficult for Renata. And with Renata. It's difficult for both of us. For all three.'

'Four.'

'Four,' she concedes. 'I don't know what I think,' she goes on, whispering at the floor. 'I don't know what I feel.'

'I think you do.'

'No, I don't,' she says, putting out a hand for him to take.

An hour later she is saying: 'We'll speak tomorrow.'

He goes back to his apartment, but from Piazza del Mercato he can see the light in his bedroom. He walks through the town, from gate to gate, and still the light is on. Four times he walks the length of Corso Garibaldi and Corso Diaz, then at last the light is out, and he can go up.

9

9.1

HE KNOCKS ON THE DOOR of the bedroom. The shriek of the hairdryer stops, the door opens an inch or two and Claire's face appears in the gap. 'Oh,' she says. 'Hello. I didn't hear you arrive.'

'Just need to get a clean shirt and a couple of things,' he says.

She steps back to let him in. She's wearing white cotton trousers and a huge red T-shirt. On the back of the chair hangs an overwashed black bra; her book is caught up in the swirl of the bed sheets. 'Sleep well?' he asks.

'Eight-hour blackout, thank you. Ready for action.'

He gathers the clothes he needs, and she restarts the hairdryer. 'I'll look for a flight,' he says.

'I'll be there in five,' she tells him.

Within a couple of minutes he has found a flight for Monday afternoon, from Pisa. Claire leans over his shoulder to look at

291

the screen. He moves aside, to let her type the credit card details; waiting for the website to process the payment, she looks up at the wall opposite, where, between posters for exhibitions at Palazzo Grassi, a frame contains a drawing of his mother and one of his father. 'Those aren't by Gideon, are they?' she asks, almost sure that they are not.

'No,' he answers.

The transaction is finished; he opens his email to find the e-ticket and print it out, and while he's doing this she goes over to the drawings. 'Who are they?' she asks.

'My parents,' he tells her.

She moves closer, to concentrate on his mother. 'You did these?'

'I did.'

'When?'

'Ten years ago. Eleven.'

Now she's peering at the portrait of his father, scanning it inch by inch. 'You still draw?' she asks.

'Occasionally. Less than when I was at art college.'

'Less than before you started working for Gideon?'

'You mean: has he crushed the creativity out of me?'

'Not quite how I'd put it.'

'I'd eased off a long time before I came here,' he tells her.

'Because?'

'Lack of time. Lack of motivation.'

'But you'd wanted to be an artist?'

'Same as every art student. But I was never going to be an artist. Same as ninety-nine per cent of them.'

'Why was that?'

'Don't have what it takes.'

She seems to feel no inclination to take issue with him. 'And what does it take?' she asks.

'Drive, for one thing.'

'And self-belief.'

'That helps.'

'Not Gideon's problem,' she remarks, stepping back to regard the two portraits together. 'So when did you give up?'

'I wound down pretty quickly after college.'

'Ever wish you hadn't?' she asks, turning.

'No,' he says, which is more or less the truth.

She nods, seeming to accept him at his word. 'And what does Gideon think?'

'Of what? My giving up?'

'Of your drawings. He must have an opinion. He has an opinion on everything else.'

'He knows I can muster a likeness. There's nothing to be said.'

And she says nothing more on the subject. He suggests that they go to the Caffè del Corso for breakfast, a proposal that is immediately approved.

The morning is very warm. Walking beside him, Claire fans herself with a hand, wafting the scent over his face. 'I'm sorry,' he says, 'but I have to ask, what is that? The perfume.'

'Après l'Ondée,' she answers.

'Say again?'

She repeats the name. 'It's supposed to make you feel that you're in the countryside and the sun is shining after rain,' she explains. 'Wet grass, damp flowers, walking barefoot in the dew, yabba yabba yabba.'

'I don't think I've ever come across it.'

'Well, it's not the sort of thing you're going to find at the local chemist's. This is one for the connoisseur,' she says, with mock self-satisfaction.

'So where did you find it?'

'My husband found it, in Paris,' she replies. 'My ex-husband.'

'I was wondering.'

'You were wondering what? Where he is?'

'Where. Who.'

'His name is Joe and as far as I'm aware he's still in London, with Philippa, who would now be twenty-seven years of age. Perhaps not quite as pretty as she was, though I should imagine the bosom continues to impress.' She cups her hands inwards, with her arms at half-stretch. 'They had a spiritual bond,' she tells him. 'Really. They bonded at a very deep level,' she insists, assuming a face of smiling piousness. 'And I don't wear the perfume for old times' sake, if that's what you're thinking. It doesn't have associations. Not any more. I just love the smell. You like it?' she asks, offering a wrist.

'I do.'

'I'm glad we agree,' she says, as if a point on an agenda could now be ticked off, then she puts out a hand to hold him back. They are within sight of the Caffè del Corso and Maurizio Ianni can be seen inside, gazing out at his dominion. 'Is there an alternative?' asks Claire. 'I'm not in the mood for the charm of Maurizio.'

Instead, they go to the *pasticceria* on Piazza San Lorenzo, where they sit outside, facing the abandoned church. A middle-aged man with spiky reddish hair and mustard-coloured trousers goes up to the façade, to take a picture of the single red flower and the graffiti around it – *Forza Juve*; *Giovanni Ti Amo*; *Ilaria Sempre*; *Juve Merda*; *Antonella Sempre*. That done, he strides to the middle of the piazza and aims upward, at the mulberry that's sprouted from the ruined roof. He seems to take about twenty shots, performing a jig as he angles the camera this way and that.

'That bloke was here three years ago,' Robert remarks.

'He's staying in the hotel,' says Claire. 'German, I think.'

'He was here for the festival. Made a real nuisance of himself.'

'You recognise him?'

'The same guy.'

'Definitely?'

'Definitely,' he says.

She looks askance at him; it's as if he had just demonstrated a diverting but futile talent, like being able to lick his own nose. 'Not sure what to do today,' she says. 'A swim appeals, but I can't risk the bees.'

Robert suggests a few places around Castelluccio that are worth a look; she can borrow his car for the day. They head back to the apartment, and at the moment that Piazza del Mercato comes into view she again tugs him by the elbow. 'Look,' she says, laughing, and there, on the far side of the piazza, is Gideon with a bedraggled and dripping Trim; at the moment they see him he stops abruptly, as if something has just struck him on the head; he rubs his brow, then walks on.

9.2

On the afternoon of May 6th, 1943, in Tunis, Lauro Pacetti was stabbed in the hand, chest, face and leg by an Indian soldier, and left for dead. He survived, but with the loss of two fingers of the right hand and damage to the muscles of his right leg. Discharged from the army, he returned to Castelluccio in July. The following week, Mussolini was arrested and replaced by Badoglio.

Lauro Pacetti had joined the army with enthusiasm: echoing the opinions of his guardian, Uncle Lino, he believed Mussolini to be the man under whose command the country would turn itself into a modern and self-sufficient nation, enriched through the efforts of men such as the industrious and canny Lino. The project of Grande Italia excited Uncle Lino; with pride he dispatched his nephew to fight for the Fourth Shore, to liberate the Italian people of Tunisia. But the war in Africa had wrought changes in Lauro's mind as well as on his body. In the bar at Sant'Agostino he announced that he was disgusted by some of the things he had seen his supposed comrades do. Again and again he would extol the virtues of the German fighting man: the Germans were better troops than the Italian rabble, incomparably better, because they had discipline and they had ideals that mattered more to them than any individual's survival. After the armistice he became a little more discreet, but from time to time he would assert to his fellow drinkers that a German was a

better fighter not only than an Italian but than an American and
an Englishman too. He declared himself ashamed of what was
happening to his country. His friends – the few that remained –
excused him: Lauro was often under the influence of drink, and
the injuries he had suffered had made him bitter. Things were
said to be bad between himself and his wife as well; the face of
once-handsome Lauro was now disfigured by a violet sink-hole
of a scar.

In November 1943 a South African POW – very undernour-
ished, with lacerated feet and a fractured forearm – was found
unconscious in a field on the south side of Castelluccio. The man
who farmed the field revived him and hid him in a chicken coop;
he dressed his feet and fed him for a week, collecting scraps from
neighbours, before escorting him out of the valley. Lino Pacetti,
suspected of being an informant for the militia, was not told
about the POW but he found out from a careless remark; he did
not offer food, though it was known that Lino Pacetti had buried
plenty of hams and oil and cheese on his land, to make them
safe from the refugees that were passing through the valley. The
following week, a rumour reached Castelluccio that the South
African had been arrested in an olive grove near Pomerance.
Two days later, in the Caffè del Corso, a man whose sister lived
in Pomerance reported that the POW had been shot as he ran
from a militia patrol. Lauro and Lino Pacetti were both present,
and neither of them, it was said, expressed any sympathy for
this young soldier, who had died alone, thousands of miles from
his home. And when, around the same time, a customer in the
Sant'Agostino bar praised, with an eloquence that touched most
of those who heard him, the Christian decency of the Italian
peasantry, Lauro was heard to scoff.

One afternoon in the last week of May, 1944, Maria Pacetti,
while foraging in woodland on the path to Mensano, observed
five men moving up the slope ahead of her; each had a gun on
his back, and one of them was walking with difficulty, supported by the men beside him. When Maria went home, she told her

neighbour what she had seen. The very same day, by the Porta di San Zeno, Lauro Pacetti was seen talking to the driver of a truck; the driver was identified, positively, as Alfonso Borsari, a militia man from Radicóndoli. The next morning, outside Mensano, an engineer at work on a broken telephone wire was approached by a man who, after some tentative conversation, identified himself as an Austrian deserter. His name was Martin, he said, and he was from Graz; he'd joined a group of Sardinian partisans, but they'd botched an ambush and become separated; acting on tip-offs, he'd been following them for two days, and he'd been told by a man in Castelluccio yesterday that his unit might have been seen in this area. There were five of them, said Martin, and one of them was wounded. The engineer, who knew that the five had passed through Mensano a few hours before, and also knew an imposter when he saw one, regretted that he could not tell him anything. But the Sardinians were killed, near Monteguidi, less than twenty-four hours later.

On Thursday nights, after little Carlo had fallen asleep, and after eating with Maria, Lauro Pacetti would leave the small apartment that he and his wife rented from a friend of his uncle and stroll to the bar at Sant'Agostino. On Thursday June 8th, 1944, Lauro was in good spirits. When someone said that the alliance with the Germans had been a catastrophe, he did not demur. He joined in expressions of hope that the war would end quickly. No disparaging remarks about the partisans were made, whereas on other evenings he had dismissed some of them as bandits whose patriotism had changed its hue as soon as it had become clear who was going to win. On June 8th he had nothing to say about the partisans, not even when the deaths at Monteguidi became the topic. 'It is a tragedy,' said one of the drinkers, and Lauro Pacetti bowed his head solemnly and nodded. He did, however, warn that there would be trouble if the Americans arrived before the British; there were black soldiers in the American regiments, and they had been raping girls wherever they went, he'd been told. 'To the British,' he declared, raising a glass. By most accounts, that was the last thing he said before bidding them all good night.

At 10pm or thereabouts he left for home. Shortly before midnight, a woman opened her front door on Piazza San Lorenzo and saw, on the far side of the square, by the church door, what she at first took to be a sack full of rubbish. It was Lauro Pacetti. Around his left arm he had a swastika armband – a genuine one, taken from a German – and in his right hand he held a piece of paper on which was written 'Justice will be served'. There was a bullet hole in his brow.

The story immediately went around that Lauro Pacetti had betrayed the whereabouts of the Sardinians to an SS officer who had been pretending to be an Austrian deserter. Nobody could possibly have been deceived by the SS man: several people in the valley had been accosted by him, and nobody had believed his story for a moment. Maria and Lino Pacetti protested that Lauro had never spoken to any German calling himself Martin; she was not even sure if she'd said anything to her husband about the men she had seen in the woods. And if Lauro had spoken to Alfonso Borsari – and she was not sure that he had, because one of the men who said he saw them talking was simply jealous, as everyone knew, because she'd married Lauro instead of him, and the other man was a spiteful idiot who'd just repeated what the other one said, and couldn't see properly anyway – the conversation, if it had happened at all, would have taken place before she'd seen the men in the woods. And what if he had talked to Alfonso Borsari? They knew each other. Lauro was no friend of the militias but he had been a friend of Alfonso Borsari, and he was not a man to turn his back on someone who had been a friend. Other men changed their friends if the wind changed direction, but not Lauro. He was a loyal man, a loyal Italian, and he had betrayed no one. He would never have assisted in the murder of a single fellow Italian, let alone five. Lauro was not a collaborator: he was a man of honour, unlike the men who had slaughtered him.

On June 10th a German motorcyclist was shot by a sniper on the Volterra road, just three hundred metres from the walls of Castelluccio. Reprisals were expected, but on June 11th the Americans arrived. Maria Pacetti was not among the crowd that cheered them along the Corso; she and her son had already left.

9.3

Gideon has visited Elisabetta: she is well, she says, '*ma un poco stanca*' – a little tired, each day a little more tired. He is chastened by the equanimity with which she is facing the end, an equanimity that is sustained by a delusion, but that has a great nobility nonetheless. He is preparing himself for her death.

Trim has crossed the stream; the water barely covers a paw. A sweet aroma of mud mingles with the perfume of desiccated grass. Gideon's gaze travels along the mild undulations of the skyline and descends to the buildings of Castelluccio; the town occupies its niche in the valley as correctly as a village in a painting by Fra' Angelico. It is a humanised terrain, durable and subtle; the air is soft; the land is full of light; but today what he sees cannot inspire him. It cannot even confer repose. He is thinking of Elisabetta and also, though it does him no credit, of himself – or rather, of the judgement that will follow his own demise, the judgement not of himself, but of his work.

He has become dissatisfied; he is repeating himself. He has not lost belief: each picture is a reiteration of what is true; a reading of the scripture of the visible world. He is devoted to the truth of the visible, but of late he has become subject, intermittently, to a desire to create something new, to bring about an image through something other than force of observation and the rigour of organisation. He has imagined, but cannot yet see, a conclusive picture, a painting of which he could say: 'This is the one by which I should be judged. It omits nothing.' He has had intimations of a moment of revelation: nothing as clear as a glimpse of the form that this work may take, but a sense of movement in the depths, as some animals are able to detect, before an earthquake, tremors too slight for humans to sense. Perhaps – the notion has often entered his thoughts – Ilaria would have brought it about? She had often made him uneasy; she may, in time, have maddened him a little, and a little more madness may have sufficed. In his mind now is the image of Ilaria, a promise of fruitful disorder.

Trim has disappeared into the stand of oaks. Gideon crosses the stream on the exposed stones of its bed; he enters the little wood, and there is the dog, running through a declivity of loosened soil, muzzle to the ground. In the base of the bowl is a thick paste of mud, now stamped with Trim's paw prints; a pungency has come into the air – an ammoniacal reek. Gideon hauls the reek into his nostrils in a powerful draught, as if it might shock him back into rationality; again and again he breathes it in, but by the fifth or sixth dose the smell is disgusting. Then Trim, legs slathered in slime, brings more of it with him. 'Sit,' Gideon orders, whereupon Trim springs forward and deposits two smears on Gideon's thigh. The stink is worse than the worst train-station toilet in Italy. They return to the town, where Ennio Pacetti, upon request, directs a hose at the dog. Trim dances away, still with a dozen berries of mud dangling from his belly fur.

9.4

The wild boar (*Sus scrofa*; Linnaeus, 1758), is native to the Mediterranean region, much of Central Europe and Asia, and the Nile Valley. Classified in 1927 by Oscar de Beaux and Enrico Festa, in their *La ricomparsa del cinghiale nell'Italia settentrionale-occidentale*, the Maremman (or Italian) wild boar – *Sus scrofa majori* – is one of two indigenous Italian subspecies, with *Sus scrofa meridonalis*, which is found in Sardinia; other subspecies, once common in northern Italy, are now extinct.

Most adult Italian boars weigh between 80 and 90 kilos, but in Tuscany male boars weighing in the region of 150 kilos have been shot. The Italian boar is generally 120–180cm in length, with a shoulder height of approximately 90cm. Its skin is thick, with deep pads of subcutaneuos fat and little blood supply, which gives the boar exceptional protection from bites and other surface injuries. Rigid bristles, in most cases dark grey or brown, cover the whole body except for parts of the head and the lower part of the legs; a finer undercoat of fur provides excellent insulation. In summer the animal will often roll in mud, which acts as a coolant, as protection from sunlight, as a balm for any wounds to the skin, and as a treatment for parasites. Should no standing water be available, the boar will urinate on the dry soil to create a muddy paste.

An omniverous species, Sus scrofa majori has twelve incisors, four canines, sixteen premolars and twelve molars. The distinctive upward-curving canines are a feature of the male only; the lower canines, which are the larger pair, normally grow to a length of between 15cm and 20cm, but 30cm has been recorded. Vegetable matter, such as grass, nuts, fruit and tubers, forms the bulk of the wild boar's diet; it is particularly partial to acorns, and thus mature oak woods are its preferred habitat. The boar is very adaptable, however, and can colonise most environments where there is surface water and the consistency of the earth makes it possible to root for food. In addition to vegetable matter, the boar will eat insects, small reptiles, eggs, carrion and fish. A notoriously aggressive animal in defence of itself and its young, the wild boar will also occasionally hunt other animals for food; Sus scrofa majori has been known to kill young deer and sheep.

Foraging discontinuously from dusk until dawn, Sus scrofa majori causes great damage to cultivated land, which is one reason that the species is so widely hunted. During the day the boar will shelter in a shallow hole; it is the only hoofed species to dig burrows. Wild boars live in groups, or sounders, that typically contain around twenty animals, but may contain as many as fifty. Each sounder occupies a territory of approximately twenty square kilometres, and usually will remain within that territory unless shortage of food forces it to wander. The boars mark the

borders of their territory with secretions from glands in the
mouth and anal area.

9.5

Plenty
Oil on canvas; 150cm x 210cm
1977
Private collection, London

It could be argued that *Plenty* is the most important work in the
career of Gideon Westfall, in that it was this picture that first
brought him to public attention, when it was exhibited at the
Royal Academy Summer Exhibition of 1978. Inspired by the
Dutch still life artists of the seventeenth century, and in particular by the work of Willem Claeszoon Heda, whom Westfall once
termed 'the supreme master of reflective surfaces', this large
painting is centred on a kitchen worktop. Carrots, potatoes,
leeks, cloves of garlic and other vegetables are heaped on the
dark stone surface, to the left of a sink in which two trout are
curled in shallow and faintly bloodied water. Three knives lie
on a wooden chopping block, beside a glass jar of olive oil and
a white porcelain bowl. Beads of oil glisten on the flank of the
jar; a bulb of water hangs from one of the taps; on the sill above
the sink, in full sunlight, stands a half-full glass of red wine,
smeared with fingerprints; a wine bottle is positioned at the
right-hand edge of the picture, next to a loaf of white bread, the
heel of which lies alongside, amid crumbs. *Plenty* made a strong
impression on visitors to the 1978 show. It's probable, however,
that certain details of the picture were not noticed by all of its
admirers. The scene is represented as if from the viewpoint of a
person standing at the worktop, looking down. And if you look
closely, you can see that someone is indeed standing there: the
artist, whose face – tiny, distorted, surrounded by the reflections
of the furnishings of the kitchen – is painted in the tap from

which the drop of water is suspended. Look closely at the wine bottle and you will make out, above the label, almost as dark as the wine inside, the reflection of a human skull, apparently floating in mid-air.

One viewer who did not miss these details was the critic James Hannaher, who cited *Plenty* in 'Nostalgia Isn't What It Used To Be', one of the essays collected in his book *Looking Backwards*, published in 1991. 'Technical accomplishment,' wrote Hannaher, 'has often been the hallmark of kitsch, and this picture is premium-quality kitsch, a bombastic and sterile pastiche, overburdened with significance.' In later years, Gideon Westfall would refer to Hannaher's essay – which was first published in *Ark* magazine, in 1989 – as 'the straw that broke the camel's back'. The viciousness of the London critics, he would say, had forced him into exile.

Plenty was sold before the exhibition closed, and still lifes by Gideon Westfall have readily found buyers ever since. It was a genre to which he returned many times, often on commission, and skulls appeared in several of these works. In the first half of his career the skull was invariably human; after the move to Castelluccio, however, animal skulls began to appear, and in the still lifes produced after 2002 one particular specimen predominates – the massive wild boar's skull presented to him in that year by Carlo Pacetti, to join the previously donated bones of a fox, a porcupine, a deer and a variety of raptors.

To an interviewer who asked him about his predilection for the motif of the *memento mori*, Westfall responded that although he may once have had a penchant for this device, the boar's skull was in fact no such thing. The great skull of the wild boar was no more a *memento mori* than an image of the hills around Castelluccio would be. 'It is a beautiful landscape, a landscape made of bone,' he said. The interview made reference to one of Westfall's most striking images: a painting of the same dimensions as *Plenty*, showing the boar's skull brightly lit against a plain brown background, in the manner of George Stubbs'

Whistlejacket. Created in 2005 and sold later that year to a collector in Berlin, it was exhibited in *Wissenschaft/Kunst* (Science/Art), an exhibition held in Köln in 2007. There it was seen by James Hannaher, who was later quoted – in an article published on the www.kunstwelt.de website – as saying that he had 'begrudgingly admired' its 'grandiloquent austerity'.

9.6

'If I don't get this bloody thing finished today,' moans Gideon, hunched on the stool, pricking Turone's picture with a tiny brush, as if lancing a pus-filled abcess, 'I'm going to take a jump off that tower and take my chances with Saint Zeno.' His mood is not the best. He has been obliged to give up half an hour to the cleansing of Trim; Robert, when asked, drew the line at shampooing the dog.

'And how is the patient this morning?' Gideon at last enquires.

'Much better.'

Gideon's response to this is silence, broken after two or three minutes with: 'The visit has not been unpleasurable.'

'Glad to hear it.'

'Rather better than might have been expected.'

'Good.'

'If she were living within driving distance, I might enjoy seeing her every month or two.'

'Get to the point, Gideon.'

'But a solid week, then extra time – it's too much.'

'It's been just a couple of hours a day. Of your choosing.'

'More than that.'

'You've hardly had to change your schedule.'

'It's too much. She's relentless.'

'I have no idea what you're on about.'

'The family,' he sighs. 'Even when she's not talking about it, the subject is there, all the time. The invisible cloud.'

'That's not true.'

'When it's just the two of us, it's there, believe me,' he states. 'But I can't unmake the past, and I'm not going to punish myself for not being Mr Happy Families. She wants a good show of remorse for not having liked her father. And she's not going to get it.' Grimly he attends to the painting, saying nothing more for a while, except to mutter: 'Christ, I hate this damned thing.' Then, after another long pause: 'So why do you think she's here?'

'She's told you. Curiosity.'

'Wanted to take a look at me before it's too late,' he murmurs. 'Strike while the iron's still lukewarm.'

'Something like that.'

Precise as a watchmaker, working with his face almost touching the canvas, Gideon continues to make minuscule adjustments. Ten minutes pass before he remarks: 'Plain, isn't she? I don't mean her appearance. Though she's no beauty. But that's not what I meant. There's a deep plainness to her. Stolid. Immensely decent, but stolid.'

'Decent, yes.'

'Literal-minded.'

'I wouldn't say that.'

'And needy, as they say in magazines.'

'Not that either.'

The sharpness of this reply makes Gideon halt his brush and turn his head, as deliberately as a CCTV camera. He smiles and says: 'Oh, I think she is.'

Robert returns the gaze indifferently, and forces it away. 'I need to update your blog,' he tells Gideon, in the tone of a doctor with a recalcitrant patient. 'We haven't added anything this month. Any ideas?'

Gideon sits upright, braced by the change of subject. Wiping the brush, he looks up at the skylight as if to receive inspiration. 'How about: Ingres and landscape – his antipathy towards it?'

'Done it. Three years ago.'

'Nobody will remember.'

'The internet does not forget.'

Hands on knees, staring at the floor, Gideon ponders. 'Well, I read something a couple of nights ago: "I have discovered that our misfortunes derive from a single source: that we are incapable of staying still in our rooms." Pascal. Words to that effect. Apply the idea to Morandi.'

'You did Morandi in January: "The intolerable struggle with bottles and paint".'

'Yes, but this is a different angle.'

'You did him twice last year.'

'Really?'

'Believe me. A break from Morandi is required.'

'OK. Maillol – I've been thinking about Maillol.'

'What do you have in mind?'

'Maillol and Dina Vierny. The idea of the muse.'

'Not sure this is the best moment to be writing about muses.'

'It wouldn't be about me. Purely Maillol and Dina. Nothing personal in it.'

'Nonetheless, circumstances being what they are, I think it's better to wait. Good topic, but one for the future.'

'If you say so.' He scans the still life, as if looking for a face in a crowd. 'Restoration – abuses of,' he proposes.

'Go on.'

'An item on that tomb in Lucca. The della Quercia. Something along the lines of: "This sculpture hasn't been restored, it's been flayed alive." Might stir up a bit of trouble. Get myself banned from Lucca.' Grinning, he wiggles his eyebrows, relishing the prospect.

'Fine. Shall we do it in the next couple of days?'

'Do it now, I say. Take my mind off this thing. Go and fetch a notebook. I'll dictate as I daub.'

And at that moment Teresa calls: 'Can you meet me at lunch-time?' she asks.

9.7

Teresa is sitting on a bench by the pool in the Giardini Pubblici. Nearby, on the grass, a boy is twirling a baton, throwing it high, catching it behind his back; another boy lies under the chestnut tree, smoking, with a snare drum beside him. Hearing footsteps on the gravel, Teresa turns and sees Robert; she takes off her sunglass and smiles, shielding her eyes with a hand. The smile is almost a wince.

'How was your morning?' she asks.

'Same as ever. And yours?'

'Unbelievably exciting.' She puts the sunglasses back on, and looks ahead, where there is nothing but the pool and some dusty bushes and the empty sky to see.

The boy with the drum starts patting a rhythm on it with his fingertips. 'Shall we go somewhere else?' Robert suggests.

'Sure,' she says, but she doesn't move. She slides a hand into his and says she's sorry.

'For what?' he asks.

Turning in the direction of the drummer, she releases his hand; she slips a finger under one lens and wipes. 'I don't know what I'm doing,' she says. 'My head is a mess.'

'It's OK,' he says. 'You'll sort it out.'

She says they should not see each other for a while; she needs time to think what is best for herself and for Renata.

'It won't be for a while. We both know that,' he answers.

She watches the boy with the baton: he passes it swiftly around his back, under a leg, then drops it. His friend laughs and smacks the drum. 'Are you angry?' says Teresa.

'Beneath this calm exterior I am a seething mass of rage,' he tells her.

She faces him, presenting his bulbous twinned reflection. 'You have a right to be angry,' she states.

But he is disappointed rather than angry, and the disappointment is not very sharp. 'No,' he says. 'This was going to happen.'

She nods, considering. 'One day,' she agrees.

They sit on the bench for a minute more. The drummer takes a call on his mobile; baton-boy takes this as a cue to make a call; they are both talking very loudly. 'Let's go,' says Robert.

They walk down Via dei Giardini, and neither of them says anything. At the Corso she kisses him on the cheek; she'll ring him in a day or two she says. Robert watches her as she hurries along the Corso and disappears into the Palazzo Campani; and that's the end. A few months from now she will have left Castelluccio and be back with her husband.

9.8

The Campani family are recorded as wine producers as far back as the early thirteenth century, when they owned vineyards around the town of Rufina, twenty kilometres to the east of Florence. By the start of the following century the Campani had also become active in Florence itself, where they put a considerable amount of capital into silk-weaving and banking, while expanding their land-holdings in the vicinity of Rufina and acquiring vineyards in northern Chianti. In 1395, Piero Campani became rector of the Arti dei Vinattieri, the city's winemakers' guild; under his guidance, the Campani vineyards became as lucrative as any in central Italy.

In 1486 the head of the Campani family, Tommaso, entered into a partnership with Cesare Marchini, a Volterra-born merchant who specialised in the importation of luxurious fabrics, particularly the heavy and much-prized silk known as *zetani*. Just six months earlier, Marchini's elder son, Piero, had married Lucrezia Vielmi, the sole heir to the substantial remnant of her family's wealth. The marriage of Lucrezia and Piero lasted little more than a year: in March 1487 he died of a fever in Barcelona, where he had gone as his father's representative. In 1490, aged twenty, Lucrezia Marchini married Michele Campani, the only son of Tommaso. Shortly afterwards, construction of the Palazzo Campani began; it was completed in 1500, and was the largest private residence ever built in Castelluccio.

Palazzo Campani is a three-storey house, with a lightly rus-
ticated façade that has an entrance arch and two round-arched
windows on the ground floor, and five windows on each of the
upper storeys; there are no columns or pilasters on the façade,
but the elegant central courtyard is colonnaded. The architect
was Simone di Foiano, whose name is associated with no other
building; it has been suggested that the design of the Palazzo
Campani might have been adapted from plans by Giuliano da
Maiano, possibly for a house in Florence that remained unbuilt.

For several years Michele Campani divided his time between
Florence and Castelluccio, then in 1525, having entrusted
control of the family business to his twin sons, he and Lucrezia
retired to the Palazzo Campani. It remained in the possession
of the Campani family until 1920, when the unmarried Paolo
Campani died there at the age of 92, almost insolvent. The
last of the Campani vineyards, having been mismanaged for
decades, had been sold by his grandfather many years before.
Nowadays the ground floor of the palazzo is occupied by the
Banca Popolare di Volterra; most of the space on the upper
floors has been leased by lawyers, doctors, a property agency
and other small businesses, but the largest room – the music
room – is unoccupied. Stretching the full width of the first floor,
the music room is notable for its trompe l'oeil fresco, painted
in 1642 by Bartolomeo Ballarini. Covering an entire wall,
the fresco simulates an ornate loggia that gives a view from
Castelluccio towards the slopes of Le Cornate di Gerfalco and
Poggio di Montieri; the young man and woman gazing over
the balustrade are Massimiliano and Matilda Campani, whose
parents commissioned the picture. Bartolomeo Ballarini was
a pupil of Giovanni Gaspare Lanfranco, whom he might have
assisted in painting the *Assumption of the Virgin* on the dome of
Sant'Andrea della Valle in Rome; Ballarini painted similar scenes
in palazzi in Genoa, Siena and Volterra. The other conspicuous
features of the music room are its two huge chandeliers, which
are festooned with glass figs and warblers; they were made on

the Venetian island of Murano, to a design by Paolo Campani. The music room may be visited, by appointment with the Banca Popolare di Volterra, every Wednesday afternoon from 3pm to 4pm, between Easter and the end of September.

9.9

Claire has been to the Biancane, and the springs and fumaroles were indeed worth seeing, as Robert had said they were, but the area was so exposed that an hour in the sun was as much as she could tolerate; and she'd been on the alert for bees all the time, which had detracted a little from the experience. Now she stands on the Corso, in the shadow of the Palazzo Campani, finishing the third bottle of water of the day. The shadows on the street are as stark as shapes painted with tar on chalk; a glass jar on a windowsill in the sun shines like a headlamp. She buys another bottle at the *alimentari*, from the boy with the blue cast on his leg, who gives her a look that seems to say she's the most bedraggled specimen he's had in the shop all day. Her hair feels like a dishcloth; her feet are slithering in her sandals, emitting tiny squeaks as she plods across Piazza Maggiore. The door of San Giovanni Battista is hot, and its paint is peeling in flakes as stiff as the scales of an old pine-cone. She spends five minutes inside, pretending to study the frescoes of Saint Zeno.

Outside Porta di Santa Maria she sits on a bench in the shade of a chestnut tree. The olive groves on the nearest slope are the colour of aluminium; the fields above are cardboard. There are no birds in the air. A cat slouches across the road and into the shade of a laurel bush; it lies there like a dropped scarf. She sits on the bench in the stupefying heat, until she feels that she cannot stay awake there. Back on Piazza Santa Maria dei Carmini she regards the church, yet again. The statue is of Elijah, she recalls, and his sword is the Word of God. Inside she would see the sculpture that Robert explained to her, but she cannot summon the will to take another look at it. She is about to return to the apartment when she becomes conscious of a whining, a pleasant whining – the sound of a violin. There are two violins, at least, playing in unison, and the music is coming from the side of the church, from beyond the wall with the arch.

The arch opens onto a cloister, and the musicians are playing in a room on the far side of it. She walks round the cloister, to a point four or five paces from the open door to the room, then she sits on the parapet between two columns. The music stops; the last phrase is repeated, and it flows on, in a quick bantering of instruments. She closes her eyes to listen, resting her head against a column.

'Hello,' says a man's voice, a deep voice, with a questioning nuance. A man in black, a priest, is standing beside her, smiling, as if amused to have happened upon a dozing woman here. There is no music.

'I'm sorry. I—'

'Please,' he says, hand raised. 'You are welcome.' The priest has a professorial air: the eyes, very dark, have an incisive gaze, and his hair – greying and wavy and profuse – is swept back from a strong brow. 'It is a rehearsal,' he explains, gesturing towards the open door. 'They are taking a break. But do stay, if you wish.' Only now does the clarity of his pronunciation strike her as remarkable.

'Thank you,' she answers at last.

'And how are you?' he asks, with a solicitousness that surprises her, and seems sincere.

'I am well, thank you,' she replies.

'You have recovered quickly,' he says. At her perplexity he smiles again, and gives her a hand. 'Father Fabris,' he says. 'Everything that happens in Castelluccio is known to me.' There is some self-mockery in the loftiness of the manner.

'Pleased to meet you,' she says, shaking his hand.

'My informant is Mr Ianni,' he explains. 'Mr Bancourt told Mr Ianni and Mr Ianni told me. That is how it works.'

'I see.'

'Have you been enjoying your stay?' he enquires; the set of his mouth perhaps betrays some irony, as if what he's really asking is a question about Gideon.

'Very much,' she answers.

A young woman comes out of the room and halts behind Father Fabris. He half-turns to nod to her. 'You will be coming to the concert?' he asks Claire, with some suavity. 'The musicians are excellent,' he says, indicating the young woman, who dips her head, embarrassed. 'They will resume in ten minutes,' he tells Claire, then with a scoop of the hand he invites the young woman to precede him. At the arch she waits for him to catch up; he says something to her, at which she laughs, as if he's a favourite uncle.

9.10

What do we know about Father Luca Fabris? From various sources we know the year of his birth – 1958 – and the place of his birth – Tirli, a village of some three hundred inhabitants, in the municipality of Castiglione della Pescaia, in the province of Grosseto. His father worked on the ferries that shuttle between Piombino and Elba; his mother was a housewife. He has three brothers: the eldest was a talented footballer, was in the squad of the Unione Sportiva Grosseto for a couple of seasons, and now works for a sportswear company; the second is a civil servant in Rome; the third, the youngest, works on the Elba ferries. A sister, Eva, two years younger than Luca, died of meningitis at the age of eight.

From Patrizia Pacetti, via Carlo Pacetti, we know that the death of Eva Fabris, though the cause of immense grief, was also the occasion of young Luca's first apprehension of eternal life. He held the hand of his dead sister and knew, as he knew the sun would rise in the morning, that her soul still lived.

From Cinzia Zappalorto, via Antonio Zappalorto, we know that Luca Fabris had not, prior to this bereavement, been an

especially devout boy. In the church of Sant'Andrea in Tirli one can
see a rib of the dragon slain by the patron saint of the village, San
Guglielmo di Malavalle (d. 1157), otherwise known as St William
the Great, the hermit saint of Stabulum Rodis. Every Sunday
the Fabris family would pray in the church of Sant'Andrea, and
little Luca would gaze at the altar on which were enshrined the
relics of San Guglielmo and he would daydream about him,
but his daydreams were not of Guglielmo the penitent pilgrim
in Jerusalem, nor of Guglielmo the pious solitary of Stabulum
Rodis, but of Guglielmo the slayer of dragons, brother in spirit
of Orlando, Rinaldo, Tancredi and all the other fabled warriors
of romance.

From Giuliano Lanese we know of another crucial incident
in the spiritual development of Luca Fabris. One day, in his
fourteenth year, Luca, alone at home, making a model boat from
balsa wood, accidentally sliced the thumb of his left hand with a
razor blade. He washed the wound, pressed ice on it, bandaged
it tightly; the bleeding soon stopped, and young Luca, examining the streak of solidified blood that had closed the cut, and
having no understanding of the process by which his flesh had
thus healed itself, decided to find out the answer. The process of
clotting, he discovered, was a dazzlingly elaborate mechanism of
multiple reactions, the removal of any one of which would cause
the mechanism to fail. When you cut yourself, Luca learned, a
protein called Hageman factor sticks to the surface of the cells
around the wound, and sets in motion an amazing cascade of
events: Hageman factor and a protein called HMK produce
activated Hageman factor, which converts another protein,
prekallikrein, to its active form, kallikrein; this kallikrein, with
HMK, accelerates the conversion of more Hageman factor to its
active form, which in turn combines with HMK to transform a
protein called PTA to its active form, which with the activated
form of another protein, convertin, works to change yet another
protein, Christmas factor, to its active form; activated Christmas
factor, together with antihaemophilic factor, converts something

known as Stuart factor to its active form, and Stuart factor, combining with accelerin, converts prothrombin to thrombin, which produces fibrin from fibrinogen; and this fibrin forms the clot, which must form quickly, and at precisely the right location, in order to stop the bleeding at the site of the wound and only at the site of the wound, because otherwise the creature's entire blood system might congeal, and the result would be death. For the young Luca Fabris, this extraordinary biochemical sequence was proof that a Creator was at work, for how else could something so complex, and irreducibly complex, have arisen? Even now, says Giuliano Lanese, Father Fabris can recite the stages of the clotting process in fifteen seconds flat. Science and religion, says Father Fabris, are 'intellectual cousins', but if one wants to understand the meaning of things, it is necessary to go beyond science.

From Fausto Nerini, supplier of stationery to the priest, we know that Luca Fabris was an admirer of Enrico Berlinguer, national secretary of the Partito Comunista Italiano from 1972 until his death in 1984, and that Father Fabris went to Rome for Berlinguer's funeral, as did Fausto Nerini and more than one million other Italians. Fausto Nerini also reports that in the study of Father Fabris's house is displayed a picture of Pope John XXIII rather than of the current pontiff. In the course of a conversation with Fausto, Father Fabris let slip a suggestion that he had some misgivings about the doctrine of papal infallibility: the slip was no more than a hesitation and a deflection of his gaze, but a slip it unequivocally was. And he was perfectly unambiguous in his criticism of the intellectual and doctrinal rigidity that, in the analysis of Father Fabris, has gained ascendancy within the Vatican in recent years. 'There will be no peace among the nations without peace among the religions, and there will be no peace among the religions without dialogue,' said Father Fabris. When reference was made to Pope Pius X, that paragon of orthodoxy, Father Fabris, with a hint of disapproval, if not of disdain, described him as 'the anti-modernist Saint'.

From the sacristan of the Redentore we know that Luca Fabris was the best tennis player at the Pontificio Collegio Nepomuceno in Rome. The same source informs us that Father Fabris, as a young man, began to write a book about Paolo Sarpi (1552–1623), the Servite church reformer, canon lawyer, Venetian patriot, opponent of papal interference in the government of Venice, author of the *Istoria del Concilio Tridentino* (History of the Council of Trent), and anatomist. Asked by the sacristan what became of this book, Father Fabris replied that he had come to see that it was a project best left to men more able than himself; at a later date he confessed that there were days on which he regretted giving it up.

From Albert Guldager, via Giuliano Lanese, we know that Father Fabris is highly knowledgeable about modern music, and has a great passion for the work of Iannis Xenakis and Helmut Lachenmann in particular, a passion shared by Guldager, at whose home Father Fabris has frequently been a guest. Albert Guldager and Father Fabris have on occasion played music together: Father Fabris is an accomplished violinist, Giuliano Lanese says Albert Guldager says. It was Father Fabris who persuaded the composer to write a piece especially for the Festa di San Zeno.

From Aldo Nerini, via Fausto Nerini, we know that Luca Fabris, as a teenager, was much influenced by a priest from Castiglione della Pescaia, who had lived in India for several years and one day delivered a sermon that took as its text the words of St Paul's first letter to the Corinthians: *And now abideth faith, hope, charity, these three; but the greatest of these is charity*. Father Fabris has described this sermon as the most eloquent speech he has ever heard.

From Elisabetta Fava, via Gideon, we know that Luca Fabris had a nickname among the seminarians of the Pontificio Collegio Nepomuceno: he was known as *il Maomettano* (the Mohammedan), because of his 'lamentable inability' – to quote Father Fabris himself – to find inspiration in the Eternal City's multitudinous marvels of painting and sculpture. Visual representation, thought Luca Fabris, is by its nature inadequate to the sacred mysteries: to Luca Fabris's way of thinking, there was an essential vulgarity, a crudity, an indecency, if you like, to any picturing of the Divine. No painting could ever make him think as words could make him think, because words are the necessary vehicle of true thought. And even thought, mired in subjectivity as it is, can not approach the ultimate truths. Of all the arts, music can best approximate the infinite, in the opinion of Father Fabris.

From Gideon Westfall we know that Father Fabris, though he generally presents to the world a smiling face, has little sense of humour. This is the conclusion drawn from a number of conversations – none of them lengthy, but none of them providing any evidence to the contrary. For example, after a concert held for the 2007 festival of San Zeno, a concert at which a young cellist from Siena had given a performance of the second and fifth of Bach's cello suites, Father Fabris, knowing of the artist's affection for the music of Bach, asked him, as the two men found themselves leaving the former refectory of Santa Maria dei Carmini side by side, what he had thought of the recital. Gideon had not been overly impressed by the cellist: her playing, he said, had been too sombre. Father Fabris, on the contrary, had been deeply moved. Father Fabris had a theory about the cello suites, which he proceeded to explicate as they walked along the Corso: the six suites, he proposed, could be heard as a sequence of devotional meditations – the subject of the second, he suggested, was the Agony in the Garden; that of the fifth, with its bleak Sarabande, might be the Crucifixion. Gideon expressed his doubts: the suites, we shouldn't forget, have their origins in dance music. And he made what he thought was an inoffensive jest: that he found it unlikely that Christ had ever danced. Father Fabris did not see any humour in the remark; he gave a vinegary little smile, and said his goodnight. Gideon is also of the view that the soul of Father Fabris harbours a little more *amour propre* than is becoming in a priest. He would direct your attention to the priestly footwear, which is conspicuously expensive and bespeaks a certain vanity; the manicure and haircut likewise.

From Robert Bancourt we know that Father Fabris finds nothing objectionable in the depiction of the female form, clothed or otherwise, as long as the image is made in a spirit of reverence rather than of concupiscence. The human form, like the form of everything else that lives, is a manifestation of our Creator, and it is right that the artist should offer praise by means of his lesser creation. This observation was made in the course of a conversation that occurred on Piazza del Mercato one Sunday afternoon, an hour or so after the conclusion of midday Mass at the Redentore, a celebration at which Robert had been a spectator for a while, sitting in the nave while the service was being conducted in a side chapel, for a congregation of no more than twenty, of whom none, other than Maurizio Ianni, was under the age of fifty-five. His presence had been noted by the priest. 'I think this is not the first time,' Father Fabris remarked, coaxing. It was not the first time: there had been several other Sundays on which Robert had been prompted to sit in the church for a while, to listen to the murmur of the voices, to watch the worshippers as they attended to the perfect performance of Father Fabris. 'Nostalgia,' the priest diagnosed, nodding in recognition of this familiar condition. 'Sometimes it is only sentimentality,' he said. 'But sometimes it is a beginning.'

9.11

Gideon orders *cinghiale*, because, as he says, he feels something of a grievance against wild boars this evening. He tells Claire about Trim and the *cinghiale*'s reeking mud-pool. Claire is too tired to do much more than smile, and Robert is subdued; Gideon can tell that he will have to shoulder the burden of the conversation this evening. When Claire's attention is caught by the poster for Federico Quattrocchi's exhibition (Siena, August 2002), he looks where she's looking, and chuckles.

Taking the prompt, she asks: 'What's funny?'

'You like it?' he asks, as if he suspects she might.

'Not especially.'

'I was worried for a moment,' he sighs, and for the next hour he barely pauses.

He had met Mr Quattrocchi, at the time of the exhibition, he tells her. An ambitious chap, almost totally lacking in intelligence. 'Not a meeting of minds, was it, Roberto?'

'It was not,' Robert confirms.

Gideon regards the poster: it shows a dirty white canvas, with some dark forms just visible beneath the surface of the white paint. 'What are these shapes?' Gideon wonders, in a tone of ponderous enquiry. 'Are they monsters? Are they our innermost fears? Because this is all about tapping into the unconscious, you see,' he continues, his features heavy with slow-witted earnestness, his hands making blossoming shapes in the air. But the unconscious is a very dull place, says Gideon. 'I have no interest in releasing my inner gorilla,' he tells her. He has a funny story, from his time as a student. One afternoon, he'd brought into the studio a reproduction of a painting he had come across in a magazine, by an artist he'd never heard of before: Dieter Müllkasten. Gideon was known as someone who didn't have much time for abstract painters, but this picture had stopped him in his tracks. He shows Claire the face he had employed in presenting Herr Müllkasten's work: grave, with a hint of contrition. His fellow students examined the picture: most were impressed, some of them very much so. Similarities with the work of Franz Kline were discerned. But Müllkasten was an invention and his masterpiece was in fact a detail, much magnified, of a painting by Corot. Gideon leans back, arms spread wide to present to her the irrefutable evidence of the collective stupidity against which he was obliged to struggle.

He has another story, related, even funnier. 'Ever heard of Pavel Jerdanowitch?'

Of course she hasn't heard of Pavel Jerdanowitch.

Well, Pavel Jerdanowitch appeared on the art scene in the 1920s. Moscow-born, Jerdanowitch had been taken to the USA by his parents, to study at Chicago's Art Institute. But he had contracted tuberculosis in Chicago, and friends clubbed together to send him to the South Sea Islands, to recover. The natives, inevitably, transformed his world view, and when he returned to the USA he went to live in the Californian desert, where he developed a style of painting to which he gave the name 'Disumbrationist'. The self-described founder of Disumbrationism exhibited his work in a number of places, and was hailed as a visionary by several critics, notably in various French art magazines. Comte Chabrier, writing in the *Revue du Vrai et du Beau* (Gideon pronounces the words as if the title in itself guaranteed the absurdity of the contents), acclaimed Jerdanowitch as a man who was not satisfied 'to follow the beaten paths of art'. This artist, wrote Chabrier, 'delights in intoxication, and he is a prey to aesthetic agonies which are not experienced without suffering.' Pavel Jerdanowitch, however, was a fake. The man who said he was Jerdanowitch was in reality Paul Jordan-Smith, a Latin scholar who had never painted anything until an art critic dismissed his wife's pictures as reactionary nonsense, whereupon Jordan-Smith had set out to prove that self-styled progressive critics were idiots, which his primitivist junk had duly succeeded in doing.

'I can't see that proves much,' Claire remarks.

'Except that Chabrier was an idiot,' adds Robert.

'Not only Chabrier,' Gideon points out. 'He was far from alone. And there are Chabriers all around us,' he goes on, scanning the room as if one of them may be present this evening. 'Hacks and flatterers. The yes-men of the so-called avant-garde. Sheep who mistake themselves for wolves.'

Three plates of pasta are presented, enforcing a pause, but Gideon has things to say about the cult of self-expression; many things. The artist in earlier times was a valued member of his society. He served his society; he was paid, you might say, to represent the best of it, to give form to its beliefs, its values, its ideas. Art was a business of the spirit, you could say. Nowadays the business is all about business and self-promotion. Whereas art was once a visual philosophy, an occasion of disinterested contemplation, of elevation into a world that was a refinement of our quotidian reality, nowadays we are required to submit to art that celebrates the individual and the trivial. Artist and public used to engage, through the sense of sight, with truths that were greater than themselves; art now is all about 'transgression' and the supremacy of the Self. We must pretend to be shocked by Nazi atrocities restaged with toy soldiers. We are asked to find evidence of genius in a diamond-encrusted skull or a film of a bowl of rotting fruit.

'But how can a bowl of rotting fruit be dismissed as self-expression?' asks Claire. The question is like a pebble lobbed into a river in full spate.

'How can it be called art?' Gideon replies. He adduces other examples of artistic inanity, fraudulence, incompetence. He decries the shallowness, venality and vanity of the failed artists and jumped-up journalists who pass for art critics today: these masters of the meretricious, these purveyors of pseudo-profundity. Some of the riper fatuities of James Hannaher are quoted: 'paintings that have a meaning, that are interpretable, are bad paintings', and so on. And it's people like Hannaher who dictate what will and what will not be shown to the public. A woman who empties the contents of her laundry basket onto the gallery floor and would have you take this gesture as some sort of artistic statement will be taken seriously, whereas a painter of Gideon's cast is excluded from the charmed circle. 'We are no longer "relevant",' he states. 'We must not be seen.'

'But you are seen,' Claire manages to interject. 'You have an exhibition at the moment.'

'In a backwater town in Italy, yes.'

'You've had shows in other countries.'

'A few. But back home, nothing.'

'That's not true, is it? Haven't you—'

'Group exhibitions – no solo shows. In Britain I'm persona non grata to the commissars of the art world. Which means I'm invisible to the public.'

'Hardly invisible. What about the website?'

'Not the same as paintings on walls, Claire. Being in a gallery is what matters.'

'But more people can see the website. And once you're in cyberspace you're there forever, aren't you? Better than being in any magazine.'

'An image is there forever, maybe, but it's not the real thing. Unless you see the paint, unless you're in the same space as the canvas, you are not experiencing the picture. And people are not being given the opportunity to experience work that doesn't meet with the approval of the self-appointed guardians of contemporary culture, if culture it can be called.' And so on and so forth, until – in the middle of a recitation of some of the less sympathetic comments that his work has provoked (he knows whole paragraphs by heart) – he interrupts himself with: 'You look tired, old chap.'

Robert, bored, apologises. He is indeed exhausted. 'If you don't mind,' he says, 'I'm going to turn in.'

'Fine. We have plenty to talk about,' says Gideon, putting a hand on Claire's. 'See you in the morning.'

'Maybe see you back at the flat,' says Claire, alarm momentarily apparent in her eyes.

9.12

Gideon walks slowly, hands in his pockets, saying little; his face assumes a mild and benign smile, as if his purpose were merely to share with her the pleasure of wandering without purpose through this tranquil little town at night. And it is pleasurable, to amble along the warm and quiet streets, under the dark purple sky, with bats wheeling in and out of the lamplight, and no sounds louder than the sound of their footsteps. They walk through the light of the Caffè del Corso; Giosuè – the only person inside – raises a hand as they pass. At the theatre Gideon stops for a few seconds and examines the building, as if to check that all is in order. 'Perhaps it'll open again, one day. Who knows?' he remarks. It's the first thing he's said for at least a minute. It's clear she's being readied for a significant moment.

As they turn away from the theatre, the owl cries. 'Let's see if we can find him,' Gideon suggests, and he takes her along the alley that ends at San Lorenzo. 'He's normally there,' he says, pointing across the square, where, when they get closer, she sees the cast-iron bracket of a defunct streetlamp, jutting from the wall. There's no owl. 'He likes to perch on that,' says Gideon, as another cry comes, from behind the houses. Gideon goes over to the church steps, where he picks a flower from the ground; he tucks it into a crack in the wall. He regards the graffiti, and has a comment to make on it: 'The world has no effect on them, so they have to impose their effect on it,' he says, with sadness.

Rather than respond, she looks at *ILARIA SEMPRE*; Gideon may think she's considering the profundity of his observation.

He descends the steps to stand beside her and join her in read-ing the message. With a movement of an arm he suggests that they continue their walk, then he says: 'Robert told me about what happened with Joe. I hope you don't mind.'

'I thought he might,' she replies.

'I sympathise.'

'No need for sympathy,' she tells him. 'Long past. Almost forgotten.'

'Almost forgotten is the same as remembered,' says Gideon.

'No,' she says. 'It's almost the same as forgotten.'

'Well, anyway,' he says, with a smile for her unconvincing but understandable protest, 'I was sorry to hear about it.'

'Thank you,' she says, wondering if the aim of their walk has now been achieved. Immediately – from the look of heavy com-passion that is being directed at her – she knows otherwise.

A ruminative silence ensues. 'You know,' Gideon begins, 'we're alike in many ways.'

'We are?'

'We are, yes. We say what we think. We have candour, which too few people do,' he says, with the melancholy wisdom of the older man. 'And you're not easily impressed. I like that.'

'You mean I'm bolshy.'

'No. Not at all. I mean what I say.'

They have come to the main street, close to the market square. 'A quick tour of the piazza, then back to the hotel?' he proposes; so he hasn't yet said what he wants to say. At the centre of the piazza he stops; he looks at the spotlit summit of the tower, rakes his neck with two fingers, and says: 'We've had similar experiences, you and I.'

'Well, we've all had similar experiences, haven't we?' she answers. 'We couldn't talk to each other if we hadn't done the same things.'

'Yes, but I'm talking about specifics. Specifically, I know how it felt, how it must still feel – the situation with Joe. The same thing happened to me.' He turns his face to her, so that she might look for the scars of his great misfortune. 'I think I have to tell you this,' he goes on. 'I wasn't going to, but I've changed my mind. It is something you should know.' Still gazing at the tower, he is like an actor taking a last deep breath in the wings before going on. 'Your mother and I,' he commences, 'were once a couple – in a relationship, as we say nowadays. I was fond of her. Very fond. We were, I think, heading towards marriage. Then, without warning, it was over. There was, of course "someone else". She confessed this, and I had no idea who it was, absolutely none. I had never suspected anything. They had met at a family gathering, and things had gone rapidly from there, very rapidly. "A bolt out of the blue", I was told, as if this made it better. No names were given, but soon I knew who it was, this "someone else",' he says, narrowing his eyes, as though the culprit might be hiding in the tower. 'It was my brother. Isn't that terrific? Betrayed by my own brother. By the better-looking, more bankable doctor. How grubby, eh? How tawdry. How squalid.' This is addressed to the sky; the memory, she is to think, is too painful to be retold face to face. Now he looks at her, and his expression – eighty per cent sorrow, twenty per cent disgust – tells her that he expects her to feel something of the pity of it.

It takes her a few seconds to find her voice. Gideon appears to believe that she is silent because she is shocked – and she is, but not as he imagines. Some words – *idiotic, selfish, complacent, tactless, insensitive* – come to mind, and are almost spoken. What she says is: 'That's it? Jesus Christ almighty – that's it? That's the great revelation? My dad stole your girlfriend? That's the thing I really had to know?'

He recoils an inch or two and does a florid frown; it's as though she'd suddenly started to speak Swahili.

'Why did you imagine I needed to know that?' she demands. 'What difference did you think it would make to anything? In what way would it improve my life? Am I supposed to be applauding your "candour" now? Am I supposed to think differently about my parents? Is that the idea? My mother went out with you and then she married my father. So what? So fucking what? Big deal. It happens all the time. But what on earth is the point of telling me? What the hell were you thinking of?'

'Well,' he says, quietly, in a low tone, as if embarking on an explanation for the benefit of someone who's a bit slow on the uptake, 'it's an aspect of our history. You wanted to know—'

'Give me strength – "an aspect of our history"? Let's get a sense of proportion here, for God's sake. We're talking about my mother chucking you, not the fall of the Roman empire.'

A man is crossing the piazza, on a course that will take him within a few feet of them; Gideon shuffles sideways, encouraging a move out of earshot; she stays where she is. 'What I'm talking about—'

'Look,' she interrupts, at twice Gideon's volume. 'I'm terribly sorry that my father nicked your girlfriend. That was a naughty thing to do. Or maybe not. I don't know how things were. But there are at least three sides to this story, two of which are now unavailable. It wasn't all black and white, I'm sure.'

'I'm not saying it was. All—'

'And the thing is, it doesn't matter. It's of no importance. None.'

'Well, in the great scheme of things—'

'And Joe swanning off with his big-chested bimbo doesn't matter either. It was a bit of blow, but I got over it. I'm better off without him. Joe was an arsehole. But my father wasn't. He was a good man. I loved him. And I loved my mother too, and she loved him. But you seem to want me to think badly of them, because of something that happened before I was born, for reasons I know next to nothing about—'

'If you'll let me get a word in—'

'I just don't want to hear it, Gideon.'

'That's obvious.'

'You shouldn't have told me.'

'I regret it.'

'No point in regretting it. It's done. Now I know: my dad stole your girlfriend, so you don't speak to him for the rest of his life, give or take the odd word once in a blue moon. You don't come to his wife's funeral because your grudge against them is your number one priority, and you don't come to his funeral because the grudge must prevail at all costs, even when there's no one left to hold a grudge against. A thirty-year sulk – pathetic, that's what it is. Totally pathetic.'

He's standing three or four paces back, arms folded, lips pursed, head angled to one side; he looks ill at ease, but not apologetic; he seems perplexed as to why his disclosure should have produced such a reaction. 'No, Claire,' he says, as patronisingly as possible. 'There's more to it than that. Much more. As I've told you already, we never much liked each other. We—'

'Well, I did like him. I liked him a lot. And I knew him. You didn't. You don't have the faintest bloody idea what he was like, because for most of his life you weren't there, not even on the end of the phone. And the same goes for my mother. It's getting on for forty years since she dumped you. It's no longer relevant, if you'll pardon the use of the word. It hasn't been relevant for a very long time. So I don't want to hear another word about it. Not one word. OK?' She's so angry, only now does she realise that she's crying. 'Jesus Christ,' she mutters, not quite to herself, 'what a man. What a fucking idiot.' She walks off, expecting to be called back, but he doesn't call and she doesn't turn to see if he's still there.

10

CLAIRE LOOKS UP from her book and there's Gideon standing in the middle of the street, presenting to her an expression of pantomime repentance. With his hands he requests permission to approach; gratefully he advances, bestowing smiles on the other customers of the Caffè del Corso. He takes a seat beside her. 'I think we should clear the air,' he says, toying with the spoon, too abashed to look her in the eye. 'I wouldn't want last night's disagreement to overshadow your day.'

'It won't,' she assures him.

'Nevertheless,' he says. 'There are things I'd like to say. To put right. Just a few words,' he requests. 'I'll wait for you outside. Take your time.'

She tries to take her time, but within five minutes she is outside, where Gideon is sitting on the steps of the church, in a slanted column of sunlight, an English newspaper spread open on his knees.

Smiling, encouraged, he stands up; a sweep of a hand ushers her in the direction of Corso Diaz. 'We said some things that would have been better left unsaid,' he begins.

'Not sure I'd agree with you,' she says.

'Well,' he answers, exuding magnanimity, 'let's agree that I said some things that would have been better left unsaid.'

'OK.'

'It's one of my greatest failings,' he goes on, sounding like a man speaking modestly of a virtue. 'I lack a self-editing function. I should count to fifty before opening my mouth, I know. I have a tendency to be impulsive,' says the champion of the daily schedule.

'Seems to me that you needed to say what you said,' Claire tells him. 'Not sure why you didn't tell me straight away, but—'

'I think I would have had to tell you before you left. But right at the start—'

'You thought you'd save it as a going-away present?'

'I felt, in the end, it would have been dishonest not to say it,' he responds. 'But honesty isn't always the best policy.'

'Oh, I wouldn't say that.'

For a couple of seconds he looks at her, as though this utterance were of sphinx-like subtlety; he looks away, with an approving smile. 'I know what you think,' he says.

'Tell me.'

'You think I'm obsessed. With what my brother did.'

'And my mother. Let's not leave her out of it.'

'I'm right, yes?'

'Can't say that's what I'm thinking at this precise moment.'

'But it's what you believe,' he states. 'And I have to admit that in many respects I am obsessive. All artists are to some extent obsessive, by definition. Which is why they can be difficult to live with. Or impossible, in many cases,' he says, opening his hands as though leaving it to her to decide if he should be placed in that category. 'But my brother is not an obsession. I am obsessed with my work, and only with my work. David is very rarely in my thoughts. I don't dwell on the past, and if I've given you that impression I must correct it. I didn't like him for what he did, that's true. But we didn't love each other anyway,' he says, then he laughs, making a noise as harsh as a shattering vase. 'Which, you want to say, is understandable in his case, with me for a brother.' The eyes do not emit good humour; they are watching her, to gauge whether his persuasion is succeeding.

'I couldn't say, Gideon,' she answers. 'I wasn't there.'

He wants her to understand that when he thinks of her mother – which, he has to confess, is not very frequently either – it's with gratitude more than anything else. It was Lorraine who brought home to him that he must live alone. There are certain things, certain comforts, that an artist cannot permit himself. Her mother had wanted a life more comfortable than he could have given her, and he did not blame her for this. Her requirements were reasonable; they were perfectly conventional; but the artist's life cannot be a conventional life. It would have been better if she had left in different circumstances, rather than doing what she did, but a hard lesson was perhaps what he needed. 'I'm not made for anyone other than myself, and she made me see that,' he says. 'Anyway, an apology is due, and I apologise,' he declares, holding out a hand. 'I mean it,' he insists, with an earnestness that does not seem insincere. 'I am sorry.' She takes his hand and he pulls her towards him, gently, to put an arm around her shoulder in a sort of quarter-embrace.

They walk into the sunlit part of Piazza Santa Maria. 'Isn't this a sight?' comments Gideon, suddenly drenched with content-ment at what he sees: the light on the upper part of the church and all of its bell tower; a young woman cycling slowly over the cobbles, with carrier bags dangling from the handlebars; a sky as blue as an Italian football shirt; a cat prowling out of the shadows, advancing towards a pigeon. Two teenaged girls are walking side by side, talking. Gideon observes them, and emits a soft snort of affectionate amusement.

'What?' Claire obligingly enquires.

'They're cousins,' he tells her, pointing to the girls. 'The one on the right is a year older than the one on the left, but if you watch the way they talk to each other you'll notice that the older one glances at the younger more often than vice versa. It's a kind of deference. The younger one is subtly dominant. And the reason for that is that the younger one is prettier. Much prettier. We instinctively defer to the beautiful,' states Gideon, ending with a pursing of the lips that might be taken to signify that he wishes this were not so, but facts are facts.

Claire is fighting the urge to tell him that she knows about Ilaria, and she is on the point of losing the fight when Gideon, in the bright tone of a man snapping out of a daydream, asks her what she'll be doing today.

'I thought I'd take a look at San Gimignano,' she answers.

'Oh Christ,' he groans, 'don't go there.'

'Why not?'

'Because it's awful. Like a department store in the January sales. You can't look at anything because there'll be six coach parties in the way. A terrible place. Leave it to another visit.'

'I don't know when there'll be another visit.'

This makes him pause. 'Your choice,' he says. 'If you're going, you can take my car.'

'That's kind. But I'm borrowing Robert's.'

'Mine's more comfortable.'

'It is. But I already have Robert's keys.'

'OK,' Gideon concedes, and he raises a hand to beckon the director of the museum, who is crossing the square.

'Signore Lanese,' says Gideon, with something like obsequiousness, 'I'd like you to meet my niece.'

'We have met,' says Mr Lanese, 'but I am pleased to meet you again,' he says, pressing a super-soft hand into hers.

'Robert introduced us,' she explains.

As if referring to the caprice of an incorrigible child, Gideon tells Mr Lanese that Claire intends to go to San Gimignano today.

'It is beautiful,' Mr Lanese says to Claire.

'But on a day like this, hell,' says Gideon.

'Purgatory, perhaps,' says Mr Lanese, fiddling with a cuff.

'But you must go, I know,' says Gideon. 'You'll be at the concert?'

'Of course. And you?'

'Of course.'

'Until later, then,' says Mr Lanese, and with a handshake for each he departs.

'And you must be going too,' says Gideon to Claire. 'The later you leave it, the worse it will be. Farewell, and have fun.'

On Corso Diaz she looks back; she sees Gideon standing in the middle of the square, face to the sun, eyes closed, grinning, as if standing under a shower head.

10.2

Giuliano Lanese, director of the Museo Civico of Castelluccio, is Italy's leading authority on the life and work of Giovanni di Paolo d'Agnolo (1409–1480), and the author of the only monograph on the artist to have been published to date. He has published papers on other fifteenth-century painters from Siena and the Sienese hinterland, notably Sano di Pietro and Sassetta, as well as essays on individual works, such as Domenico di Bartolo's *Madonna delle Nevi* (Our Lady of the Snows) and Vecchietta's *Arliquiera*, the painted wooden reliquary that was created for the Spedale di Santa Maria della Scala in 1445. He has also curated a number of exhibitions, the most ambitious of which was *Ex-Voti: arte e devozione popolare*, held in Volterra in 2008.

In addition to running the town museum, Mr Lanese plays one other significant part in the civic life of Castelluccio: for the last three years he has been the chairman of the committee that organises the celebrations for the Festa di San Zeno. It was

Giuliano Lanese, in his capacity as chairman of the committee, who proposed to Gideon that he take the part of Domenico Vielmi in this year's parade. After some consideration, Gideon consented, a decision not uninfluenced by his hope that Castelluccio's museum will one day have a room dedicated to his work – just as Mr Lanese's proposal was at least in part a consequence of the artist's suggestion, first made a year ago, that the Museo Civico might gain some allure by having a room devoted to the work of a living and, in some quarters, celebrated painter.

The idea, in its original form, as put to the director over lunch in the Caffè del Corso, was that the museum might like to acquire a number of studies plus a painting or two at a greatly reduced price – for a nominal fee, in fact. Mr Lanese, though grateful for the offer, felt obliged to decline, with regret: any fee, however generous the discount, would be beyond the resources of the Museo Civico, an institution so under-funded that its very survival is a cause for constant concern. Gideon sympathised; he wondered, then, if they should discuss the feasibility of a bequest of some sort. In return for a guarantee that a room would be set aside for the purpose, he might be prepared to donate a number of his works on his decease: a selection of pieces, in various media and genres, from the beginning of his career to the present. What he had in mind was something akin to the Severini room in Cortona's main museum – not, of course, that he was a huge admirer of Severini. Touched deeply by the gesture, Giuliano Lanese said that he would discuss this extraordinary offer with the people who would have to be involved in any decision on the matter – there were colleagues in the town hall, for example, and others higher up, as he was sure the *maestro* would understand. Gideon of course understood.

Eventually, after many consultations in the town hall, Giuliano Lanese reported to Gideon that the consensus was that the museum would be greatly enhanced if it were able to offer to the public an exhibition in which were displayed not solely works by *maestro* Westfall but also the creations of other eminent artists of, as the director expressed it, 'the same tendency'. It had been suggested, for instance, that Lanese might approach Gunther Diedrich or Vassily Bartnev or Pierre Medina (to name but three of the most celebrated practitioners of 'the new classicism' or whatever one may like to term it) about the possibility of their making bequests to such a collection. This counter-proposal was not well received by Gideon. Leaving aside the fact that he was highly surprised to hear that anyone in the town hall had ever heard of Pierre Medina, let alone Diedrich and Bartnev, Gideon was little short of amazed that anyone should seriously consider hanging his work alongside the productions of any of that trio. Mr Lanese was at pains to clarify that it was not being suggested that the works of Medina, Diedrich and Bartnev were of a merit comparable to that of his own, and indeed believed that most people would share Gideon's distaste for much of what they did, but he would argue nevertheless that there was some value – a great deal of value, perhaps – in endeavouring to represent the global scope of 'the phenomenon' of anti-modernism, a phenomenon to which he was by no means entirely antipathetic, sharing as he did many of Gideon's misgivings about certain aspects of contemporary art – not all aspects, of course, but many. And he reiterated that he was simply representing the collective opinion of his colleagues, as he had an obligation to do. Gideon, mollified, agreed that such a project would be worthwhile – but not, please not, with the involvement of that trinity of hacks. Further discussions would be held, promised Mr Lanese; and there the matter rests.

There is no doubt that Giuliano Lanese is well inclined towards Gideon: he admires his dedication; he is impressed by the force of his personality; he has immeasurable respect for his expertise in the matter of painting, as he has told Robert on a number of occasions. Precisely what he thinks of Gideon's work, however, is a matter of speculation. He is a man of great delicacy; he never raises his voice, and speaks spontaneously in sentences as perfect as a sixth draft; Gideon finds him evasive and prolix. 'Talking to Mr Lanese,' he once remarked, 'is like walking through perfumed fog'. Works of art, for Giuliano Lanese, are 'interesting' or 'rewarding' or 'of significance'. Nothing is good or bad. The 'phenomenon' of Gideon Westfall and others of his 'tendency' is, says Mr Lanese, 'worthy of study'. Asked directly by Robert if he actually likes the paintings that the *maestro* produces, he replied that he was not a critic, and had no desire to be a critic, because the assignment of value, in his opinion, is the work of a whole culture, not of any individual. This was said gently, but with a light finality; to press the question further would have been discourteous.

A little under a year from now, a week after his forty-second birthday, Giuliano Lanese will leave Castelluccio to take up a new post at the Pinacoteca Nazionale in Siena; not a single painting by Gideon Westfall will be on show in the Museo Civico of Castelluccio when he leaves, nor anything by any artists of his tendency.

10.3

Yesterday, Gideon now discloses, he'd had the most powerful sense of déjà vu as he was crossing Piazza del Mercato: a woman's bag slipped from her shoulder at exactly the same moment as a crate of empty bottles crashed onto the floor of a van outside Alle Torre, and the feeling that precisely this combination of events had happened before was so strong that he'd known, a split second before it occurred, what was going to happen next: a yellow car would drive in front of him, with a dog on the front seat – which was in fact what happened.

'You'd already seen the car in the corner of your eye,' suggests Robert.

'No,' states Gideon. 'It suddenly appeared, on cue. And there's another thing,' he goes on. 'This morning, on Piazza Maggiore, after Claire had gone, I saw Martin Calloway.' Sitting on a stool, with the self-portrait on the easel, he turns to show a face of bewilderment and dread.

Robert, opening the morning's post, answers without looking up: 'And what exactly do you mean by that, Gideon?'

'I saw him.'

'Could you be more precise? Given that the person in question is deceased, in what manner did you see him?'

'I saw someone walking onto the piazza and it was Martin Calloway. His face, his build, his walk—'

'You mistook a man for Martin Calloway.'

'He was his double.'

'It happens.'

'But then, a few seconds later, he wasn't like him at all. Hardly any resemblance.'

'OK. So, your brain misfired.'

'It was a perfectly lucid moment: for several seconds, he was there, as clearly as everything around him.'

'Can't see what imagining Martin Calloway has got to do with a woman dropping her handbag,' says Robert, moving to the door of his work room.

Focusing his gaze on the face on the easel, Gideon answers: 'Signs. They were signs.'

'Of what? That you're losing your marbles?'

'Not funny, Robert.' He tilts his head as he looks at the painting, and sorrow comes into his face, as though he were at the bedside of an ailing parent. 'I'm not far short of the age at which my father died,' he says. 'And my brother.'

'You'll live to be ninety.'

'I'm overweight. The Westfall men have a track record. And I get breathless. Frequently.'

'Yes, but there's nothing seriously wrong.'

'Not yet, maybe. But I feel tired.'

'Take a few days off.'

'No,' says Gideon, drawing his hands down his face, then blinking like a man waking up. 'It's not that kind of tiredness.'

'But you could give it a go anyway. Allow yourself a rest.'

'Another year, two at most, and you'll be free.'

'Free already, Gideon. Free already,' Robert sings, going into his room.

A few minutes later, Gideon appears in the doorway. 'Is there something you want to tell me?' he asks.

'Not especially,' Robert answers from the computer.

'I detect something. An undercurrent. Trouble with Teresa?'

'Not any more.'

Gideon knits his fingers across his midriff; he bows his head, as discreet as a priest. 'I see,' he says. He waits while Robert attends to an email, then asks, when it becomes apparent that no more information will be offered: 'Anything else?'

'Nothing comes to mind, no.'

After a slow exhalation, which may be intended to be expressive of sympathy but sounds more like relief, Gideon says: 'I can't pretend to be greatly surprised.'

'Neither can I,' Robert replies, setting papers in order.

'Never did see the attraction of that one. Apart from the obvious.'

'I know you didn't.'

'What's the story? Another man?'

'Yes.'

'That's disappointing.'

'I was the other man.' Robert glances up, to see Gideon awaiting elucidation. 'I have things to do,' Robert tells him, gesturing at the computer.

'You can do a lot better,' remarks Gideon, leaving. 'That Agnese was an impressive young woman.'

'She was.'

'I liked her. Not many of her calibre around here.'

'Indeed. Perhaps I need to fish in a bigger pond.'

Gideon ambles away, and that's the end of their conversation for the morning. In the hours before lunchtime, it appears, Gideon does nothing but make some desultory alterations to the background of the self-portrait; in the afternoon, whenever Robert leaves his room, he sees Gideon leafing through the sketchbooks of the past few months, as though in the hope that an idea will rise from the pages. A sheet is torn out of one of the books, as Robert is passing; what's destroyed is barely a sketch – half a dozen lines of charcoal that had failed to become a figure. Robert makes no comment, and neither does Gideon. Later, he's gazing on a drawing of Ilaria that's been placed on the floor in front of the stool, so that he's peering down onto it as if onto the deep-lying water of a well. 'Perhaps Mr Guldager's music will cheer us up,' he remarks.

10.4

Nude 126
Oil-tempera on canvas; 105cm x 75cm
2010
Private collection, Krákow

The naked female form is a subject that recurs frequently in the work of Gideon Westfall: from the mid-1970s onwards he produced several paintings of this type every year, as well as scores of studies in pencil, charcoal, ink and oil-tempera. Each of the finished paintings bears a number, a sequence that begins with *Nude 1*, from 1975; *Nude 1* was not his first such work, but all examples preceding it were destroyed in that year, including several for which the model was Lorraine Daventry, later Lorraine Westfall. The series ends with *Nude 126*, which shows Ilaria Senesi, seated on a plain wooden chair against a white wall, gazing – 'with something like the fascination of Narcissus at the first encounter with his own reflection' – at a small black oval which she holds loosely in her right hand, upon her thigh. The oval is a Claude mirror, manufactured in 1856 and bought in New York by Milton Jeremies, as a gift for the artist; it was in its original packaging, complete with explanatory text – *Claude Black Glass Mirrors: These are very useful for the young artist, as they condense or diminish the view into the size desired for the intended picture, and all objects bear their relative proportions.* The model's expression is not wholly a simulation: she was as intrigued by the black mirror as a child might have been. It was like looking into the underworld, she said; when she looked at it, she saw herself as a vampire or the queen of the night. Peering into the dark depths of the glass, she could hold her pose without strain for an hour or more.

Nude 126 was bought at auction in 2011 by a Polish film producer, to augment a collection that contains, in addition to pieces by Balthus and Delvaux, the most extensive array of Kitagawa Utamaro *shunga* prints in Poland. The sum paid for *Nude 126* has to date been exceeded by only one other Westfall work of this genre: *Nude 115* (2007), the last of six paintings produced during the ten months in which he worked with Laura Ottaviano.

In one sense Laura Ottaviano was Gideon Westfall's most successful model: every painting of Laura sold immediately, as did many of the drawings that came out of his sessions with her. She was, furthermore (and unlike some), always patient, punctual and uncomplaining. Silence for her was not – as it was for many others – an ordeal. Only on the first afternoon was there anything like friction between artist and model: she had ideas as to how her body could be best presented, ideas that owed everything to the aesthetics of calendar photography; she believed that these alluring contortions and provocative half-coverings and head-tiltings not only accentuated the virtues of her form – they projected most powerfully her personality too. Of this misconception she was quickly disabused. Her form needed no accentuation, she was told. She should simply be herself, Gideon told her, and leave it to him to show what she was. After a brief discussion, she acquiesced.

In the body of Laura Ottaviano, to paraphrase the artist, the tenets of classical form were made flesh. She was a young woman of 'exemplary beauty'. But the form of Laura Ottaviano was also, as he remarked after their collaboration had ended, rather more eloquent than her speech. At the start of a session, to relax, she would talk while he made ready; she rarely said anything that

it was thought worthwhile to report. Often she would complain
that she was cursed: she was burdened by her own appearance,
she wanted him to believe, though it appeared that the burden
was light. It seemed, she said, that she attracted only men who
saw the skin and nothing else; most men are idiots, experience
had taught her. But if an idiot was what she was going to have to
settle for, she was at least going to make sure she landed herself
an idiot with some money and decent looks: a footballer, maybe,
though nearly all footballers are really thick and you don't get
many of the good ones in this part of the world – you need to be
in Milano or Torino or Roma to catch the best of them, so that's
what she might do one day, though it would be hard to leave
Siena because that's where she was born and grew up, and all
her family were there, et cetera, et cetera.

She had been working with Gideon for nine months when
she embarked on a relationship with his assistant. 'But nobody
would ever mistake Robert for a footballer,' Gideon remarked, on
the morning his suspicions were confirmed, and Laura laughed;
her laugh was strangely ingenuous. It was true, she had to agree:
Robert wouldn't last two minutes at the San Siro; on the other
hand, he wasn't stupid, and that counted for a lot. It took her
less than a month to discover that, disappointingly, Robert in
fact was yet another of those men whose gaze cannot penetrate
the skin. And Robert, after almost four weeks of Laura, was not
inclined to rebut the charge, however inappropriate it might
have been. 'What did you find to talk about?' Gideon enquired,
incredulous. 'Until last week there wasn't a great deal of talking,'
was the answer.

Earlier that day Laura had informed Gideon that it would
no longer be possible to continue to come to his studio. She
preferred to say no more, and Gideon was happy to respect her
discretion: he accepted her resignation with a regret that was
not wholly for form's sake – Laura had proved to be, after all, a
lucrative subject. He was, however, not entirely happy with any
of his paintings of her: they had a certain inertness; they were

too decorous; there was a whiff of the academy about some of them, which was perhaps to be expected when the model was a young woman as conventional as Laura. Nevertheless, he decided to complete the painting that had been interrupted by her departure, even though it had barely advanced beyond tracing on the canvas; it was finished by using sketches he had made in the preceding months – the only instance in which he produced a figure painting in the absence of the model. This was *Nude 115*, which was bought by a Russian businessman who had previously bought *Nude 111*, another image of Laura Ottaviano. His wife was jealous, reported this aficionado of the feminine, but she had to admit that 'this young lady is very special'. He had, he informed the artist, a 'gallery of beauties' in his apartment in St Petersburg, and for purposes of documentation he would like to have some information about the 'lady depicted with such art'; Gideon provided none. In addition to his gallery of beauties, the Russian owned a Fabergé egg, and his great ambition in life, his 'Holy Grail', he confessed, was to find one of the missing eight 'Marie' eggs. Many Renaissance princes, Gideon had to remind himself, were terrible vulgarians too.

10.5

After a hasty meal at the Antica Farmacia, they arrive at the former refectory of the convent of Santa Maria dei Carmini less than five minutes before the start of the concert, but there are several unoccupied seats, most of them close to the front. Gideon does not want to sit at the front: musicians should be heard and not seen, he says, directing Claire into a row near the back. The acoustics are better here, he says; the sound is more balanced. His arrival has been noted: people nod to him, and a man she's never seen before reaches back to shake his hand. '*Maestro*,' says the man, and Gideon smiles in acceptance of the tribute. A woman taps Gideon on the shoulder; she is enthusing about the exhibition, Robert explains; Gideon's mouth twitches with self-deprecation; you can almost hear him purr.

On each seat there's a programme, a single sheet of paper, listing the works to be played and the names of the musicians, above adverts for La Cereria, the Ottocento hotel and a restaurant in Mensano. On the reverse are three paragraphs – Italian, German, English – about the music of Albert Guldager. The first sentence informs the reader that *La luna, quasi a mezza notte tarda* was 'inspired by the local legend of Mad Ginevra, though in no way a representation of the story', and is dedicated to Father Luca Fabris, from whom the composer first heard the tale. Thereafter, the text becomes more opaque. Perusing it, Gideon begins to mutter. 'What is this tripe?' he asks nobody in particular. Then, to Robert: 'Have you read this? "Evaporation into nothingness . . . blah blah blah . . . a paradise of glaciers." What in God's name is this supposed to mean? "Time is here a point, not a line. There is no before and after." Drivel. Utter gibberish. What's the Italian like?'

Robert scans the Italian paragraph. 'No better,' he answers. The musicians – three young women – are emerging from a doorway in the end wall. A spatter of applause greets them.

Gideon, as if hearing nothing, continues to read. 'Jesus,' he murmurs. 'How could anyone write this guff? "The body of sound is opened by Guldager's scalpel of micro-intervals." Any idea what that might mean?' he enquires.

'We'll find out in a while, Gideon,' Robert tells him.

The musicians are tuning their instruments. Clutching the sheet of paper, Gideon looks around the room as though trying to locate the person responsible for the nonsense he's had to read. He's still indignant when the musicians begin, with a trio by Boccherini, but the scowl dissolves quickly, and by the second movement he is, apparently, in a state of bliss.

Claire, by the third movement, is keen for this particular item to end: it's pleasant enough, but it sounds like background music – she imagines lords and ladies, bewigged, playing cards in candlit rooms, with the fiddlers at work in an alcove. The second piece on the menu, by someone called Felice Giardini (1716–1796), is not dissimilar. She finds herself, for all her efforts to concentrate, glancing to left and right. Several faces are façades of attention, with tedium visible through the eyes. Gideon, however, appears rapt: he smiles as though the three musicians had been nurtured by him and were acquitting themselves brilliantly. For Claire, the demeanours of the young women are the principal diversion: the cellist is all blithe virtuosity, her expression nonchalant throughout; the violinist stares at the score on her music stand, with a concentration that is almost fearful; the eyes of the viola player – the young woman she saw with the priest – keep flickering to the side, as though she's taking prompts from an invisible tutor. They are, as far as she can judge, a very well-drilled trio.

As soon as the last note of Giardini's composition has died, Gideon exclaims: 'Bravo'. Others follow suit. 'Terrific stuff, eh?' he says to Claire, with a passion that cannot be countered.

Next come two études by Albert Guldager. The first, for cello, commences with a sprightly phrase that might have been taken from one of the trios they've just heard, but then the music disintegrates into a sequence of gestures, of squiggles and scrapings and pluckings and brief catches of melody, or the beginnings of melodies, becoming quieter and quieter in the course of its six or seven minutes, until finally there's nothing more than a tentative scribbling on one string. The response to Guldager's étude for violin is cautious, and the applause is done in twenty seconds; Gideon's hands remain locked in his lap. The violin étude, after a bar or two of old-fashioned tunefulness, is similarly strange, if more abrasive: glaring at the score, the violinist hacks at the strings; she makes them screech and wail and moan; a crescendo of ascending spirals is succeeded by spirals descending towards silence.

Robert glances at Gideon, who is examining the ceiling, and at Claire, who has a slight frown, as if experiencing a sensation, like a low-voltage electric shock, that may or may not be enjoyable.

Now every note is at the instrument's upper limit, like an electric whispering; then there's a long slow slide, down to the lowest reach, and the piece is finished. The violinist, smiling with the satisfaction of having overcome the music, puts a hand out and Albert Guldager rises from the front row to take it. He bows, before standing aside to direct his applause at the performer; about two-thirds of the audience follow his lead.

Gideon waits for a minute before remarking, out of the side of his mouth: 'Sometimes, you know, less really is less.'

This, it seems to Claire, is probably not the first time this joke has been aired. 'I liked it,' she says.

'No you didn't,' Gideon tells her.

'I did.'

'Really?' he says, as if she'd just said that she likes to eat frog spawn.

'I wasn't the only one,' she says. 'They did, definitely,' pointing to a small cluster of enthusiastic applauders, Mr Lanese among them.

'They are pretending, believe me,' says Gideon. 'Never underestimate the fear of appearing stupid.'

'Well, I thought it was interesting,' says Claire. 'I've never heard anything like it.'

'We're agreed on that,' says Gideon. 'I've never heard a monkey running over a keyboard either, but that doesn't mean that a monkey running over a keyboard would be an event of any significance.'

'I'm not saying it was of any significance,' answers Claire, calmly obdurate. 'I'm saying that I liked it.'

Gideon looks into her eyes, to ascertain if this is a disagreement that has any foundation other than a compulsion to disagree with him. Appearing to achieve no conclusion, he continues: 'There was no reason for any of it. Noodling, that's all it was. Pseudo-clever noodling. It began in the middle of nowhere and finished in the middle of nowhere.'

'But a different nowhere,' Robert suggests.

'It could have gone on for twice as long or half as long and it wouldn't have made a blind bit of difference.'

'Yes it would,' says Robert. 'It would have been half the length or twice the length.'

'And just as pointless,' Gideon responds, scanning the programme.

'Robert, what did you think?' asks Claire.

'I'm staying for part two.'

Claire directs at Gideon an amiable smile of triumph, but he doesn't see it. '"We do not think of the music's architecture – its sounds are constellations, disconnected yet of a oneness",' he recites. 'The composer's own words,' he informs them, like a prosecutor leaving the jury to draw its own conclusions from the defendant's incoherence. 'I'm off. Enjoy the noodling.'

'Gideon,' Robert protests. 'Stay. You've got another dose of Corelli afterwards.' The tone is what you might use in trying to persuade an obstreperous teenager.

'They've put the Corelli at the end to stop people buggering off after the interval,' answers Gideon. 'But in this case the bait is insufficient. *Buona notte tutti.*' He tiptoes out, aping the crouching hurry of a man regrettably called away.

The violinist comes out, on her own, to make an announcement, which Robert translates: for this performance of *La luna, quasi a mezza notte tarda*, the very first, the main doors of the hall and the windows are to be opened, as requested by the composer; she makes a respectful gesture towards the front row. As the doors and windows are being opened, the musicians take their places.

The tam-tam player, wielding a club with a massive head of dense white fluff, strikes the soft initial note, which is allowed to expire into silence – or near-silence, because inside it there's the whine of a scooter, two or three streets away. Again the percussionist caresses the metal, with slightly greater force, and the bassoonist makes a sound like a quiet snore. Next the saxophone joins in, contributing a sigh, and the violinist taps the wood of her instrument with her fingernails, as if sending a message in Morse code. Sequences of slowly rising tones, separated by silences, come from the flute; they suggest to Claire an image of bubbles rising through oil. It's all strange: the cellist swipes the strings with the pads of her fingers, before bouncing the bow off the strings; the flautist exhales exhaustedly, and a moment later is blowing as if firing a dart from a blowpipe; the violinist generates a noise like a bee swarm; the saxophone murmurs like a dove; violin and cello together make a soft hissing and clatter, not unlike the sound of the porcupine's quills. In one of the silences she hears an owl, a real owl, far off; a car door closes with a thump; the percussionist, putting a hand to the back of the tam-tam, makes a similar thump. When it ends – with flute and saxophone and violin adding tiny squeaks and squeals to the slow-dying boom of the tam-tam – she's not sure if the last sound, a barely audible scrape, has come from the musicians or the audience or the piazza. For fully fifteen seconds the musicians remain motionless, with bow to strings and mouth to mouthpiece, making not a sound. They relax at last; Guldager takes another bow, modestly; he shakes the hand of Father Fabris, who is seated in the front row; half a minute after rising, the composer is back in his seat; the applause stops almost at once.

10.6

One day in the year 1245 or 1246, a man known to us only by the name of Michele, a pedlar of knives and pots and other items of metalwork, approached Castelluccio from the direction of Volterra. He had come to the town for its weekly market, and was accompanied by his son, Luca, who was fifteen years of age, and his daughter, Ginevra, a year younger. They were within sight of the town when a pack of dogs came howling through a field of wheat beside the road and leapt upon the family. Fighting furiously with knives and axes, Michele and his children succeeded in putting the animals to flight, but all three were bitten in the struggle. At the stream outside Castelluccio the father washed the blood from their wounds. The injuries were numerous and painful, but none was grave, or so it appeared. Michele dressed the cuts with herbs and closed them with bandages of sacking, then he led Luca and Ginevra to the market place, where they remained until late into the afternoon. They slept that night in a granary.

In the morning Ginevra had not enough strength to raise herself from the ground and her eyes could not tolerate the light of day. Her skin was as hot as a piece of metal that has been under the summer's sun for many hours, and there was foam in her mouth. By sunset she was dead. Ginevra was buried in a shallow grave outside the walls. Later the same day, Michele and Luca set off along the road to Massa.

On the following Sunday, as the moment came for the elevation of the Host in the church of San Giovanni Battista, a most extraordinary incident occurred. A cry from the rear of the church made the priest pause. He looked towards the door, which had come open. There, on a track of sunlight, stood Ginevra, the pedlar's daughter. Worms writhed in her hair; her shroud was torn and muddied; as she approached the altar, serenely as a bride, crumbs of soil were scattered behind her; she exuded a sweet stink of corruption. She spoke: which was the man, she enquired, who had consigned her body to the earth? The question was put gently, as if she were requesting a cup of water. The priest stepped down from the altar, and stated that he had conducted the burial. Ginevra moved towards him; at arm's length, she stopped; she bowed her head; she raised her arms, on which the wounds were turning green; she placed her hands on the priest's shoulders, drew him closer, and kissed him, softly, on each cheek. That done, she raised her face. Tears were streaking from her eyes, yet she was smiling. In a voice so quiet that few but the priest could hear her, she said to him: 'Jesus Christ is not our saviour.' In the next instant she collapsed, falling so suddenly it was as though she had been struck dead for her blasphemy. But she breathed as she lay on the floor in front of the altar, and one of the worshippers – a widow – stepped forward to request of the priest that the girl should be carried to her house.

For a week the widow and her sister tended Ginevra. They bathed her every day; they dressed her wounds freshly every morning; they fed her and they talked to her, but she spoke little, except to murmur, again and again, that she had seen things that would make anyone marvel. What these things were, she did not yet say. She slept for many hours, and began to recover her health. She was calm, and courteous, and grateful for what had been done for her.

News of her resurrection had been conveyed to her father and brother, who duly came back to Castelluccio. Michele entered the room in which his daughter was sleeping, and waited for her to awake. When at last her eyes opened, the look they gave him was strange. She smiled, but it was as if, instead of seeing her father at her bedside, she was looking upon an image that had given rise to tender memories of him. They embraced, and then she told him that because of what had happened to her she could no longer be his daughter. Like the blessed Chiara, she told him, she must renounce all possessions and family. She revealed to him what she had so far revealed to nobody: what her soul had experienced in the hours in which her body had been lying in the grave.

She had, she said, journeyed to the domain of the dead. It was a plain of perfect flatness that had no end to it, and the dead were going about in a violet twilight that never changed. And everyone who had ever died was there, the sinful and the good, all together. Charlemagne was there, and all the Caesars of Rome. The popes were there, every one of them, with Saint Peter and John the Baptist and all of the Apostles. She had seen so many of the holy martyrs, and so many evil men – she had seen Nero and Herod and even Judas himself, and he was not in torment. Nobody was in torment and nobody was in bliss. Noah and Moses and the Queen of Sheba – she had seen them all, everybody who has ever lived, and though there were thousands upon thousands upon thousands of them she could see them all so clearly, it was as if her sight could fly over any distance and lose none of its strength. She closed her eyes and smiled, and seemed to be seeing once more that infinite plain of the dead.

For a full day Michele reasoned with his daughter, but she was immovable: she could not go with him. So, as soon as Ginevra's body had recovered, Michele bound her wrists with twine and placed a halter around her neck, and he led her back to Volterra. She submitted to capture, and followed her father as meekly as a calf following its mother. But on the second night she escaped from him. Two days later, she reappeared in Castelluccio.

She begged in the streets of the town, and in return for alms she would tell her benefactors what she had seen when she had been dead. 'We must live, we must live,' she would repeat, as if she had discovered a wonderful secret. Pitying the mad girl, many people gave her food and drink. A carpenter built a hut for her, against the town wall, near the Porta di Volterra. Some days she would walk through the streets from dawn to dusk, singing songs that were inaudible or made little sense. Her walk – erect, dignified, slow – at times made it seem that she was following a sacred procession that was invisible to everyone but her. Sometimes she would pass through one of the town gates at first light and re-enter many hours later, having walked the hills all day long, circling Castelluccio again and again, without pause; she could be seen in the distance, crossing the fields with her steady tread. The townsfolk feared for the girl, but no mischance ever befell her. 'No misfortune can harm me,' she would tell them, 'because I have been dead.' Every day she would bathe in the stream, and it did not concern her that she might be seen. A priest remonstrated with her, upbraiding her for immodesty. She rebuked him for his lechery.

The girl's behaviour became wilder. It became her custom on a Sunday to wait outside San Giovanni Battista while Mass was being celebrated, and to scorn the worshippers as they emerged, or to dance lewdly in front of them. On market day she would dance on Piazza del Mercato. People at work in the orchards and vineyards would come across her, bathing in the sunlight as if its heat were the highest blessing of God. The dead, she proclaimed one morning on the steps of San Giovanni Battista, do nothing but watch the living, and spend eternity in a gloom of envy and regret.

A farrier's wife, after discovering her husband disporting with Ginevra at the stream, climbed onto the scaffolding of the Palazzo del Podestà and from this pulpit she condemned Ginevra for her lasciviousness and her blasphemies. A butcher stepped forward to inform the gathering that his son had been tempted by the young woman when he came upon her yesterday, outside the Porta di Massa, at noon. But this was not possible, said another man, because at noon yesterday he had been riding along the road to Volterra and had seen Ginevra rooting in the earth like a boar. Yet it was a fact that at noon she had been at the Porta di Massa, said the first man; and it was a fact, responded the other, that at noon she had been on the other side of the town, by the Volterra road; and so it was ascertained that the girl, beyond doubt, had been at two different places at the same time.

It was decided to bring Ginevra before the magistrates, and the company of townspeople set off immediately to find her: they looked by the Porta di Volterra and by the stream; they searched the orchards; they went up onto the walls to scan the land around the town; for the first time since the day she had come back to Castelluccio, she was not to be seen anywhere. It was as if she had known that she was about to be sentenced. Darkness came down, and the town gates were closed. Either the girl had fled, it was reasoned, or she would return to her shelter in the course of the night. Two men were dispatched to keep watch at the Porta di Volterra, and there, at midnight, Ginevra was seen, moving across the grass so lightly, it was said, that she left not the slightest mark of her passing. She was seized; forty or fifty people gathered around her. She listened in silence to their accusations, then turned upon them in fury. She decried them as hypocrites and liars and fools. She spat and cursed, and she tore apart the rags in which she was clothed until she stood as naked as Saint Francis when he divested himself of his garments before the bishop of Assisi. Clawing at her captors' eyes, she broke free, and was pursued through the town. The farrier whom she had seduced was at the head of the mob, and as the girl raced across the market square, with her long black hair flowing behind her like a pennant, he sprang forward to take hold of her. His hands reached into the hair, but they grasped nothing, as if her hair had become smoke. The girl ran on, towards the Siena gate, and there the farrier sprang again. But again she eluded him, because in the blink of an eye Ginevra di Michele vanished like a fume, with a sound like the clatter of an owl's wings.

10.7

As is customary on the night before the Festa di San Zeno, the streetlights have been turned off. All along the curve of Corso Diaz, candles are burning on windowsills in lamps of blood-red glass; illuminated by the lantern that has been hung in the bell-chamber of the Palazzo Comunale, an arch of brick glows in mid-air, a hundred feet above Piazza Maggiore; on the façade of San Giovanni Battista, the statues lean into the light that strikes them side-on from the Caffè del Corso.

Claire walks out into the centre of the piazza, where she turns slowly, admiring the star-strewn sky. 'This is a great idea, turning the lights off,' she says. For a minute she stands there, face upturned.

'Nightcap?' Robert suggests.

'You're not going to Teresa's?'

'Not tonight,' he says.

She looks at him.

'Not tomorrow, nor the day after,' he answers.

'Ah,' she says. 'I couldn't decide if you were preoccupied or bored,' she says, with a robust sympathy.

They take an outside table and Robert requests an *amaro*; asked, he explains what it is; she's doubtful, but orders the same.

'Definitely kaput?' she asks.

'She's decided to give her husband another chance,' he tells her.

'Rarely a good move,' says Claire. 'I gave mine another chance.'

'So Philippa wasn't the first offence?'

'She was not. There'd been a fling with a secretary from the office. Started at a Christmas party – stationery cupboard scenario. Unbelievably tacky. When he was rumbled we had the full works: tears, remorse, self-hatred, more remorse, more tears. "It'll never happen again," and so on. After a few weeks I cracked and let him back.'

'And he did it again.'

'Twice. Philippa was number three. And the reason he didn't want kids is that he wanted it to be just the two of us. Oh, the irony,' she says, in a mordant drawl. She takes a sip of her *amaro*, winces, reconsiders, takes another sip. 'But I'm fine now. It doesn't rankle at all,' she assures him, with a clenched-teeth smile.

'But you still use your married name.'

'Laziness. Haven't got round to changing it. But I will.'

'And it helped with the element of surprise, I suppose.'

'Sorry?'

'Well, if Maurizio had taken a booking from a Westfall, Gideon would have known about it within the hour.'

'Oh, yes. I suppose so. Didn't think of that.' Over Robert's shoulder she can see the woman who served them, standing at the counter, stretching cling film over a bowl. The woman is deep into middle age but she has a trim figure, and the tight-fitting grey skirt looks good on her. She's taking great care over what's she's doing, smoothing the cling film into the belly of the bowl, as if this action were a craft, like making a drum with a superfine skin. And as her hand passes over the bowl for the fifth or sixth time, she glances up, perhaps at the reflection of herself in the mirror beside the till, and her hand stops.

Robert says: 'So, you really did like the music? Guldager's stuff, I mean.'

'I did,' she answers, presenting to him a mild smile as her attention returns. 'But don't ask me why.'

'Just what I was going to ask.'

'Well, I can't tell you. I enjoyed it. It held my attention. It surprised me. That's all I can say. You didn't?'

'I wouldn't say fascinating. Interesting, maybe. I don't think I'll be able to remember it in the morning, though.'

'Neither will I. Does that matter?'

'Not sure,' he says. 'Gideon would say it does.'

'Gideon isn't always right.'

'True.'

'He should have stayed. Might have given him the odd moment of pleasure. Something new for his ears, at least. Perhaps something to think about. Shouldn't artists be open to new experiences?'

'Up to a point. But if you're open to everything you don't get anything done. That would be Gideon's line.'

She tilts her head and purses her lips, acknowledging the point, but unconvinced. A smile appears. 'He thought I was only pretending to like it, to get a rise out of him, didn't he?'

'Possibly.'

'Well, you can tell him I wasn't,' she states. 'If anything, I was playing it down. If anyone else had asked me, I'd have been more enthusiastic. But with Gideon I couldn't, because I didn't want an argument. And I knew I'd look stupid if I had to talk about it. But you can't really talk about it, can you? You can't persuade someone to like something you like. Especially music. Maybe. All you can do is ask them to listen. Same with Gideon's pictures. You can tell me what he's trying to do, and you can tell me how he does it, but even if I understand all that, I can't be persuaded to love it, can I? Does that makes sense? I'm talking drivel – that's what you're thinking, isn't it?'

'No.'

'I think you are,' she says.

He halts and looks at her. 'No,' he repeats, 'I agree with you. All you can do is listen.'

They walk down Corso Garibaldi, between the tracks of red candlelight. As they are about to turn into Piazza del Mercato he notices, in Via dei Falcucci, about thirty metres off, silhouetted against the lantern-lit stone of the Porta di Siena, a shape on top of a cable that spans the street from gutter to gutter: an owl. 'Look,' he says; he touches her elbow and they creep a few steps closer. 'He's often here,' he whispers, 'even when the lights are on.' He explains that the building at number 27 has been empty for years, because various members of the last owner's family have been squabbling in court over their inheritance, so now the place has a resident population of rodents. 'A steady supply of snacks,' he says. Then, putting out a hand: 'Near enough. They can be dangerous.' For five minutes or so they keep a watch on the bird; it remains motionless.

'That's enough for me,' whispers Claire.

'Two more minutes.'

She waits for two minutes more; the bird could be made out of plastic. 'I'm off,' she says. 'You staying?'

'I'll give it a bit longer,' he answers.

'OK,' she says. 'Good night.'

'Sleep well,' he says. He counts to sixty before turning: she's almost out of sight, striding across the piazza, head up, apparently marvelling at the sky. He stays in Via dei Falcucci for another half-hour, waiting for the owl to swoop; it doesn't budge.

10.8

The tawny owl (*Strix aluco*), which was first classified by Linnaeus in the 1758 edition of *Systema Naturae*, is a sturdy and medium-sized owl, being 37–43cm (14.5–17in) in length, with a wingspan of 81–96cm (32–38in); the female is about five percent longer and twenty-five percent heavier than the male. Common to woodlands in much of Eurasia, the tawny owl is an opportunistic nester, occupying sites such as holes in tree trunks or the abandoned nests of other species. It is a nocturnal bird of prey, eating rodents and other small mammals, as well as frogs, insects, worms and birds. Many of the subspecies are so poorly differentiated that there is no agreement as to how many subspecies there are: some authorities list fifteen, but most accept eleven. The owl of Via dei Falcucci is a male *Strix aluco sylvatica*, a subspecies identified in 1809 by the English naturalist George Shaw.

The eyes of *Strix aluco* are large, with densely packed retinal rods (almost 60,000 per square millimetre), but many researchers contend that the owl's night vision is only slightly more sensitive than a human's, and that the bird's prowess as a nocturnal hunter is attributable chiefly to its sense of hearing. In common with other owl species, the tawny owl has ears that are asymmetrically placed and differently structured; the discrepancy between the way a sound is perceived in each ear enables the bird to locate its source precisely. The hearing apparatus of the tawny owl has been estimated to be approximately ten times more sensitive than the human ear.

The tawny owl is typically monogamous, though some males are polygamous. The territory of an established pair varies little from year to year, and is defended strongly, especially in the spring, when there are fledglings to protect. Attacks on human intruders are not uncommon: the bird invariably aims for the face, descending at speed with talons extended, and as the tawny owl is virtually silent in flight its approach in the darkness is rarely detected until the last moment. People have been injured while imitating the owl's call, or after unwittingly wandering too close to a nest. Wildlife photographer Eric Hosking lost his left eye to a tawny owl in 1937; since then, bird photographers have often worn a fencing mask or similar protection when taking pictures of these birds.

10.9

'Robert,' his mother says, as if surprised to hear his voice, though only two weeks have passed since their last conversation.

'Not in bed, are you?' he asks.

'No, love. Not yet. You know me.'

'So how are you?'

'Ach, you know,' she sighs.

'Tell me,' he says.

'Not getting any younger.'

'But you're well?'

'I'm OK,' she concedes.

'And dad?'

'The knees are giving him terrible trouble,' she says. 'This morning, he couldn't get out of bed. Couldn't bend his legs. I keep telling him he's got to do something – give up the bowls or get the doctors to take a look.'

'Well, he's not going to give up his bowls, mum.'

'But he won't go the doctor either. Doesn't want an operation. Bit of stiffness in the morning is par for the course at his age, he says. But it's ridiculous, Robert. It's not a bit of stiffness. He could hardly get out of his chair this evening. He's got to get it seen to. I've told him a thousand times, but he won't listen.'

'Shall I have a word?'

'Won't do any good. You know what he's like.'

'I'll have a word anyway.'

'Next time, maybe. He's turned in for the night. Took him ten minutes to get up the stairs. You should see him. Walks like he's got broken glass in his legs.' She pauses, and he knows what's coming next. 'Pity you live so far away,' she says.

'It is,' he responds, as always.

'Have you thought about Christmas?'

'Mum, it's the middle of August.'

'I know. But the flights book out fast. You don't want to leave it too late.'

'There's plenty of time.'

'We'd love to see you. You know that.'

'I do.'

'Mary and the family are staying for a couple of days, we hope. Boxing Day and the day after.'

'OK.'

'The children will be really disappointed if they don't see you. They haven't seen you for ages.'

'Well—'

'It feels like ages to them.'

'I know.'

'See what you can do, Robert. Just for a day or two. I know you're needed there as well. But a brief visit, that's all. Think about it.'

'I will, mum. I will.'

'Thank you,' she says, in a humble murmur – like an acquitted defendant thanking the magistrate – that always grates, but can still give him a twinge of guilt. 'And how's Tania?' she asks.

'Teresa, you mean.'

'Sorry. Teresa. How's Teresa?'

'She's fine.'

'She won't mind if you're home for a few days,' she says, more as a statement than a question.

'No, ma, she won't.'

'And Gideon. How's Gideon?' she asks, in the tone that's customary for this question, a tone that one would use in asking after an unruly but likeable acquaintance whose life is regularly punctuated by wacky escapades.

'Working away,' he answers. 'Another American wants a portrait. A lady with a plastic face. And someone has vandalised one of his pictures.'

'Oh no. Who? Where?'

'At the exhibition,' he says; there is no response. 'The show I was telling you about. In the town hall. Someone wrote a rude word across one of the paintings, but we don't know who. Not yet.'

'Who would do a thing like that?'

'They're very passionate about their art over here, ma.'

'Gideon must be upset.'

'He's OK. I fixed it. Only a bit of ink. Not as if it was ripped.'

'It was ripped?'

'No, ma – I said it's not as if it was ripped. The damage was minor. It's fixed.'

'That's good,' she says. 'It's the parade soon, isn't it?'

'Tomorrow.'

'What are you going to wear?'

'I'm not in it, mum. Gideon's taking part, but I'm not. Looks like Charles Laughton doing Henry VIII. I'll send you a photo.'

'And send me a picture of you.'

'But I'm only watching. I'm not in fancy dress.'

'I know. But send me one anyway.'

'I look the same now as I did last year, give or take a wrinkle.'

'Nevertheless.'

'OK, ma. I'll send one.'

'I'd like that. Thank you.'

She's never been one for long conversations on the phone; it's time to wrap it up. 'I do have one bit of news,' he tells her. 'We've had an unexpected visitor. Gideon's niece.'

'He has a niece?'

'Daughter of the brother who died last year. He hasn't seen her since she was a kid. Just turned up on the doorstep. Thought it was time to reintroduce herself.'

'Gosh. And was he pleased to see her?'

'It was quite a surprise.'

'I bet. How did it go?'

'It's still going. She's here at the moment.'

'She's staying with Gideon?'

'Sort of. She's here.'

'You mean with you?'

'My apartment, yes.'

'Robert—'

'Separate rooms, ma, separate rooms. She has my room; I'm on the sofabed.'

'Is she nice?'

'She is. Very agreeable.'

'I see.'

'Nothing is going on,' he says, to which she answers with a doubtful hum. 'I promise you,' he adds.

'Attractive, is she? Pretty?'

'I told you. She's nice.'

'You said "Very agreeable". I distinctly remember a "very".'

'Indeed you do. She is. But nothing is going on.'

'You behave yourself, Robert.'

'For God's sake, ma. I lead a sedate life.'

'I know. But the girlfriends come and go, don't they?'

'Not as often as you seem to imagine.'

'I'm not imagining, Robert.'

'Nothing is going on. Nothing will go on.'

'But you like her. I can tell.'

'Yes, I do. I said so.'

'You know what I mean. What's she do, this—'

'Claire, mum. Her name's Claire.'

'Oh, I can hear something. I can tell,' she says again.

10.10

Gideon has been in her mind all day. Even in San Gimignano, amid the hundreds of people trudging towards the main square as if under orders, she could not rid herself of his voice. She picks up her book, but cannot concentrate on the page. He has had the last word. He has scrawled on the image of her mother and father: it was self-serving what he told her, and certainly false in some way, but the mark is there. Only the words of her parents could remove it quickly. She hears his voice clearly: 'The same thing happened to me'. The flabby face, drooping with bogus sympathy, appears before her. She wants to be at home. It's not possible to read, nor to sleep. She decides to take another lap of the town to tire herself; the Corso café should still be open.

At the door to the living room it occurs to her to tell Robert that she's going out; she is about to knock when she realises that the sound she's hearing isn't the television, it's Robert talking. She registers the word 'mum' and a tone of affection. Then she hears 'agreeable' and 'nothing is going on', and 'she's nice'. Again he says: 'nothing is going on'. She isn't sure what she should do. 'For God's sake,' says Robert, raising his voice; she tiptoes back to the bedroom.

10.11

Gideon has failed to quell his indignation at the effrontery of that absurd music, and to work in such a state of mind has proved impossible. A walk is the only way to regain his composure. Trim is summoned.

As he reaches the end of Corso Diaz, Gideon begins to sense that he is being followed; he looks back; he's the only person on the street. He crosses Piazza Maggiore and passes the Caffè del Corso. At the Teatro Gaetano he seems to hear footsteps, a little quicker than his own, approaching from behind. Again he turns; two people, a couple, are moving towards him; he lets them overtake, and when there's nobody on the Corso between himself and Piazza Maggiore he starts walking again. Now he hears only the sound of his own feet. He turns into Via dei Giardini; as he passes the gardens, the leaves make a sound that recalls the ridiculous scratchings of the violin. At the Porta di Volterra he turns left; he follows the walls to Sant'Agostino, where he stops. The little piazza is dark; the streetlamp is off, and in the surrounding apartments only three or four windows are lit; a shadow moves across the ceiling in Teresa's place; from somewhere comes the crooning of a male voice, then applause.

He looks at the church, at the buildings around it, and it occurs to him that he might use this place for a night scene, with a high viewpoint, perhaps. The black glass of the rose window could be juxtaposed with the white disc of the moon, or maybe the piazza itself should be the focus, viewed from the campanile. The latter idea has the feeling of a beginning: something should happen here, on the piazza, something with the atmosphere of a dream. He envisages a scene: a figure stalking another one (one of them death-like; perhaps not the pursuer but the one being stalked?), and a third, in a dimly lit window, watching. Then a man is standing in front of him, ten paces off; he's stocky, and is wearing a dark top with a hood, which is up, and topped with a baseball cap. In the gloom it's not possible to make out the face. His presence having been registered, the man starts talking, quietly. Gideon can't hear him clearly and cannot understand the sounds that he does hear; this character appears to be drunk. 'What do you want? Who are you?' Gideon asks, so disconcerted that he asks in English. The man recoils and says something, as he raises his arms and bends them inward, so the fingertips rest on his chest. Now it sounds as if he's reciting a list; he appears to be ticking off points on his fingers. The fingers look like gargantuan termites and his lips have a strange way of moving up and down, in and out, as though testing the fit of his teeth. Gideon knows who this is: it's Ilaria's father. And in that instant, as if seeing that he's been recognised, Alfredo Senesi approaches. With two rigid fingers he taps firmly on Gideon's breastbone, forcing him to take a step back. '*Cosa vuoi?*' shouts Gideon. Senesi, aghast, emits a scream. Behind him, a light goes on, in a room on the second floor; a silhouette appears. Gideon repeats his question: '*Cosa vuoi?*' Another light goes on, high to the right, with two silhouettes in front of it. Senesi scratches his chin and nods, dourly, as though this charade of not understanding were just the sort of trick he should have expected. A fist comes up and batters twice into Gideon's left eye. He totters, putting a palm to his face; when he takes the hand down he sees blood on it. The lights in the apartments go out and Senesi is jogging out of the piazza, hands held high at his sides, like a boxer on a training run.

10.12

A chapel is known to have stood on the site of the church of Sant'Agostino as long ago as the first decade of the twelfth century, when a community of monks lived here, in obedience to the Rule of Saint Augustine. Following the papal bulls *Incumbit Nobis* and *Praesentium Vobis*, both of which were issued by Pope Innocent IV on December 16th, 1243, many monastic communities in Tuscany were consolidated within the reformed Augustinian order. In the wake of this consolidation, the small chapel in Castelluccio was rebuilt as the church of Sant'Agostino, with a monastery being raised on the adjacent orchard. Not until 1370 was the church completed.

The façade's rose window is the most substantial visible remnant of the fourteenth-century building. The church was greatly modified between 1580 and 1650, when the façade was embellished, an elaborate *baldacchino* was raised over the high altar, the side chapels were constructed, stucco-work was applied throughout the church, and the gilded ceiling was put in place. The pictures on the walls above the columns of the nave, illustrating sixteen scenes from the life of Saint Augustine, were painted in the 1650s by followers of the Sienese artist Raffaello Vanni (1590–1659); in style they bear similarities to the work of Pietro da Cortona, to whose work Vanni himself was considerably indebted.

Between the first and second altars on the left-hand side of the church is the memorial to Tommaso Galli, which takes the form of a marble stele; Galli's profile is sculpted on a medallion held by Melpomene, the muse of tragedy, and Thalia, the muse of comedy. Of the numerous memorial stones in the cloister, the most conspicuous is the wall plaque for Domenico Vielmi (1350–1424), which features a finely carved panel depicting the three crosses of Calvary, with an angel descending to take the soul of the good thief.

II.I

ON CORSO GARIBALDI people are on ladders, stringing pennants across the road in readiness for the parade; the shutters of the Caffè del Corso are half raised, and Giosuè is outside, smoking a cigarette while talking to a young man who wears crimson and gold silken pantaloons and white stockings below his denim jacket. A dog with a rosette on its collar lies in a sunny corner of Piazza Maggiore. Barriers are being put in place beside the Palazzo Comunale, and scarlet and gold banners have been unfurled from its windows.

Robert pauses on Corso Diaz to listen to the trills of a flute, coming from a room opposite an alley from which a woman now hurries, bearing a bright blue dress on outstretched arms. It's Agnese. She stops, and looks at him as though her eyes are having difficulty in adjusting to the light. 'Hello Robert,' she says, in the tone of a teacher encountering a former pupil who was disruptive but bright.

'Nice outfit,' he comments.

She examines it for a few seconds. 'It's been altered by Signora Nerini,' she tells him. 'I'm a centimetre wider than last year.' It's said as a simple statement of fact, as you'd remark on the growth of a plant in your garden.

He pretends to inspect her waist for thickening. 'Looking good,' he tells her, which is true. The narrow black-framed glasses are subtly different from the last pair; they go well with her frown.

'And how are you?' she asks. 'Well?'

'I'm fine.'

'And Mr Westfall?'

'Fine too. How about yourself?'

'Very well.'

'Haven't seen you for a while,' he says.

She's been to a conference, she says, in New Zealand. They made a holiday of it – Filippo came too.

Surprised to hear that Filippo is still on the scene, he asks: 'And how is Filippo?'

Filippo is well, but very busy: there are big problems with acid leaking from one of the mines. Before he can think what to say to this, she asks: 'Have the police been to see you about the girl?'

'They have.'

'I saw her,' she says. 'On the day she disappeared. I gave her a lift.' She'd been driving to work and had passed her outside Radicóndoli, walking along the road. The girl wasn't hitching, but she'd given her a ride and dropped her off in Castelnuovo. 'She didn't want to talk,' remarks Agnese. 'It didn't strike me that anything was wrong. Have you heard anything?'

'Not a thing, no.'

Agnese shrugs. 'I must go,' she says, raising the dress by way of explanation.

'Of course. Nice to see you.'

'And you,' she says. Nobody observing them would have guessed that they had been close, not so long ago.

II.2

Of the various women with whom Robert has been involved since the move to Castelluccio, Agnese Littarru is the one that Gideon most liked, and he liked her because, as he told her in the course of their conversation in the Antica Farmacia, on the first and penultimate occasion on which the trio ate together, she possessed a clarity of purpose such as one too rarely encounters. 'I admire that,' he told her. 'I admire it immensely.' The compliment was received with something less than the gratitude he had doubtless anticipated: Agnese nodded slightly, as if taking note of a disclosure that had nothing whatever to do with herself.

She had given him a synopsis of her career, a story as full of purpose as a fable. Her grandfather, born in the heart of Sardegna, in the village of Desulo, had been a partisan; wounded by a grenade, he'd been nursed in the cellar of a farmhouse near Massa Maríttima until the Americans passed through and patched him up. Back home, he stayed in touch with the family who had cared for him, and promised he would visit them one day, but he had a family to raise and no money, so that day was a long time coming. Eventually, though, Agnese's father landed a good job at Cagliari airport, and he paid for the grandparents to come with the family on a holiday across the water. And on the day that her grandfather and grandmother went to the village near Massa Maríttima to be reunited with his saviours, Agnese and her brother were taken to Monterotondo. She was only twelve years old, but the course of her life was set by that afternoon: she stood by the fumaroles at Monterotondo, with the wisps of pungent steam flying around her face, and her father telling her about the eruption of Krakatoa, an explosion so loud that it was heard three thousand miles away, and as she listened, and breathed that chemical air, she experienced a thrill that she had never experienced before. She was an intelligent child, and she'd known that studying would be her future; now she knew what it was that she would study – the earth, the substance on which we lived. From that moment, said Agnese, it was inevitable that she would do what she went on to do.

Gideon had first noted her among the spectators of the 2007 San Zeno parade: a young woman conspicuous initially for her height, her maelstrom of brass-coloured and windswept-looking hair (though the day was becalmed), and her concentratedly observant demeanour, which gave her the appearance of an anthropologist conducting fieldwork, rather than of a participant in the festivities. Her beauty was remarked upon by Robert; Gideon judged her to be too severe – he could imagine that face, he later remarked, on a forty-foot statue of a Heroine of Soviet Industry, sledgehammer in hand. Enquiries were made: it was learned that her name was Agnese and she was a new arrival; she lived outside the town, on the Volterra road; she worked at Larderello, at the power plant.

Later that year, in the Palazzo Comunale, Agnese Littarru gave a talk on energy conservation and new initiatives in power generation. It was an eloquent and passionate lecture, an hour long, delivered without notes, and was well received by the great majority of the twenty or thirty people in attendance, with one vociferous exception: Maurizio Ianni, whose objections to the 'leftist consensus' on the subject of global warming were denounced robustly by Carlo Pacetti, speaking from the floor, before being skewered with exquisite precision, and an impressive array of memorised statistics, by Dottoressa Littarru. Afterwards, Robert caught up with her halfway down the staircase of the town hall, to congratulate her. 'Thank you,' she answered, continuing to descend.

'It gave me a lot to think about,' he said.

'I am glad,' she replied.

'My carbon footprint is around a size 40, I'd say,' he told her, failing to amuse, 'but it could be smaller.'

She gave him a glance. 'It can always be smaller,' she said.

'You work at Larderello?' asked Robert, to which her eyes responded: 'That's what it says on the poster.' They were now at the door. Holding it open for her, he asked: 'What exactly do you do?'

She stopped, and delivered her answer as if identifying herself to a persistent journalist: she was at the Centro di Eccellenza per la Geotermia di Larderello, an institution that functions as a point of reference for research into all aspects of geothermal energy.

'That sounds very interesting,' remarked Robert.

To this fatuity she responded: 'It is.' Her eyes regarded his as if they were items in a cabinet, but he chose to be encouraged by a movement, a very small twist, of the corner of her mouth, and was on the point of asking if she had time for a coffee, because there were some things he'd like to ask her, when her look took on an unambiguous meaning, which was: 'Will that be all?' She was very pleased he had enjoyed the talk, she told him; she shook his hand, and clamped her document folder to her side; and she departed, alone, at speed, as if another audience awaited.

It was discovered, soon after, that an open day at Larderello would be featuring a talk by Agnese Littarru of the Centro di Eccellenza per la Geotermia. Robert attended, taking a seat at the back of the hall, lest he appear too eager. 'Beneath our feet is an unexploded volcano,' announced Agnese, arms and hands spread in tension, as if to counteract the pressure of the earth. Pacing the narrow stage, demonstrative as a Pentecostal preacher, she showed pictures of the torrents of steam that shoot out of the ground here at 200 degrees Celsius, of the turbines that those torrents propel, of the drills with which the even hotter strata, 4,000 metres down, would be tapped. She made them comprehend how remarkable this engineering was; she explained how it was that geologists and seismologists could predict where the untapped wells were located. Robert was entranced by her: by her flashing eyes, her floating hair, the immensely flattering glasses, the provocative trousers.

Questions were invited at the end. Robert didn't speak, but stayed behind to ask her, as she was gathering up her papers, a question which, she pointed out, had been answered by her talk. 'But perhaps I spoke too quickly for you?' she suggested.

'No,' he assured her. 'I was following.'

'You are English, yes?'

'I am.'

'And you are interested in geothermal technology?'

'It's an interesting subject.'

'What do you do? What work?' she asked, putting the contents of her briefcase in order. He told her. 'OK,' she said, as though he had applied for a job for which being an artist's assistant did not automatically disqualify him. 'And is that interesting?'

'To me, yes,' he answered.

'Good,' she said, with a bright and professional smile; within a minute he was alone.

But one Friday evening, the following April, he was in the Caffè del Corso, sitting at the table underneath the painting of Tommaso Galli, reading the *Corriere della Sera*, when Agnese came in. She appeared not to notice him, and he made no attempt to attract her attention; he carried on reading his newspaper, and she came over to him, coffee in hand, to ask if she might join him. And straight away, as though their acquaintanceship were well established, she told him she'd been for a meal with a friend and her new husband, and it hadn't gone very well, because the husband was such a fidgety and irritating little man, like a jockey, and he'd clung to her friend's arm all evening, as if he'd thought she might run away if he let go of her. 'Which is what she should do,' she said, 'because he has nothing to say.' She gazed at Galli without looking at him, shaking her head at the recollection of the evening. 'Tell me about what you do,' she said, which he did, and she in turn told him more about herself, about her studies at the National Institute of Geophysics and Vulcanology in Rome and her work at Larderello. 'Who's that guy?' she asked, inter- rupting herself to indicate the portrait of Galli.

'He used to be the boss of the theatre,' Robert answered; he added a few details.

'How do you know all that?' she asked.

So he gave credit to Cinzia Zappalorto, and his admiration for the eccentric Signora Zappalorto appeared to improve significantly his standing with Agnese Littarru.

They talked until it was time for Giosuè to lock up. 'I live on the Volterra road,' she told him. The house was cheap, and it had a large garden – she couldn't live in a place that had no garden. It was a forty-minute drive to work, which wasn't ideal, but she had to admit that she enjoyed driving, and it was a small car, which did a lot of kilometres to the litre; and she'd fitted solar panels to her house, to redress the balance. 'It's a nice place,' she said. 'I'll show you one day, if you're interested.' This was said in a tone and with an expression so devoid of flirtatiousness that it did not seem impossible that all she had in mind was showing him the solar panels and the highly productive garden.

'Thank you,' he answered, as if in response to a business proposition.

To which she responded, still with no smile: 'How about now? It's not late.'

She drove fast, with one hand almost constantly on the gear-stick, braking late; it was a performance of great concentration and insouciance; the face was that of a woman watching a mediocre show on TV. She had learned to drive from her brother, who raced go-karts, she explained. 'He isn't as good as me,' she added, with a quick smile of victor's sympathy. Regular and high dosages of adrenaline were, it turned out, essential to the well-being of Dottoressa Agnese Littarru. Whitewater kayaking was a favourite activity, as was hang-gliding: they spent a weekend in the Monti Sibillini, where he watched her wheeling in the sky above the Piano Grande, higher than all the others. They went up to the Dolomites, to clamber along the Ivano Dibona *via ferrata*; he edged along the Ponte Cristallo without risking a glance at the abyss below him; fearless Agnese strolled across as if it were the path to her front door. She played tennis as though she thought the purpose of the game was to destroy the ball; being driven by her – she couldn't bear to be a passenger – was like riding in a rally car.

And in bed too she was energetic, and brisk. When he proposed that there might be benefits in taking things a little more slowly, it was as if he'd suggested that it might be nice to let their food go cold before eating it. What would be the point in delaying, when they could achieve the desired result so readily? He should be pleased to get such a response, surely?

There was another problem: it soon became apparent that, although she could muster some interest in the technologies of art, in the materials and techniques of it, she believed that art, in the final analysis, was a form of entertainment: the highest form, one might argue, but nonetheless frivolous, in essence. An hour with Robert in the Museo Civico, learning how the old paintings were made, why some had lasted better than others, was more enjoyable than she would have thought possible, she said, and she could concede that pictures of saints and Bible stories did once perform a valuable social function. In the twenty-first century, however, art was no longer a source of information about anything except the artist; to her way of thinking, she had to say, it was too often a self-indulgence. She didn't see much point in what Gideon produced, and didn't warm to him; when Gideon asked if he could draw her, she laughed.

Agnese Littarru was as conscientious as she was intelligent. At weekends she brought work home; on any evening she might spend two or three hours on the various online forums to which she contributed lengthy postings that were as tightly argued and thoroughly referenced as an academic paper, on climate change, conservation, recycling, et cetera, et cetera. She was entirely admirable, as Robert came to tell himself frequently in the last weeks of their relationship.

The night it ended, she was at her laptop, and had just pressed 'Submit' after writing five hundred words on the prospects for electric cars. It had taken her less than twenty minutes – it was the sort of thing she could compose as quickly as she could type it. Two more postings and she'd be finished for tonight.

'I think,' said Robert, 'that there's something missing here.'

He had her full attention: she encouraged him to continue, in the expectation, it appeared, of being be able to refute whatever point he was about to make.

Deploying as many Italian approximations to 'spark' as he could find in his vocabulary, Robert made his point.

Agnese looked at him as though he were reciting the lyrics of some inane pop song, and not even getting them right. 'We have a good time together,' she reminded him, which was largely true.

'I'm not saying we don't.'

'Is there someone else?'

'No,' he stated.

For a minute or more she stared at the computer screen; she said nothing; he moved to her side, and saw that she was crying.

'I would like us to be friends,' he said.

She smiled, as at a weak gesture of consolation. 'Thank you,' she said, selecting a Favourite from her browser menu. 'But no.'

Less than a month after this, on Corso Diaz, Agnese greeted him as you would greet a former colleague with whom you'd had a good working relationship, and introduced him to Filippo, a thin and anaemic-looking individual with a slight wilt to his stance, like a week-old stick of celery. His pale eyes directed an incurious attention onto Robert. Filippo worked for the Parco tecnologico e archeologico delle Colline Metallifere grossetane, for which organisation he was employed to investigate the condition of the abandoned mine workings of the Colle Metallifere, particularly with regard to the pollution of the water table by acid drainage and the reconstitution of the topsoil. This information was proffered by Filippo as if reciting a paragraph of his CV, and delivered in a voice as unmodulated as the hum of a generator. While he was speaking, Agnese gazed at him as if he were a war hero modestly admitting to an action that some might call brave.

Filippo was not a frivolous man, evidently, but he looked so flimsy that one blow from a tennis ball struck by Agnese could lay him out. 'I give it two months at the outside,' thought Robert.

11.3

Carlo Pacetti and the *maestro*, like a pair of senior security guards on patrol, are ambling across Piazza Santa Maria dei Carmini. The subject of the previous night's attack has been exhausted; Gideon has accepted, several times, that his friend had indeed warned him that the Senesi girl would bring nothing but trouble. Now Carlo has another criticism to make: he had been a little disappointed when he'd heard that Gideon was to take part in the parade, and he is still disappointed. A man of Gideon's good taste should not have consented to participate in an event that is merely a show for the tourists. '*Maestro*,' he says, 'you must promise me that you will not do it again.'

Gideon regrets that he can make no such promise. As he has often done before, he invokes the concepts of community, of ritual, of continuity. What the tourists see is not necessarily what the festival is, he tells his companion.

There are not ten people in Castelluccio who believe that a boy called Lodovico di Piero once fell out of a window and was saved by Saint Zeno, argues Carlo. 'It's make-believe, a stupid fantasy,' he says.

'I don't think it's stupid,' says Gideon.

'We have become a circus,' grumbles Carlo. 'We are making ourselves into clowns. The clowns of the history circus,' he says. This formulation gives him some satisfaction; he walks on in silence, along Via Sant'Agostino, his jaws working as if on a little cube of hard rubber.

And here are some tourists, coming out of the Cereria: two children and six adults; Dutch. Within half a minute one of the adults has taken a photograph, of a boy in particoloured stockings and tabard, sitting on a step.

Travellers no longer have a use for memory, says Carlo. They don't use their minds at all. People used to travel to a foreign country and write down what they saw, or draw it. Now you just press a button: no effort is involved, no engagement. Gideon agrees with this thesis, for perhaps the tenth time this year. One of the women, having pointed her phone at a basket of flowers, takes note of the two older gentlemen, one limping, the other with a black eye. Grabbing Gideon's wrist, Carlo says: 'Let's give her a show.' With great vehemence, and much operatic flailing of an arm, he tells his friend that he agrees with those Africans – or whoever they are – who think that they lose a bit of their soul whenever someone takes a photo of them. 'Every damned snap takes away a bit of the soul of Castelluccio,' he shouts, with complicated finger gestures that do not mean anything. 'Death by a million photographs.' Abruptly he calms himself, and presents to the woman an over-bright smile; she smiles uncertainly and rejoins her companions, as a friend of the Cabrera boy appears, with a snare drum slung at his hip, twirling drumsticks between his fingers. A photo is taken. Carlo links an arm with Gideon's, and they continue to the Porta di Siena.

11.4

Hell, a Tuscan poet once wrote, would smell like a tannery. The production of leather at that time was indeed a noxious business: hair was removed from the hides by steeping them in vats of urine, or by allowing them to putrefy for weeks, before the skins were softened by being pounded in a stew of animal excrement. For many years, nevertheless, the largest tannery in Castelluccio was located within the town walls, in the building that nowadays contains the holiday apartments of the Antica Cereria. Then, in the early 1300s, fearful of the effects of the bad air that emanated from the vats and troughs, and of the filth that the place discharged in such quantities, the *comune* banished the tanners to a site downstream from Castelluccio.

The vacated building became a wheelwright's workshop, which it remained for several decades. A vintner was the next occupant, then a blacksmith and farrier. In the 1550s, after it had been put to a multitude of other uses, the building in Via Sant'Agostino became a candle factory, or *cereria*.

The candles used most widely at that time were of tallow, which was made by rendering animal fat; these candles dripped, gave off a lot of smoke, required frequent trimming, and smelt vile. The *cereria* of Castelluccio manufactured only beeswax candles, which burned slowly and cleanly, with very little smoke, and produced a pleasing perfume. These candles were, however, expensive, as the raw material is not in plentiful supply: bees have to consume around eight kilos of honey to produce one kilo of wax, and it takes the nectar of more than thirty million flowers to make that quantity of honey. The Castelluccio candles were of the highest quality, and were supplied to churches all over the region, as far away as Siena, as well as to the area's wealthier families. Deliveries were made every week to the Palazzo Campani, and in 1728 the *cereria* of Castelluccio achieved its highest accolade, when it was commissioned to make candles for the wedding of Cornelia Barberini – the daughter of Urbano Barberini, the last male Barberini – and Prince Giulio Cesare Colonna di Sciarra. Some of the Barberini candles were as tall as the eleven-year-old Cornelia, and every one was adorned with the emblems, in painted wax, of the two families: the three bees of the Barberini and the crowned column of the Colonna.

The candle-making industry changed rapidly in the nineteenth century. Stearine, a wax first described in 1814 by the French chemist Michel Chevreul, was used to manufacture candles that burned more slowly than tallow, were odourless and smokeless, and were far less costly than beeswax. In 1834, Joseph Morgan created a machine that could turn out 1,500 candles per hour, and in 1850 the Scottish chemist James 'Paraffin' Young filed a patent for the process of extracting paraffin from coal.

Consequently, inexpensive and high-quality paraffin wax candles were soon being mass-produced. Just four years after Young's patent, George Wilson – brother of William Wilson, the founder of Price's Candles – carried out the first distillation of petroleum oil, from which paraffin could also be extracted. By the end of the century, Price's had become the world's biggest manufacturer of candles.

Though business declined with these advances in technology, the *cereria* of Castelluccio continued to function until 1891, making beeswax candles, mostly for local churches, as well as producing polishes and modelling waxes. After the factory closed, the premises were used as storage space by the Teatro Civico before becoming a warehouse for timber. While working on the town's war memorial, Achille de Marinis had his studio here. When bought by Maurizio Ianni in 2004, the bottom storey of the building had last been used by a welder, who had left Castelluccio twelve years earlier; families lived on the upper floors until 1997.

II.5

La Cereria, Castelluccio, midday, April
Oil-tempera on canvas; 100cm x 134cm
1993
Jeremies Collection, Boston, Massachusetts

The Cereria was the subject of the first painting completed by Gideon Westfall in Castelluccio. Walking around the town on a Sunday morning, a few days after his arrival, browsing for scenes that might have the makings of a picture, he was arrested by the sight of this workaday building. He could not remember if he'd passed it before, during those two days in Castelluccio when he had decided that this was where he would live. As he must have walked along every street in the town, it was probable that he had seen it, and taken no notice of it. It was, after all, not

a distinguished thing. The churches, the theatre, the town hall,
the Caffè del Corso, the town gates – these would have made
a stronger claim to the attention of someone who was new to
Castelluccio. But on this quiet Sunday morning, with the pale
April mid-morning light striking a pattern of small shadows from
the rough, silver-yellow stones of the wall, the Cereria made him
stop. A splintered wooden gate, painted myrtle green, occupied
the arch that today is glazed with a sheet of thick glass, on which
L'Antica Cereria has been inscribed in gold. Above the gate were
four small windows, a pair for each storey; the shutters of the
upper pair were half-open, and from one of these windows hung
a towel, maroon and yellow – a detail that became the focal point
of the painting, in which the colour of the gate was darkened a
little, and the graffiti that then defaced it was omitted. The next
day, he set up his easel in Via Santa Maria, and began work on
what was to become a series of sketches in watercolour and oil;
by the end of the month he had completed La Cereria, Castelluccio,
midday, April.

It was while he was at work on these sketches that he came
to the attention of Carlo Pacetti. Their first encounter was inaus-
picious. It was again a Sunday; Mass was in progress at Santa
Maria dei Carmini, the Redentore and San Giovanni Battista;
the streets were so empty that in an hour Gideon saw no more
than half a dozen people. Then he became aware of a man in
a blue shirt, loitering a short distance away, smoking, possibly
watching him. Gideon glanced his way, raised a hand, and was
ignored. A couple of minutes later, the blue-shirted man ambled
past, behind him; Gideon turned and observed a sniffing kind
of expression, as if the man had expected to be unimpressed,
and duly was. Later that day, around five o'clock, the man again
wandered past; he looked at the picture, looked at the wall, and
gave a begrudging grimace, as if to say: 'Could be worse'.

The following week, on Piazza del Mercato, where he was
making a drawing of the loggia, Gideon perceived the blue shirt
passing close to him, risked a 'Buongiorno', and received, or so

he thought, a blink of acknowledgement. When they next met, again on a Sunday morning, this time on Piazza Maggiore, an exchange of words occurred: 'On holiday?' Gideon was asked, in Italian, and he replied 'I live here,' in English, then in Italian. The man frowned, making Gideon wonder if he'd not said precisely what he had intended to say, or was it that his pronunciation was even worse than he feared? 'Is good,' said the man, indicating the watercolour of the Palazzo Comunale. Gideon thanked him, and the man departed. Seven days later, by the Cereria, names were exchanged; Carlo Pacetti tried to explain to the Englishman what this building had been, and where he worked. Soon after, late in the afternoon, Mr Pacetti stepped out of his garage for a cigarette and saw Mr Westfall seated on the grass embankment, sketching the walls and the Porta di Siena; he brought the artist a glass of wine, in an oily beaker.

One other immensely significant relationship in the life of Gideon Westfall is associated with his first painting of the Cereria. In May 1994, Milton Jeremies, a partner in a Boston law firm, was on holiday in Tuscany with his new wife, Jane. On May 12th he and Jane stopped for a coffee at La Costarelli in Siena; they sat on the terrace, overlooking the Campo, and Gideon was at an adjacent table, with a sketchbook on his knee. From where he was sitting, Milton Jeremies could see the page on which Gideon was drawing: it was covered with sketches of the waiter who had served them. Every time the waiter reappeared on the terrace, Gideon did a sketch – a dozen lines or less, fluid, interwoven, capturing the essence of a movement. When the waiter brought a glass of water, Gideon set the sketchbook aside, whereupon Milton Jeremies struck up a conversation, with: 'You've been here before.' It was almost a question. 'You're not looking at it,' he went on, waving an arm at the Campo below them, 'so I assume it's familiar.' Gideon confirmed that it wasn't new to him.

'We're walking round with our mouths open all the time,' said Jane, though it was impossible to imagine that this refined young woman would ever gawp. Milton made some remarks about the cathedral, which they'd visited that morning: his comments were far from banal; he was astute, and very personable. Jane told Gideon that they'd been in Florence for a few days. 'Wonderful, but too many people like us,' she said, with attractively dry self-deprecation. 'And there's just too much, you know? Like eating caviar all day.' They talked about the restaurants they'd eaten at, and then, without a pause, Milton asked if he could take a look at the sketchbook. Studying the drawings of the waiter, he made no comment, but his silence seemed thoughtful and complimentary. He passed the sketchbook to Jane, and told Gideon how much he liked Rembrandt's drawings. There was no pretension in the remark. 'If I could own one piece of art, just one, I think it would be that sketch of Saskia asleep,' he said. Now Jane murmured 'Wow,' and handed the sketchbook back to her husband, opened at a drawing of Carlo Pacetti, which Milton studied for a full minute, without speaking. He did not yet tell Gideon that he was something of a collector, and that he'd begun to consider commissioning a portrait of Jane to mark their marriage, but the conversation continued for an hour, at the end of which it had been agreed that Milton and Jane, after taking their planned drive through Chianti, would tomorrow take a diversion to Castelluccio. The result of that visit was that *La Cereria, Castelluccio, midday, April* became the first picture bought by Milton and Jane Jeremies, whose collection of Gideon Westfall paintings was to become the most extensive in the world.

The following year, Gideon was flown to Boston to paint a portrait of Jane Jeremies. He took with him another Castelluccio scene, *Porta San Zeno, dusk, November*, which had been bought on the strength of a photograph. By 2009 Milton and Jane Jeremies had acquired fifteen paintings of Castelluccio, which were displayed in one room, arranged in such a way that the visitor's progression from picture to picture corresponded to a walk through the town, starting from the Porta di San Zeno and ending with the painting that hung on the opposite side of the door, *La Cereria, Castelluccio, midday, April*.

There is scarcely a street in Castelluccio that Gideon Westfall did not at some time paint or sketch, and there are several parts of the town to which he returned many times. The church and piazza of San Lorenzo, for example, appear frequently in his work, and between Sant'Agostino and Santa Maria dei Carmini there's an alley of which he was very fond, because it contains a house that dates back to the fifteenth century and has been modified so many times that its walls, as he put it, have become 'a palimpsest in brick and stone'. His favourite episode in the townscape of Castelluccio, however, was the façade of the Cereria, of which he made no fewer than twenty-two paintings, plus scores of watercolour and pencil sketches. 'Morandi had his bottles, I have this wall', he once remarked. Only when Maurizio Ianni bought the building and 'restored it to death', did he cease to paint it.

II.6

'I need help with the headgear,' says Gideon in the doorway, presenting a huge whorl of scarlet fabric. He's wearing a high-collared scarlet velvet *cioppa*, floor-length, over a thickly pleated and loosely belted black doublet, with a white linen shirt underneath; white stockings and his best black brogues complete the ensemble.

'What the hell happened to you?' Robert asks, indicating the bruise.

'A contretemps,' Gideon answers, depositing the cloth on his head; from the pocket of the *cioppa* he takes a plastic box of pins and clips, and a piece of paper on which is printed the Jan van Eyck portrait of a man with an extravagant red *chaperon*. 'This is the effect we're after,' says Gideon, putting the picture in Robert's hand.

'A contretemps with whom?' asks Robert.

'A drunk chap,' says Gideon.

'Where? Who? How?'

While his assistant constructs the headdress, with much folding and pinning, Gideon lies about what happened at Sant'Agostino.

'You've never seen him before?' asks Robert.

'If I have, I've forgotten him. But one sensed an element of personal grievance,' says Gideon, with a single-note laugh. 'I'm pretty sure he was the one who scrawled on the picture.'

'Have you reported it?'

'No.'

'But you will, yes?'

Gideon looks out of the window, as though tracking the flight of a squadron of birds. Eventually, with a rueful scowl, he answers: 'I don't think so.'

'What?'

'I don't think so. It doesn't matter. The picture doesn't matter.'

'Gideon, this does not make sense. Explain.'

'I can't be bothered,' sighs Gideon, watching the invisible flock.

'I spend hours cleaning the picture, and now it doesn't matter. Terrific.'

Gideon bows his head, acting out a meek acceptance of the rebuke.

'And the punch in the face?' Robert goes on. 'What about that?'

'Just a slap.'

'Looks like more than a slap to me.'

Again Gideon turns to the window; he narrows his eyes, going through the motions of considering what should be done. He raises a hand to scratch at the back of his head, and dislodges the headdress, which slides ten degrees to starboard. 'Let's leave it,' he says.

'Leave what? The drunk or the hat?'

'Not the hat,' Gideon replies. 'Vielmi must have his hat.'

Robert resets the *chaperon*, altering a fold or two. 'Gideon, is there something you're not telling me?' he asks.

'No. Not a thing,' he says, rebutting his assistant's gaze with a glance of pure honesty, then he bows his head once more. Four months later he will tell the truth about the encounter on Piazza Sant'Agostino, but we'll never find out who it was who scrawled on the picture.

II.7

On entering Robert's apartment she sees Gideon at the table, resplendent in a red velvet gown, crowned with a fantastic swirl of red, like a gigantic carnation. He turns to greet her with a limp and courtly wave; one eye socket is dark grey and damson. 'We require your assistance, my dear,' he says, in an over-ripe voice.

'Strewth,' she says. 'How did you get that?'

The story is that Gideon (tired at the end of a long nocturnal bout in the studio and not paying as much attention to the placement of his feet as he should have been) and Trim (for once not perfectly anticipating his master's movements) had tangled at the top of the stairs, with the consequence that head and banister had come into collision with some force. Though this explanation is delivered with a more than plausible guilelessness, it seems unlikely, and a glance at Robert – who glances at Trim – confirms that it isn't true.

'Quite a shiner,' she remarks.

Gideon strokes the bruised skin, as if he might wipe the damage away. 'We were hoping you may have something in your arsenal of womanly substances that we could employ as camouflage,' he says.

'Do I look like a woman with an arsenal?'

'Some foundation, perhaps? Is that what you call it?' Gideon asks.

She steps up to the chair and takes his chin between thumb and forefinger; securing the headdress with a hand, Gideon closes his eyes and leans back, assuming the passivity of a man submitting to a dentist. 'Foundation is what you call it, but foundation won't do,' she diagnoses. 'Not strong enough. Stage make-up is what you need.' She touches the bruise; his expression of trust does not change. 'I have some concealer with me,' she tells Robert. 'That'll help.' She fetches it.

Gideon appears not to have moved a muscle in her absence. 'I submit to restoration,' he says, closing his eyes again. As the concealer is worked into the skin, his face takes on the drowsy smile of a man under massage.

'Open,' she instructs. Robert passes a CD to Gideon, to use as a mirror.

'Much obliged,' says Gideon, after prolonged inspection, and he kisses the hand that holds the concealer. He rises, removing the hand from the *chaperon*. 'How's the turban?' he asks Robert.

'As it was.'

'You look splendid,' Claire assures him.

Gideon takes the compliment with a terse bow. 'My public awaits,' he announces, retreating towards the door, whisking florid shapes in the air.

As soon as the door has closed, she asks: 'Come on then – what's the story with the eye?'

11.8

The parade, having received its blessing from Father Fabris at the Porta di San Zeno, has processed around the walls and re-entered the town through the Porta di Santa Maria, and is now on Corso Garibaldi. Two drummers are at its head, then there's a gap to Fausto Nerini, who is walking alone, as the Muzio Bonvalori always must do. His cloak is white, and the gown he wears underneath it is adorned with a red cross from throat to navel and armpit to armpit; he alone bears a sword, and he rests one hand on its pommel as he accepts with humility the acclaim of the citizens of Castelluccio, who have gathered to congratulate the reformed tyrant upon his return to the path of virtue. Behind him, Ercole and Maria Bonvalori – Gianluigi Tranfaglia and his wife, both new to their roles – wave to the bystanders like actors who, rather late in their careers, find themselves on a red carpet for the first time. Eliana Tranfaglia and her husband follow closely; it's possible that they've argued again this morning; Eliana's gaze is fixed one way, her husband's the other, and at no point along the whole length of the Corso do they so much as glance at each other; she is wearing white trainers, which at each step stick a nose out from underneath the hem of her plum-purple dress. More concerned with authenticity, Mr Lanese has posted his eyewear into the pocket of his cloak; Beatrice Lanese, like her husband, does not appear to be wholly comfortable in her colourful but cumbrous attire – they have the demeanour of dignitaries performing a civic duty which, while not exactly onerous, is not exactly pleasurable. Antonietta and Giulietta Lanese, each six feet tall and recognisable as the daughters of their mother from a range of a hundred metres, are by contrast as relaxed as two young women unhurriedly on their way to meet their boyfriends, taking time to chat and enjoy the fine weather of this summer day; clad in tight-fitting bodices of honey-coloured silk, they attract comments from several young men along the Corso, comments which – walking demurely arm-in-arm, their strides in easy synchrony – they ignore with arch disdain. They precede by half a dozen places Agnese Littarru, who is escorted by Antonio Perello; she wears a snowy wimple, which contrasts fetchingly with the stark black frames of her glasses, and her face is downturned, perhaps in emulation of medieval modesty, perhaps in thought – Robert thinks he sees, for a moment, that familiar smiling frown, as if she's been pondering a problem for hours and senses that a solution is within reach.

And here, after a pair of drummers, comes Gideon. As the Domenico Vielmi, he should be on horseback, but the horses of Vielmi and Muzio Bonvalori have always been loaned by Alfredo Senesi, who this year, at the last minute, informed the festival committee that, regrettably, none of his animals would be available on the day. But Gideon is happier on foot than he would have been in the saddle: replete with well-being, he returns the good wishes of the citizens of Castelluccio with a perpetual, slow and lordly wave, donating a smile to every last one of them. The headdress has retained its shape, and is the most spectacular in the whole procession; when he passes through a buttress of sunlight he flares like a flame. Claire takes a photograph of him, of Robert, of Giacomo and Cecilia Stornello, of Giovanni Cabrera, who swings by on his crutches, in the wake of the flag-hurlers, one of whom chucks his flag to gutter height and catches it with insolent aplomb. Applauded by a gang of teenage girls, he does it again, forcing a halt on the back half of the parade. Maurizio Ianni, stepping out of position to watch the soaring flag, notices Claire, who notices his cloak of iridescent turquoise before realising who's inside it. Holding his head high, Maurizio preens with some self-mockery, running his hands down his shining torso and giving her a smirk that says: 'So what do you think of this, lady?' Beaming, he proceeds along the Corso, the target of many cameras and phones; he stops often, arms spread to allow a clear shot of his magnificence; the man in the mustard-coloured trousers jumps out in front of Maurizio, fires off half a dozen pictures, shakes his hand, jumps back. Maurizio, apparently affronted, wags a finger, and says something that raises laughter from the people around the snapper, who smiles uncertainly. After two more drummers and Marta Alinei's parents, Teresa and Renata pass by. It's Renata who spots Robert; she waves, as if taking part in a victory parade, and nudges her mother's side; Teresa smiles at him, abashed, then she notices Claire and her smile changes to encompass both of them. They move on, with Stefano Granchello at their heels, stern as a man at a high religious ceremony; alongside him, Arianna is doing her best to mimic the solemnity of her husband, but cannot entirely resist the distractions of her audience; her fingers wiggle in greeting, out of her husband's line of sight. Giosuè, handsome in azure and scarlet stockings, points a leg for the benefit of heckling friends.

On Piazza Maggiore the crowd is joining the tail of the procession. 'We should get to the finish line,' says Robert.

Squeezing between the spectators and the wall of Palazzo Campani, Claire calls to him: 'Is it always like this?' It sounds as if she's saying she may come back next year if the answer is Yes, which it is. He puts out a hand to ease her through the crush. They overtake Gideon as he's passing the English watercolourists, two of whom appear to recognise him. Turning away, he aims some goodwill at the people on the other side of the road, before turning back to offer the lady amateurs a wave of pontifical condescension.

In the centre of Piazza del Mercato a long rectangle has been enclosed by thick red ropes, which at one corner open out to form a corridor down which the parade will walk, to the benches that flank the enclosure; at the other end, against the railings of the Redentore, the target has been erected for the crossbow competition, raised on a platform; another platform, forty paces from the target, awaits the competitors. Hundreds of people have assembled on the piazza, most of them gathered in the area between the enclosure and the Torre del Saraceno. It's no longer possible, at ground level, to get a view of the point at which the angel and the falling boy will meet, but Robert has a plan. He strides towards the loggia, looking up. On that side of the square, several apartments have a balcony, and every balcony now is occupied. Towards one of these – on which a young boy and two couples are standing – Robert directs his attention. A whistle of shocking volume secures the attention of the boy at the second attempt; the boy tugs the arm of the nearer woman, who, having picked out Robert amid the crowd, beckons him to come up. She is waiting at the door on the second floor; introductions are made, so quickly that Claire doesn't catch the name; glasses of wine are handed over; they are ushered at haste to the balcony.

The drummers are hammering away as the end of the procession enters the enclosure, under an arch of flags. Even in that multicoloured enclave Gideon's carnation-hat stands out: she sees him step onto one of the benches and turn to face the Torre del Saraceno. Everyone turns to the tower, where, in the uppermost window, a red cross appears – the cross on the chest of Fausto Nerini. A cheer goes up from the piazza; Fausto/Muzio withdraws, to reappear a minute later, holding something at arm's length. Binoculars are passed to Claire by one of the men: the object held by Fausto, she can now see, is a hessian-clad mannequin – little Lodovico, who, as Robert explains, sleeps for 364 days of the year in a cabinet on the top floor of the Museo Civico. From behind Fausto a hand comes out to do something to the mannequin, then Fausto steps aside so that adjustments can be made to a wire that falls vertically from the window. A nudge from Robert diverts her attention to the campanile of the Redentore: there, in the bell chamber, stands Marta the waitress, her body silver and glittering between silver wings. A man is beside her, fastening her harness to the cable that descends from the bell chamber to the road below the Torre del Saraceno; three times the man – it's Ennio Pacetti – circles Marta, checking the fastenings; a crescendo of murmuring begins. Claire hands back the binoculars, and at that moment an explosion cracks the air of Castelluccio: a geyser of golden fireworks erupts from the parapet above the bell chamber. For fifteen seconds the geyser is in full spate, then in an instant it subsides, and Marta the angel emerges, wings smashing the sunlight. Under the control of Ennio, she slides to earth in slow motion, blessing the throng with whisks of her silver wand, cheered through every second of her descent. Almost at the ground, she looks up to the summit of the Torre del Saraceno and raises her arms, whereupon the mannequin of Lodovico, flung out by Fausto, plummets on its wire down the wall of the tower, limbs flailing in the rush of air. Marta is in place, arms cradled in readiness; at an altitude of ten metres his fall is arrested; he slides smoothly into the embrace of the angel – the cheers become a roar, and fire pours again from the summit of the campanile. A trumpet is raised at the foot of the Torre del Saraceno; a fanfare blares, and is answered by another within the enclosure, to which everyone now turns.

'Well?' asks Robert. 'Worth staying for?'

'My thanks to the bee,' she answers.

They stay on the balcony for the Palio della Balestra. Maurizio Ianni, the third man up, puts his bolt on the edge of the gold, and for fifteen minutes, until Fausto Nerini takes his turn, nobody improves on his effort. Ennio Pacetti betters Fausto's attempt. Giuliano Lanese is next; as director of the festival he is obliged to have a go; he extracts his glasses from his pocket, dons them with a great deal of fussing, takes aim, and sends his shot into the grass beyond the railings; sympathetic applause breaks out briefly at the front of the crowd. Three contestants remain. The second of them is Giovanni Cabrera, whose injury necessitates a modification to the firing platform: a chair is put there, so that he can shoot sitting down. Alessandra Nerini, who took up her post at the rope two hours ago, to ensure the best position, gives Giovanni a thumbs-up, despite being under her father's gaze. Giovanni raises the crossbow slowly and holds it level for as long as a person could go without blinking, perhaps imagining that the gold is the forehead of Gideon Westfall, or his assistant, or even Ilaria.

The noise that comes off the piazza is like something from a football stadium. When the din collapses, Giovanni's friends, surrounding Alessandra, start to scream a song that seems to have his name in it. Five minutes later, Giuliano Lanese is presenting Giovanni Cabrera with the Trofeo Arrigo Pepe, which takes the form of a silver crossbow mounted on a plinth of mottled black Portoro marble.

II.9

Arrigo Pepe (1848–1927) was not a native of Castelluccio: he was born in Borgo San Dalmazzo, near Cuneo, the illegitimate son of an unknown man and a seamstress named Carlotta, who surrendered him immediately to a home for foundlings. He worked for a blacksmith in Cuneo, before volunteering, at the age of eighteen, for the Cacciatori delle Alpi. A matter of weeks later, at Bezzecca, he sustained wounds that cost him two fingers and damaged his right leg so badly that he had to wear a brace for the rest of his life. He became an itinerant farrier, and in 1870 he came to Castelluccio, where he met Agata Serredi, a thirty-year-old widow, whose husband, a miner, had been killed in an accident at Montieri the previous year. Two years later he married Agata and settled in Castelluccio, where he stayed for the rest of his life.

Prior to his exploits at the Festa di San Zeno, Arrigo Pepe was renowned in Castelluccio for his adventures with the Cacciatori delle Alpi – or perhaps it would be more accurate to say that he was renowned for talking about those adventures. Almost every evening he would spend an hour or two at the *Pergola*, a tavern that used to occupy a corner of Piazza Sant'Agostino, and there, 'enthroned on his rustic bench,' in the words of Tommaso Galli's diary, he would, in return for a bottle of wine, regale any newcomers with tales which, on each retelling, were 'garnished with fresh exaggerations and outright lies'. He had fought at Bezzecca, and been wounded there – this much was indubitably true. And it might have been true that the missing fingers had been removed by a bullet during the defence of the church at Locca, and that, having been bandaged, but still bleeding copiously, he had straight away rejoined his comrades for the assault on Bezzecca, where a burst of shrapnel had given him the scars on his legs, which would inevitably be displayed to his audience. Perhaps he had killed a man at the church and another one at Bezzecca, and it was not impossible that he had, as he would sometimes claim, shot an Austrian at Locca with the Austrian's own gun, having overpowered him with his bare hands after the firearm had jammed. Most were inclined to believe him when he swore that the maiming of his leg was so severe that the doctors had despaired of saving the limb – indeed, of saving his life. Some were convinced, or almost convinced, that Arrigo had, as he claimed, been present in the piazza at Bezzecca when, on August 9th, Garibaldi had received news of the armistice and had given his famous one-word reply to the order to end his campaign.

And some were even persuaded that, in the aftermath of the battle, Garibaldi himself had commended Arrigo for his valour. The credulity of most, however, expired when assured that the bloodstained glove that Arrigo Pepe would on occasion produce from his coat pocket had belonged to the Hero of the Two Worlds himself, who had insisted that Arrigo keep it. Nevertheless, for many years Arrigo Pepe was known in Castelluccio, with varying degrees of affection, as 'our little hero'.

Arrigo was a small man; in the one authenticated photograph of him, taken in 1905, he is standing between the grandsons of Silvio Ubaldino, who were then aged ten and eleven, and Arrigo is the tallest of the trio by less than a hand's span. The photograph was taken after the crossbow competition at the conclusion of that year's festival, and it commemorates the achievement that has perpetuated the name of Arrigo Pepe. A year before, Arrigo had been cajoled by Tommaso Galli into participating in the shooting contest. His reluctance to compete, it had been assumed by many, was explicable by the ageing hero's fear of damaging his self-sustained reputation of having been the best shot in the history of his regiment. So there was some astonishment when the less than robust veteran of Bezzecca placed a bolt in the very heart of the target, calmly reloaded, and fired a second bolt with such accuracy that, according to Galli's diary, 'a sheet of paper could not have been slipped between the two'. The marksman acknowledged the applause, wrote Galli, 'with the curt bow of a man who had silenced his slanderers.'

The following year, Arrigo Pepe consented to take part again, and on this occasion he achieved a feat that was even more remarkable: his first bolt landed in the centre of the gold; his second split the first right down the middle. At the instigation of Tommaso Galli, the trophy bearing Arrigo's name was commissioned. Arrigo was allowed to believe that most of the money for the trophy had been raised by donations from the common people of Castelluccio, whereas in fact nearly all of it had been donated by Paolo Campani, the one person in Castelluccio who

was despised by the little hero, partly because of Cambino's ef-
feminacy, and partly because of his exalted social position.

Arrigo Pepe never competed again in the Palio. The newspaper
report on the 1906 event makes reference to an 'infirmity'; the
pain of his wounds, it was written, had never ceased; the death
of his wife, in the winter of 1905, had reduced him. In 1909 it was
reported that Arrigo Pepe was absent from the festivities. In 1910
he died.

He was buried in the cemetery at Castelluccio, beside Agata.
He had attended the church of Sant'Agostino regularly with his
wife and their children and his stepson, but it had been known
that, like his revered Garibaldi, he had held anti-clerical opinions, and his recorded utterances are indicative of a philosophy
that did not accord with the tenets of the Catholic faith. Asked if
he had ever feared death on the battlefield, he had once replied:
'Where death is, I am not; where I am, death is not; we shall
never meet.' A few months before Arrigo's death, a neighbour,
concerned at his frailty and despondency, encouraged him by
telling him that, if only he would take better care of himself,
he might live for another decade or more. 'Nothing awaits us,'
replied Arrigo. 'Another year of life doesn't reduce eternity by
one jot.' His heart was weak. A doctor told him that he must
not exert himself, and on no account should he ever try to walk
further than one kilometre at a time. On the day of his death he
walked to Radicóndoli, a distance of four kilometres; he returned
without resting, and collapsed and died within sight of the Porta
di Siena. The priest of Sant'Agostino adjudged that the death of
Arrigo Pepe was not to be regarded as suicide. As Arrigo had
requested, the glove of Garibaldi was buried with him.

11.10

Having taken a call from a miserable-sounding Teresa, Robert
has left the Antica Farmacia first, with apologies, promising to
be livelier in the morning.

'He's preoccupied,' Gideon tells her.

'I'd noticed,' says Claire.

'Never knew what he saw in her, I have to say,' he remarks. 'What did you make of her?'

'Attractive woman.'

'Of pleasing lineaments, certainly. But an empty vessel, if you ask me. Half-empty, at best.'

'Well, other people's choices are often baffling, aren't they?' she answers. 'We can't see what they see.'

'True,' he says, staring ahead pensively, like a man who has been cast aside.

'Come to that, if Joe Yardley walked in now, and I'd never met him before, I don't think I'd give him a second look.'

It takes Gideon a full five seconds to register who Joe Yardley is, then he smiles as you'd smile at someone who's putting on a brave face. 'Oh well,' he sighs, rising from the table.

Out in the street, he proposes a last ramble. Within a couple of minutes they are on Piazza Maggiore, and the enigma of Teresa and Robert seems to be troubling him no longer. Stopping in the centre of the square, he raises his face as if to receive the beneficent rays of the moon of Castelluccio. He loves this town, he says, with the fervency of a man declaring his love of the woman to whom he's been married for many years. Everything he needs is here, he declares. In the first few years of living here he had thought, now and then, that one day he'd be going back to London; he'd had this fantasy that only after leaving and returning could he truly belong in England. 'But I'll never leave,' he says, as though making a vow to her. 'This is my natural habitat.' He needs to have the hills around him. When he was a boy, he goes on, he used to sleep in the garden on summer nights, and in his teens he'd sometimes take the train out into the countryside at the weekends to go camping, on his own, usually. 'But I went camping with your father once,' he says. 'Did he tell you about that?'

'He didn't.'

'Funny story,' he says. 'Before it was time to turn in for the night we'd argued, inevitably, and David took himself off to sleep in the open air, leaving the tent to me. David was a very heavy sleeper – he could sleep anywhere. We'd pitched our tent at the edge of a wood; David went in a bit farther, but what he didn't know was that he'd put his sleeping bag close to a path. I was woken up in the morning by a terrible scream: a woman had been walking along the path and she'd seen my brother lying in the bracken, mouth open, pale – and she'd thought he was dead.'

'Which now he is,' she almost responds, but instead she smiles effortfully; tomorrow she'll be home.

'But you like London?' he asks, as if requesting verification of a strange predilection.

'Couldn't live anywhere else,' she says.

'I had to go there last year. I found it unbearable.'

'Comes with getting older,' she suggests.

'You may be right,' says Gideon. 'I'm getting tired,' he admits. He fears he may not have many more paintings left in him. The unavoidable distractions of the artist's life – the commercial side of things – have become increasingly burdensome. He would like to be left alone now, but he cannot afford to: he has to sell himself.

'Doesn't Robert take care of all that?'

'The worst of it, yes. He does the donkey work. But I have to be involved. Nowadays, in the age of the infernet, you have to have a presence. You have to project a personality,' he complains, performing a mime in which his innards are disgorged through his abdomen. 'The business of self-promotion is a distasteful racket,' he says. 'But it has to be done. If you don't sell, you don't work, and I have to work. That's my justification. "You see that a man is justified by works, and not by faith alone",' he proclaims, laughing. He proposes a last drink at the Caffè del Corso. 'Come on,' he urges, nudging her towards the light. 'One for the road. And I'll tell you one last story. It'll amuse you. It doesn't reflect well on me,' he says, though clearly, from the forgiving slant of his smile, it doesn't reflect too badly either.

Gideon's last story – for her ears only, though told in public – concerns his degree show at Camberwell. For a young artist, he explains, the degree show is a big event: it's an opportunity – in most cases, the last – to make people take notice. 'You have to sell something, if you're to have a future,' he says, seizing a block of space with both hands. A few people in his year, by the time the show closed, had sold a single picture; Gideon had sold six of his eight. 'I was the one person in my year who could really draw – let's not be falsely modest,' he says. 'And I was the only one who sold so much work. I was the hit of the show. People talked about me. I'd made my mark.' He pauses, basking in remembered glory. 'But it was a con,' he goes on. 'Not completely a con, but a semi-con, because in fact I'd sold only two pictures, not six. The other four buyers existed solely in my imagination. In the course of the first day of the show I placed a little yellow dot beside the four pictures I least liked. I'd thought up a description of each of my buyers. I'd given them jobs and addresses, so I could spin a good story if anyone asked. And it worked. People saw the four little dots and they thought: "This chap is being taken seriously. Let's give him a closer look." Opinions are modified by success, you see. Fake success brought real success. And when the show was over, to cover my tracks, I destroyed the four that I'd sold to myself. So there you are,' he concludes. 'The tricks to which one feels obliged to resort. Disgraceful. And you and Robert are the only people in the world who know about it.' Hands raised in surrender, he awaits her judgement; and, to her surprise, she finds herself smiling.

He ushers her into the Caffè del Corso and towards a corner table. For himself he orders a *grappa*; when Claire requests an *amaro* he nods approvingly – 'Gone native, I see,' he remarks. Then, with a sudden change of register, he gives her the sort of look you might give an employee who has come into your office for her annual assessment, an employee whom you like but haven't quite fathomed, and he says: 'You find people disappointing, generally, don't you?'

'No more than average, I'd say.'

By means of a small smile he answers that what she's said may be true, but is an evasion; he wrinkles the skin around his eyes, signifying kindliness. 'It'll happen,' he says.

'What'll happen?'

'You're a good person,' he tells her; he seems to be saying that this is a realisation at which he has only now arrived.

'That's nice to know,' she replies.

'What happened with your husband was a blow, I know. And when your parents have gone, it's difficult. But you'll be all right. Someone will come along.'

'Ah, I see. You're telling me not to worry about being left on the shelf.'

'Not how I'd put it.'

'I'm not worried, Gideon.'

'Good,' he says. 'Just give it time.'

'That's what I'd planned to do.'

He laughs and chinks his glass on hers, as if they've reached an agreement. 'Now,' he restarts, leaning back, 'tell me more about the new job.'

For half an hour she talks about the new job, and Gideon interrupts only to ask questions. He appears to remember every remark she's made about her work since she's been here; he remembers every name she's mentioned, however briefly, and he remembers what these people did, and to whom, and when. 'I'm sure it'll be a good move,' he says, when she's finished. 'A sympathetic woman with a clear head – you'll be perfect,' he says, and his directness momentarily disarms her. 'I couldn't do what you've been doing,' he states. 'Too absorbed with my own dramas.'

And as they are strolling back to the apartment, along the Corso, he tells her that a woman once remarked to him, at a private view, under the misapprehension that he was one of the other artists in the show: 'I have nothing but respect for Westfall's talent; I just don't like what it does.' He chuckles at the recollection. 'And that's your view, more or less, isn't it?' There is no accusation in the question.

'It's not—' she begins, but he touches her shoulder to stop her.

'That's OK,' he says. 'The world would be intolerable without variety. You're not keen on what I do, and that's perfectly all right. You are not alone. Universal acclamation I do not need. Small applause suffices,' he assures her. They are passing the old theatre; he halts to look at the façade of the building; it seems that he is finding it difficult to continue with what he's saying, and needs a distraction in which to compose himself. Still facing the doorway, he goes on: 'And I'm not quite your cup of tea. Personally, I mean. I know this is the case. I'm a little too rich for your palate, shall we say. At times, to tell you the truth, I'm a little too rich for my own palate.' He turns, presenting to her a face of wistful resignation. 'To some people, sometimes, I am preposterous. I am aware of this. On the other hand, I can also be entertaining, I hope. I try not to bore. Occasionally I fail. I overdo it, I know. But,' he declaims, walking on, raising a forefinger, 'as the sage of Rotterdam once put it, "fictions and illusions are what hold the gaze of spectators". I rest my case.' A hand goes out, to hook itself under her arm; she lifts an elbow to let the hand in. 'I'm very glad you came,' he says.

II.II

She can't settle to read. Robert isn't back, so she goes into the living room and turns on the TV. On one channel there's an Italian rapper; on the next one it's three men talking earnestly – about football, it turns out; then it's an excitable man strolling around a huge warehouse of leather furniture, being admired by a comely twenty-year-old whose skirt is the size of a handkerchief; a film, dubbed into Italian; an interview with a depressed-looking elderly man; a young man dancing badly between two leggy specimens in spangly bikinis. She watches the dancers until they have finished; the audience – in which there are some very

beautiful young women, almost as glossy as the ones on stage
– claps and cheers in a delirium of happiness. The dancing man
goes to a desk, and the leggy specimens perch on it, pouting at
the cameras while the man gabbles. It's appalling and fascinating
and incomprehensible. She watches for another quarter of an
hour, then returns to the bedroom. It's still very warm; she starts
to pack her bag. A notion occurs to her; she will go to the pool.

To the east the hump-backed horizon is revealed against the
low glow that rises from Siena. Across the valley, a dozen tiny
lights are strung across the lower hills; above them, two villages
show as clots of yellow, and above the villages the stars are like a
scoop of salt thrown onto blue-black paper. It's a richer sky than
she will see at home; tomorrow she will be sorry, a little, not to
be seeing it. The moon, almost full, gives a slate-grey top to a
narrow veil of cloud underneath it, and there's no sound, almost
no sound – just the buzz of a scooter shrinking into the silence.
Standing neck-deep in the water, she moves her arms slowly,
like weeds in a stream, and a few seconds later she can hear the
water moving in the gutter, as quiet as a small fish breaking the
surface.

In the benign night air her thoughts of her uncle turn benign:
she can admire his expertise; he is generous, with his money
at least; and she can imagine that she could, in time, find his
extravagances more palatable. His dedication to the image of
himself is impressive, in a way, and almost pitiable too. She
recalls their afternoon in Siena and in her mind she takes his hand
again, but differently. This scene is sentimental and nonsensical,
she knows; she stops it, instead bringing to mind the worst of
him – the self-absorption and the pettiness; the bombast. And
from this arises the image of her faithless husband. His spectre
appears, and she regards him as he cringes in the attitudes of
guilt; the hands wrestle with each other, but his eyes are the eyes
of a man whose mind is on the imminent day of release. She
holds him there, in the pen of her memory, and she feels nothing.
It is true: she feels nothing, and this is new. So perhaps she is not

identical to the woman she was two weeks ago. The things that she has observed and heard: it is possible that they have had an effect. How could they not have? She recalls being waylaid by grief when she walked out of the town on the third or fourth night here, the night she saw the porcupine. Her father has gone: she reiterates the fact; she sees it in its entirety, she thinks, and the sadness of it is grievous. But what she feels at this moment is something different from the grief that she recalls being pierced by before, on that evening; it is not acceptance, but perhaps the beginning of it – his absence is becoming a part of who she is. Acceptance is a condition she will never fully achieve, she knows: her mother's death, after so many years, can still make her stagger. But a change may be happening; or this may be only an interlude, she warns herself – a simulation of change, not change itself. Nothing significant, she tells herself, can have happened in so short a time.

She swims for a few minutes, slowly, barely ruffling the pool. She swims towards the glow of Siena and back towards the light-sprinkled hills. Floating in the cool water, her skin to the warm dark sky, she watches a ribbon of cloud becoming longer, thinner, and breaking apart. Again she thinks of Gideon, of his forcefulness, of his consistency, of his lack of doubt. He is always who he is, and she is not sure if she envies him. Gideon will be this Gideon until the day he dies.

A shape cuts across the moon at speed and disappears against the sky. She waits, vigilant, then it passes over the pool, like a scrap of black paper in a gale: a bat. It swoops back down, closer, bouncing an inch above the surface of the water, and zigzags up, across the moonlit cloud. It's a pipistrelle, she can tell by its flight: fluttery, like a butterfly, unlike the flight of a noctule bat, as Robert explained. Again and again the pipistrelle skims the water; then there are two, three. She gets out of the water and sits on the edge of the pool, watching the bats as they scribble on the air, taking insects. She is watching when she hears someone walking towards the gate of the villa: a heavy tread, a male tread, on gravel. She pulls the towel towards her, but the person passes and carries on down the lane.

11.12

The common pipistrelle is a species of the *Pipistrellus* genus, in the subfamily *Vespertilioninae* of the family *Vespertilionidae* (commonly known as vesper bats), and was given its binomial, *Pipistrellus pipistrellus*, in 1774 by Johann Christian Daniel von Schreber (1739–1810), in his *Die Säugethiere in Abbildungen nach der Natur mit Beschreibungen*. The name is derived from the Italian *pipistrello*, meaning 'bat', which in turn is derived from the Latin *vespertilio* (from *vesper*, meaning 'evening'), via the Old Italian *vipistrello*.

The common pipistrelle is found across most of the European continent, as well as North Africa and southwestern Asia, and it is the smallest European bat, with a body length of 3.3–4.8cm, a wingspan of 19–25 cm and an average weight of 4–8g. The maximum lifespan is about 15 years. It is common in woodland and agricultural areas, but is also found in shrubland, semi-desert and urban settings. Summer nursery colonies, which generally occupy buildings and trees, usually comprise 25–50 individuals, but colonies of 200 have been observed. The pipistrelle hibernates in winter, sometimes in caves or cracks in addition to the summer sites, and it often hibernates alone or in small groups, although huge populations – up to 100,000, by some estimates – have been recorded in caves in central Europe. The diet of the common pipistrelle consists primarily of diptera, such as mosquitoes, gnats, midges; a single bat may forage as far as 5km from its roost, consuming as many as 3,000 insects in one night. Most common pipistrelles are not migratory, though movements in excess of 1,000km do occur.

In 1999 the soprano pipistrelle was officially differentiated from the common pipistrelle, on the basis of the frequency of its echolocating calls: the frequency of the call of the common pipistrelle is 45kHz, whereas the soprano pipistrelle's is 55kHz. Differences in appearance, habitat and diet were subsequently observed. The bats at the pool outside Castelluccio, on this particular evening, are common pipistrelles; their roost is in the ruined roof of San Lorenzo.

12

12.1

TRIM RUNS AWAY across Piazza del Mercato, to be petted by Luisa Fava, who is sitting on the bench by the loggia, scanning a magazine. Seeing Gideon, she puts a hand to her mouth in alarm. She wants to know what has happened to his eye, now no longer masked by make-up. Gideon sits beside her and tells her a tale about the altercation; he permits her to put a fingertip to the edge of the bruise.

'You must report it,' she says, and he tells her that he will.

She asks if his niece enjoyed the festival.

'Very much,' he answers.

'A nice woman,' Luisa comments; Gideon agrees.

They pass a minute looking at some pictures in the magazine, of a TV presenter and a football player on a yacht. Then Luisa says: 'Time to open up.'

'I'll take a turn along the Corso with you,' says Gideon, and he walks with her to the shop.

'You are in a very good mood today,' she remarks.

'I am,' he says, and he gives her a kiss on the hand before leaving.

This episode will be repeated two hundred and forty-four days later. Gideon and Luisa will chat by the loggia for a while, then Luisa will look at her watch and say: 'Time to open up.' And Gideon will escort her, because he has to call on Fausto Nerini. He will not reach Luisa's shop: outside the Palazzo Campani he will collapse. In the ambulance, as the paramedics work on him, he will speak these words: 'Nobody knows what has really been at the centre of my life.' His eyes will then close and he will smile. 'What do you mean, Gideon? What do you mean?' she will ask him, over and over again, but she will not receive an answer.

In accordance with his will, Gideon is to be cremated. Claire will be there for the service, as will Luisa Fava and Carlo Pacetti. Each will be bequeathed a painting; Robert will receive five; the rest of the estate is to be auctioned, with the proceeds going into a fund to support young artists 'working in the classical tradition'.

12.2

The Loggia del Mercato was built between 1420 and 1422 at the behest of Domenico Vielmi, to replace the wooden shelter that had previously occupied this corner of the square. Designed by an unknown architect, it is a rectangular brick structure, roofed with terracotta tiles, with a façade of three pointed arches, each of which extends from the pavement to within a metre of the eaves. The thick, ten-sided columns that separate the arches have acanthus-leaf capitals of Istrian stone; a stone relief of Domenico Vielmi's insignia – a ship with a star above its central mast – is set into each of the columns; the relief of the Madonna and Child, above the middle arch, is probably by the same un-known hand.

The loggia was severely damaged in 1840, when part of the building that adjoined the rear wall collapsed; two of the arches were subsequently filled in with brick, and new tie-beams were inserted between the back wall and the façade. After that, the loggia was used intermittently by the town authorities as a storage space. Demolition was regularly proposed, as was restoration, but the loggia was always deemed too precious to be destroyed, and too expensive to repair. Money from central government finally allowed restoration to proceed in the late 1980s, when the façade was reopened and the internal frescoes restored; further restoration of the fresco depicting the dreams of Ablavius and the emperor Constantine was undertaken in 2010.

The frescoes on the rear wall of the loggia were painted by Giovanni di Paolo d'Agnolo and his workshop in the 1450s; they depict Saint Nicholas (patron saint of apothecaries, bakers, bankers, brewers, butchers, candle makers, chandlers, clerks, coopers, drapers, embalmers, grocers, haberdashers, millers, pawnbrokers, shipwrights, shoemakers, shopkeepers, tanners, vintners and various other classes of merchant) and scenes from his life. In the centre of the wall, a faded image of Saint Nicholas shows him as a bishop, with his crozier in one hand and three purses in the other. The purses are an allusion to the story of the impoverished man whose three daughters were able to marry thanks to the charity of the saint, who secretly, under cover of darkness, threw three purses of gold coins through the window of their father's house. This episode is depicted to the right of the central portrait of Saint Nicholas, but only the scene showing the man's discovery of the purses is now clearly legible. To the left, the best preserved frescoes show Saint Nicholas appearing in a dream to the emperor Constantine and, simultaneously, to the sleeping prefect Ablavius, instructing them both to release three innocent men who had been condemned to death.

Underneath the figure of Saint Nicholas, a small fountain is set into the wall, with a large marble bowl in the shape of a scallop shell. The marble panel below the bowl shows another of the saint's miracles: the resurrection of three small boys who had been slaughtered by a butcher, whose intention had been to sell their flesh as ham. Local folklore has it that the face of the butcher is disfigured because the people of Castelluccio, having named the figure of the butcher Muzio, after Muzio Bonvalori, used to beat it with sticks.

12.3

Taking her leave of Castelluccio, she strolls along the Corso, past the theatre and Palazzo Campani, across Piazza Maggiore, past Santa Maria dei Carmini, Sant'Agostino, the museum, the Porta di San Zeno, Porta di Volterra, the Redentore, the loggia. Because she has time, she sits for a while on a bench in the gardens; the morning is balmy, the little park is lovely, but she is not entirely in it; she is both here and in London already. Opera music starts playing somewhere nearby, and the effect of the music is to make the scene a little more unreal; it's as if a soundtrack has been applied to it. She hears the music, she feels the warmth of the sun, she hears the jostling of the leaves, yet she feels like an actor playing the part of herself on holiday.

She moves on, to San Lorenzo, the war memorial, the old candle factory. Skim-reading the town, she returns to the Corso, where she exchanges a '*Buongiorno*' with Cecilia Stornello, by whom she'll be remembered next year as Gideon's niece and the lady who was stung by the bees, which will become a small swarm in the course of the intervening months. At the Teatro Gaetano she turns into Via del Teatro, and here she finds a cranny that she's somehow missed: an alley that's narrower than a car, which she's walked past on other days and taken to be a cul de sac. It turns out not to be a cul de sac – it makes a jack-knife turn and opens into a courtyard that's bounded on one side by a high blank wall, which she assumes to be a wall of the theatre. It's a surprise to find, in a town so small, a pocket that she's over-looked, but it's not what you'd call a photogenic spot: some new

window-shutters, some geraniums in flowerpots, a square of
blue sky to top it off. Turning to leave, she notices a small plaque
above a door:

QUI IL X MARZO DEL MDCXXXVI
SI ESTINGVEVA
Giovan Antonio Ridolfi

The name has a weak aura of familiarity, but she's not inclined,
this morning, to test her memory on it.

Back on the Corso again, she hesitates, unsure what else to
do with the time that remains, and Gideon goes lumbering past
with Trim, heading towards Piazza del Mercato. He's smiling
and is talking to himself, it appears, and he stirs his stick in the
air as if to dislodge a piece of litter from the end of it, where
there is no piece of litter. He passes within five yards, but doesn't
notice her. The shirt is untucked at the back and the hat is awry;
he looks quite bonkers. Keeping her distance, she follows him
onto the piazza; the stick keeps flicking out; the head is bobbing
as though in agreement with an invisible companion; the dog
glances up repeatedly, perhaps wondering if the mutterings are
intended for him.

At the loggia Gideon stops; he peers into it, noticing something unusual, it seems. He smiles; the dog sits down at his feet;
the smile becomes a laugh, and the laugh gathers momentum,
as though at the approach of a punchline; his head jerks back,
almost dislodging the hat; a hand goes down to Trim's head,
and together they head home. The laughter was so hearty and
so strange that she wonders if he had in fact known she was
watching; when she looks into the loggia this idea becomes difficult to dismiss, because there's nothing in the loggia that isn't
always there, and nothing that's remotely funny. Then her gaze
travels up, to her favourite piece of art in Castelluccio: the small
Madonna and Child in the centre. She's no expert, but she can
see that as a sculpture it's unremarkable, yet the way the hand is

pressed to the infant's chest, to stop him toppling off her lap – it makes her eyes begin to smart, even now, though she's looked at it a dozen times.

12.4

It is evident, the moment Robert arrives in the studio, that something has happened. A large sheet of paper is pinned to the wall, and Gideon – charcoal stick in hand – is prancing as he works at it: he swipes a fat black line from top to bottom, steps back to inspect it, steps forward, strokes another line across the first, steps back. He snarls at what he has done, as if confronting an intruder and demanding that he explain himself. With his free hand he grips his brow, putting a smear of charcoal onto his forehead. He prances forward again, adding some diagonals to a corner.

Unobtrusively, Robert moves towards his room, from where he can see what is being drawn: a bird's-eye view of a square, with a church in the centre and streets slanting away to the side of it. He opens the door, goes in, closes the door silently.

Ten minutes later: 'Good morning,' Gideon booms.

Robert emerges; Gideon, his face streaked with black dust, has taken down the sheet and is pinning a new one in its place. 'We have lift-off,' he says.

'So I see,' answers Robert.

After a rapid scrutiny of the blank paper, Gideon, arm extended like a fencer, advances on it and scores a dozen small loops in a line across the centre, close together.

When he retreats, Robert takes the opportunity: 'Lunch at 12.30,' he reminds him.

'Yes,' says Gideon, with a frown that imposes silence.

At 12.20, having remained in his room in the interim, Robert comes out. Now another sketch is on the wall: a cluster of cloaked figures in the midst of the whiteness, faces raised, perhaps screaming. Six or seven sheets are on the floor. Gideon, arms crossed, glances at him.

'Time to go,' says Robert.

Gideon directs a look of discontent at the wall. 'I'll join you,' he mutters.

'We'll need to be on the road by two, so—'

'Noted.'

'She'll—'

'I'll be there,' states Gideon, in a monotone. 'I cannot stop at this precise moment.'

'OK. But—'

'Enough, Roberto,' he says, pinching the bridge of his nose, then he rips the sheet off the wall.

12.5

Gideon comes into view, as if being chased through mud, shirt untucked, belly on the bounce. At the door he pauses to gather some air; in he comes, with an exhausted wave of greeting for Giosuè. 'Have you ordered?' he asks, swiping the perspiration off his face with three quick passes of the hand. He's breathing like a man just saved from drowning, and Claire can see the pulse in his neck.

Robert, regarding Gideon coolly, waits for the gasping to subside. 'Yes, we've ordered,' he says. 'Of course we've ordered. We've been here for forty minutes.'

Gideon glances at his watch and does a wince of embarrassment, before turning to call for a coffee and a glass of water. 'Sorry,' he says to Claire. 'I lost track. I was in the middle of something.'

'On a roll,' says Claire.

'I think so,' Gideon agrees.

'Robert told me.'

'Bad timing,' says Gideon, with a helpless shrug. 'I'm sorry.'

'It's OK,' says Claire; Gideon appears to hear only sympathy, and gives her a grateful smile. 'Don't feel you have to stay,' she says.

'I won't linger,' he accedes. 'A quick coffee, then I'll get back.'

'Mustn't lose momentum,' says Claire.

'Precisely.'

Robert has said nothing; now, seeing Carlo Pacetti – hands thrust into pockets; face a parody of disgruntlement – making his way along the Corso, he mutters: 'There goes your mate. On the lookout for communists.'

The laugh that Gideon releases has no mirth in it; it is intended, it appears, to placate Robert. 'He's not that bad,' he says.

'He'd be dangerous, given the opportunity,' answers Robert, tracking Carlo Pacetti till he's out of sight.

Gideon only smiles, at Claire, as if to apologise for Robert's hostility. The coffee is delivered, followed by two plates of tortellini.

'So,' she says, 'inspiration has struck.'

'Perhaps,' Gideon replies. 'We'll see.'

'Anything you can tell us?'

Gideon squints into his cup, as if seeing there, in miniature, the emerging image of his painting. 'Something to do with the festival,' he murmurs. 'The parade, spectators. There'll be a part for him in it,' he says, pointing to the picture above her head.

She swivels to look at it; Robert eats.

'Tommaso Galli,' says Gideon, 'the real—'

'—patron saint of Castelluccio,' Robert butts in, completing the sentence as you'd complete a cliché.

'Exactly,' says Gideon, failing to prevent a momentary appearance of annoyance. He proceeds to give her a few facts about the real patron saint of Castelluccio, and makes reference to a famously beautiful actress called Lydia Borelli, whose style was imitated by young women all over Italy.

'Lyda,' Robert interrupts. 'Lyda Borelli, not Lydia Borelli.'

'I defer,' says Gideon, giving Claire another quick smile of apology. 'I shall hand you over to my trusted assistant,' he says. 'Duty calls.' He stands up, and bows to Claire. 'Before you go, come upstairs. I'd like five minutes.'

'Sounds ominous,' she remarks, to which he replies with a hammily enigmatic wrinkling of the eyebrows.

'*Ciao tutti*,' he says, and they watch him jog along the Corso as if hurrying to catch the post.

12.6

The career of Tommaso Galli might be said to have begun on an afternoon in June, 1871, when his father, in celebration of Tommaso's sixteenth birthday, took him to a production of Vittorio Alfieri's *La congiura dei Pazzi* (The Pazzi Conspiracy). Gianpaolo Galli, a notary, felt an especial affinity with Alfieri, in part because of the dramatist's devotion to the cause of liberty, in part because of his love of horses, a love which Gianpaolo shared, and to which he gave voice in many of the poems that he composed of an evening, when his wife and children were asleep. Gianpaolo Galli dreamed of publishing his poetry, and in his poetry he dreamed of his childhood in the Pisan hills – an idyll, as he now recalled it, of freedom and virtuous poverty. His father, though he could barely read or write, had known hundreds of lines of Tasso and Ariosto by heart, which he had recited to the young Gianpaolo as other fathers would recite nursery rhymes, and Gianpaolo had in turn read them to his children, of whom one – Tommaso – had come to respond to poetry with an enthusiasm that more than compensated for the indifference of the notary's other offspring. That Tommaso might become an actor, however, seems never to have been considered until that day in 1871, when, at *La congiura dei Pazzi*, he suddenly recognised his destiny. 'Watching those actors,' he wrote many years later, 'I understood, as clearly as if I were standing before a mirror for the first time, what it was that I was.'

Quick-witted and handsome, Tommaso was the favourite of both his parents. They had always indulged him and they did not oppose him strongly when he informed them that he was determined to make a career for himself as an actor. It had been assumed that he would follow his father's profession. The life of an actor promised no prosperity, his father warned him, before confessing that neither did the life of a notary. His mother, whom life had not dampened as much as it had her husband, prophesied success and fame, a fame as great as that of Tommaso Salvini. Her Tommaso was a better-made young man than Salvini. His voice was beautiful: it was the voice of an angel, Father Simone had told her, though he had added – foreseeing where the admiration of so many girls would lead the young man – that Tommaso had, unfortunately, the face of angel too.

The beautiful face and voice eventually, in 1879, obtained for Tommaso Galli a contract with a Florentine company that was to tour with an adaptation of Sardou's *Séraphine*. This position lasted only a few months: he was dismissed after becoming involved with the leading actress, a young woman whose uncle, the manager of the troupe, so strongly disapproved of the liaison that he ejected his niece's lover on the very day he discovered what was going on. The dismissal occurred in Bologna, where, by the start of the next season, Tommaso found employment with a company that took him back to Florence, then on to Rome, Genova, Verona, Padova and Venice. The following season, with a different ensemble, he appeared in no fewer than twenty theatres, from Naples to Milan. He worked for ten companies in as many years, specialising in *amoroso* roles. From time to time the critics took note of him. His voice and fine figure were praised, though a certain stiffness of gesture was remarked upon.

Though he was a competent actor rather than a remarkable one, Tommaso Galli never struggled to find employment. He was attractive and had a certain panache. He had ideas about stagecraft that were adopted by several of his managers. And he proved to be adept at editing and rewriting material to better suit the taste of the audience. For example, a number of speeches written by Galli were interpolated into his company's production of *Romeo and Juliet*, in the final act of which, in what many held to be an improvement upon the original, Juliet momentarily revived to give the dying Romeo one last embrace. He proved to be an exceptionally effective publicist: full houses became the rule for shows in which Tommaso Galli was involved. And, having inherited his father's scrupulous eye for detail and distaste for profligacy, he showed himself to be of invaluable assistance in the administration of the company's budget: more than one manager was happy to entrust to Galli the paperwork of the multitudinous taxes to which the travelling players were subject.

In effect, Tommaso Galli was the joint manager of the company with which, shortly after Easter in 1891, he came to Castelluccio's Teatro Civico, bringing a play – co-authored by himself – that bore a very close resemblance to Paolo Giacometti's *La morte civile*. On the opening night Paolo Campani, on whose subsidies the Teatro Civico had come to be heavily reliant after two markedly unprofitable seasons, held a reception for the actors at the Palazzo Campani. Galli made an extremely favourable impression on the theatre's chief benefactor – so favourable, indeed, that by the time he left the gathering he had been assured, in effect, that the managership of the Teatro Civico could be his for the asking. Tommaso Galli had a wife – Giacinta, who had been Juliet to his Romeo – and a child, and another child was due in October. The touring life no longer appealed to him. Within a matter of weeks, he became the manager of the Teatro Civico.

Under the guidance of Tommaso Galli, the Teatro Civico of Castelluccio enjoyed its most successful years. Making use of the contacts he had established during his decade of travelling, he attracted high-calibre companies to the town. The Teatro Civico, Galli proclaimed in a newspaper item soon after taking up his post, was to be 'a theatre of a new and vital nation . . . a theatre of contemporary life.' He staged works by Achille Torelli, Giuseppe Costetti, Roberto Bracco, Marco Praga, Gerolamo Rovetta and Giuseppe Giacosa, whose *Tristi amori* was one of Galli's first offerings at Castelluccio, and whose *Come le foglie* was one of the last. He disliked declamatory acting, and encouraged a naturalistic style of staging: the Teatro Civico's production of Torelli's *I mariti*, in 1893, caused something of a stir by having an actor turn his back on the audience while speaking. The sets at the Teatro Civico became noted for their realism, and scene changes were swift and smooth, thanks in large part to stage machinery that Galli helped to design. He wrote plays as well. In 1895, at Milan's Teatro Manzoni, he saw a production of Ibsen's *Ghosts*, which inspired him not only to bring the great Norwegian's work to the attention of his audience in Castelluccio but also to create dramas of his own, in a similar philosophical vein. He wrote two, which were published at Paolo Campani's expense: *La figlia di Matteo* (Matteo's Daughter) and *Fiamme* (Flames). They were not well received in Castelluccio, but the great Eleanora Duse, upon receiving a copy of *Fiamme*, sent him a complimentary letter.

Tommaso Galli worked so hard, as Campani wrote to a cousin, 'that it was as if he thought the devil would take him were he to rest for an hour'. After fifteen years in Castelluccio, he was exhausted. He became ill: for days at a time he would be unable to eat anything except bread. One evening in September 1907, an hour before curtain-up, he could not be found in the theatre. A member of the theatre staff was dispatched to his house, but Giacinta had not seen him since breakfast. The play went on without him; still he did not appear. He remained missing until the next morning, when a shopkeeper came upon him, sitting on a bench by the Porta di San Zeno, as grey as a dead man, and weeping. A week later, he resigned, on grounds of poor health.

There were other reasons for his resignation. Receipts at the theatre had been declining. Ibsen was not to the taste of the land-owners and mine-owners whose subscriptions were the theatre's chief source of revenue, after Paolo Campani's donations. The people of Castelluccio wanted Italian plays, as they had been promised, and they wanted stuff that was more uplifting than this Nordic gloom-mongering. Galli gave them a comedy once in a while, but not often enough. Paolo Campani had also started to take issue with his protégé's programming, but whereas the

general populace called for a leavening of their diet, Campani
– who, as Galli wrote at this time, liked to regard himself as 'a
man of the future, to atone for his name and for the privileges he
has inherited' – wanted the opposite. Specifically, he wanted the
people of Castelluccio to be elevated by 'the divine D'Annunzio',
whose La gloria he declared to be 'a masterpiece of sublime audacity'. Galli detested its 'spurious profundity', and argued his
case with Campani with such passion that for a month afterward
they did not speak to each other. 'I have done all I can do here,'
he wrote to a friend in Rome, the day after the disagreement.

Another factor was the loss of his parents, to whom he had remained close. They had died in the previous year, within days of
each other, and their deaths had prompted him to re-appraise his
life. His dissatisfactions had come into sharper focus: 'The truth
is,' he wrote to his Roman friend, in the same letter, 'I have tired
of the theatre. And I am almost as tired of this town as it is tired
of me.' It perhaps would have been truer to say that the town
had come to disapprove of him. Many had been scandalised by
the way he had conducted himself with a young actress by the
name of Eugenia Mollica, who in 1906 had appeared at the Teatro
Civico in Bracco's Una donna. Tommaso Galli was enchanted by
her, and made no attempt to disguise his enchantment. Shortly
after Eugenia and her fellow actors had left for Florence, Galli
went to Florence, ostensibly for a meeting with the manager of
the Teatro delle Antiche Stinche. Some months later, he took a
trip to Milan, where Eugenia Mollica was performing that week.
Giacinta Galli bore these desertions with demure grace, and gave
nobody any reason to think that she did not believe that her husband's stated reasons for his absences were genuine, but many
in Castelluccio were insulted and enraged on the wife's behalf.

Giacinta's serenity was well practised: the affair with
Eugenia Mollica, if such it was, was far from being Tommaso's
first infatuation. At a ball in the Palazzo Campani he had met
Ingrid Puppa, whose image he knew from the figures created
by her husband for the interior of the Teatro Civico. He found

her even lovelier than he had expected, and over the succeeding months he subjected her to many amorous declarations. His letters were returned; the husband objected, threatening a duel; Galli at last desisted. But the following year, again in Campani's house, he was asked to accompany, on his mandolin, a singer from Forlì named Giovanna Edel, and the correspondence that was discovered among Giovanni Edel's possessions many years later made it clear that in this instance the ensuing attraction was not unreciprocated. On another occasion, he was found in a compromising situation, in his office, with a pretty Swiss actress. There were others. They were mere flirtations, Giacinta maintained – 'once an *amoroso*, always an *amoroso*,' she remarked. 'Tommaso is a genius, and for a genius there are different rules,' she would say, and everyone knew that the excuse had been learned from her husband. Campani defended him in similar fashion. 'If it were not for Tommaso Galli,' he upbraided the accusers, 'this town would lack all distinction.' More than once, exasperated by the small-minded complainants, he would declare that Galli was like a son to him. Gossip had it that the elderly and unmarried man's affection for the still handsome manager of the Teatro Civico was not paternal.

Tommaso Galli and his wife and children left Castelluccio in the autumn of 1907. In the week before his departure he told a journalist that, having seen *La presa di Roma* (The Taking of Rome), he had been galvanised by a new enthusiasm: 'The Kinetograph is the future,' he said. 'The theatre is dying.' He went to Rome, to work initially for the production company of Filoteo Alberini – maker of *La presa di Roma*, inventor of the Kinetograph and owner of Rome's first cinema – then with the producer Arturo Ambrosio. Between 1910 and 1915 more than six hundred and fifty films were released by Ambrosio, and Tommaso Galli was involved in dozens of them, mostly as an adviser on design or direction. The rapid pace of production in the studios did not suit him, however, and the triviality of much of the material with which he had to work depressed him. In

1915, as his health deteriorated sharply, he parted from Ambrosio and devoted himself to drafting a number of scripts for more ambitious projects, several with Biblical subjects. None was ever filmed. Having become an admirer of Lyda Borelli, whose *Rapsodia Satanica* he saw six times in as many days, he wrote for her the outline of a film to be entitled *Lilith*. There is no record of her opinion of it. Later that year, following her marriage to Count Vittorio Cini, Lyda Borelli retired from the cinema. In the same month as Borelli's wedding, Tommaso Galli and his wife returned to Castelluccio.

They had been back to the town at least once every year, as guests of Paolo Campani, and now they moved into an apartment on the upper floor of the Palazzo Campani. Occasionally the three of them attended performances at the Teatro Civico, which – thanks to the generosity of Paolo Campani – was still in business, barely, but the comedies preferred by the current manager were not to Galli's liking, and the pain of his illness made concentration difficult. In September 1919 they saw a revival of *Come le foglie*; Galli recognised the sets, and some of the gestures utilised by the actors. At the interval the audience stood, as if at a signal, and began to applaud; it took Tommaso Galli a moment or two to understand that the applause was directed at him. This was the last time he was at the Teatro Civico: he died of stomach cancer on December 24th, 1919, in the Palazzo Campani. Paolo Campani died two months later, at the age of 93. Giacinta Galli lived for another fifteen years, and died in Modena, her place of birth.

Galli's tomb is in the church of Sant'Agostino and his portrait hangs in the Caffè del Corso. He has a third memorial as well, which takes the form of a performance. The saint's day of Saint Zeno has been celebrated in Castelluccio for centuries, but before 1903 the celebrations comprised little more than a special Mass and a communal meal in Piazza Maggiore. The present-day festival is largely Galli's creation. It was Galli who devised the spectacle of the descent of the Falling Boy and the Angel, and the costumed parade, and the crossbow contest.

12.7

Gideon opens the door and looks at her for a second, saying nothing, but smiling as a man might smile at a daughter who's about to leave home for good. Wiping paint from his hands with a rag, he stands aside. 'Come in, come in,' he says.

'I really do have to be going,' she tells him.

'Plenty of time,' he assures her. 'Come in. Just for a minute.'

She follows him into the living room. At the table he stops and turns around to prop himself against it, still working the rag between his fingers. Inspecting his hands, he says: 'I'm very glad to have met you. Or re-met, I should say.'

'It's been interesting,' she says.

'Itching to get back to the crowds and the fumes, I'm sure,' he says.

'Not quite itching,' she answers. 'But it'll be good to be home.'

'Of course,' he says, 'of course.' You might almost think he'd rather she stayed for a few days more.

'I've enjoyed myself,' she says.

'Bees excepted.'

'Apart from the bees,' she agrees.

He folds the rag and places it on the table. 'Before you go,' he says, and he reaches down to take something from the seat of the chair beside him. 'A going-away present,' he says, putting a small framed picture into her hand, its back facing upward.

She turns it, and sees herself, in pencil, sitting on grass, intent on the book that's open in her hands.

'I framed it myself,' he tells her. 'Robert would have done a better job.'

She tilts the picture to get the reflections off it. Much of the drawing – the grass, her dress, her legs – is lightly sketched, but the face and hands are crisp and dark; and the face, though it's obviously herself, has a composure that she does not recognise as hers. 'This is on the hill, isn't it?' she says. 'The day we had the picnic.'

'It is.'

'But you didn't do it then, did you? I'd have noticed.'

'No, I did it then,' he says. 'I made improvements later, but essentially it was done on the spot.'

'But how? You weren't looking at me.' Her perplexity pleases him, clearly. She doesn't know what to think: he has been sly, and she is annoyed by the deception; and part of her is flattered, perhaps; and it's a good drawing; and he means to please her with the gift – and to please himself, of course. 'I look like I'm in church with my prayer book. Pious. I look pious.'

'No you don't,' he tells her. 'You're concentrating.'

'You've done some nip and tuck on the face, haven't you? That's what you mean by improvements.'

'It's you, truer than a photo,' he says; it sounds more like a compliment than a boast.

She angles it one way and then another, seemingly a little unsettled by herself, but intrigued as well.

'If you don't like it,' he says, 'you could always sell it. It's signed and dated on the back, so you could get a decent amount of cash for it.'

'Thank you,' she says, continuing to look at it, not knowing how to look at Gideon.

'My pleasure,' he responds, making out that it's nothing of importance, then he puts a palm to her shoulder and turns her towards the door, as if there were a risk of their getting tearful were they to linger.

Robert starts the engine the instant they appear on the steps. Beyond the car, at one of the tables of the Torre, Marta from the restaurant is chatting with a young woman who's recognisable, but not precisely, until she takes her glasses from the table to look at Marta's phone, and then Claire knows her – she was in the museum, at the desk. Marta waves and calls out 'Ciao'; her friend is too fascinated by the phone to take note of anything else.

Having opened the passenger door, Gideon is looking her in the eye; evidently he has something conclusive to say. His mouth opens, he breathes in, and he lets the breath out, closing the door.

His arms go out and he advances. The embrace cannot be avoided: he gathers her to his belly and presses her tightly, one hand in the small of her back, the other between her shoulders; the pressure is peculiarly even and mechanical – it's as if his torso were a bed of soft clay and he is trying to take an impression of her. Several seconds later he releases her, with some solemnity. The embrace has marked a sort of pact, it would seem, and he appears to be moved: the lower eyelids are moistened.

'I hope you'll visit us again,' he says, reopening the door.

She finds herself answering: 'I will,' and if this is not quite a definite intention, it doesn't feel like a lie either. She gets into the car and winds the window down; she puts her arm on the sill, and Gideon pats it, once.

'OK,' he says. 'Back to work,' he cajoles himself, with a sigh of mock-reluctant compliance. She will never see him again.

12.8

Marta received a call less than half an hour ago, from Ilaria, in Florence, from a new number. 'Don't tell anyone,' Ilaria had said at the end, but Marta was so annoyed by what Ilaria had told her that she didn't feel obliged to keep her promise. And even if she hadn't been annoyed she would have had to tell someone and that someone would have been Sofia. As soon as she'd finished talking to Ilaria, she gave Sofia a call; Sofia was at the museum, chatting to her sister, doing nothing. 'Can you come to the Torre?' asked Marta. 'Something interesting has happened.'

Sofia is wearing a dress – sky-blue, with thin straps – that Marta has never seen before, and she looks so lovely that Marta's heart does a stutter at the sight of her. The past few months have been a sweet misery, because she has come to realise that she loves Sofia and cannot do anything about it. Sofia has been a friend for years, but Marta now knows that what she feels for Sofia is more than friendship, and you could say that she's been able to accept that she loves Sofia because of what happened with Ilaria last year, in a way. Ilaria had argued with her boy-friend and had drunk a lot of wine before she met up with Marta; they bought a bottle and went out into the fields, and they ended up messing around. For Ilaria it meant nothing; it was just some fun, as Marta knew. And for Marta it was fun too – that's all it could be, with Ilaria. Those kisses with Ilaria, though, were what changed everything: they turned a suspicion into a fact; she now knew why no boy had ever interested her as boys were meant to interest a girl. But it was one thing for Marta finally to understand and accept herself – it was something quite different for her family, her friends and the town to understand and ac-cept. 'Not a word to anyone,' Ilaria had said, and Marta had said nothing. It hadn't been too difficult to keep the secret: but now, with how she feels about Sofia, it's very difficult.

She and Ilaria had hardly ever spoken about their evening, but they didn't regret what they'd done; they weren't even embarrassed about it. And they had stayed friends – better friends than ever, in fact, which is why, every day since Ilaria disappeared, a dozen times a day, Marta has been trying her number. Every day Ilaria's phone has been switched off – and now, suddenly, here she is. She's sent a picture of herself in Florence, up on Piazzale Michelangelo, with a man who looks about forty, with eyes like a lizard and a mouth like a gash. 'He's wearing eye-liner, and he's a hundred years old,' Sofia comments, with a disgusted flicking of her tongue against her teeth, as if trying to scrape off a horrible taste.

As Sofia says, the man looks like a pimp, but Ilaria says he's a photographer and he knows loads of people in television. 'His name's Uli,' says Marta.

'Uli,' Sofia repeats, making it sound like the most ridiculous name a man has ever had.

'That's right. A lot of girls on TV have this guy to thank for their first break, apparently.'

'According to Ilaria.'

'Yes.'

'That girl's an air-head,' says Sofia. She takes off her glasses and rubs her eyes, as if the stupidity of what she was hearing were giving her a headache. 'So Lizard-Face is the reason she ran?'

'And she wanted to give the old folks a scare.'

'The old folks and her friends,' says Sofia.

'That's what I said. But she thought I'd tell the parents if I knew she was OK.'

'Are you going to tell them now?'

'Don't know. If I do, she'll never talk to me again.'

'You have to tell them,' says Sofia. 'It's not fair. Her dad's a pig, but it's not fair, even for a pig. If you don't tell them, I will.'

'Please don't,' says Marta. 'I promised her I wouldn't. If you tell them, she'll know I told you. She says she's going to call them.'

'When?'

'Soon.'

'Soon could mean anything,' says Sofia. 'Enough is enough. Ring her back, right now. Tell her that if she doesn't call them tonight you'll call them yourself. It's just not right.' She picks the phone off the table and places it in Marta's hand. 'This is a stupid game to be playing. People are worried. Call her.'

'I'll ring her this afternoon.'

'No, Marta. You'll ring her now.'

She rings, and it goes to voicemail; she tells Ilaria to call her back, because they need to talk.

'Good,' says Sofia, and Marta feels as stupid as Ilaria, and for a moment hopeless, because Sofia is so decisive, and right, and so gorgeous, and whatever happens she is about to lose Ilaria as a friend.

That afternoon she speaks to Ilaria, who can only give her a few minutes: she's waiting for Uli and he'll be here any minute. In the background there's an announcement for a train. 'You have to talk to your family,' pleads Marta. It is cruel what you are doing.' Ilaria, losing her temper, promises she'll call them.

Four days later, Sofia passes Ilaria's mother on the Corso, and, seeing immediately that the poor woman still knows nothing, tells her all she knows. Eight days after that, Ilaria returns to Castelluccio. True to her word, she refuses to have anything to do with Marta. She's seen in town a few times, but never in the Torre; none of her former friends gets a call from her; neither does Gideon.

One morning, unloading a van, Giovanni Cabrera comes face to face with her, and she looks at him, he says, as if she's searching for someone to murder. 'How are things?' he asks. Things are terrible, she says. Her father has hit her and her mother yet again has done nothing, just standing there and wringing her hands and whispering her weepy little prayers, as if she thinks Saint Zeno is going to come flying out of the clouds to sort things out, after a few hundred years of unemployment. But Ilaria has plans, she says.

And some time in October she leaves again; her mother, failing to avoid Sofia on Piazza del Mercato, informs her curtly that Ilaria has gone, and that her departure is best for all concerned. And that's all we know, though Giovanni Cabrera hears a rumour in March that Ilaria is dancing in a club outside Florence and is making a lot of money, 'because men really go for a redhead'.

On a foggy morning in November, not long after Ilaria's second and – it is safe to assume – irrevocable departure, Gideon is setting off for his morning walk with Trim when he sees in the murk a lone figure sitting on the bench by the loggia: it is Marta, in a blue tracksuit. They chat for a few minutes. She's been for a run, she tells him; she's taken up running because she needs to lose some weight.

'No you don't,' Gideon replies.

She loves this kind of weather, she says, running her hands down Trim's back. 'Everything is familiar but a bit wrong. Like a dream.'

'It is,' he agrees; Marta seems glum. 'May I sit down?' he asks.

'Of course,' she answers.

They sit side by side, facing the foggy square. The Redentore is a dark cliff; footsteps traverse the piazza; someone moves from left to right, like a big slow fish under muddy water.

'It really is like a dream,' says Gideon.

'It's lovely,' says Marta. There is a strange kind of intimacy to the situation, sitting together on the cold bench, in the quietness, with ghostly people passing through the fog in front of them. 'Ilaria has gone,' she says. 'Did you know?'

'I'd heard,' says Gideon.

Marta admits that she is disappointed – not that Ilaria has left, but that she was not, in the end, a real friend.

'I never understood her,' says Gideon.

'But she was fun, sometimes,' says Marta.

'I can imagine,' says Gideon.

Trim trots off into the greyness, dwindling in seconds to a no-coloured dash. 'She wasn't happy at home,' says Marta. 'Her father – he wasn't a good father.'

'So I believe.'

Then Marta, as though talking to herself, utters the words that run through her mind a hundred times a day: 'I don't know what to do.'

Gideon turns to look at her; his smile is kindly, and his eyes are very tired. 'Go on,' he says.

The dog returns, its coat gleaming with beads of water; she brushes his brow. She is sure, as Ilaria had been sure, that Gideon is gay, so he will understand; and the fact that his Italian isn't great makes it easier too. So now she says what she has said to nobody else: 'I'm in love.'

'That's good,' Gideon replies, and the smile does not change. He knows what she's about to say, because of what Ilaria had once told him, no doubt thinking she'd give the old man a bit of a jolt.

'With a girl,' says Marta.

'That's good,' he responds. 'But she doesn't know – is that it?'

'Nobody knows anything,' she says, with a long look to make sure he understands exactly what she's saying.

'I see.'

'My mother thinks I have no luck with boys.' She laughs, and for a moment Gideon joins in. 'I don't know what my father thinks,' she adds.

'And this friend – you think she doesn't feel the same way as you feel?'

'I know she doesn't. It's not possible.'

'Nothing is impossible.'

'No. Believe me. It is impossible.'

'OK,' he says, 'but you want to tell her?'

'I want her to know how I am. Maybe not that I love her. But I want her to know me. I need her to know who I am. If I can't tell her, I'll explode.'

'But if you tell her, it's possible she will not stay a friend.'

'Exactly. Ilaria is bad enough. I can't lose two.'

He cradles the dog's head and gazes into its eyes. 'If she does what Ilaria did, she's not a friend,' he pronounces, then he turns to her again. 'You have to tell the truth, Marta. And if you love her, I'm sure she's a good person. So tell her. Tell her how you are. Perhaps don't tell her everything. If you think it's too dangerous to tell her that you love her, don't say it. Perhaps later. See how it goes. But don't explode, Marta. The Antica Farmacia needs you,' he jokes, and he puts a hand on her knee and gives it a small squeeze. He stands up, wincing at the effort of straightening his legs.

'Thank you,' she says, releasing her gratitude with a rough rub for the dog.

'See you tonight,' says Gideon, and he walks into the fog.

So a month or so later she finally tells Sofia that she is not at-tracted to boys, and Sofia doesn't miss a beat: she had suspected as much – more than suspected, to be honest. They talk for hours, and in the end Marta has to confess that she has deep feelings, very deep feelings, for Sofia. 'I've sometimes wondered,' says Sofia. But she's totally frank with Marta: it can't happen, she tells her; she's touched; she's flattered; but she likes boys. If Marta can live with this situation, though, so can Sofia. They talk into the night, and it's all OK. Sofia swears she'll not say anything about what Marta has told her, not even to her boyfriend. They remain good friends. But at the back of Marta's mind, as she admits to Gideon, there lurks the notion that maybe, after all, something will happen one day. Sofia has boyfriends, it's true, but Marta has heard about situations where a woman one day wakes up and realises she's not what she thought she was. 'A person is a river, not a monument,' Marta tells herself; it's a phrase of which she's very fond; she heard it from Gideon.

She tells her family, and they are fine about it: they had guessed, says her father, and her mother nods, not overjoyed. Her father gives her a mighty hug, and that's that. Marta loves her father, and her mother, and could not bear to live far from where they are, yet she knows she will have to get away from Castelluccio some day soon. London is where she wants to live, she thinks; she is thrilled by the idea of a big city, and of this big city in particular. In London she could be herself with no hassle at all. She once talked to a DJ who had lived there, and he'd made it sound fantastic. But what would she do in London? She lacks the courage of Ilaria, and has no talents that could help her. People tend to like her, she knows. She is a good waitress: she does not make mistakes and can smile at people she doesn't much like. The thought of being a waitress in Castelluccio when she's thirty, however, makes her despair.

She says as much to Sofia, sitting outside the Torre. When she was up on that wire, she tells her, with the whole town spread out below her and the cemetery beyond, she'd felt a great wave of dread. Looking down, she'd seen all those faces smiling up, and it was as if someone had thrown a net over her. To loud applause, and the flash of dozens of cameras, she'd descended to Piazza del Mercato, feeling ill with the thought that sliding down a wire on a Sunday afternoon, dressed up like a fairy, was the most exciting thing that was ever going to happen to her. She gazes through the gates through which Gideon's niece has just been driven. 'I can't stay here forever,' she tells Sofia, thinking: *But I love you.*

12.9

The Falling Boy
2011
Oil-tempera on canvas; 100cm x 212cm
Dexter Rutherford collection, Albuquerque, New Mexico

In what turned out to be his last interview, with Gary Yerolim, for Yerolim's *Brushwork* blog, Gideon Westfall remarked that if he were to be told that he was going to die the next morning and, in accordance with the convention of granting a condemned man his final request, were to be allowed to spend the coming night in the presence of one painting, that painting would be *The School of Athens.* Several times since moving to Italy he had gone to Rome primarily to study that picture. It was, he thought, the Renaissance's 'supreme masterpiece of anachronistic verisimilitude', a work of 'the most subtle strangeness', in which the 'wildest invention is perfectly reconciled with the rules of harmony'.

And in this interview he expressed some regret that he had, as he put it, 'imposed too much constraint' on his own powers of invention. He acknowledged that he had been discouraged by the reception given to some of the more overtly imaginative works of his early career, such as *Epicurus in Hell.* One particular journalist's response to this painting had, he did not mind admitting, wounded him deeply. Several years had passed before he had attempted anything in a similar vein, and he had destroyed this painting before completing it. Later 'experiments' had likewise been adjudged, by himself, to be unsuccessful. As many as a dozen canvases had been destroyed. But he had come to wonder if his judgement might not have been clouded by too great a concern to preserve the overall cohesion of his work.

These forays into the fantastic were perhaps rejected chiefly because he'd known they would have appeared to a future public as outcrops that disrupted the landscape of his oeuvre, so to speak, like boulders in a meadow. He now wished that he had found the courage to spare more than one of these 'erratics'. The one that had escaped the cull – the *Landscape with Dead Horse* – was, in his opinion, one of the half-dozen works on which his reputation would depend. *The Falling Boy*, recently finished, was another.

Of the paintings that had been destroyed, he regretted the loss of three: *The Laureate* (1987), in which a procession of black-gowned men and women, in double file, some involved in intense argument, crossed a wide and moonlit square, following an elderly man who wore a laurel crown and white gown and had the look of a criminal on his way to the scaffold; *The Gathering* (1992), set on a grassy hill, swathed in mist, with a crowd, backs turned to the viewer, gazing towards an isolated figure that was all but lost in the fog of the upper slope; and *The Somnambulists* (1999), another nocturnal scene, in which – seen from a rooftop vantage – a street and two small squares were occupied by twenty or thirty figures, a few in small groups, most alone, some clothed, some naked, some with eyes open, some with eyes closed, a few weeping, most expressionless, and one – a young woman, clad in a blood-red robe – looking directly at us, with preternaturally large eyes and a ghastly smile. The circumstances in which this last detail had been added, he revealed, were most unusual, for him. After a long day's work on *The Somnambulists* he had gone to bed at one or two o'clock, drained; at some point in the night he had got up and gone into the studio, where he'd stayed for he didn't know how long; when he woke up again, he was conscious of having returned to the painting in the middle of the night, but had no idea of what he'd done to it; with some trepidation he went up to the studio, and found that he'd created the figure in the blood-red robe. 'The picture,' he told Gary Yerolim, 'had told me how it should be completed.' He sometimes wished, he confessed, that he had more often surrendered himself to such subconscious promptings.

There are several points of resemblance between *The Somnambulists* and *The Falling Boy*, most obviously that of viewpoint. A parade is crossing Piazza Sant'Agostino and we are looking down on it from a position in space that is opposite the church, at about the same height as the ceiling of the nave; in reality, no viewer could occupy such a position. The people in the parade are all wearing their everyday clothes, but some are carrying flags and banners which are adorned with images of the boar of Saint Zeno; others are playing trumpets or beating drums; at the head of the procession is a priest, who holds aloft a silver chalice, tarnished. The stones of the piazza and the façade of Sant'Agostino are brightly lit, and the celebrants cast stark shadows on the ground, yet the portion of the sky that we can see, in the alleys that flank the church (alleys that are not in reality there) is ominously dark. A look of stern concentration, like that of soldiers on parade, is on the face of most of the participants, and it is as though an invisible rope were tightly encircling the procession, so closely packed are the bodies: the trumpets are almost touching the shoulders of the people in front; one man has put a hand out to create more space for himself; a woman is about to tread on the priest's golden surplice. Only one person – a portly man, balding, an unidentical twin of the artist – has room in which to walk unencumbered: he is preceded by a void which is as conspicuous as a missing tooth. A figure who is unequivocally the artist – this painting's sole portrait of a citizen of Castelluccio – appears elsewhere, among the crowd that lines one side of the piazza; standing at a slight remove, with a mud-caked dog at his feet, he is the only person among the throng who is not applauding or cheering: his gaze is directed into one of the alleys, at the end of which, displaced from its true location, rises the Torre del Saraceno. Silhouetted against the pale stone, a tiny figure is falling from the tower, observed by nobody else; no saint is swooping out of the oily sky. And in the mouth of the alleyway, herself detached from the crowd on that side of the piazza, stands a young woman in a red gown, fixing us with a look that is perhaps desperate, or accusatory, or deranged; above her head, the alley is spanned by a stone arch, and into this arch is set a stone plaque, inscribed with a text in letters so small that a lens is needed to read it. The text, in Latin, may be translated thus: *We must first descend if we wish to be raised*. There are two other isolated figures in the scene: on the extreme left, in a doorway, a skulking man, with a rolled newspaper sticking out of a jacket pocket, holds a bloodied handkerchief to his nose; and on the opposite side, visible through a window, a bearded man sits at a paper-strewn desk, with a pen in one hand and the other resting on a mandolin.

In his interview with Gary Yerolim, Gideon made reference to the late style of certain old masters, a style in which the experience of a lifetime was distilled into gestures of great boldness. Titian, Matisse and Picasso were cited as exemplars of this 'supercharged simplicity', as he termed it. 'I'm going in the opposite direction,' he jested. *The Falling Boy*, he continued, was 'busier' than anything he'd produced since he was a very young man. He disclosed that he'd inserted into the painting a sly allusion to his advanced years: the owl in the campanile of the church might be thought of as a reference to Hegel's owl of Minerva, which 'spreads its wings only at dusk'. He declined, however, to explicate any of the picture's other tantalising details, such as the man with the bloody nose, or the small cloud of grey smoke in the alley to the right. When he'd begun work on *The Falling Boy*, he had thought he was embarking on his '*summa*', his '*opus ultimum*,' a synthesis of everything that he had learned in the course of his life as an artist. The finished canvas had fallen short of that, he admitted, but he was satisfied with it.

Giuliano Lanese, having been invited to view *The Falling Boy* as soon as it had been completed, pondered the picture in silence for a long time, before pronouncing that it was 'extremely interesting'. It was somewhat hermetic, he said, but very interesting. He used the word 'allegory', to which Gideon, understanding what Lanese was really telling him, took exception. *The Falling Boy* was not an allegory, he informed the director of the Museo Civico – it was a vision, 'a lucid dream in paint', and dreams always resist the sort of analysis that allegory demands. Giuliano Lanese listened, and nodded a lot, as though being persuaded by the point that the painter was making. 'This has given me much to think about,' he said.

Milton Jeremies was no less equivocal. Upon receiving a photograph of *The Falling Boy*, and a promise of first refusal, he emailed immediately, declaring it 'a great picture'. Two days later, he emailed: 'this painting has knocked me sideways – Jane too'. After another week he was 'unsettled' by it – which was, he hastened to add, 'not a bad thing'. Soon he was wondering how it would fit into his collection, and while he was wondering he mentioned *The Falling Boy* to an aquaintance of his, Dexter Rutherford, founder of Rutherford Solar, manufacturers of photovoltaic systems in Albuquerque, whose collection of visionary art – a collection that included work by James Ensor and Alfred Kubin, to name just two – might, Milton Jeremies ventured to suggest, be a more suitable home for this 'bizarre and wonderful creation'. It duly came about that Dexter Rutherford bought *The Falling Boy*, just three weeks before Gideon Westfall died.

Dexter Rutherford intends to bequeath his collection to the University of New Mexico Art Museum in Albuquerque; and so *The Falling Boy* may one day become the first Westfall painting to enter the permanent collection of a public gallery.

12.10

'You knew nothing about this?' Claire asks, holding the drawing on her lap.

'Not a thing,' Robert answers.

'I thought he told you everything.'

'Evidently not.'

She raises the picture and squints at it, doubtfully.

'Don't you like it?' he asks.

'What do you think?' she replies, turning it towards him for another glance as they wait at traffic lights.

'Good,' he says.

'You think it's me?'

'It's not anyone else.'

'I think he's been kind,' she says.

'Let's see again,' he requests, leaning over. He looks closely at it, but does not look at her. 'No,' he states. 'Don't agree.'

A minute later she asks: 'You really didn't notice what he was doing?'

'Honestly, I didn't. He's very adroit, you know.'

Another silence; she directs her face towards the pines that line the road. Then she resumes with: 'What do you think of him?'

'Of Gideon?'

'Obviously.'

'I like him.'

'But as an artist. What do you really think? You can tell me now. Last chance.'

'He's a brilliant painter.'

'You're being slippery again.'

'No, I'm not,' he says,

She gives him a glance of stern admonishment. 'Do you think he's a brilliant artist? That was my question. As you know perfectly well. Do you think he's important?'

'In the great scheme of things, none of us is important.'

'Is that what you think?' she asks, as if having half a mind to be scandalised.

'Well, yes,' he answers.

'Gosh,' she says; it takes a few seconds to come to terms with this revelation. 'OK,' she continues, 'do you think anyone will be looking at Gideon's pictures in a hundred years time?'

'They're built to last. So – yes, someone will be looking at them.'

'But do you think he will be appreciated a hundred years from now? That's what I'm asking.'

'I don't know. I can't possibly know. But I think he'll still have his admirers. Perhaps more than now. Perhaps fewer.'

'And what about you? Do you really like what he does?'

'I work for him, don't I?'

'Yes, you do. But does everyone love their work? They don't. You could like working for him, but still have your doubts. So: do you really like what Gideon does?'

'Some of his pictures are excellent, in my opinion.'

'What about the stone walls?'

'I like them.'

'The cogs and bottles?'

'Not so much.'

'The portraits?'

'Some.'

'The naked ladies.'

'But of course,' he replies.

'Seriously.'

'Not all of them,' he answers.

She smiles at his profile, as if she's uncovered something. 'OK,' she says. For several minutes, neither of them speaks. She has the window down, and places her face into the moving air. Then she remarks: 'He does rather play up the part, doesn't he?'

'Sometimes,' he agrees. 'He plays it well, though.'

'He does,' she says, and she turns away again.

At the airport she tells him to just drop her off – there's no point in hanging around to watch her queuing at the check-in. He could do with a break, he says; he'll stretch his legs for a few minutes, then get going. In front of them in the queue there's a fine-looking Italian woman, over-tanned, athletic, thirty-ish, saying goodbye to a man who is at least fifteen years older; he's done some complicated things with his hair, to mask the thinning on the crown, and he's wearing half a bottle of after-shave. They kiss: left cheek, right cheek, then lips, but the movement of her perfectly manicured hand on his back – it flaps softly, rather than presses – tells you everything. Now a family of Brits arrives behind them; between the parents some tension is evident; words of disagreement are spoken, *sotto voce*; the woman is twitchy, on the alert for queue-jumpers. 'For God's sake, relax,' whispers the husband. The woman drags the kids off to the toilets, and as soon as she's out of the way the husband takes out his phone and within seconds he's saying: 'I tell you, mate, it's been an absolute fucking nightmare.'

Claire kneels to open her suitcase and pack the picture in the midst of her clothes. 'I'm not doing this again,' says the man on the phone. 'No fucking way. Not in a million years,' he says, and Claire angles an ear in his direction and gives Robert a wide-eyed stare of comical amazement.

The queue has moved one pace in ten minutes. 'This is silly,' she says. 'Don't stay any longer. Go.' She stands up. She extends a hand, looks down at it, then takes a small skip forward to give him a moth-weight kiss on the cheek, as if she had just re-membered that a kiss is what politeness requires in this country. 'Thank you for everything,' she says.

At the sliding doors he looks back, expecting to see her wav-ing, but she's busy with her bag.

12.11

Occasionally, during the drive from the airport back to Castelluccio, a thought of Claire breaks into Robert's conscious-ness: her face during the concert, or in the Antica Farmacia, taking issue with Gideon. More frequently, an image of Teresa presents itself: Teresa in the parade; Teresa in bed; Teresa in her office, on the phone, blowing kisses while talking to a client. He sees the face of Renata, regarding him with no affection what-soever. For much of the drive, however, his mind is registering nothing other than the road.

At the stand of cypress trees beside the Volterra road, a kilometre to the north of Castelluccio, the road swerves. He stops the car by the trees and gets out. The tips of the cypresses are flexing in the breeze; the air pours through their branches with a sound like fingers stroking paper. This is the place where, in 1603, Giovan Antonio Ridolfi was attacked by a snake. Tommaso Galli liked to read and write in the shade of these very trees. Teresa Campani, during her years of confinement, told her brother Tullio that she often called to mind the day on which the two of them, in a carriage, had seen a doe and her fawn at the cypresses, and had stopped to watch them; she had come to think of it as the happiest day of her life, she said; Tullio, though he had no recollection of any such day, smiled with her at the thought of it.

I have passed forty, thinks Robert, *and have done nothing of any significance.* He is, as Teresa would put it, a servant; yet he is not discontented. He is fond of Gideon; he has a good life, a life that many would envy. It is a fine day, he observes. The sunlight flashes across the bright grey walls and russet roofs of Castelluccio; the flag of Saint Zeno wriggles against the complicated sky. And already, he tells himself, that flash of sunlight is a memory; it was becoming a memory in the moment that he perceived it. The present barely exists – it is as tenuous as a membrane between the future and the past: something happens, and instantly it's gone into the circuitry of the brain, and is of the same substance as a dream. A bird traverses the sky above Castelluccio and flies into his memory, joining the body of Laura Ottaviano, a walk in the mountains with Agnese, the concert at Santa Maria, Teresa dancing.

The time is 5.45pm and the temperature is 24° Celsius, with fifty per cent humidity; a steady breeze, averaging twelve kilometres per hour, is driving a flock of cumulus clouds eastward.

The following May, in similar weather, he will again drive from Pisa airport to Castelluccio, this time with Claire. They will talk first about Gideon. She says that she had come to realise that she'd liked him rather more than she'd thought she had at the time. 'He was unusual,' she says.

'He was,' says Robert, a little surprised at the reaction he has to her voice, to the slight creak in it.

'How's Luisa taken it?' she asks.

'Distraught,' he answers.

'And how about you?' she asks.

'Coping,' he says.

She glances at him, nods, and says no more. Her perfume is fresh and slightly smoky, woody, with vetiver in it. 'That's not the same one, is it?' he has to ask. 'The perfume.'

'Timbuktu,' she answers. 'You approve?' she asks, and for a moment it seems she's going to lean closer, but she doesn't.

'Nice,' he says. 'Expensive?'

'An arm and a leg.'

'You wear it for work?'

'I do.'

They pass Volterra. She recalls the strange man, and wonders if he is still there.

'We could stop for lunch,' suggests Robert.

'No,' she says immediately. 'Let's unpack, then eat.'

Near Cásole d'Elsa I remark: 'Good to see you again.'

'Pity about the circumstances,' she says. Then, after a long pause: 'But ditto.'

12.12

Though commonly known as the Italian or Tuscan cypress, the evergreen *Cupressus sempervirens* is not native to Italy; it is likely that the tree was brought to Tuscany by the Etruscans. There is no agreement as to its place of origin: Greece, Turkey, Crete, Cyprus, Lebanon, Iran and Syria have all been proposed, with most experts favouring Iran and Syria. It takes two forms: fastigiated, which is the tall and slender Tuscan cypress; and horizontal, which is widely believed to be the only form that existed prior to human activity. The so-called Tuscan cypress, in other words, is to be regarded as a cultivar rather than as a subspecies.

In the tenth book of his *Metamorphoses*, Ovid relates the tale of a prince named Kyparissos, to whom Apollo, as a token of his love, gave a magnificent stag; Kyparissos lavished great care on the animal, but accidentally killed it with a javelin when the stag was resting in the shade of a forest; in his remorse, Kyparissos pleaded with Apollo to be allowed to grieve for ever, whereupon he was transformed into a cypress, which perpetually weeps tears of sap. The Greeks esteemed the cypress as a tree that was sacred to Hades. The Romans likewise associated it with Pluto, and mourners at funerals carried branches of cypress as a sign of respect; prior to burial, eminent citizens were laid upon a bed of cypress branches. Believing that the fragrant wood had the power to repel evil spirits, the Etruscans planted cypress trees around their burial grounds. In more recent times, cypresses have customarily been planted in cemeteries, to freshen the air and comfort the bereaved with their scent.

The hard and close-grained wood of *Cupressus sempervirens* is extremely durable, and has long been used for coffins and sarcophagi. In ancient Egypt, cypress wood was used for mummy cases. The doors of the temple of Diana at Ephesus were made of cypress wood, and Pliny states that these doors were still perfect four centuries after their construction. The statue of Jupiter in the Capitol was carved from cypress wood, and lasted even longer. The doors of the first Basilica of St Peter in Rome were made of the same material, and were said to have served their purpose from the reign of Constantine to the time of Pope Eugenius IV, who was elected to the papacy more than a millennium later.

The tree reaches a height of 20–25m on average, but considerably taller specimens are numerous: in the Samariá Gorge, on the island of Crete, there are cypresses that have grown to approximately 35m (115ft). *Cupressus sempervirens* can live to be more than one thousand years old. The cypress at Somma Lombardo, in the province of Varese, was revered as the oldest tree in the world, having been planted, reputedly, during the reign of Julius Caesar. Reaching a height of 36.6m (120ft), it was also the tallest known specimen. Napoleon is said to have diverted the course of a new road in order to preserve it. A storm toppled the Somma Lombardo cypress on September 2nd, 1944, a date recorded on the war memorial in Piazza Scipione; subsequently it was estimated that the tree had been planted around the start of the ninth century.